PRAISE FOR *THE VOODOO KILLINGS*

A BookNet Canada "Lone Stars" Pick

A *Canadian Living* "10 Hot Canadian Reads" Pick

"*The Voodoo Killings* is such a spectacular mix of urban fantasy and mystery it kept me up to two in the morning. Give me more Kincaid Strange."

—Faith Hunter, *New York Times* bestselling
author of the Jane Yellowrock series

"Kristi Charish grabs the zombie novel by the throat and drags it back to square one, creating a voodoo zombie mystery that is a fresh and fantastic take on a whole genre. A must read!"

—Peter Clines, author of *The Fold*, *14*
and the Ex-Heroes series

"What a rush! Highly entertaining, original, and brimming with wit—and zombies in closets—I loved *The Voodoo Killings*. Can't wait for the next!"

—Julie E. Czerneda, author of *This Gulf of Time and Stars*

"This was an absolute delight to read. With a smart, cynical hero and zombies whose morals are as grey as the brains they snack on, *The Voodoo Killings* offers a fun and creepy new world—or two—to get lost in."

—Patrick Weekes, author of the Rogues of the Republic series

"If you're a [...] use, you'll
definitely li[...]

[...]*dian Living*

"A masterful urban fantasy 'whodunit.' It is one of the best, if not the best book I've read so far this year."

—*One Book Two* (blog)

"With an electric end and a dramatic cliffhanger that made me swear out loud in surprise, *The Voodoo Killings* manages to make magic accessible and scientific at the same time. It's a fun ride with an original setting and good attention to world-building."

—*All Things Urban Fantasy* (blog)

THE VOODOO KILLINGS

A KINCAID STRANGE NOVEL

KRISTI CHARISH

VINTAGE CANADA

VINTAGE CANADA EDITION, 2018

Copyright © 2016 Kristi Charish

Originally published by Vintage Canada, a division of
Penguin Random House Canada Limited, in 2016. Distributed in Canada by
Penguin Random House Canada Limited, Toronto.

Vintage Canada with colophon is a registered trademark.

www.penguinrandomhouse.ca

LIBRARY AND ARCHIVES CANADA CATALOGUING IN PUBLICATION

Charish, Kristi, author
The voodoo killings / Kristi Charish.

Issued in print and electronic formats.

ISBN 978-0-7352-7312-2

eBook ISBN 978-0-345-81589-7

I. Title.

PS8605.H3686V66 2018   C813'.6   C2017-900652-5

Book design: Five Seventeen

Cover images: Shutterstock.com (Pink powder © RedGreen;
Dark alley © Jon Bilous; Woman © Olena Bloshchynska)

Printed and bound in the United States of America

2 4 6 8 9 7 5 3 1

Penguin
Random
House

VINTAGE CANADA

To anyone I know who is stuck on the Otherside

CHAPTER 1

BETTER OFF DEAD

My cellphone rang six times before I managed to fish it out from underneath the stack of receipts scattered over the desk. I swear to god, if my ex, Aaron, is trying to get a hold of me again . . .

It wasn't Aaron, though. It was a number I didn't recognize.

I picked up. "Hello?"

A squeaky, barely pubescent male voice replied, "Umm, hi there. We need a zombie."

I scrunched my forehead and leaned against the kitchen counter. "Uh-huh."

"Yeah, umm, one who isn't too gooey, still looks pretty normal, can walk—" He snuffled like he had covered the receiver. Muted whispering followed. "It also has to have its ID. How much would that be?"

I pinched the bridge of my nose. "Look, kid—I'm not raising you a zombie so you can send it to buy beer. Now hang up or I'll track your parents down." I tossed the phone back on the counter.

Damn kids. I closed my eyes. I never should have put that line about zombies in my listings. Apparently zombie mascots were in this season.

I reached for the half-finished mug of Japanese noodles. The mug, a souvenir from my own college days, had been crazy-glued back together more times than was healthy—for me or the mug. The handle more so than the rest. And, as if that very thought was action, it snapped off, sending what was left of my dinner over the desk.

Damn it. I swept most of the broth onto the floor with my arm, but not before it reached the curse book I'd left open. I picked it up to assess the damage. The corners of the pages and back cover were soaked through with Japanese chili broth. Of everything on the desk the noodles could have soaked, it had to be *Curses of Louisiana*, the sole book I had buyers for on eBay.

Great. Just spectacular. I tossed it on the couch. Maybe I could hair-dry or microwave it back to sellable. . . .

The phone rang again. "Oh, you've got to be kidding me." I grabbed it. "Listen, kid, I don't care which one of your little friends you stick on the phone, I'm not raising you a beer zombie. Got it?"

"Ahh-hi," an uncomfortable, unmistakably adult male voice said. "Is this Kincaid Strange, practitioner? I was told you handle zombies."

I sighed. "Look, buddy, I don't do zombies for parties, and when I do do zombies, it's permits only. The best I can give you is a ghost: no kids, no suicides. If you want one of those and can construct your request in a way that doesn't involve Elvis or Marilyn, I might be able to help you."

"Uh, you don't understand. I mean, I am a zombie . . . I think . . ."

I ran through the possibilities in my head. One, he was nuts. Two, I was talking to a ghost who'd accidentally possessed a phone and then confused itself. Seattle had banned pay phones three years back—way too easy to possess—so that was unlikely.

Still, it was more plausible than the third option: that I was speaking with a newly raised zombie who carried a cellphone.

Real zombie or imaginary, I'd be the last number the cops saw in his call list, and if he started biting people . . . I had to go take a look.

I rifled through the desk drawer until I found a pen and paper. "So . . . what did you say your name was again?"

"You didn't ask. Cameron. Or that's what the wallet says."

"Okay, you can still read. That's a good sign. Listen, Cameron, where are you?"

"I'm not sure. . . . I'm near a bar. But I don't remember it."

If he really was a zombie, that wasn't surprising. Short-term memory goes fast. Still, zombies tend to wander back to familiar places, like homing pigeons.

"That's okay, Cameron. Any landmarks? Signs, the waterfront, interesting buildings?"

I heard boots scrape against wood. "There are docks across the road, and trains." Each word was deliberate and careful. The more he spoke, the more I was convinced this guy might be the real thing. It sure as hell wasn't a ghost calling me, since it wouldn't be able to generate the background noise. Well, unless it was a poltergeist . . .

I pushed that thought aside. With a poltergeist, the call would have deteriorated to insults by now.

A bar by the docks. "Is there a yellow banner hanging above the doorway, below a burnt-out set of neon lights?"

"Yes. The bartender—he gave me your card and said to call."

Randall would do that. So Cameron was outside Catamaran's, the local sports bar. I was not happy Randall hadn't bothered to call me himself, but at least he'd know what to do with the zombie until I got there.

"Okay, Cameron," I said as I slung my leather biker jacket over my shoulders and tied my black curls into a messy ponytail. "Do exactly as I say. Walk back inside. Find Randall, who is likely the one who gave you my card. He's the big Asian guy with tattoos. Tell him Kincaid is on her way. He'll tell you where to sit. No talking to anyone else, and no eye contact. Can you do that?"

After a hair's breadth of a pause, he said, "I—I think so."

He didn't sound that far gone. Never hurts to spell things out, though. "One last thing—and it's important. Whatever you do, no biting. If you bite someone, I can't help you. Got it?"

"Sure," he said, with less hesitation in his voice. Not that far gone.

"Repeat it back to me, Cameron—all of it." He did, and then I made him repeat it three more times until I was satisfied he'd remember.

As soon as I hung up, I called Catamaran's. Randall and I went way back; his family had been big in the Seattle practitioner community, though Randall never took it up. I used to babysit his kids when I was back in high school. He and I were still friendly, but he made no secret that he didn't approve of my career choice. Said no good ever came of using Otherside, that tapping the afterlife is a crutch the living use so they don't have to let go of the dead. Eventually, you get to the point where you can't stop using it or it drives you mad, he said. I didn't quite buy it, though I couldn't blame him for having an allergy to practitioners, considering his wife ran off with a voodoo priest ten years back.

"Kincaid," Randall said.

The joys of caller ID.

"Wondered how fast you'd be calling," he continued. He had the low, intimidating voice of a full-contact-sport referee. "He one of yours?"

"You kidding? I put them back when I'm done. I sure as hell don't let them go walkabout in Seattle with cellphones."

Randall snorted.

"Think he's the real thing? Not just pretending, or messed in the head?"

"Kid, trust me, he's a zombie. Can you help him?"

I let out a long breath as I fumbled my keys off the stand. "I don't know, but just don't call the cops until I get there."

I heard the door chime in the background; I hoped it was Cameron walking in. I pictured Randall weighing the baseball bat he kept behind the bar. "Just get down here fast before one of my customers figures out what's up with him." He hung up.

I headed into the washroom to leave a message for Nate, my roommate. I grabbed the red lipliner in Manhunt I always left by the sink and began to write backwards on the mirror: *Nate. Going out. Back in an hour or so.*

I waited for a response.

Nothing. He was probably still pissed about my most recent

comments on nineties-era grunge music. Piece of advice? Don't argue with the ghost of a deceased grunge star about his contribution to the modern music landscape. It doesn't go well.

I added, *Stop being a princess.*

Still nothing.

I stuck the lipliner back in the toothbrush holder. He'd hold out for another day at most. Ghosts might be stubborn by nature, but the modern ones love their electronics and suck with combination locks. Too tactile. If Nate wasn't jonesing for his PlayStation by tomorrow, then I'd get worried.

Before I headed for the elevator, I opened my freezer and carefully removed the blue ice trays and shelf, and reached for one of the three silver Thermoses I kept hidden there. I rolled it over and checked the date. June 2015: three months old, so still good—or good enough in an emergency. I tucked it in a discreet compartment of my backpack and grabbed my bike, a red 1990 Honda Hawk GT 650 in desperate need of an overhaul. As I locked up, I couldn't help wondering what the hell was waiting for me at Catamaran's. Some start to my Friday night.

I live in a converted warehouse by the Seattle docks that was originally used for sugar- and rum-running in the 1800s; the boats had sailed right in where the cargo could be unloaded away from prying eyes. It wasn't until 1950 that they infilled the slough and converted the warehouse into studio apartments. The one feature they'd left intact was the freight elevator, which I was partial to because it let me take my bike upstairs. No, I don't trust my neighbours.

The building attracted a revolving and seemingly endless roster of artists and musicians. I had my suspicions there was a witch three floors down, but people in my business tend to keep to themselves. I'd pieced together from snippets of laundry room conversations I'd overheard that tenants in the building thought I was a drug dealer or a stripper. It's the leather. The bike doesn't hurt either.

As I rode the elevator down to the main floor, I composed a mental list of everyone in Seattle still capable of raising a zombie. It wasn't long. Since the new laws kicked in, restricting what kind of dead you could raise and when, there were only two of us left in town that I knew of: me and Maximillian Odu.

Max was the genuine article, a traditional voodoo priest from a long New Orleans family line. He was very good. I'd been Max's apprentice for a number of years, an arrangement I'd terminated almost a year ago at Halloween. Max was a stickler for tradition and didn't appreciate some of my more creative modifications when it came to raising the dead. And unlike me, Max outright refused celebrity seance gigs. As he'd said many a time, it went against every fibre in his body to capitalize that way. Given the new laws, his wallet had to be hurting too.

I'm not so picky. This is Seattle: do you have any idea how many calls I get for one-on-one time with famous dead grunge rockers? It's called making rent.

I was not keen on zombie shoptalk with my old teacher—my leaving him was still a sore point between us—but I found Max's number and hit Call; even if it wasn't his zombie, he'd know if anyone else in Seattle could have pulled off a raising. He was a hell of a lot more up to date on the local scene than I was these days.

The phone rang six times before it went to voice mail.

"Max, it's Kincaid. Get back to me ASAP, will you? Business-related question."

The freight elevator hit the ground floor and I kicked the grate open—hard; it had a bad habit of catching on its hinges. One of these days I'd oil them, since our building manager sure as hell wasn't about to. I pushed the bike out and weaved between the haphazard art installations—an impromptu art gallery for the artistically inclined in the building, or a display of every piece rejected by the legitimate dealers of Seattle. Take your pick.

By the back entrance, the front wheel of my Honda Hawk rammed into the side of a new installation. I swore, and backed the bike up to try again. The piece in question was an ornate six-foot mirror painted to look like a ghost summoning, complete with a detailed depiction of a frozen Renaissance-era man with an authentic Otherside ghost-grey cast.

I shook my head. No wonder none of the art galleries took it. First off, ghosts don't last that long; they can survive a century and a half, tops. And they sure as hell don't stand there and watch the world go by.

I negotiated my bike past it and out the door into a perfect mid-September Seattle night: drizzle with a touch of seaweed in the air. I hopped on, kicked it into gear and took off up First.

*

Catamaran's was only a few blocks from my place, and I knew the route well enough to hug the alleys. The last thing I needed was some cop spotting me en route. A zombie by nature is unpredictable, doubly so if the practitioner who raised it is MIA. It was a distinct possibility all hell would have broken loose by the time I got there . . . which brings me back to wishing to avoid a patrol car on the way. Even if I had twenty rock-solid alibis, in the event of a zombie mishap I'd be an immediate suspect. A vision of one of those Monopoly "Go directly to jail" cards comes to mind.

I veered into Pioneer Square, the trendy historical part of town. In my experience, the cops usually left Pioneer Square alone. At least until after midnight.

As I crested the hill, I noticed floodlights a block away on the other side of Pioneer Square park. The streets were crowded with people heading to the clubs, but there was a notable gathering around one of the popular coffee shops, one I liked to frequent. I hadn't heard about any movies filming in town this weekend; most of that action had moved north to Vancouver. So what gave?

I spotted the two unmarked black sedans tucked by the curb, the silently flickering red and blue lights set just inside the windshield.

Shit.

I turned into the nearest alley. Most of the detectives wouldn't recognize my Hawk from this distance, but my ex, Aaron, and his partner, Sarah, would. I checked out the scene unfolding behind me in the side mirror. No sirens, no ambulance—a break-in?

I stuffed my curiosity. Even if I rode up and asked the uniforms, they probably wouldn't give me the time of day, even though I used to be a department consultant. Like I said, the new paranormal laws outlawed five-line, permanent zombies and also restricted the four-line, temporary zombies used in police investigations and legal disputes. That changed a lot of things in Seattle, especially for me. One day you're raising ghosts and zombies to help the police catch killers, the next you're *persona non grata*.

I reached Catamaran's and glided the bike around back, where I stashed it beside the overflowing green Dumpster. I reached for the canvas tarp Randall kept out back to further conceal my bike and was rewarded with a hiss. Randall's fat yellow tabby growled as I uncovered its hiding spot before bolting off to find another refuge from the rain. I shook my head. Randall really needed to stop feeding that thing. It's rare you run into a cat that hates the Otherside so much it reacts to the trace scent I carry with me everywhere.

I slipped in through the kitchen's back door—and by kitchen, I mean a deep fryer and dishwasher wedged into a corner. I squeezed by the deep fryer, trying not to think how many health regulations Randall was breaking. It was his bar, though, so I suppose they were his rules to break. . . .

The many widescreen TVs out front were all playing the Mariners' home game against the Oakland Athletics. They were heading into the sixth inning, Mariners up to bat and the game tied 2–2. I doubted even a zombie would get the crowd's attention, and they certainly paid me no mind as I stepped out through the tropical-coloured yellow and green kitchen push door. The doors stuck out like a sore thumb, but Randall had taken to decorating the place in a tropical theme to complement the bar's name.

I spotted my zombie immediately.

He was sitting at the far end of the bar—the one spot where you didn't have a clear view of one of the TVs—and was wearing a faded Mariners sweatshirt with the hood pulled down over his face. It was at least two sizes too large, so Randall must have given it to him. An untouched beer sat in front of him. Randall himself stood nearby at the sink, cleaning glasses when there was no shortage of clean ones hanging overhead. He saw me and waved me over.

"Randall," I said, taking a stool one over from the zombie. I crinkled my nose as the smell hit me, but it wasn't strong enough to alert anyone not trained to pick it up.

Randall poured me my usual Pilsner and placed it on the bar beside the zombie's untouched drink, no coaster. It wasn't a coaster kind of place. "He's all yours, Kincaid," he said. Then the Mariners game hit a commercial break and without another word Randall headed to the crowded end zone of the bar, as people clamoured for more beer.

I took a sip of mine and turned my attention to the zombie. "Cameron?"

His head didn't move and with his face obscured by the hoodie, I couldn't gauge whether he'd heard me or not. I didn't dare check his bindings—the focused lines of Otherside energy that were holding him together. Not that anyone would see me pull a globe to check, but Cameron would feel it and I didn't want to startle him.

Instead, I touched his forearm. In the early stages, zombies respond to touch better than sound. Has to do with how the different parts of the brain break down. "Cameron?" I said again, applying a little more pressure.

He lifted his head and turned it to face me.

An untrained person would figure him for a homeless guy Randall had taken pity on and let sit at the bar while the game was on. Not bad-looking, either—still had all his teeth, minimal decrepitude. But to me? It's in the eyes. A new zombie watches you as if he's grasping to remember something on the tip of his tongue and you might have the key. It's when he stops searching your face that you need to worry. I don't know if it's even possible to bring a zombie back from that. . . .

The way Cameron's pupils focused on me, part of him still had to be in there. There was no way he was a four-line, permit-friendly zombie—the temporary kind you were still allowed to raise for will disputes and such. The kind who have just enough brainpower to recite pertinent info from memory, but not enough to appreciate their predicament, so when they've served their purpose you can put them in the ground, no problem. Cameron was a five-line, permanent zombie. The illegal kind.

Shit.

I quickly scanned him, top to bottom. There was no obvious trauma, no bullet holes, no darkening of the lips from lack of oxygen . . . no obvious sign of foul play. Nine times out of ten, the reason a zombie is raised is to cover up a murder. Makes proving time of death a real bitch.

I couldn't be sure with the hoodie up, but it didn't look as if his shoulder-length red hair had started to fall out yet.

Young, too. Not a day over thirty, if that. Shame he was dead.

I heard a bat crack on TV, signalling that the game was back on. I tensed as Cameron's focus shifted away from me and towards the noise. In profile, there was something familiar about his face. . . .

"Cameron?"

He slowly turned back to me, narrowing his zombie faded green-white eyes. "Are you . . .?" He struggled to remember my name. Zombies aren't known for their short-term memory.

"Yes, I'm Kincaid," I said. "You called me, remember? I'm here to help you."

His frown deepened. His cellphone was on the counter. I fished out a business card and picked up the phone, flipping to the last called number. I held my business card up beside it, showing him the identical numbers. "See? We spoke less than a half-hour ago."

Cameron took the phone from my fingers and stared at the screen.

"Do you know why you're here?" I asked.

After a moment more of staring at the phone, he nodded. "I have to stay here," he said. He picked up his beer and peered at the contents, as if undecided whether he should drink it or put it back. His indecision morphed into frustration, and I watched his knuckles turn white as if squeezing the glass would somehow make the decision easier. I counted another ten seconds before he looked back at me again. "I'm waiting for someone," he said.

Afraid the glass would shatter, I gently pried it from his hands. In general, alcohol is a bad choice for a new zombie: wreaks havoc on the intestines, accelerates bloating, decay . . .

I glanced around, but everyone was still fixating on the Mariners' home game. Randall, smart man that he was, was making a point of not glancing in my direction. I removed the metal Thermos from my bag and unscrewed the cap, out of sight under the lip of the bar.

I leaned in close to Cameron and passed the Thermos right under his nose so he'd be sure to smell the contents; frozen brains aren't nearly as aromatic as thawed. "Drink this instead," I said, keeping my voice low.

Cameron's nose crinkled as he grasped the Thermos, trying to figure out the smell. The hairs on the backs of my arms shot up. It wasn't every day I had to get close and personal with a zombie I didn't control.

He took a first hesitant sip, and winced.

"Trust me, it'll make you feel better," I said.

He gave me a critical stare—or as critical as a zombie in his condition could manage—but took another sip. The emergency mix of cow, pig and sheep brains would stop Cameron from deteriorating further but wouldn't fix him. To fix him, I needed to get my hands on real brains—human ones—which was a serious problem since it was highly illegal to feed real brains to zombies. Life-sentence illegal.

It was also the only way I'd get any useful answers from Cameron, such as who the hell had raised him.

I took another sip of my Pilsner and motioned for Cameron to drink from the Thermos. I'd worry about finding real brains after I got him back to my place.

I then realized where I'd seen him before: on local TV. I was looking at one Cameron Wight, the up-and-coming Seattle artist. . . .

My beer went down the wrong pipe and I started to cough.

Cameron jumped at the noise, his movement jerky from a deteriorating nervous system.

I swore under my breath. A stray zombie was one thing, but a famous stray zombie? I racked my brain for details about him from the interview I'd seen, but I'd been more concerned with watching the eBay bids on one of my voodoo books than listening to the plastic-fantastic host read cue card questions to a painter. Cause of death could be anything from suicide to accident to, well, worse. How had this man ended up a zombie?

I studied his features and tried to gauge a timeline. I figured he was no more than three days dead but no fewer than two, so he'd died between Tuesday and Wednesday.

I leaned back in my seat to check the closest TV screen: near the end of the sixth, Mariners up, bases still loaded. The bar might be oblivious, but eventually someone in Seattle was bound to notice Cameron was missing, if they hadn't already. I needed to get Cameron out of here now.

I took the half-finished Thermos of mixed brain slushie, re-fastened the steel lid and shoved it back into my bag.

I placed a hand on Cameron's arm and kept it there until he looked at me. "We need to go now," I said.

He glanced down at my hand and back up at me, then nodded and stood. I silently thanked the universe I'd got lucky, and wasted no time steering him towards the kitchen and door.

We were almost there when someone tugged at the sleeve of my leather jacket.

"What the—?" Startled, I let go of Cameron.

A man, maybe late thirties, with tobacco-stained teeth, was hanging on as if my jacket were a handle. A baseball hat shadowed a face that would have verged on handsome if not for an ugly scar running down the side.

"Hey gorgeous, have a seat," he slurred.

"You've got to be kidding me." I yanked my sleeve back, but Yellow Teeth just smiled and stepped closer.

Of all the lousy nights—

Two more men appeared behind him, the one to his right sporting an MMA faux hawk and the one to the left sporting no hair at all. They weren't regulars at Catamaran's, as far as I knew. Figured. Liquid courage and relative anonymity do wonders for pushing boundaries.

Wrong girl, wrong bar.

Faux Hawk made a grab for my jacket next. I jumped back and readied my boot to strike.

Cameron stepped in front of me. "Leave her alone," he said.

Shit. If this idiot managed to hit Cameron and a chunk of skin peeled off, it'd be game over.

The three men edged around us, forming a small circle. Damn it, I hate assholes.

I inserted myself between them and Cameron. Thank god his hood hadn't fallen back.

Slam.

The four of us froze as a wooden baseball bat hit the bar beside us. The entire room fell silent and turned to us as one.

Randall primed the bat over his shoulder as he addressed the three men. "She said she isn't interested."

I don't think they even breathed as they stared at the bat.

It came down on the bar again. "So scram already," Randall said.

He didn't need to say another word. They obediently filed out of the bar, never taking their eyes off Randall and his baseball bat. The door shut behind them and I breathed in deep, holding the bar to steady myself. My hands were shaking, but not from the three idiots; it's not like I've never had a punch thrown at me. It was the narrow miss of having Cameron exposed. I managed to smile at Randall. "I owe you one," I said.

Randall didn't smile back. "Kincaid, get him the hell out of here or you can bet your ass I'm calling the cops." He pointed the business end of the bat at Cameron's head.

"Don't have to tell me twice," I said. I grabbed Cameron's hand and led him out through the kitchen. When we reached my Honda Hawk, I started the bike and passed Cameron my helmet. I figured he was more likely to fall off than I was, and it wouldn't do either of us any good if he cracked his skull open. Cameron didn't put the helmet on, just ran his fingers over the red detailing on the cracked leather seat.

"Never been on a bike before?" I asked.

"Never on the back," he said, "and usually on better bikes."

Tough, I thought, you're dead. You don't get to turn your nose up at my bike. Besides, he had no reason to be turning his nose up: my Honda Hawk was a work of art, despite the scratches. "Just get on before Randall sends a mob of crazed baseball fans after us."

I scooched forward, and Cameron got his leg up and over then settled in, placing his hands on my waist. I suppressed a shiver at having a zombie that close. If he came unhinged on the short ride back, hopefully he'd fall off. . . .

CHAPTER 2

NO SUBSTITUTE FOR THE REAL THING

Cameron grimaced and wiped his mouth with the sleeve of his Mariners sweatshirt. "That's disgusting," he said, and slid the second empty silver Thermos towards me across the kitchen table. I stopped it before it careened over the edge.

"Cameron, the taste is the least of your worries right now," I said, handing him the last Thermos from the freezer. Well, maybe not so much "handed" as "threw." Best way to check his reflexes.

It sailed past him and smacked into the backsplash of the kitchen sink.

Yeah, those reflexes were nowhere near what they should be after two Thermoses of brains. I retrieved the Thermos and handed it to him. "Keep drinking," I said.

His face contorted into what I figured was a look of disgust—it was hard to tell as all the muscles didn't move—but he opened it and tipped it back.

I took my seat across from him. "Remember anything?" I asked.

He swallowed and shook his head, and stared down into the Thermos.

I closed my eyes. All these brains and Cameron still had no idea what had happened. But he looked better. His eyes were now a shade of green that would pass for alive, and his smell had improved to a "trace of musk." Both big pluses in my books, even if his nervous system was slow on the regeneration uptake.

I sighed. He needed human brains. Hard to come by and not cheap.

I glanced down at my cellphone. Still no new messages. Come on, Max. What the hell could be taking you so long?

I checked the time: 10:30 p.m. Screw it, I couldn't put off calling Mork any longer.

"Back in a sec, Cameron. Stay put." I ducked into my bedroom. I grabbed a fresh burner phone from the bottom of my underwear drawer and dialed Mork's number from memory. No one picked up, but then no one ever picked up. I let it ring five times then hung up; no one ever left messages either. I slid the phone into my pocket, turned, then jumped a foot in the air, my heart racing. Cameron loomed in the bedroom doorway, holding the Thermos of brains.

"Cameron, I swear to god, don't sneak up on me. . . ."

He looked down at the Thermos and then around my bedroom.

Conscious of the mess, I slipped past him and gently closed the door. No sudden moves allowed; they unnerve zombies.

"Can I take a shower?" he said, his eyes following me back into the kitchen. "I smell awful."

I shook my head. "I'm sorry, but not until we fix you up a bit more. Water causes—" I stopped. There didn't seem much point explaining that water would warp his skin until it peeled away like birchbark. "Let's just say it won't help any."

He followed me back into my less disastrous kitchen.

"Look, as soon as I have you fixed up, you can have a nice long shower and start getting your life sorted out."

"I'm dead."

"Being dead doesn't mean you get out of paying rent. I need to get you functional," I said, sliding back into my chair.

Cameron frowned. I got the distinct impression that the tidbits of his personality filtering through the zombie fog didn't appreciate my dry sense of humour.

"Okay, Cameron, this is what I know. Yes, you are dead. You were—*are*—a Seattle artist, an almost-famous one. By the looks of it, you've been dead a couple of days and you were probably animated this morning."

I waited for him to respond, then prodded: "Any of that ring a bell?"

He stared at me as if on the verge of remembering something, and then it was gone, like every other time I'd asked him. "No," he said. "I'm hungry. Why am I so hungry?"

God, I needed Mork to call me back right now. Mork was never this slow—and neither was Max.

Every single zombie I'd ever raised—and I'd been a full-fledged practitioner for almost a decade—remembered exactly how they'd died. Heart attack, murder, overdose, even dying in their sleep—a zombie always remembered. Hell, it was the first thing they wanted to talk about. Yet Cameron didn't have a clue.

Maybe if I took a little peek at his bindings . . .

In polite paranormal circles you only look at someone else's work if you have permission from the zombie or binder. Since Cameron's binder was nowhere to be found and Cameron was in no condition to be giving permission to anyone for anything, polite was impossible. The bigger issue was that Cameron would feel it, and for all I knew, his bindings were already unravelling him into one big dangerous zombie mess.

Which was all the more reason to take a look.

"Cameron, hold still a sec," I said. Before he could respond one way or the other, I pulled a globe.

Pulling a globe—being able to breach the barrier to the Otherside—isn't some kind of special talent or gift. Most people dabble in college but then give up because they don't actually want to deal with what they see past that barrier. Me? I dabbled too, but I'm stubborn, persistent, and I have a strong stomach. And then there was the fact that there weren't a lot of jobs out there for history majors who dropped out before they got their degrees. Whereas there was a substantial and surprising niche for practitioners willing to call up ghosts and zombies for law enforcement, for lawyers, and for good old entertainment value. And then it turned out I was already in a prime location for practitioners. Seattle is the North American mecca for all things paranormal. I blame it on the violent gold rush history and the 1990s heroin-obsessed grunge scene, though it's probably more the geographical location of the city itself. Near water—and all of Seattle is pretty near water—the barrier to the Otherside is paper-thin.

Tonight, as soon as I tapped it, cold Otherside flooded my head in a rush. I bit back the usual wave of nausea and waited for Otherside energy to fill my skull. Once I had stabilized my globe, I opened my eyes to a world bathed in the telltale grey Otherside haze. I looked at Cameron as I let Otherside expand around me like ripples from a raindrop.

As the first wave of energy hit Cameron, he drew in a sharp breath and gripped the arms of my kitchen chair. He started to stand but sat back down as I sent a second wave at him.

"Cameron, just stay still," I said, my teeth clenched. "You just need to put up with me for a few seconds."

I searched first for the gold glow of his bindings. I picked up the four anchoring lines, heavier and brighter than the rest, running through his arms and legs. All four lines coalesced in one spot, Cameron's heart, in a bright gold beacon typical of Western and African bindings. Then the secondary lines flared into view, branching off the main lines and into his fingers and feet, getting thinner and thinner until they were fine gold threads that reminded me of nerve endings. It was good work. Most practitioners wouldn't have bothered with the fingertips. They'd have called it a day at the wrist, maybe the palm if they were feeling generous. So with such careful bindings, why the hell was he in such bad shape?

I checked his head next. I expected to see a fifth line, but there was none.

Shit. He was one line short of a full deck.

Without a fifth anchoring line in his head, no amount of human brains could fix him. I'd been sure he was a five-line, but whoever had raised Cameron had meant him to be temporary. With the detail on the hands, it had to be Max, or else there was another very good practitioner lurking around Seattle.

Not that it mattered. I couldn't leave Cameron up and running with only four lines. I'd have to put him back myself.

I took a deep breath, pushed the Otherside nausea down, and readied to untie his lines.

"Kincaid?" Cameron said through clenched teeth. He was still gripping the arms of the chair.

"Not much longer, Cameron," I said. *Almost over.*

I pushed more Otherside through his lines and flushed out the symbols: traces of the incantations used to write the bindings onto Cameron's body, the bolts that were holding his lines together, so to speak.

Cameron winced as the symbols flared a gold only I could see. Sweat collected on my upper lip. One more push and then everything would unravel, and whatever was left of Cameron's ghost would siphon back to the Otherside. He'd never know what hit him. Or at least that was the plan.

I sent the final wave at Cameron.

And that's when things got weird.

The four main animation symbols, all ones I recognized from classic voodoo, floated up from each of the anchor lines. I expected that. But then six more symbols flashed to life inside his head.

Cameron arched as if in the throes of a seizure, his head twisting. The six new symbols flared brighter and brighter. Celtic? Norse wasn't out of the question either. Then a fifth line leading from Cameron's heart to his head, the one I'd expected to find in the first place, flickered into existence. The six strange symbols brightened as Cameron convulsed, and then they began to spin slowly, like gears in a clock.

"Kincaid." Cameron's voice was strained. No kidding.

I sent another wave of Otherside towards him, hoping the symbols would stop their revolutions. Instead, they sped up, and all five main anchoring lines wavered. Cameron convulsed again.

Shit, I was hurting him.

I might not recognize the architecture of that fifth line, but Cameron sure as hell wasn't a four-line zombie.

I dropped my globe, letting the Otherside flood back across the barrier before any more of Cameron's bindings could destabilize. He slumped back into the chair, his face covered in sweat as he gasped for air—not that he needed to breathe anymore. A long moment passed before he glanced at me.

"That was more than a few seconds," he said. "And it hurt like a son of a bitch."

I shook my head. "Cameron, I hate to break this to you, but—"

"But what?" he said.

I started again. "What just happened—it should be a physical impossibility. Your bindings . . ." Damn, how to explain instability of bindings to a barely compos mentis zombie? "Look, I don't know how to put this exactly, but I don't think you were made right."

Cameron just stared at me.

I tried again. "Imagine if you were building a car, except instead of ordering all the right parts, you just used whatever you had lying around. You're one massive jerry rig." Or, more accurately, like a bomb ready to go off . . .

Cameron didn't take his eyes off me. "That doesn't strike me as particularly comforting."

Well, his faculties were working a little better than they had been, probably from the massive hit of adrenalin caused by the seizure. One little chemical, so many wonders. "It wasn't meant to be comforting."

"Can you fix it—me?"

"I have no idea."

The burner rang, and I grabbed it. "Mork, what the hell?"

"Ms. Strange," Mork said. "To what do I owe this pleasure?"

I frowned. I hated people using my last name. Mork only used it to piss me off. "I need a delivery. Now."

"Now will cost you. High grade? Low grade?"

"High, and don't mix. I'll smell the formaldehyde."

"Five hundred, Strange. I'll see you in an hour. You know where."

"Five hundred? Are you out of your—Goddamn it!" Mork had hung up on me. I tossed the phone and Cameron jumped as it hit the floor.

"Sorry, Cameron. I didn't mean to scare you," I said.

It took him a second to look away from the phone. "Who—what was that?"

"Negotiation, or lack thereof," I said, nodding at the phone. "Mork's special—he manages to piss everyone off."

It wasn't just the price I'd wanted to negotiate. Mork's "you know where" was the underground city. Which meant I had to either drag Cameron with me or lock him up here. Neither of those options appealed to me. It was like flipping a coin: heads, get caught with a zombie outside, tails, have a zombie discovered in my home. . . .

Though the underground city did have Lee, and she'd seen more zombies come and go than anyone else in Seattle. Maybe she'd know what the hell was wrong with Cameron's bindings.

Cameron cleared his throat.

I glanced up. I was used to zombies, but they have a tendency to stare.

"Where can I get—whatever it is I need to eat?"

It was my turn to stare.

"That's what you were talking about, wasn't it? Food?" he said.

Right. If Cameron had regained enough cognitive function to not only deduce the subject of a one-sided conversation but analyze it with respect to an unrelated, earlier conversation, there was no way I was leaving him alone. Chances were too good he'd get bored and take off. And losing him would not be good, not with those unusual bindings. I checked the clock: 10:30. One hour to meet Mork.

"Come on, Cameron," I said, and tossed him a leather jacket out of the closet, one that Aaron had left behind. He managed to catch it. If I'd had any doubt that my meddling with his unusual bindings had had an effect, the recovered reflexes sealed it.

"Stay right there," I said, and headed into the bathroom. I grabbed the red lipliner out of the toothbrush holder and held it up to the mirror.

Mirrors are the easiest way to send messages to the Otherside. Ghosts are bored by nature and drawn to any mirror they come across. It's like a voyeurism TV channel for ghosts: look but don't touch. If the mirror is primed—and this one was—they can send messages across to the side of the living or, with a practitioner's help, come through themselves.

Nate, going to Damaged Goods. If you can swallow your ego for half an hour I've got a gig for us Sat. night, I wrote.

At last, a reaction. *Not interested, Kincaid,* scrawled backwards across the glass in ghost-grey fog.

Like hell he wasn't interested. Nate never passed up an opportunity to schmooze with diehard fans. *I'll give you the next six episodes of* Lost, I wrote. I wasn't above bribery.

As I left the bathroom and ducked into my bedroom, I saw that Cameron was able to track me. "Stay put," I called, and closed the door.

I pushed my queen brass bed frame to the side then pried the loose floorboard up and retrieved the white envelope. My stash of emergency cash. I pulled out the five hundred I needed for Mork and pocketed it. I counted what was left. Fifteen hundred. Shit. I knew it was going to be low, but not that low. If seances were sparse between now and Halloween, I'd be hard pressed to make rent let alone restock my brain slushie supply. Whoever raised Cameron was going to get one hell of a bill at the end of all this.

I slid the paltry fifteen hundred back under the floorboard and made sure the brass bed was in place. Where the hell was I going to scrounge up more work? The cops were out until they lifted the ban on paranormal advisers. The university frat houses? Only if Nate got over his hissy fit.

The door opened. I spun, grabbing my keys out of my pocket, wielding them like a weapon.

Cameron stood there, calm and alert. In the time it'd taken me to retrieve the five hundred, he'd managed to slide the old jacket on.

It looked better on him than it had on Aaron. "Jesus, Cameron, stop sneaking up on me," I said.

His brow furrowed as he took me in. "We know each other, don't we?" he said, focusing on my face. "Is it Kincaid?"

I sighed. "Yes. My name is Kincaid. You're Cameron and we just met." I walked over and did up the zipper on his jacket for him. "Come on."

"Where?" Cameron asked.

"Out for dinner," I said.

Not for the first time, I was happy the freight elevator had been left a wide-open safety hazard, not renovated into something small, modern, and enclosed. Zombies don't do well in confined spaces. The elevator clanged to a stop on the ground floor. Before I opened the grate, I looped my arm through Cameron's so I could steer him towards the door. Or that was the plan. As soon as he saw the art installations, he veered towards them.

"Cameron, we don't have time for this. You can look when we get back," I said, and attempted to tow him along. But Cameron was on a mission. Ignoring every single garish sculpture in the lobby, he headed straight for the ornate standing mirror.

The same young man in Renaissance clothing stared out in perfect mimicry of a ghost. The most striking feature of the work was the ghost-grey cast to the image; even his blue eyes had the right layer of grey to them.

Cameron stopped just inches away from the Renaissance man's face.

"Cameron, be *careful*," I said. Not socializing with the artists in the building was one thing; pissing them off by breaking their artwork was something else entirely.

Then I noticed something that I hadn't seen before—a single word scrawled backwards across the glass, as if drawn in condensation.
Help

Maybe it was meant to be avant-garde, but the combination of the ghost man and the message . . . I shivered.

Cameron brushed his fingers against the foggy script. "I don't know why, but I like this one," he said. "The others are trying too hard."

Well, Cameron's memory might be a loss, but his aesthetic sense was intact.

"It's a good rendition of a ghost in a set mirror," I told him. "You were a decent artist. Who knows, maybe there's something to the whole realism-in-art thing . . ."

I trailed off as the Renaissance man turned his head towards me and blinked twice.

Son of a bitch, the mirror was real . . . which meant the ghost had to be real too. I grabbed Cameron by the arm and moved him a step back.

"What the hell is that?" Cameron said as the ghost turned his attention from me to him.

Cameron now took his own step back, dragging me with him. His reaction didn't surprise me. He was dead. What he saw in the mirror was a far cry from the Renaissance man I saw. Ghost or zombie, when the dead see the dead, it isn't pretty. "Cameron, say hello to your first ghost," I said.

"I'd rather not," he whispered, as if afraid he might cause the ghost to jump out at him.

The ghost tipped his head to study Cameron, a movement that looked as though he was fighting against molasses. What could cause a mirror to do that? A faulty set?

Cameron tensed again as the ghost, with a great deal of effort, turned its attention back to me. Since he couldn't be more than a hundred years old, he was probably an actor who'd died in costume—or, worse, onstage. Not a pleasant way to go. "Don't worry, Cameron, it can't hurt you," I said. That was more or less true.

Even in Cameron's basket-shy-of-a-picnic zombie state, the look he shot me said he wasn't buying it.

"Just don't make eye contact with it, okay?" I said, trying to decide what to do. On the one hand, I was not okay leaving a ghost in some art exhibit. On the other hand, I had enough trouble dealing with Cameron. The ghost wasn't going anywhere; chances were he'd still be there when we got back.

Oh hell, five minutes wouldn't kill us.

"Cameron, hold tight for a minute," I said, and tapped the barrier. The nausea hit me hard this time, not surprising since this was the second time I'd tapped it in an hour. I held on to my stomach as cold Otherside flooded my skull. Ghosts are mostly harmless, but I did not like the way this one was now sizing me up. I clenched my teeth as another wave of nausea hit, stronger than the last one. I was going to be feeling the after-effects later.

Still, I forced myself to hold the Otherside until my globe finished forming. When it did, my view of the mirror shifted.

Not one piece of inscription had been placed on the mirror to filter it. A mirror without any filter is like, well, an open flame to a moth. The mirror was a giant grey beacon broadcasting to every ghost in a hundred-mile radius. No ghost could resist the chance to communicate across the barrier with the living. No wonder the Renaissance man was moving with so much effort. Who knew how many ghosts were jostling behind him for a spot?

I was looking at a ghost trap.

What kind of asshole would do such a thing? It was like turning a bear trap into art. No wonder the ghost looked pissed. Who knew how long he'd been stuck there. And who the hell in my building could have set it? Anyone who'd sat for more than twenty minutes in a community college paranormal class, that's who. All you had to do was learn the most rudimentary setting inscriptions and tap enough Otherside without passing out. Now adding filters, that was trickier. . . .

The logical, obvious solution was to go meet Mork, take care of Cameron, and deal with this later. But I couldn't bring myself to leave the mirror like this; I'm not that mean.

I glanced at Cameron, who was still watching the ghost from a safe distance. His bindings seemed stable enough.

I switched my attention back to the mirror. First things first: get the ghost out of the way. I focused on the Renaissance man. "Sorry you ended up here tonight, buddy. I'm sure this was the last thing you expected," I said. I might not be able to hear him, but he, and all the rest of them, could hear me. One push ought to do the trick.

Before I could force the ghost out of the way with Otherside energy, he stepped back into the grey cloud of fogged nothingness and disappeared.

What the hell?

A jumble of backwards-written messages uncoiled over each other as the ghosts in the mirror fought for space.

Help

Please

Stay

Is anyone there?

Call my girlfriend — please?

I suppressed a shiver. The Renaissance man hadn't been trapped at all; he'd been holding back the flood of ghosts. I shook my head. Ghosts aren't exactly an altruistic bunch.

The messages kept unfurling over each other until I couldn't make sense out of any of them. Like I said, moths to a flame.

"What is all that?" Cameron said.

"Hold on, Cameron, I'm going to fix it."

Time to add some parameters. No red lipliner, though. Nate might see it and walk straight into the trap.

I placed both hands on the glass and swallowed the bile that rushed up as more Otherside reached through the mirror into my hands, attracted to the energy I already held. The cold hit me full force. I'd never actually tried to reset a mirror this way before, but I figured the principle had to be the same as setting an unset one. I breathed on the mirror until it fogged up and then began tracing the most common voodoo filter symbol I knew: *This is a mirror*.

Otherside arced at my fingertips as I etched the image into the fogged glass. For a moment I worried the mirror would resist the simple filter, but it absorbed the symbol like a sponge. I frowned. Huh. Whoever set the mirror in the first place hadn't known what they were doing, otherwise they'd have made it a lot harder to reset than that. I traced a second message into the fogged glass, just underneath the first: *Beware. Carnival trick. Don't get caught.*

I stood back to admire my handiwork and couldn't help smiling. Whoever set up this mirror in the first place was going to be pissed when they tried to show it off. Fifty to one they'd have no idea how the hell to undo it.

Just to be sure the ghosts in the mirror got the picture, I closed my eyes and felt around with my globe. There was still a captive crowd reaching out to me, curious, and I picked up the odd angry curse, but mostly just cold apathy and disappointment. The frantic crowd was gone.

Apathy and disappointment are something ghosts are well equipped to deal with. That I could live with. I dropped my globe and sighed with relief as the nausea dissipated.

"All right, Cameron, time to get out of here." But before we could move, one last message scrawled across the glass.

Good deed for the day?

I took a closer look. No ghost should be able to do that after what I'd just done, but the fact that a flood of messages weren't coming through meant my set had to be working. I thought I saw the Renaissance man's face pass in front of me, but it vanished in the fog before I could be sure.

"Kincaid?" Cameron said.

The last thing I needed was to pull another globe. I'd check later.

I touched Cameron's arm and steered him towards the back door. The drizzle was still going strong but hadn't morphed into rain yet, so I left my hood down. As soon as we were past my building's floodlights, I let out a breath and tried to relax. I couldn't. I'd dealt with hundreds of ghosts, dozens of zombies, and I'd never seen something as ugly as that ghost trap—or a ghost that could bypass my filter.

I checked the time on the disposable cell: 11.

I tightened my grip on Cameron's arm and picked up my pace. I still had one hell of a night ahead of me.

CHAPTER 3

UNDERGROUND

The alley out back of my apartment building ran towards First Avenue and up into Pioneer Square. For an alley, it was well lit; people didn't want their businesses and apartment buildings getting broken into. Thieves tend not to like lights, or so Aaron and Sarah once told me: more chance of getting caught on someone's security camera.

Tonight the alley was filled with the scent of stagnant water and wet cobblestones. Like everywhere in Seattle, it had a permanent accumulation of puddles. Even more so here, because we were in one of the older sections of the city, and the drainage was lousy. The only time the puddles dried up was during the summer heat waves, and even then the ground looked as if it was just begging for someone to turn on a garden hose. As if dry was an affront to the natural order of Seattle.

It took us fifteen minutes to reach our destination: the dead-end brick wall of the Downtown Mercantile. It was the only heritage building in the city I couldn't stand. It wasn't just the lack of upkeep that irked me, and the way the walls had settled at weird angles, breaking more than a few building codes I'm sure, but the odd mix of bricks and stones that had been used to build the walls in the first place. It never ceased to amaze me that the Mercantile had managed to drag itself into the twenty-first century. It sure as hell hadn't deserved to. Adding insult to injury, the store itself sold Chinese-made souvenirs to tourists and served bad coffee. . . .This was Seattle, home of the green mermaid logo; there was no excuse this side of the mirror for serving bad coffee in this city.

Cameron stared up at the refitted antique flood lamps illuminating the wall, completely fixated. I scanned the nearby windows checking for late night onlookers. Not that I'd ever seen any, but there's a first time for everything.

I felt the buzz in my jacket pocket from my regular phone and swore under my breath as I fumbled it out of the pocket. I glanced down at the number. "Shit." University campus. Probably that frat house calling about Nate. They'd been hounding me for a week to run a seance on Saturday night. I'd have to corner Nate about it later; we needed the money. That is, if he swallowed his pride and showed up at Damaged Goods.

Cameron broke free of whatever silent communion with the lamppost he'd been caught up in. He reached above me to run his hand along a charred brick, a remnant of the great fire.

Tactile and visual observation. He might keep forgetting my name, but something was working.

I made a last scan of the windows around us, and when I was confident that no one was watching, I crouched down and grabbed a corner of a four-by-four sheet of plywood leaning against the wall just below an antique grated window. "Cameron, help me with this," I said.

He gripped the other side of the plywood sheet.

"On the count of three. And make sure you don't hurt yourself. I don't know how well you'll heal."

He nodded without looking up.

"All right, one, two, three—"

The plywood came free, exposing a pair of cellar doors with rusted hinges and a lock mechanism in the green copper plate that held the doors closed. The lock was recessed into the copper plate and looked like a rotating puzzle piece with Chinese characters etched around a central ring. Unless you had the combination, nothing short of a grenade would open it—and I'm not sure even a grenade would do the trick.

I knelt down, closed my eyes and tapped the barrier, slowly this time, so the nausea didn't overwhelm me, and funnelled the Otherside into the lock. When the energy bound to the lock arced back, I opened my eyes.

Three rings of Otherside-etched symbols circled the locking wheel outside the Chinese characters, along with an arrow in the central ring that reminded me of a feather. This was a damn good way to keep people out: not only did you need the combination, you had to charge the symbols too.

Now, let's hope Lee hadn't changed anything in the month since I'd last been here. I began turning the outer wheel, setting the Otherside-etched symbols on the central arrow from memory. Each time the right symbol lined up with the arrow, a new vein of gold Otherside spilled into the shallow metal trough that kept the doors sealed shut. When I reached the last symbol in the sequence, the copper plate groaned and the doors opened with a hiss of air. I pulled my penlight out and used it to illuminate the white cellar stairs.

"After you," I said. "Make sure you don't bump your head."

Cameron looked down the steps. "What's down there?"

"The underground city," I said.

He glanced one last time at the sodium lamps overhead and took his first hesitant step, testing the stair for stability. I lit the way for him so he didn't fall and break his neck.

"It looks more like a pit than a city," he said when he was halfway down.

"Lesson one. Things are rarely what they seem down here, Cameron," I said as I followed him to the bottom, crouched to avoid smacking my own head on the low ceiling. The cellar doors closed behind us on one of Lee's set time springs. As soon as they clicked shut, the metal lock whirled back into place and the metal strips hissed shut, sealing away any residual lamplight from outside.

The cellar ceiling was only five feet high. The room was originally built to hold slabs of salted ice, so height hadn't been an issue. Two people could fit, but without much manoeuvring room. There was also no obvious way out except back up the way we'd come. Claustrophobia at its best. But Cameron seemed to be holding it together. Too tall to stand, he crouched by the foot of the stairs as I turned the penlight on the far brick wall of the cellar and reached out to tap the barrier one last time. Four times in less than an hour? I was in for one hell of an Otherside hangover tomorrow.

I took a good look at each brick, searching for the one that glowed with Otherside. Unlike the lock outside, the symbols on the brick wall rotated on a constant basis. The only way to know which one to push was to tap the Otherside and scan them all. Again, great security since only experienced practitioners could tap the barrier back to back like that. Pushing the bricks by trial and error was a bad idea. Think cave-in.

Now where the hell was it?

Cameron had started to fidget, so I began talking while I scanned to distract him.

"There's a public entrance to the underground in Pioneer Square. The ruins of the old Seattle are nice down there. All spiffed up for the tourists." Or so I'd heard; I hadn't set foot in the tourist section of the underground since the late nineties. "But that's not the part we're heading to."

"This doesn't look like an entrance to anything except someone's basement," Cameron said.

"That's the idea." At last I caught the gold glow of an etched Chinese dragon on one of the bricks—one of the four symbols Lee used to mark the passageway. Holding the penlight in my mouth so I could use both hands, I put my back into pushing on the brick.

Almost immediately, large gears somewhere behind the wall began to grind and Cameron almost tripped over himself backing up to the stairs as the sound of large metal plates colliding rang through the cellar. The room began to shake as the wall rattled against the mortar.

"Don't worry, it's supposed to do that," I shouted. Not surprisingly, it didn't have the calming effect I would have liked.

At last, bricks separated down the length of the wall and cold air seeped out, filling the cellar. The gears kept grinding until the wall was fully retracted, exposing the passageway.

I shone the flashlight down the tunnel, taking note of all the dust in the air. I shook my head. "Lee needs to get someone to sweep this out."

I did up the collar of my jacket as far as it would go to ward off the chill and stepped inside. Not for the first time, I was glad I'd never told Aaron about this place. Aaron might be sympathetic to the paranormal, but I wasn't sure how far that would stretch now that everything to do with permanent zombies was illegal.

Cameron was halfway back up the stairs. "Come on," I said. "The tunnel ceiling is higher. You can stand straight and not hit your head." I started down the passage.

"You're out of your mind if you expect me to follow you in there."

I glanced over my shoulder. Cameron was glaring at me, his arms crossed over his body as if that would protect him from whatever was in here.

I shrugged. "You have a choice. Stay there in the dark or follow me. Up to you."

I didn't get two feet before I heard Cameron coming after me, brushing up so close against my shoulder it made the hairs on the back of my neck stand up. I knew Cameron probably wouldn't go feral, but that didn't stop the reaction.

Twenty feet into the tunnel, I picked up the faint scent of metal, the kind I associated with stagnant water. God, I hoped Lee had cleared the rainwater from the tunnel this week. Last time through, I'd almost ruined my leather boots when I'd had to wade. I kept my penlight and eyes on the ground, just to be sure.

The entire Seattle underground was constructed of brick, one of the only reasons so many of the buildings survived the 1889 fire. The tunnels all looked the same: red-brick arches that had faded to a dull brown. Every now and then we passed a section boarded up with wood that led to buildings that had been closed off at the surface and abandoned. I shone the flashlight through the cracks of each as we passed by. I don't care how long a building has been abandoned; between the rats and the poltergeists down there, it pays to be careful. Fifteen boarded-up buildings later, I smelled the sixteenth before my light revealed it. Rotten eggs. It was the old sawmill. I covered my nose, knelt down beside the entrance, and shone the flashlight into the space.

"Cameron, unless you want to see another ghost tonight, I'm going to recommend you turn around and face the wall until I say 'all clear,' understand?" I waited until I heard Cameron turn.

"Des?" I whispered. "You in there?"

No answer. Damn it, he was probably holed up somewhere lazing around or drinking. Lee wouldn't be happy about that; Des was paid to guard the entrance, not take breaks. I could get him back to his post through a pocket mirror, but I didn't want to tap the barrier again tonight.

I tried again, whispering louder. "Des, I mean it. If I have to pull another globe to find you, I'll—"

A loud, derisive snort. "You'll what, Kincaid?" Des said from somewhere inside the ruined sawmill.

The ghost of a man in his mid-fifties with a logger's beard and a pair of wire spectacles—real wire spectacles—balanced on his nose floated out from behind a pillar. Or the head and upper torso did. The rest of him trailed behind like tendrils of smoke.

"You aren't that tough, Kincaid," Des said, his eyes glowing red behind the glasses. Unlike Nate and most ghosts, Des had no problem carrying a pair of glasses around; he was a poltergeist.

"Des, for Christ's sake. The least you could do is put your pants on," I said.

Des snorted and disappeared right in front of me, re-forming a moment later inches from my face. "You're noisy enough to wake the damned dead," he said.

"Des, you are the damned dead. And the dead don't need to sleep. Now hurry up and let me by."

He smiled. It wasn't friendly. "Know the new password?"

"Fuck off?" I tried.

His eyes glowed a brighter red and the air around me chilled. "Don't take that tone with me, young lady—"

"I'm not a lady, and if you don't let me by, I'll tell Lee you're the one sneaking rotten eggs into the tunnels." I had no idea why, but Des was obsessed with stealing eggs. It's not like he could eat them. He just left them. Everywhere. To rot. Lee still figured it was the work of rats. The only reason I knew it was Des was that Nate had caught him stealing a jar of eggs from a bar once and had followed him out of perverse curiosity.

Des regarded me through the spectacles. "You wouldn't dare."

If Des had still been alive, I'd have been a hair's breadth away from his face. "Try me."

Des growled, "You're lucky I'm in a good mood, Kincaid." As quickly as he'd appeared, he disappeared.

I shook my head. Poltergeists are ghosts with serious anger management issues. The older they are, the more powerful; they've had more time for their issues to fester. Unfortunately—or fortunately, depending on your perspective—poltergeists are the only ghosts that can exert any real will this side of the barrier, including causing actual physical damage. Hence, Des's sentry duty.

"Come on, Cameron," I said, crawling through the opening. When he hesitated, I added, "Don't worry, it's safe." Well, that was mostly true.

Cameron was partway through the crawl space when Des reappeared. "Who the hell is this?" he said, diving in to get a better look.

Shit. "It's a zombie, you idiot."

Cameron scrambled back and raised his arm to cover his face.

"Des, stop it, you're scaring him."

Des turned on me, eyes blaring poltergeist red. "That, Ms. Strange, is my job."

"I'm taking him to see Lee."

The poltergeist wavered in front of me before turning to stare down my terrified zombie. If ghosts look bad to the undead, poltergeists have to look worse. I felt sorry for Cameron: barely dead, no memory, and he'd already had to deal with two ghosts in one night.

Des hovered for a long moment, snarling at Cameron.

"Des," I said, warning in my voice.

Finally, he tore his eyes off Cameron. "Fine, Kincaid. Take him to see Lee. But next time, tell me you got company." He dissolved into a grey cloud and flew at Cameron, who backpedalled faster than I thought a zombie could move.

"Asshole," I said under my breath.

"I heard that," Des said, but his voice was faint and he didn't reappear.

Cameron stared at the spot where Des had been a moment ago.

I sighed. "Not fun, but the worst of it is over. Come on."

He didn't move.

I tried again. "If you stay here, Des will come back. He's a bit of an asshole that way. All poltergeists are."

That did the trick. Fear, the almighty motivator.

I stuck the flashlight in my mouth, and we crawled through the collapsed sawmill until we reached the log chute. "Through here," I said.

Cameron took one look over my shoulder. Even without shining the flashlight in his face, I could tell he was glaring.

"I'm dead. That doesn't mean I have a death wish," he said.

I rolled my eyes. "Look, I'm going first. Just follow me. The city is on the other side. Promise."

Cameron swore but crawled after me.

When I said it was just on the other side, I meant it. The chute was only a few yards long. Halfway along, I started picking up the thrum of the city, amplified by the tunnels ahead. At the end, I lowered myself down the four-foot drop into another brick-lined tunnel. The difference between this tunnel and the previous ones was that it was lit by a trail of yellow paper lanterns. I figured it was Lee's way of saying, "If you've made it this far, chances are good you belong. If not, we'll probably kill you, so no point making your last few moments miserable tripping through the darkness." Lee was nothing if not polite.

Once I helped Cameron down, we followed the trail of paper lanterns. The noise of the city became louder with each step, and soon the lanterns gave way to lampposts. The tunnel started to widen and the dusty brown bricks turned bright red, as if someone here bothered to take care of them. Then the tunnel stopped, the red bricks turning into a spiral stairwell.

At the bottom was the start of a floodlit boardwalk with storefronts on one side and a market on the other. The underground city. No one was passed out on the steps yet, which meant I didn't have to worry about Cameron stepping on one of them and scaring himself as he descended.

I motioned for Cameron to carry on. He gripped the railing beside me and stared down, speechless. I gave him a second to catch his breath. Memory or not, it's not every day you stumble onto an entire city hidden underground.

Finally, he said, "It's beautiful."

Not the exact descriptor I'd use, but I'm not a zombie. "Keep hold of the railing and try not to trip," I said, and we started down the spiral steps into the city.

The city unfolded in a series of wide tunnels with stores and apartments recessed into the walls all the way up to the arched ceilings. Those ceilings were high, considering how far down we were. Wrought iron lampposts reached out over the tunnels, gaslight lending the vibrancy of a city that comes alive at night.

The twenty smaller tunnels, or streets, spilled out into First Street, a "main street" that stretched out for a mile. As on the other streets, the shops and apartments here resembled their frontier Seattle roots, even though they'd been built after the great fire. The only section of the city that had escaped the flames was the market, a large alley off to our left as we stepped off the stairs onto the city boardwalk. A dead-end offshoot of First Street, it was one of the few places large enough to accommodate rows of stalls.

"Try not to stare, Cameron," I said, and pushed him along the boardwalk and away from the staircase, which descended for two more levels, each with an identical layout. The second level wasn't somewhere I went often, because it catered to zombies and ghouls. As for the third level? Well, the third ended at the subterranean docks. If you found yourself needing to go down there, you had big problems.

I kept a hand on Cameron as we moved through the crowds coming out of the market. The pedestrian traffic rivalled that of any busy street in downtown Seattle, except that nothing here ever really shut down. Nate compared it to Las Vegas for zombies, though I didn't see it. Not enough lights and the gambling broke out into fist fights more often than not, which was one of the reasons Lee didn't keep poker tables in her establishment anymore.

I held my breath as we passed by the food stalls that catered to zombies and ghouls. It wasn't the smell that bothered me, but the fact that it reminded me of chicken noodle soup. I did my best not to look, either. I can handle dead bodies, but not a lot of unidentifiable hanging . . . things.

We passed by zombies who looked almost normal and others where no way they were passing topside without a gallon of paint. I almost lost Cameron once when he stopped to stare at a ghoul, a type of zombie, sitting on a bench.

"Sorry," I said to the ghoul in apology, and towed Cameron back along the boardwalk. "You wouldn't have stopped to stare if you knew what the serrated teeth were for," I said.

Halfway down the boardwalk, I turned down one of the narrower side streets, and after five more minutes of weaving through the foot traffic, we reached our destination: a dusty, gold-coloured shop window next to a set of saloon-style red doors. Gold Chinese characters decorated the doors and the edge of the window, and hanging above the entrance, also written in gold letters, was a sign announcing Damaged Goods.

I noticed a pair of Chinese paper lanterns hanging just inside the window, white with red characters. Hunh, those were new. Either

Lee got bored with the old ones or there'd been another fight. I was betting on the fight.

"Well, Cameron. Here we are. What do you think?"

Cameron examined the shopfront painstakingly. Then he turned to face me, confused. "You're taking me to a dive bar?"

I shrugged and pushed him ahead of me through the red saloon doors. "Depends on what you consider a dive bar."

CHAPTER 4

DAMAGED GOODS

We stepped straight into a set of beaded curtains suspended over the entrance—not your classic hippie beads, but strings of bamboo painted white and decorated with red Chinese characters. Hmm, those were new too, and, oh . . . phew.

I covered my mouth with the sleeve of my jacket; the air was loaded with paint fumes. Well, that explained why the place was empty for a Friday night. As I stood there giving my eyes a chance to adjust to the newly dimmed lantern light, I took in the scene that lay before me. Lee really had been redecorating.

White Chinese paper lanterns had been strung across the entire ceiling, in the windows, and wrapped around the wood pillars, all of them covered with the same red characters that decorated the bamboo curtains. Each lantern gave off a warm yellow glow much dimmer than the gas lamps Lee had been partial to, which were nowhere to be seen. Besides the addition of the lanterns and beaded curtains, the walls, table, chairs and bar stools had also been given a new coat of bright red paint—from the smell of it, exterior enamel.

"Hunh, Lee's been spiffing the place up," I said. The wisdom of that was suspect in my mind. The underground isn't what I'd call a haven for interior decorators. It reminds me of a living, breathing thing more than a place, and tends to rebel against any and all change. Think of bathing a cat: there's a good chance it'll bite you.

Lee was nowhere to be seen in her white and red extravaganza, and barring a handful of sketchy patrons clinging to recessed corner booths at the back, the place was dead—no pun intended. Then again, any human practitioner with any respect for their lungs would be taking their business elsewhere tonight. Even most zombies wouldn't put up with these fumes. While they didn't have to breathe them in, the fumes still smelled bad.

I'd have turned tail, but I needed brains from Mork and I wanted Lee Ling to see Cameron. And then there was the small problem of Nate, my prima donna roommate. Just maybe he'd actually show up.

I caught Cameron covering his mouth. "You can just stop breathing and you'll be fine," I told him. "Trust me."

He frowned at me then gulped twice as the muscles in his throat and chest fought with the idea before all motion in his chest stopped.

I focused on the smells filtering through my sleeve. Turpentine, paint . . . and was that tar? Yup. Paint, solvents, tar and next to no ventilation.

I glanced at Cameron as he started to pull his hood up and shook my head. Best not to hide your identity in the underground. The zombies like to know whom they're dealing with.

"Well, what do you think?" I asked Cameron, my voice muffled by the sleeve of my jacket.

He scanned the bar from one end to the other, and then his eye was caught by a red and gold poster taped to the wall behind the bar and obscured by a string of white lanterns. One of Lee Ling's wards against evil spirits—a real one, loaded with Otherside. Unnerving if you were dead. "It's harmless," I said, half expecting an argument. I'd been telling Cameron an awful lot of things were harmless.

Cameron only stared at the ward, hypnotized. . . .

"Cameron?" I said, touching his arm and taking one big step back, just in case.

At the sound of my voice, he tore his eyes off the ward and turned a face, void of any recognition, towards me.

Shit. I took another step back. I did not want to pull another globe tonight to undo Cameron's bindings, unless I really had to. Tapping the barrier for a fifth time in one night meant I'd stand a good chance of knocking myself unconscious. Cameron took an unsure step towards me, and I reached behind me and found the back of a chair.

That'd do. I readied to swing if Cameron didn't snap out of it. . . . Damn it, Lee was going to be pissed with me bringing her a dead body. Speaking of which, where the hell was she?

Cameron's chest began to move again as he picked up a scent. Sniffing the air, he took another slow step towards me. I lifted the chair and got ready to strike. No time to feel sorry for him now, I could do that later. . . . Damn it, this was going to be messy.

"Kincaid, to what do I owe this pleasure?" Lee's low, throaty voice carried through the bar. Her voice had too rough a texture to be feminine, but it was refined with a hint of a British accent.

It wasn't much of a distraction, but it was enough. Cameron turned to stare at the petite silhouette standing behind the bar, back-lit by the lamps in her office. The blank expression disappeared as he turned back to me, frowning at the chair I still held. "I don't think this is the kind of place I hang out," he said.

I exhaled and put the chair down. "Cameron, you have no idea how close you just got to having a very short afterlife." I turned to Lee. "Nice timing," I said.

She snorted and ducked back into her office.

"And when did you start redecorating the place?" I called after her. No answer.

I grabbed the nearest bar stool and double-checked to make sure the paint was dry before sitting down. Cameron reluctantly came to join me.

"Hey, Lee, what the hell do I need to do to get a drink around here?"

"Patience is a virtue, Kincaid," Lee yelled back. I heard the sounds of rustling papers and a desk drawer closing.

"What I was saying—earlier—about this place not being somewhere I'd go?" Cameron interrupted.

I glanced at him.

"You don't seem like the kind of person who hangs out here either," he said, glancing back down at the bar.

"Six months ago I'd have agreed with you, Cameron." I propped my elbows on the bar and craned my head to get a better look in the office. "Hey, Lee? How about a whisky sour?" I sat back, but my elbows met with glue-like resistance. Damn it, I'd forgotten about the tar smell. The entire wood beam that made up the bar had been coated in creosote, a tacky preservative Lee Ling used to hold back water rot. I tried wiping my elbows off on the side of the stool, to no avail. "I knew there was a reason no one was sitting at the bar," I said.

"Yet here you are," Lee said, stepping out of her office and into the bar's lantern light. Tonight her hair was tied in a low knot and she was wearing a red silk Chinese dress. The colour was a lovely contrast against her pale skin and dark hair. It also drew attention away from the scars that ran across her face like cracks in porcelain—grey rivulets that were difficult to camouflage. The pale green-blue eyes, however, ruined any chance Lee had of passing for the living. Granted, her eyes had been bought and paid for. Dearly. The originals had been ruined more than a hundred years ago, after all.

I held up my creosote-covered sleeves. "Would it kill you to put up a Wet Paint sign?" I said.

She arched a single, perfect black eyebrow. "Everyone else figured it out. I fail to see why you should receive special treatment. . . ." Her voice trailed off as her eyes moved to Cameron. It didn't matter that he didn't show any outward signs of decay. Any dead worth their salt can spot another dead; unlike the living, they don't need to tap the barrier to see Otherside. Her eyes narrowed as she continued to examine Cameron, at the same time as she mixed my whisky sour with the deft grace that came from a hundred years of practice.

She passed me my drink without betraying any of her thoughts. Only a few of the muscles in her face still worked; Lee had turned that state of affairs into a gift of sorts.

"Nice zombie, Kincaid," she said, the unspoken question heavy in each word.

I took my first sip. Lee made the best whisky sour in Seattle, topside included. "So you caught the same binding anomalies I did?"

"Your work?" she asked, her face still unreadable as she searched my eyes.

"Not mine, Lee, and you won't believe where I found him. Outside Catamaran's."

Cameron cleared his throat. "I'm sitting right here."

"Yes, but I have to explain it to Lee as you currently have the memory of a goldfish—"

Lee cut me off. "And who are you?"

He pushed his mind to pull the detail up. "Cameron Wight," he said. Wonders never ceased, he remembered his name.

Lee flashed Cameron a smile. "Somehow that strikes me as appropriate," she said, and continued to ignore me as she studied his bindings. I wondered if Cameron could see Lee Ling's bindings yet and, if he could, what the hell he'd make of them.

At last, Lee turned her attention back to me. She inclined her head towards Cameron and lifted a frozen draft glass.

I nodded. "Yeah, on my tab—and top shelf, Lee, no formaldehyde. He'll need more than one glass."

"He's new. Best to start slow. It is also less intimidating than a pitcher," she replied.

"Just keep them coming," I said. I polished off the remainder of my whisky sour.

As she stepped out of the cooler carrying a grey, frothy concoction reminiscent of a milkshake and topped with a red umbrella, I asked, "Hey, have you seen Maximillian lately?" Lee liked to make all of the zombie and ghoul mixtures look like tropical drinks. She placed the glass in front of Cameron, who leaned as far back from it as he could without toppling off the stool.

"No, I have not seen Maximillian Odu in quite some time," Lee said.

I slid two twenties across the bar. The bills disappeared into Lee's dress. Without another word or glance at me or Cameron, she left to handle the other patrons. Sparse as they were tonight, they still expected something resembling service.

Cameron eyed his brains.

"Cameron, there's an easy way or a hard way to do this."

He still didn't touch the glass.

"Right now, you're doing it the hard way."

His nostrils flared and the muscles in his throat contracted as he involuntarily began to salivate. A big part of the new Cameron wanted to drink it.

I shook my head. "Stop thinking."

He closed his eyes, grabbed the glass and slammed the drink back, forcing the grey liquid down his throat with the commitment—if not the enthusiasm—of a frat pledge. He made it halfway through before something between a gag and a whine escaped him, but he finished it all. He set the glass back down and wiped the remnants off his mouth with his hand, then coughed as he began to breathe again. "That was disgusting," he said, staring at the glass.

"Less chugging, more sipping: this isn't a kegger."

He coughed again. "*You* try sipping it, then."

I'd have come up with something witty to say, but just then Lee stepped back behind the bar well and began mixing drinks. I caught a whiff of formaldehyde. I'd been right: only zombies putting up with the fumes tonight, probably ones who couldn't pass for human anymore.

I figured Lee would offer her opinions about Cameron when she was ready to, so I switched topics. "Care to tell me what the redecorating is about? And don't tell me you found the undead, Chinese version of IKEA."

She glanced around, as if seeing the lanterns and paint for the first time. "I had a premonition of bad luck. Red and white will help to change that."

I looked around the bar. Considering what happened the last

time Lee had a premonition, luck was something she had to take very seriously.

Lee Ling Xhao had died during the summer of 1889, the year the great fire destroyed most of Seattle. An entire city built of lumber on wooden stilts—even the drainage pipes were made of wood. Add to that the driest summer in fifty years and a carpentry shop full of turpentine. The surprise wasn't that the city burned down; it was that no one had seen it coming.

Lee didn't die in the fire, though. She had been murdered three weeks before the carpenter had the bright idea of downing a bottle of whisky and striking a match.

At the tender age of fifteen, Lee had had a flourishing career as a high-end courtesan in Shanghai. Known for her gold-coloured eyes, a coveted symbol of freedom from worldly cares, she expected to have a long and illustrious career . . . until her twin brother, Lou, was exposed as a practitioner of the dark arts. Perfectly acceptable in China at the time, but not so much so with her predominantly foreign and very Christian clientele. A witch hunt ensued, and the two fled to San Francisco, where they once again set up shop, Lou selling his talents and Lee selling hers. They eventually followed the gold rush up the coast to Seattle.

To hear her tell it, Lee had quite the distinguished clientele, all of whom she and her brother planned to extort and blackmail into comfortable retirement. Things probably would have gone exactly the way they'd planned if it hadn't been for Isabella, the wife of one of Lee's more ardent customers, who got wise to where her husband's money was going.

Stories of Whitechapel's infamous Jack the Ripper murders had reached the northwest coast by then, and had inspired Seattle's own copycat, who was attacking crib girls—indentured Chinese prostitutes—by the Seattle docks.

I shivered, remembering how Lee had described for me the way the merchant's wife had drugged her with chloroform in the dark of an alley, her single scream muffled by the noise of the crowds out enjoying an unusually warm summer night.

She'd still been lucid when the woman began slicing into her beautiful porcelain face with a paring knife. The last thing Lee saw before she died was the knife coming towards her golden eyes. She'd been found in pieces the next day and carried to Lou. Lee's brother did his best to stitch her up before raising her as a zombie. The grey china cracks running over her beautiful face were what was left of his handiwork.

I asked her once why she hadn't found a pair of golden eyes, like the ones she'd lost.

"I like green," she'd said. "It is a good reminder that I am not free from worldly cares. And Isabella had such beautiful green ones."

I know when not to push for details.

I lifted my empty glass. Lee mixed me a second and then held it just out of my reach. "Quid pro quo, Kincaid," she said, and nodded at Cameron. "You want your drink, you tell me about him."

"That's why I'm here."

I told her everything, including my suspicion that Cameron was either one of Maximillian's or a botched murder cover-up . . . or, however strange it might sound, both. Lee listened intently, stopping me only for the odd clarification. This time Cameron made no protest, but listened as if it was all news to him.

"The amnesia and slow regeneration is the strangest part, along with how he reacts to Otherside."

Lee nodded. "As if his bindings are tentative at best. Are you certain Max is involved? It seems . . ." She tilted her head to the side and chose her words carefully. "Unlike him."

"I know. But who else would it be? Unless you know of any other practitioners hanging around Seattle, down here or otherwise, who could rig those symbols. Have you ever seen anything like them? I mean, they look like a clock."

She pursed her lips, considering. "With the lines set so precariously over the anchors, I'd say they were meant to destabilize, which doesn't sound like Max. But there are traces of his work. If you were not telling me this story, I would have added you to that list of who could have done this."

"Why would anyone want to set up a zombie like that?"

Lee eyed Cameron. The muscles around her eyes twitched with indecision and I realized she knew more than she was letting on. "Lee? What are you not telling me?"

"It is none of your concern, Kincaid."

"*Lee*, I have an unstable zombie here—"

But she only shook her head. "It is irrelevant and of no value to your current predicament."

Like hell it wasn't relevant.

"My advice to you, Kincaid, is to find Max and soon. Cameron's bindings are unstable. If he didn't raise Cameron himself, he will know who did. That is all the advice I can offer."

"Bullshit."

I didn't get the chance to press my argument. With more grace than most professional dancers, Lee picked up another tray of formaldehyde-laced drinks, pivoted and headed over to the corner-pocket zombies.

"Great. Back to exactly where we started," I said. Find Max, who wasn't returning my phone calls.

I sipped the whisky sour. If Lee wasn't going to part with the information, there was no chance anyone else in the underground city would, whether I was willing to pay or not. Zombies are worse than a secret society that way.

I checked my watch: 11:45. I glanced around the bar on the off chance I'd missed Mork toting his metal cooler. Nope. It was usual to wait a few minutes for him . . . just not this long. I also didn't like holding this much cash down here. I think Mork knew that— probably why he was late.

"Is Mork back there?" I asked Lee as she came back around the bar. Cameron had finished his brains, so I slid his empty glass towards her.

"Hold on a sec, I'm not drinking any more of . . ." He trailed off when both Lee and I shook our heads at him.

"No, I haven't seen Mork," Lee said, taking a fresh glass and filling it with a mixture that matched the blue umbrella she decorated it with before passing it back to Cameron. "And with luck, I won't," she said, retreating to the cooler.

I snorted. Mork, Lee's business partner, was many things. Zombie was not one of them. I wondered if that's what led to all the strife between them. On the other hand, it could just be Mork: he had that effect on people.

Rumour had it that five years back Lee had hit a rough spot when the morgue technician she'd been using skipped town and her brain supply dried up. Enter Mork, stage right, with a bottom-less supply of high-quality, fresh brains. A tenuous partnership was born out of desperation.

Normally I'd agree wholeheartedly with Lee's aversion to Mork. But I needed supplies for Cameron.

I finished my second whisky sour. Two options faced me: stay here and make small talk with Cameron until Mork arrived, or try once more to make nice with Nate and get him to agree to the uni-versity gig tomorrow night.

I slid myself up off the bar stool. Time to see if the late great Nathan Cade had swallowed his pride and reached something resembling a reasonable frame of mind.

"Lee, watch Cameron for me, will you?" I said, and didn't wait for her nod. "I'll be back in a sec," I said to Cameron. "Stay put. If you forget something, ask Lee. And I want that second glass gone by the time I get back."

He swore but pulled the umbrella out and took a sip.

The washrooms were outside the back door, off a small courtyard that occupied the space between the natural rock wall of the cavern that formed the city and the back of Lee's bar. It was a throwback to outhouse days. Lee and Mork kept generous-sized mirrors in the bath-rooms, pre-set for summoning. Just another service for their clientele.

"Kincaid?" Lee called, raising her voice just enough that I could hear her. Door handle in hand, I glanced back over my shoulder. She was leaning around the cooler door.

"Tell Mr. Cade I'm calling in his bar tab tonight," she said, and smiled, slow and wide, like a very dangerous cat.

I shook my head. It wasn't like I hadn't warned him.

The electric heaters—Mork's doing—buffeted me with warm air that smelled of stale peat moss as I closed the door behind me. They were supposed to beat back some of the dampness that permeated all of Seattle and was especially potent down here. The jury was out as to whether they worked, but the smell of decaying moss drove home a crucial detail practitioners who visited the underground for too long tended to forget: the city was never meant to suit the living. It was a place for the dead to rot.

CHAPTER 5

THE LATE GREAT NATHAN CADE

Lee's improvements had extended into the courtyard.

Christmas lights, tiny white ones, clung to everything, including the two gas lamps hanging over my head. Strings of them had been woven into a haphazard canopy that stretched all the way to the three outhouse-style washrooms along the rock wall. It was like a night garden filled with fireflies, minus the plants, which wouldn't grow down here anyway.

I shook my head. Cheap Christmas lights were not going to scare off bad luck, only the odd drunk zombie or ghoul catching a nap behind the trash. Though I had to admit it was pretty.

I pushed open the door to the first stall, turned the lamp on and wiped the mirror down with glass cleaner I kept in my bag. Satisfied any residual stains were gone, I pulled out the red lipliner I kept in my backpack in order to contact Nate.

Nate, you there? I wrote in the top left corner of the mirror.

I counted thirty seconds before the ghost-grey glass fogged up and letters from the Otherside etched themselves underneath my note in a tight, slanted, capital-letter script—the only way Nate's writing was legible.

YOUR LATE, K. WHERES MY APPOLOGY?

Oh, for the love of . . . Well, at least he'd had the decency not to write backwards. Just below Nate's fogged note, I wrote: *Learn to spell and maybe you'll get one.*

I waited. A minute passed with no reply.

I rolled my eyes. Hold a grudge much? *Nate, get out of the mirror.*

STILL WAITING, came Nate's fogged reply.

I glared at the mirror. "Come on, Nate," I said, knowing full well he could hear me. Down here the barrier was thinner. Something to do with proximity to water and magnetic fields from the west coast plates.

SAY IT.

I sighed. Eventually, Nate would get bored and come out on his own. Unfortunately, if we had any hope of making rent this month, I needed him for a seance. Tomorrow.

I caved in word if not in spirit. "Fine. Seattle grunge rock reshaped the international music scene. There. Happy?"

. . . AND?

I swore. "Nate—"

SAY IT.

Oh, for crying out loud. "And grunge style had significant societal influence that reverberated through the fashion world. Truce?" I gave my grey reflection in the mirror my best stop-screwing-with-me expression. I couldn't see Nate yet, but I knew damn well he could see me.

TRUCE was finally scrawled across the mirror.

"Thank god," I said. I stepped to the side to give him room.

Watching a ghost materialize is a rush, even if you've seen it a hundred times. An ash-grey fog slid out of the mirror and coalesced in front of me. A pair of red Converse sneakers formed first—Nate usually materialized from the feet up—followed by ripped jeans and a bright-yellow happy-face T-shirt with a red plaid flannel shirt tied around his waist. I don't think Nate had ever actually worn the damn plaid shirt, just figured it was part of the grunge package.

His head came last, complete with his dated brown shag. So many things went through my mind. "Can't afford a haircut?" topped the list, followed closely by, "What idiot gave you a pair of nail clippers?" Ghosts can't create things. They're dead, so it's beyond their scope. But mimicking from memory is well within their repertoire, meaning Nate was perpetually stuck in 1995.

"Hey K," he said, grinning ear to ear.

I crossed my arms. "I hate it when you goad me like this, Nate."

His grin widened. "You apologized already. Can't take it back now."

"I mean your haircut."

Nate's smile faltered and he turned to study his reflection in the mirror. "What's wrong with it?"

"Nothing at all, if you meant it to look like you scalped a ferret and stuck it on your head."

He ran his fingers through the mess. "It does not look like a ferret."

"While drunk. With a pair of nail clippers."

Nate frowned at me. "It's a social statement against conformity. You just admitted—"

"I know, I know. No need to rub it in. Now come on," I said, and opened the door. "I'm having a lousy night." I gave him and his outfit a sideways glance. "Do people still seriously buy that nonconformity shit?"

"All the time. Whoa." Nate darted around me to get a better look. "What's with the Christmas lights? I haven't been out of the game that long, have I?"

By "out of the game," Nate meant how much time had passed since he'd crossed the barrier. It's easy for ghosts to lose track of time on the Otherside. Nate was better than most, but he still got jumpy when I moved the furniture around while he was gone, worrying a week had in fact been a month.

"Lee Ling's been redecorating. Just wait till you see inside. Now move, I don't have all night," I added when Nate blocked the door, the tips of his ghost Converse sneakers brushing the ground. He

knew I hated walking through him. Roommates had to have some
boundaries, and besides, the rush of cold unnerves me.

Nate got out of my way then fell in step—or float—beside me.
"Nice to see you too, K. I've been doing all right. Keeping a positive
attitude and all. Found out my ex-girlfriend married my drummer.
Appreciate the heads-up on that one."

I winced. I'd meant to break it to him gently. "If you hadn't spent
the last week moping, I'd have told you." Well, maybe. "And my
week's been worse."

"How the hell do you get worse than the evil ex marrying your
drummer?"

"Oh, come on. That is not the worst thing that's ever happened
to you. It's not even the worst thing that's happened to you in the last
two months. And besides, weren't they already sleeping together
before you died?"

Nate frowned. "Yeah, but now they're getting married. That's
totally different. Look, Kincaid, I don't ask for much—"

"You ask me for shit all the time."

"Just take me over to Mindy's. Five minutes, just so I can talk to
her—"

"No."

"*Please*, Kincaid?"

"Nate, I said no!" Talking to his ex-bandmates and -girlfriend was
the stupidest idea he'd had in a long while. Not everyone comes
back as a ghost; in fact, most people don't. Ghosts tend to be those
who died young and/or violently, though no one knows exactly why,
physics-wise that is. Not only had Nate been young, he'd drowned.
It doesn't matter whether it's your fault or someone else's, drowning
is always violent, especially where the lungs are concerned.

He'd died on December 31, 1998, a couple of years before I'd hit
junior high and been introduced to the wonderful world of peer
pressure and acne. Grunge was in full swing and Nathan Cade, lead
singer and front man for Dead Men Tell No Tails (Nate's spelling
sure as hell hadn't improved any since he'd died), was partying as
if there was no end in sight. On New Year's Eve, he'd had the

misfortune to pass out drunk on the front of his boat and slide into the ice-cold Seattle harbour waters. His body never turned up.

"Kincaid, you're killing me," he pleaded.

I shook my head. A ghost's impulse control is minimal and Nate had had very little to begin with. "Nate, stop it with the bad puns."

"There is no *way* your week's been worse than mine."

I stopped short of opening the back door. I crossed my arms and turned to face him. "Three hours ago I got a call about a stray zombie wandering the streets of Seattle."

His eyes narrowed like he was trying to figure out if I'd made that up. "No shit?"

"I've got Lee watching him right now, and I've spent the last hour trying to get enough brains into him to stop him going feral while I figure out who made him."

Nate's brown eyes turned a darker, ghost-grey shade. Some ghosts can tell if you're lying. Nate was one of them.

"Shit," he said. "Okay, you win." He paused, but then couldn't resist: "See, it's not so hard admitting you're wrong."

I swung the door open. "Inside, twinkletoes. You're helping me babysit."

"What do I get out of it?"

"Beer?" I said.

"Keep talking."

I shook my head. If men are the sum of their parts, ghosts, who have no parts, are the sum of their vices. If someone had told me I'd be rooming with a co-dependent ex–rock star . . .

Two years ago, back when I could still raise zombies for a living, grunge hit a resurgence. Open ads to find the ghost of Nathan Cade flooded the paranormal trade journals. Only problem was, no one could find Nate because he wasn't interested in being found.

Prompted by the challenge and a need for cash, I made it my business to find him. It turned out that the people who'd tried before me had been offering the wrong incentive. It amazes me how fast practitioners forget ghosts were people, and in a lot of ways still are.

I spent weeks writing notes on every set mirror I encountered and shamelessly leveraging the local ghost network. Finally, three weeks into my campaign, Nate agreed to talk to me out back of Damaged Goods.

Saying Nate had been pissed off is putting it mildly.

I'M NOT SIGNING YOU'RE GODDAM ALBUM, Nate had written.

Don't want your autograph, I'd written back. *Just want to talk.*

There'd been a pause. Then: *I'M NOT DOING ANY CREEPY GHOST SEX THING EITHER.*

Wow. Okay. *Umm . . . Yeah . . . I don't even want to know.*

UNLESS YOUR REALLY HOT—LIKE VICTORIA SECRET MODEL HOT . . .

Yeah, that's not creepy at all. Seriously—I only want to talk. If you don't like what I have to say, we go our separate ways and I won't contact you again—promise.

A second later, Nate had materialized in front of me. It'd been a small bathroom, so it'd been cramped, and Nate was dressed like he was on a ghost bender. I think he'd been trying to scare me off.

"What could you possibly have to say to me that I'd want to hear?" he'd said.

I'd pursed my lips. Nate had trust issues. Couldn't blame him, since his old band was trying to rope him into a comeback tour. "I have a proposition for you, one where you can make some money and it doesn't involve reuniting with your band."

The no-comeback-tour clause clearly got his attention . . . and the money part too. My ghost contacts all said Nate was broke, even by their standards. Worldly possessions are a lot harder to give up than you'd think. And then there's beer. Ghosts carry appetites from their real life into the next, and anything they've done repeatedly—like, say, drinking a cup of tea every day at noon—they'll muster enough energy to do as a ghost. Nate drank beer. No one in the underground city was letting a ghost skip out on a beer tab.

"What if I'm still not interested?" he'd said.

I'd shrugged. "Then I turn around, head back into the bar and take this with me." I showed him the six-pack of Steamworks in my backpack. His favourite.

He'd glanced down at the beer and back up at me.

"Just come into the bar, have a beer and hear me out," I'd said, and crossed my heart.

I don't know if it was because Nate was bored out of his mind, or there was beer involved, or the fact that I had a passing resemblance to trustworthy. My money was on the beer. But he'd agreed.

We worked out a mutually beneficial deal then and there. I'd be the exclusive provider of one Nathan Cade, but only for jobs he wanted to do. In return, I'd cover his outstanding bar tab and he'd get paid. I'd also give him free passage from the Otherside to this side through my apartment and keep his real name a secret. Did I mention that his real name was the other thing I'd managed to dig up? Ghosts have a bitch of a time ignoring them. The only reason Nate's ex-bandmates hadn't succeeded in calling him before I did was that Nathan Cade was a stage name. He'd never bothered telling them the real one.

A few months into our partnership, I started charging Nate rent. Word to the wise: never let a ghost store a PlayStation at your house. No good can come of it. Nate's not a bad roommate, and he's a halfway decent friend, too . . . when he isn't broke. Nate's not what you'd call good with numbers.

"What are you smirking at?" Nate asked.

"Oh, nothing," I said as the door closed behind us. A day would come when Nate would pay his beer tab on time, since, statistically speaking, at some point the day his bar tab was due had to land on a day he had money. In the meantime, I'd keep Lee's earlier threat to myself.

"I've got us a gig for tomorrow night."

"Really?" Nate perked up. "Where and how much?"

"Five hundred. Two hours, a couple songs. Frat house up at the university."

Nate groaned. "You're whoring me out to university kids again?"

"Guitar lessons are hardly whoring you out. Scheduling a Dead

Men Tell No Tails one-night-only reunion concert? *That* would be whoring you out."

"You wouldn't dare," Nate said, though he didn't sound so sure.

"Skip the gig tomorrow night and you'll see just how far I'll go to make rent."

"Turncoat," he said.

"Get over it. You like talking shop, and chances are good they'll buy you beer."

Nate rolled his eyes but didn't offer up any more arguments. "Any other jobs in the pipeline?" he asked.

I shrugged. "A D&D group e-mailed me about you."

Nate made a derisive sound. For someone who loved video games as much as he did, he harboured an unnatural hatred of Dungeons and Dragons.

"I made a point of explaining I can't *make* you play D&D—"

Nate stopped me dead by pulling the ghost equivalent of a three-sixty in the bar's narrow back hall, his body turning translucent grey as he searched for whatever scent he'd picked up on. I had to jump out of the way to avoid getting frosted by a stray arm. "Hey!"

He whispered, "You didn't tell me Mork was here. Sorry, Kincaid. You know my Mork policy. I'm riding your coattails till that asshole disappears."

"Nate! Don't you dare—" But it was too late. Before I could dodge out of the way, Nate dissolved into fog and dove at me.

I winced as the ice cream headache hit. Damn it, I hated it when he hitched a ride. "Get out of me, you little toad!"

No answer. I swore again. "As soon as I sit down at the bar, I want you the hell out—"

"Want whom out?" a male voice, just shy of nasal, said behind me.

I half jumped, and spun. Mork. Lounging in dark corners. Typical. And I could have sworn he hadn't been there a second ago.

I was the one who had nicknamed him Mork, after the alien on TV I remembered from reruns when I was a kid. His real name was Michael, but the nickname had caught on. Like Nate, Mork hadn't changed his shag haircut since the late nineties, but what set him apart from the rest of his high school grunge cohort was his uncanny knack for taking that Seattle stereotype to the point of absurdity. Tonight, for example, he wore a leather duster with a pair of ripped blue jeans and a pair of yellow Doc Martens. Underneath the coat I caught sight of blue scrubs: med school dropout meets grunge cowboy. The look brought to mind an old Stephen King novel, the scary one about the dark tower. . . .

Mork grinned. His teeth were straight and bleach white—easily his best feature—yet he somehow managed to make good teeth cringe-worthy.

I don't know what was worse, Nate hitching a ride or Mork being so close.

"Trouble with your scaredy ghost?" he said.

"Nate's fine, thanks. He just doesn't like you." I felt the mental kick from Nate but ignored it.

A slow smirk spread across Mork's face as he gave me the once-over. A chill ran down my side, and for a second I thought it was Nate, until I realized a draft was coming from an open side door I'd never noticed before. It wasn't hidden, exactly, it just blended into the wall. I glanced inside: a walk-in fridge of some sort.

I was about to say something less than pleasant when I noticed the portable cooler in his hand.

And that was why everyone, including Lee, put up with Mork. Mork was creepy, but he knew his brains. Clean, professional, no questions, and—most importantly—no trail. Where did the brains come from? Who knew? Scratch that. Down here, who cared? My best guess was that Mork was a coroner's assistant.

I nodded at the cooler. "I take it that's for me?" I said.

His smirk didn't falter as the steel cooler clanked to the floor. He flicked the lid up and, using the tip of his boot, slid it across the floorboards towards me.

"Watch it, Mork. You scratch Lee's floors, she's going to be pissed."

A heavy cloud of carbon dioxide flowed over the edges. When the cloud dispersed, it revealed a dozen or so vacuum-sealed bags nestled amongst dry ice. I counted the bags.

Twelve.

I counted once more to be sure, then glanced back up at Mork. "You're three vacuum bags shy."

He shrugged. "Price went up. Had to add a few security measures." His eyes narrowed and he glanced in the direction of the bar. "Every time someone raises a new zombie . . ."

I hate being accused of shit I didn't do. I'd grown up in a household that was more concerned about apologizing nicely than figuring out who was actually at fault, which made it a real sore spot for me. I did not need accusations from Mork. I picked up the cooler and tossed him the envelope. "Not my zombie, Mork. I'm on cleanup duty."

"Not like I care one way or the other," he said, and counted the money in front of me—twice—before stuffing it inside his leather duster. "Nice doing business with you, Kincaid. I'd say it was a pleasure, but . . ." He put his rubber work gloves back on and tipped his hat, then headed back into the walk-in.

As soon as the door clicked shut, I felt a pull like someone stretching an elastic. There was a snap and Nate formed in front of me.

"I hate that guy," he said.

I didn't exactly hate Mork, but I sure as hell wanted out of that hallway.

"You're a ghost, Nate. Mork isn't even a beginner practitioner. He can't do anything to you—"

"Dude, he's terrifying."

I shook my head and pushed open the door into the bar. A few more zombies and practitioners had filtered in; other places in town must have filled up. My eyes went straight to where I'd left Cameron. A trio of zombies trying to order drinks blocked my view, though that had to be his blue hoodie just past them.

"I'm not a dude. . . ."

I trailed off as two of the zombies moved. The one in the hoodie wasn't Cameron. Where the hell was he? I scanned the rest of the bar. There was no sign of Lee either.

"Son of a bitch, she promised she'd watch him." Well, she hadn't *promised* to watch him, but she hadn't actively disagreed. This was exactly where trying to do the right thing got you. "Nate, come on, he couldn't have gotten too far."

A light ghost tap on my shoulder stopped me from sprinting out the front door.

"Over there," Nate said.

At the end of the bar, enclosed by a set of photo-booth curtains, was the pinball machine. Zombies love pinball machines: the lights, the chimes, the rapidly careening metal balls. Since Lee had brought them in, they had proven a huge draw, but therein lay the problem: when sitting out in the open, they were irresistible to the zombies, like sticking a bottle of whisky in front of a recovering alcoholic. Too many of them spiraled into an all-consuming pinball bender, doing anything to keep the quarters coming. I'd seen zombies blow years' worth of savings. For that reason, Lee kept the pinball machines along with their bright lights hidden from sight.

I followed the line of curtains to the floor. A pair of sneakers, like the ones Cameron wore, stuck out underneath.

I strode over and swung the curtain back.

The pinball was careening around the top corner, setting off a cacophony of alarms and lights, and it took a moment for Cameron to register me.

"You okay?" I asked.

He raised an eyebrow and his glass of brains before turning back to the game.

"Cameron, where did you get the quarters?"

"Lee Ling," he said, not bothering to glance up this time. "She said I could waste my time just as well playing pinball as staring at her."

Another free-game ball had dropped into his queue. "All righty, then." I dropped the curtain, leaving Cameron in peace, and headed for the bar.

Nate circled me. "Umm, not that I want to tell you what to do . . ."

"Then don't."

"Should you be leaving him there?"

"He'll run out of quarters soon enough, and he won't have his short-term memory back until I get this into him." I held up the cooler. "Way I figure it, he can't do any serious damage."

Nate glanced back at the curtain before darting ahead of me to grab a seat at the bar. "Man, I need to stay on your good side."

"Better believe it."

I made a point of not putting any part of my jacket on the bar this time as I scanned the room for Lee, who was missing from the bar well again, even though a line of zombies were waiting for service.

I gauged the distance to the taps and stretched myself over the bar, careful not to touch it. I picked up two pint sleeves and reached for the tap. Bingo. I poured a beer for Nate and one for me.

I passed one to him. "Bottoms up."

Nate stared at the full glass with something akin to reverence. You'd only catch it if you were looking for it, but his hands and face took on more substance. Not quite solid, but close. It took a hell of a lot out of a ghost to solidify even a little, but he had to use the energy if he wanted to drink.

"Thank you, Jesus," he said, and gunned back the beer.

I doubted very much Jesus had anything to do with it.

The metal cooler safely tucked under my feet, I hazarded one more glance at the pinball alcove. Then Nate's empty glass clinked on the bar and I turned to see him eyeing me.

"What?"

Nate leaned in close. "At what point were you going to explain to me why you have a dead artist playing pinball? You aren't starting a collection, are you?"

I choked on my beer. "How the hell do you know who he is?"

"Ummm, what self-respecting Seattle native *doesn't* know who Cameron Wight is?" When I didn't immediately respond, he added, "Cameron Wight? The modern, contemporary—whatever the hell you call it—artist? Has a penchant for art, drugs, women. In that order."

"I know who Cameron Wight is. I watch the news, but you don't, so how do you know who he is?"

He shrugged. "There's a set mirror in one of the art galleries. It's not one I can stroll out of, but the view's decent. I've seen his work, and him." He stopped to focus on his hand, solidifying it so he could set his empty glass spinning. "I think he's sleeping with one of my exes."

"You think?"

Nate solidified the tip of his hand and rested a finger on the rotating rim. The glass sang like a wind chime. "It was foggy," he said.

"Are you referring to the mirror or the patchy memory that is the result of your short life?"

He stopped the glass spinning and arched an eyebrow at me. "You really want to know?"

I rolled my eyes. "Annnddd so we mark your descent into cheap voyeurism."

Nate looked up at the strings of lamps. "Nah, I was always into cheap—"

"*Nathan Cade.*" Lee Ling's voice rang out through the bar.

"*Shit.*" Nate spun around with inhuman speed, scanning the room as the muted roar of conversation came to a halt. Lee stood at the back of the room holding two frosted blenders full of what I can only describe as green zombie mojitos, her green eyes on Nate.

Nate turned to me, eyes wide in panic. "Kincaid, you got to spot me two hundred bucks."

"What?" It came out louder than I'd intended, garnering even more attention from the zombies on either side of us. "Are you out of your mind?"

"This is an emergency—"

Lee was making her way towards us at a clip, the tight skirt barely slowing her down.

"Lee already warned me once," he said.

Oh, for the love of—Lee had even less patience for Nate's total lack of financial awareness than I did. I glared at my roommate. "Nate, I don't have two hundred bucks."

"We did a gig a couple weeks ago—" Panic edged his voice.

I shook my head. "Most of that went to rent, and then remember you begged me to buy Call of War and Demon Run."

"Shit." Nate slumped down onto the bar; he didn't have to worry about getting creosote on his coat sleeves. "Please, Kincaid."

"Nate, I'm *broke*."

"You just blew five hundred on brains!"

"What the hell? Were you watching Mork count it over my shoulder?"

"Kincaid, I'm desperate—"

"Nate, no."

"Pleeaasseee—"

Too late. Lee leaned across the bar so her face was mere inches from Nate's. "Nathan Cade. Where is my money?"

Nate's expression was immediately sheepish. "Hi Lee, how are you? Been, what, two, three weeks now?" Nate glanced at me, pleading.

Lee turned to look at me too. Waiting.

I sighed. "How the hell did you get so irresponsible?"

"More money than sense and an army of professional handlers?"

"You're doing the D&D gig next Sunday," I said to him.

Nate held up both hands. "Totally. I'm in. They can dress me up as a fairy queen for all I care."

"It's elves. And they might." I turned to Lee. "I'll cover it."

Lee nodded and gave Nate one last even stare. "You are lucky, Nathan Cade. Usually I would not have been so generous."

Done with Nate, Lee started to pour the green, mojito-like contents of one of the blenders into glasses when something caught her attention in the office. She abandoned the drinks and headed for her door. On the way, she shouted what was clearly an order in Chinese, and Mork stepped out of the back hall, removed a thick leather apron and came behind the bar to finish filling drink orders for the increasing crowd of zombies.

Wonders never ceased. Mork not only understood Chinese, he was actually pulling his weight at the bar.

"Line up, already," Mork shouted. "This isn't a feeding trough."

So he didn't quite have Lee's grace, and if the place hadn't looked like a Chinese western before . . .

"Incoming," Nate said.

I checked over my shoulder. Cameron had abandoned the pinball machine and was heading our way.

"Ran out of quarters," he said when he reached us, doing his best not to look at Nate.

Nate may have been irresponsible, but he was not insensitive. He knew the effect ghosts have on zombies, especially new ones. He finished off his beer and nodded at Cameron. "Nice to meet you. See you at home, Kincaid." He dissolved off the chair to find his own way back to the mirror.

The zombie sitting on the other side of Nate glanced down at my cooler as Nate vanished. He looked away as soon as he caught me noticing.

I slid off the stool and grabbed the cooler. "I don't know about you, Cameron, but I'm about ready to blow this Popsicle stand." I would have beelined out of the bar right then if Lee hadn't reappeared at the entrance to her office. She inclined her chin and motioned for us to follow her.

There were some things you didn't do in the underground city; ignoring Lee was one of them.

Cameron in tow, I made my way around the bar and deposited him outside Lee's office door. "Stay right here, Cameron. I'll just be a couple minutes." I hoped.

Lee stood at her desk, her back to me. No redecorating in here; it hadn't needed it. Lee's office achieved a level of tidiness I wouldn't ever aspire to. The only thing that was out of place was a desk drawer with an ornate antique lock I'd never noticed before, which was standing open.

I cleared my throat. "Lee?" I said. "Thanks for letting Nate's bar tab slide so long."

She glanced over her shoulder at me, a frown twisting her scars. "Oh—that."

"Yeah, well, if you wanted to do me a real favour, you'd cancel Nate's tab."

She turned to face me. "Why on earth would I do that? I make a great deal of money off Nate. Besides, when he can't pay, you do."

I was about to shoot back about basing her business model on Nate's irresponsibility when I noticed she was holding a small gold cellphone. I don't know why I was taken aback; I mean, I have a whole drawerful of disposable cellphones. While Lee didn't exactly make a point of keeping up with the times, she wasn't a Luddite, either.

"Kincaid, I have received some . . . disturbing news." Her blue-green eyes drifted down to the gold phone. Without a word, she put it in the drawer and closed it. "Marjorie Secord, a friend of mine—I believe you know her?"

"Marjorie's Coffee Shop? In Pioneer Square. Everyone knows that place."

Lee nodded. "Someone broke into the shop this evening. Marjorie is dead."

It took a moment for it to sink in. I thought back to the commotion at that end of the street. "So that's what the police were doing there."

She nodded.

"I'm sorry, Lee."

She took an uncharacteristic breath. Her fingers played with the key to her desk drawer. "Kincaid, I need you to visit the murder scene for me."

That . . . was not what I'd expected. "Umm, Lee, I don't work for the police anymore. They fired me. Remember? I can't go near *any* crime scene."

"No one will be investigating. Her shop will be left alone."

"I highly doubt that, not from the number of cop cars I saw tonight. Aaron and Sarah are good. They might give me information on the murder if I ask." Well, Sarah would. Aaron would attach strings. . . .

Lee frowned at me.

"I can try and get a hold of her ghost, but seriously, that's all I can do." I didn't add that talking to the ghost of a murder victim rarely sheds any light on what happened to them; they're usually batty from the shock and trauma.

Lee shook her head again. "There will be no investigation, Kincaid, and no ghost. Marjorie was a zombie, like me."

"What! How is that even possible?"

"Marjorie became a zombie shortly after I did. A bout of smallpox."

I thought back to my visits to the coffee shop. I'd never once got a zombie vibe off Marjorie.

"She was very careful," Lee said, reading my thoughts. "Especially around practitioners such as yourself. You give off a signature. Faint, but distinct to a zombie looking for it."

"It's not that I don't believe you," I said. "I just thought I knew every old zombie in Seattle."

"Apparently you were mistaken," Lee said.

"Apparently."

"Kincaid, all I need you to do is scan the scene for any traces of Otherside—any at all, however insignificant."

"Lee, this is more up Max's alley. He's got way more experience with bindings than I do."

Lee just looked at me. "You stand a better chance. And if you get caught, the police like you."

"No, they hate me right now."

Lee's eyes narrowed and the fine scars gathered around them like shadows.

I sighed. Walking by a crime scene and pulling a globe wasn't illegal . . . yet. But if Aaron saw me . . .

"Lee, look, I'm sorry. It's too risky. Things are bad enough right now without me sticking my nose over the police tape—"

"I'll pay you," Lee said. "Fifteen hundred just to look. I know you need the money."

"Lee, that's not fair—"

"No," she said, "it isn't. But you need the money and I need to know what happened to Marjorie."

"Why?"

Lee stared at me for a long moment. "I owed her some favours," she finally said. Her fingers absently brushed the drawer key again. I don't think I'd ever seen Lee perform an action that wasn't conscious and deliberate. Marjorie's death had really rattled her.

I tried one last time. "Lee, you don't need me, you need a private investigator with a practitioner on retainer. Scrap that—you need to talk to Aaron. I've got enough of a problem with this zombie without poking my nose into Marjorie's murder—"

"Kincaid, now that they know she was a zombie, you know there will be no investigation."

I closed my eyes and worded what I said next very carefully. "They'll investigate the break-in and treat what happened to her as aggravated assault. I'll talk to Aaron. If he knows she was part of the local underground community—"

Lee actually hissed. I stopped. She was right. No matter how you dice it, zombies can't be murdered. Since they aren't technically alive, no one can "kill" them. California was the only one of the states even close to figuring out the legal quagmire of zombies, and only because it was full of them. A lot of people in show business really don't want to die, even if that means chugging brains for the next hundred years.

"Please, Kincaid," Lee said. "I do not ask many favours."

I checked to see if there was a hint of ulterior motive in her green eyes, but no. Just grief—or as much grief as someone like Lee ever shows.

I sighed. Why do people always have to be so sincere when they ask me for favours? If someone broke Marjorie's bindings, there might be a trace left at the coffee shop. Or a flood of jumbled emotions, maybe an image or two.

"All right, Lee. I'll take your fifteen hundred. But just to look. If I don't find anything, I don't find anything, got it?"

Lee nodded. "That is all I need you to do."

"I've got to deal with Cameron first. I'll let you know what I find."

"What do you plan to do with him?" Lee asked.

I wanted to find out what the hell Max had done and give him shit for it. At least, that was at the top of my list. That and keep him out of Aaron's sight. "I'll figure it out," I said.

"A piece of advice, Kincaid? Find who made him and return him to that person as soon as you can."

"What do you know about his bindings that you're not telling me?"

"It's just advice. Take it or leave it."

I nodded and closed the office door behind me.

Cameron was still leaning against the wall. Cooler in hand, I led him out the side entrance into a narrow alley. "Remember anything else about your life yet?" I asked.

"Bits and pieces, images at most. Nothing coherent."

Yeah, but he was using words like *coherent* now. With luck, the fresh brains would do the trick.

We started back through the crowds towards the stairs. The whole way back to the City Gate, I wondered what it was Lee wasn't telling me about my zombie.

CHAPTER 6

DEAD MEN TELL NO TALES

When we were back above ground, I headed down the alley towards First. If I was lucky, the police tape would be gone and I could take a look at Marjorie's tonight, before any Otherside traces at the scene dissipated. What was one more globe after the night I'd had?

But Cameron didn't follow. "We came that way," he said, nodding down the alley in the direction of the docks.

So he picks now to get his bearings back. I fished the penlight out of my pocket. "Cameron, look at me, will you?"

"Wha—? Jesus!" Cameron threw a hand up to try to shield his eyes as I shone the penlight in his face. "Will you get the damn light out of my eyes?"

"Humour me," I said. Both his pupils constricted. All systems relatively normal. I moved my finger back and forth, checking to see if both his eyes could follow it.

"Will you stop it?" Cameron said. "You said something about police, I remember that much—Jesus, why does that have to be so bright?"

So his eyes were good as new, or as close as they needed to be for Cameron to pass for normal on the street.

"You're thinking critically again and your short-term memory is back. *This*," I said, flicking the light off, "was for checking how your eyes reacted. Peripheral cranial neurons—the ones in your face— regenerate faster than the ones in the rest of your body. They're closer to the brain."

Still wincing, he said, "Couldn't you have just asked me to smile, or blink, or, I don't know, wiggle my nose?"

"Too easy. Eyes are more complicated." I headed towards First. Again Cameron didn't follow.

"Are you sure we should go out there? There are . . ."

"People?" I said, filling in the obvious blank.

"I can smell them," he said, as if admitting a dark secret.

"I just need to take a look at something. It won't take long."

After a moment, he nodded and fell in step beside me. "Will I get all of it back? My memory, I mean?"

"Honestly?"

He thought that over, then nodded.

"At this point, your guess is as good as mine."

Pioneer Square still hummed with nightlife—people, cars, even the closed storefronts blaring with neon lights. The dinner crowd had gone home, leaving the area to a younger, louder bunch of club-goers and hipsters. I wasn't worried about anyone spotting Cameron. With his hood up, he looked like everyone else still out on a Friday night.

I looped my arm in his. "Just avoid staring at anyone," I told him. "If you get nervous, stare at the logo on my jacket." On my shoulder I'd fixed a red hawk badge in honour of my bike.

We dodged around a group of kids stumbling along the sidewalk and then ducked under the awnings that lined First. Marjorie's was on the opposite side of the square, so we waited at the crosswalk along with the motley crew looking to catch the night bus at the stop on the other side. I could see that the yellow tape marking the crime scene had been removed. But if everyone was gone, what the hell were the lights still doing on inside the shop?

The signal to cross flared and we all piled into the street. I led Cameron across the intersection, avoiding the Pergola, an intricate wrought iron leftover from the 1909 Expo. Though it was built decades before the barrier had thinned between here and the Otherside, no one in their right mind should ever have stuck an iron walkway in one of the rainiest port cities in the world—iron is too good a conductor of Otherside—unless they actually wanted ghosts strolling through the barrier on their own. Thankfully, the drizzle tonight wasn't enough to trigger the iron. Still, I didn't want to push our luck and run the risk of Cameron having yet another ghost encounter, even though he'd kept it together the first two times.

Once we were directly across from the shop, I stopped to scope it out. Cameron came to a jarring halt beside me. Why were the lights on? For all I knew, an employee could have been called in to clean up. Still . . . I stepped off the curb and crossed the street a few doors down.

"Shit."

I grabbed Cameron and pulled him into a deep doorway.

Tucked in the adjacent alley was a black sedan, in all its unmarked glory. Discreet if you didn't know what to look for, but I couldn't forget that licence plate number if I tried.

"Son of a bitch."

Cameron was studying me, so I pointed out the sedan. "Homicide detectives," I said. "They shouldn't be here." Were Aaron and Sarah trying to piss off the new captain? No, they weren't that stupid. It had to be something else.

"So?" Cameron asked. When I shot him an incredulous look, he said, "There are people all over the sidewalk. Why don't we just walk past?"

I weighed how much to tell him. "These homicide cops know me," I said. "I used to work with them." I didn't mention that I'd been avoiding Aaron like the plague the last few weeks and had ignored his last three voice messages.

I considered my options. There were a whopping two: I could go home, come back in the morning and risk that any trace of Otherside bindings would have dissipated, or I could take my chances and stroll by now. If it was only Sarah in the car, I could bluff my way past her— *if* she spotted me. Aaron, not so much. Aaron had an unfortunate knack for picking me out in a crowd. I still hadn't figured out how. Still, that didn't mean he was in the car.

"Wouldn't they be more inclined to help since you've worked with them?"

"We're not that friendly anymore," I said.

Ah, screw it. Like I said, patience isn't one of my virtues. I grabbed Cameron and headed for the coffee shop window, keeping my eyes on the car, watching for any movement. Nothing.

As we drew close, there was still no indication of anything amiss. No noise, no moving shadows, just a warm, inviting yellow glow.

"Shit." I tightened my grip on Cameron's arm as Aaron got out of the driver's side. I swear, if I didn't know for a fact he couldn't see Otherside . . . I forced myself to keep going at the same pace, my eyes on the ground. We were almost at the window.

"Who's the blond?" Cameron whispered.

"No one. Why?"

"Because he's looking straight at us."

"Well, stop looking back," I said.

"It's impossible not to—*Oomph*. What the hell was that for?"

"Keep your eyes down, Cameron. Stare at the hawk patch."

Cameron snorted but fell silent. I stopped in front of the window, pulled out my cell and pretended to check messages as I pulled a globe faster than I should have. A streak of nausea seared through me. As the edges of my globe stopped wavering and settled into place, I pushed thoughts of Aaron away. I focused on the window and opened my eyes.

Nothing. I let out a pulse towards the shop glass, and it crashed against the window like a wave and came back at me. I chewed my lower lip. I'd stuck to working with mirrors so much over the past year, I must be out of practice working with windows. I loosened my globe and gave the wave of Otherside a push, adding another mental kick when it hit the glass.

This time I caught sight of the barrier before the Otherside ricocheted back at me, even harder. I grabbed the sill to steady myself and swore as the nausea hit me. Why the hell hadn't I thought to check for a ward? Marjorie was an old-school zombie living on the surface of Seattle; of course she'd had someone ward the hell out of her place to stop prying eyes like mine from doing exactly what I was trying to do. "Damn it, this is so not my night."

I shook my head, trying to clear the nausea while not dropping my globe; I wouldn't be able to manage another one. I waited a few seconds then made a second, gentler and much more explorative probe of the window blocking me. Now I knew what to look for, it didn't take much for me to pick out the symbols holding the barrier in place. They had been carved into the wooden windowsill with anchors placed at the four corners of the frame. Subtle but effective. Good work, too—an old collection of Celtic symbols. And they'd been there for at least five or six decades, considering there were no signs of the modern shortcuts.

Question was, could I break it?

I focused on the nearest corner and waited until the entire anchor floated out of the tangled mess of Otherside threads holding the ward over the window. It was a Celtic knot I knew how to break. Anything more intricate would have been out of my realm.

A girl's shriek of laughter tore my attention away from the window. I let my globe go as a group of twenty-somethings darted past us and across the road, chasing after a bus as it pulled away from the curb.

"He's still watching us—the blond," Cameron whispered.

I checked the reflection in the window. Sure enough, Aaron stood on the corner with his hands in his pockets, facing our way. I could have sworn he looked straight at my reflection, but then he took a call.

Regardless of whether I *could* break the ward around Marjorie's shop, it wasn't happening tonight—not without supplies and not with Aaron hanging around.

Another group of students were heading our way, probably to join the crowd huddling at the bus stop.

I looped my arm in Cameron's again and made a beeline for the bus stop, trying not to look as if I was dragging him. If Aaron suspected it was me, seeing me with someone would throw him off. That and he knew I hated buses.

When we reached the stop, I pulled the hood farther over my face, feigning cold, then waited, watching the traffic light. It turned green as a bus pulled up and cars angled around and into the intersection. The front door opened and the throng of people pushed to get on. Cameron tensed beside me.

"Kincaid, I don't think I can get on there. The smell—" Cameron said, shuddering. The overpowering scent of fresh brains. Dinner.

"Steady, man. Just wait."

The bus door closed just as the stoplight turned red.

One, two, three, four . . .

I dragged Cameron behind me, keeping count in my head. Thirty seconds to cross the park and duck back into the alley before the light turned green. It was doable.

"Walk fast, Cameron, and don't look back."

Twenty-one, twenty-two, twenty-three . . .

Halfway across the park. "Almost there," I whispered.

We reached the other side of the park and bolted across the crosswalk.

Twenty-eight, twenty-nine . . .

I heard the bus gasp as it switched into gear. Time's up.

Only a small group of people stood between us and the alley.

"Excuse me," I said, and shoved past a slender girl a few inches taller than me even with my chunky-heeled boots on. She glanced down at me, first in anger, then with recognition.

She was one of the artists who lived in my building—twenty-two, maybe twenty-three, short pixie cut with dyed neon-pink tips. I wasn't used to seeing people from my building on the street, though I shouldn't have been surprised. Our place was stumbling distance, all downhill. She looked about to say something to me then stopped and stared at Cameron. Of course she'd recognize him—all the art students knew who he was.

"Sorry, in a rush," I offered, and darted past with Cameron before she could recover.

Before ducking into the alley, I allowed myself one glance back at Marjorie's. The car was still there, but Aaron was no longer watching me. *Safe*.

Still, I didn't let up the pace until we'd turned the corner.

"Why so scared of the cops?" Cameron asked.

"I'm not scared of them. Just keeping things uncomplicated."

Cameron stared at me.

"Look, just forget it."

I didn't know why, but I couldn't shake the feeling someone was still watching us. Probably left over from that last globe. I doubled around back of the warehouse and opened the glass door for Cameron. While I held it open, I caught sight of our reflection in the window. What the—

I spun around and scanned the sidewalk behind us. I could have sworn I'd seen someone behind me, a man. . . .

I went numb. I'd seen the ghost from the mirror.

No, that wasn't possible. First off, this window wasn't set, and second, the barrier here wasn't so thin that ghosts could cross over by themselves. I'd checked before signing the lease.

My mind had to be playing tricks on me.

Inside the lobby, I checked the gilded mirror. No sign of any ghosts.

Fantastic. It wasn't enough I worked with ghosts, now I was imagining them.

The freight elevator was sitting on the ground floor and I dragged Cameron in. We rode up, and after minimal cursing and negotiating with the lock on my front door, I was home. All I wanted to do was crawl into bed.

"Kincaid?"

I slid the cooler onto the kitchen island and flicked the kettle on before attending to Cameron. "Come on. You're sleeping in the spare bedroom. I'll show you where."

They don't really need to, but it's a good idea for zombies to sleep; without it, the neurons in their brains tend to get overtaxed. I grabbed three extra blankets and a pillow from the cupboard so he could keep his feet warm. With minimal circulation, zombies are prone to opportunistic infections of the extremities. I shoved them into his arms and swung open the door. Cameron stared at my spare bedroom/storage room with trepidation.

"Don't worry, you'll fall asleep, and you'll wake up again too. And you'll remember more in the morning."

"You sure about that?"

I shrugged. "No, but it beats thinking you'll wake up worse off. Besides, this is the only door I can lock from outside. Otherwise, if you do go downhill, you could get out and . . ." No need to be graphic.

Cameron nodded and stepped inside. I locked the door behind him and bolted the three padlocks, checking twice to make sure they were secure. When I'd got into raising zombies, I'd had the foresight to make one room zombie-proof.

I needed this night to be over. The kettle boiled. I made myself a tea and opened my laptop. One last thing I needed to do before bed.

I warmed my hands on the mug as I scanned the police missing persons listings. I wasn't supposed to have access anymore, but the department was overworked and had a non-existent tech department.

No sign of Cameron Wight anywhere on the list. Which meant that no one was looking for him. What had he done to deserve that?

I finished my tea, closed the laptop and headed into the bathroom. I draped the large hand towel over the mirror. Ghost roommate–speak for "stay out." Not that I had anything to worry about. I was so not his type, it wouldn't occur to Nate to take a peek.

I was brushing my teeth when something brushed against my shoulder. I yelped and spun around, half expecting to see Cameron.

There was no one there, but the towel I'd hung over the mirror was now on the floor.

"Nate."

Nate's reflection hazed into focus. He wore a giant grin.

"Don't ever do that again. You scared me—"

"To death?"

I threw the towel back over the mirror.

It didn't help. In a rare show of self-sufficiency, Nate slid out of the mirror without my help. Must be all the damn fog off the water this last week. But it was a stupid waste of energy. He was going to burn himself out before half a century was up.

I grabbed my sweats off the rack and motioned for him to turn around.

"How's the zombie?"

"Locked in the spare bedroom. How the hell else do you think?"

Nate didn't usually hang around in the bathroom to chat but headed straight for his PlayStation.

"Okay, what do you want?"

"I need someone to play co-op."

"I need sleep. One of us is still alive."

"What about the zombie? Can I have him? I promise I'll put him back—"

"*Good night*, Nate."

He gave a dramatic sigh. "Fine." His extremities dissolved into streams of thin fog before coalescing into a thick cloud that made its way back up the sink to the mirror. On his way, he said, "You really need to stop going to bed angry, Kincaid. Ever since this whole Aaron thing, you're, like, ten times worse to deal—"

"*Nate*."

"Like seriously. A nightmare—"

I launched another towel at where Nate had been floating, but it only struck the cabinet.

I stomped to the kitchen, returned my laptop to my desk and then checked the office door locks one last time. I figure it can't be OCD when zombies are involved. As an afterthought, I went back to the living room and flipped on the PlayStation, just in case Nate came back out. He could run the controller about as well as he could handle a guitar, since it was something he'd done every day of his life. But if they ever changed the controller design, Nate was hooped.

I locked my own door and crawled into bed, pulling the duvet up to my neck. Warm and familiar. I flipped the lamp off.

My phone buzzed. Damn it. I fantasized about ignoring it but checked, just in case it was Max.

It was a text from Aaron.

Call me.

My stomach turned as I stared at the message. Screw it, I was too tired to deal with him right now. I tossed my phone back on the nightstand.

Less than a minute later, it buzzed again, casting the room in a ghostly grey-blue light. I shut my eyes and buried my face in the duvet. The phone kept buzzing, though. I grabbed it.

Nice night in Pioneer Square.

"Fuck." I read the text again to be sure my sleep-deprived eyes weren't playing a trick on me. Another message popped up.

Your light went out less than five minutes ago. I know you're awake.

I slid out of bed and headed over to the window. Sure enough, Aaron's black sedan was there, and Aaron was leaning against it. He waved his cellphone at me and my gut tightened. If he'd been watching Cameron . . . No—if Aaron thought for one second I had a zombie in here, I'd be having a conversation with the wrong end of a SWAT team.

I dialed.

"Hi, Kincaid." Aaron sounded pleasant, even friendly. "So you are still awake."

I stuffed "go to hell" and forced out a civil response. "Aaron, I've had a really rough day. Can this please wait until tomorrow?"

"How about you tell me what you were doing in Pioneer Square."

"No."

I saw Aaron tense up. Score one for me. Damn it, I was scoring our fights now.

"Kincaid, you can't ignore me indefinitely," he said. He actually sounded defeated. Though I wasn't going to let myself put much faith in that. I had a track record of being wrong when it came to people I thought I loved.

I took a deep breath and pulled my verbal filter out of the cob-webbed pocket of my brain before any accusations flew out. "Aaron,

I'm going to say this once and only once. You want to know why I was in Pioneer Square tonight? It's none of your damn business anymore."

I heard him take a deep breath on the other end. "Kincaid, this is important."

"It can wait until tomorrow."

He paused, then said, "Fine. Tomorrow. Before noon."

"Fine."

As I turned away from the window, I pulled the drape shut, something I didn't normally do. Before I could hang up, Aaron's voice came through.

"How much longer are we going to do this?"

I froze as emotions I'd been keeping carefully in check flooded me. Say something civil, Kincaid, something civil.

"*Good night*, Aaron," I said, and hung up.

How much longer? Try a goddamned apology and maybe then we could talk.

I stopped just short of launching my phone at the bedroom door and instead tossed it back on the nightstand. I got into bed, pulled the duvet up and hoped no one else called me tonight.

Max, Aaron, Cameron, Lee—it seemed as if everyone wanted something from me. You know how the saying goes: when it rains, it pours, especially in Seattle.

CHAPTER 7

HANGOVERS

I woke up to the phone ringing.

Oh man, did I ever have a headache. I reminded myself never to tap the barrier so many times in one night ever again. I peeked from underneath the duvet. Enough light streamed through the blinds that it had to be past seven.

Max wasn't above calling me this early. . . .

I grabbed my cell off the night table to check the number. Aaron. Scratch my previous assertion that pulling too many globes guaranteed the equivalent of a bad hangover. This was much worse.

I declined the call, shoved the phone under the pillow and pulled the duvet back over my head. He'd said before noon.

The phone started to buzz again, but with the pillow between us I had no problem ignoring it. I'm functional that way.

As I lay there attempting to get back to sleep, I registered a smell in the apartment. Smoky, salty, crispy. Bacon. Reaching out to me like a lighthouse beacon through fog. My stomach growled.

Wait a minute. I didn't have any food in the fridge. And what the hell was Nate doing cooking bacon?

I threw my duvet off and slid out of bed as fast as I could manage without face planting on the floor. The room was spinning. Oh why did the room have to spin? I fumbled the lock on the bedroom door twice before I got it open. "Nate, if you've so much as burnt a piece of toast . . ."

Cameron, not Nate, was standing in front of the stove wielding an assortment of cooking utensils I didn't even know I owned. At the sound of my voice, he turned around, frying pan in hand.

"Morning," he said. "I made breakfast."

Reaction times normal, no twitching, eyes focused . . . I nodded towards the open office door. "How did you get out?"

"The ghost—Nathan. I woke up at daybreak and he heard me moving around. He asked me a lot of questions before he let me out, but he said I was fine."

I had to agree—Cameron did seem fine. I picked up the smell of coffee and spotted a full carafe tucked behind the kettle. I didn't have coffee. . . .

It was then I noticed the collection of plastic grocery bags on the counter.

Cameron caught me glancing at them. "You needed stuff," he said.

I started rifling through: eggs, ketchup, milk. I held up the bag of espresso with the green and white logo I loved so dearly.

He fumbled a pair of aviator sunglasses out of his sweatshirt pocket. My aviators. The ones I kept by the front door. "Nathan told me to wear these. And use cash. I kept my hood up the entire time and I only went as far as the corner store. No one noticed me."

That was debatable. Cameron would be hard to miss, zombie or not. I was sure he'd garnered more than a few looks, even on a short morning walk.

I made a mental note to check the missing persons postings again as soon as I had a cup of coffee in me. "You should be careful how much advice you take from Nate. In case you hadn't noticed, he didn't exactly win the 'living' lottery."

Cameron glanced down at the sunglasses, handed them to me, then turned back to the stove. "Neither did I," he said quietly.

"Point taken," I said. My sensitivity leaves a lot to be desired. I migrated to the coffee pot and started to fill a mostly clean mug from the sink. I thought I heard the radio over crackling bacon and spotted my transistor on the desk, balanced on another pile of books destined for eBay.

"I turned the radio on—I hope you don't mind," Cameron said.

How the hell had he found it? I'd wedged it on top of the fridge behind a pair of phone books I'd never bothered to unwrap. "It's fine," I said. "News just depresses me." Cameron had it tuned to the local generic pop/rock station.

I ducked my head into the living room to check for Nate.

"So I'm a zombie," Cameron called after me.

It was a statement, not a question.

"Yup," I called back. The PlayStation was still on, but there was no sign of Nate. "You sound like you're dealing with the new status quo."

"No, but there's not a hell of a lot I can do about being dead."

"Not really. To be honest, though, I'm used to more . . . resistance on the issue." Screaming, throwing tantrums, other assorted unpleasantness. I checked the bathroom next. Hunh, no Nate here either, and no message . . .

"Exactly how much do you remember from last night?" I called.

"Not much. Snapshots with no context, though they get clearer closer to the end of the night."

To be expected with regeneration.

"When I woke up this morning, I half convinced myself last night was just a bad alcohol-induced dream. That was before I realized I wasn't breathing. I held my breath for ten minutes straight before giving up. No heartbeat either."

I rifled through the toothbrush stand—where was the lipliner? "Yeah, your eyes will keep fading, too. No blood flow messes with pigment deposit. Happens to every zombie. I know someone who can get you contact lenses, special ones that won't peel off. . . ." There it was, behind the toothpaste. I wrote *Nate?* in the top corner of the mirror and waited. Where the hell was he?

I left the bathroom to find Cameron standing in the kitchen doorway holding a still-sizzling frying pan. Watching me.

Doesn't matter what kind of dead they are, they always want the same thing: affirmation from the living that they're still there.

I shrugged. "Look, Cameron, it's an adjustment. You're doing about as well as can be expected."

It wasn't the answer he wanted. It never is. Still, he nodded and headed back to the stove.

"Hey, did Nate say anything to you before he bugged out? Like where he was going?"

"Yeah, he said he had someone to visit."

I snorted. Nate was a recluse; he didn't have anyone to visit. I flipped open my laptop to check the missing persons section of the police database again. The browser was already open, to Mindy May's website, with a second tab open on her Facebook page.

Nate was stalking his ex-girlfriend again.

Cameron glanced up from the frying pan. I closed the pages and clicked on the police database. "My roommate is being an idiot. Again." There wasn't a chance in hell Nate's ex had a set mirror hanging around her place, so how would he even catch a glimpse of her?

Still no missing report filed on Cameron. A thought struck me: if my access to the missing persons list hadn't been revoked, maybe I still had access to the paranormal cases. It was worth a shot. I typed Marjorie's name into the search window and, sure enough, I found her listed in the open paranormal cases. But there was next to nothing on the break-in or her murder. It was within the realm of possibility that they simply hadn't had a chance to enter the data yet, though Aaron and Sarah were both usually better about getting the staff to update new case files. . . . I closed the browser down.

"How do you like your eggs?" Cameron asked.

I still had one hell of an Otherside hangover, but far be it from me to turn down a breakfast I don't have to make. I slid into one of the chairs at my two-person kitchen table so I could watch him. "Over easy. Bacon, extra crispy."

The frying pan sizzled as two eggs went in. Cameron deftly flipped them, gently deposited an egg on each plate, then passed one to me along with a set of cutlery. Where he'd found the forks and knives in my sink's bottomless pit was beyond me.

He looked from his plate to mine. "I can still eat . . . normal food, right?"

I snagged a piece of bacon. "Yes, but put your plate back down on the counter for a moment and don't turn the frying pan off." I popped the bacon into my mouth and nodded to the silver cooler sitting by the fridge.

Cameron followed my eyes, then swallowed. "I was afraid of that."

I bit into another piece of bacon. I don't know exactly how long it'd been since someone had made me breakfast, but it was far too long.

Cameron picked up Mork's metal cooler and set it on the counter. I'd have to throw the frying pan out after this, or maybe send it on its way with Cameron.

"Okay. Open it up."

He kept the cooler at arm's length as he undid the catch. Gas from the dry ice flowed over the rim. "Now what?"

I dipped my second piece of bacon in the egg yolk and ate it. "Take a knife out of the very bottom drawer." I kept my tools of the trade separate from the cooking appliances. I'm messy, but not that messy.

"Next, grab one of the sealed bags. That's dry ice in there, so—"

Too late. He'd reached in with his bare hand.

"Ow! Jesus—" He dropped the vacuum-sealed bag on the cutting board and stared at his ice-burned fingers.

I shook my head and got up. "You may be dead, Cameron, but shit still hurts."

He headed to the sink to run his fingers under cold water. "No, really? I hadn't figured that one out yet."

"Here, let me take a look." I went over to him and shut the tap off, then lifted his hand to examine it. Cameron swore. I ignored him.

The tips of his fingers were covered in circular white welts the colour of cooked chicken breast. Brilliant. Just fantastic. With no circulation, they'd take a long time to heal, even with an infusion of fresh brains. I wrapped a clean dishtowel around his hand and sat back down with my coffee. "Be happy the skin didn't peel off."

"No offence, but this is like the mother of all benders."

I took another sip of coffee. "None taken. Now cut the bag open and try not to get any—Never mind," I said as the contents spilled onto my clean cutting board. I'd be throwing that out as well.

"Now what?"

"What do you think? Cut it up, put it in the frying pan, give it a good searing, then stick it on your plate."

He placed the knife he'd used to open the bag beside the cutting board and covered his face with his unburned hand. "I was afraid you were going to say that."

I pushed my now-empty plate towards the side of the table and cradled my coffee mug. "Those disgusting little packets are all that's standing between you and turning into a walking worm bag. Eat them or not—it's your choice."

Cameron stared at me, then at the knife, then at the brains on my soon-to-be-disposed-of cutting board. "Un-fucking-believable," he said. One big breath later—out of reflex, not necessity—he'd diced the brains into cubes and dumped the whole lot into the frying pan. He jumped back as the pan sizzled.

I stuck my nose over the coffee to mask the smell. "For Christ's sake, hit the fan."

Cameron looked as though he was going to hurl. "Seriously? I'm about to eat the most disgusting thing ever and you're worried about the smell?"

"It's no worse than what you drank last night."

Cameron swore and hit the fan.

"And add ketchup. Lots of it. At least until you get used to it."

He stirred it for a few minutes then dumped the mess on his plate beside the eggs and bacon and toast. He grabbed the brand new bottle of ketchup from the counter and squirted what had to be half the contents on top. He put it on the table and, after finding a clean mug in the sink, poured himself a cup of coffee and took three large sips before sitting down in front of his plate.

He picked up his fork and dug in with the same kind of Hail Mary grace he'd shown chugging Lee's brains concoction.

While he ate—or, more accurately, scarfed down his food in between giant gulps of coffee—I kept watch for a twitch, a miscue. After five minutes I had to concede that if Cameron remembered to breathe and got a pair of coloured contacts, short of pulling a globe, I'd never guess he was a zombie.

But he should have been like this last night. And the strange clockwork symbols mixed in with his bindings had to be causing problems, otherwise Lee would never have commented on them—or, rather, refused to comment on them. Part of me wanted to send Cameron on his way, with that cooler and the cutting board, but he'd taken so long to stabilize, what if he came unstuck?

I sat back and sipped my coffee, keeping him company as he got it all down, keeping one ear on the morning news. No reports of murdered or otherwise missing artists. Also no report about events at Marjorie's Coffee Shop, not even the break-in.

Cameron chased the last bite down with another gulp of coffee and set his fork on the plate.

"So, now that you've got most of your cognitive skills back, Cameron, I need your help with something."

"What?"

"Who turned you into a zombie and how the hell did you end up wandering around the docks by yourself last night?"

Cameron picked up both our plates and headed to the sink. He started the water and let it run for a minute, staring at the flow. Just when I figured I'd overestimated the return of his cognitive skills, he said, "I don't know."

"Well, start with how you roped Max into doing it."

He turned the taps off with more force than was necessary and faced me. "That's just it. I woke up this morning and remembered who I am, where I live, what I did last weekend. I remember my credit card pin, for Christ's sake. But I have no idea how I died or how I ended up a zombie. I have no idea who Max is, or whether I roped him into anything." He shook his head.

I searched his face for the lie. There wasn't one. "Let's start with what you do remember. Raising zombies usually doesn't happen last minute on a Friday night. It takes weeks, sometimes months to plan. And Max doesn't come cheap."

He shook his head again. "I don't know anyone named Max."

Something I'd seen Aaron do with witnesses gave me an idea. "You say you remember what you did last weekend. So walk me through this week, starting with Tuesday." By my estimation, that was the absolute earliest day Cameron could have died.

Cameron concentrated hard. "Monday night I was at an opening, Gallery 6. I club-hopped with the owner, Samuel, who's a friend, for a few hours afterwards, than we hung out at my place—"

I'd heard of the owner of Gallery 6. Samuel Richan. He was a middle-aged Argentinian infamous for travelling the globe finding new and talented artists who initially earned him only the ridicule of the art community but eventually garnered him a fortune. He'd settled in Seattle a decade ago and opened a space near the convention centre. I followed Richan because predicting art trends with any accuracy was like pegging a World Series winner two years ahead of time: you either were some kind of savant, had one hell of an in with the mob, or had figured out a way to use Otherside.

"And then?" I asked.

"What do you mean?"

"Well, what time did he leave? What time did you wake up Tuesday?"

He frowned. "I think I slept in, met a friend for coffee . . ."

"You don't remember, do you?"

I could see him concentrate and then give up. "I can't remember what I did Tuesday night either."

His memory was patchy. It was known to happen, but mostly in zombies raised from corpses that had been in the dirt too long, not fresh zombies like Cameron.

"What's the next thing you can remember?"

"Wednesday night. A girlfriend of mine was in town. I picked her up, we went out . . ."

A girlfriend. As in one of many. "What about Thursday morning?"

He shook his head.

"Okay, did you drop her off at the airport? A hotel?"

"I have no idea."

Still, that was two people now who'd been with Cameron around the time he'd died: the gallery owner and the girlfriend. Short-term memory loss was consistent with serious head trauma, but I'd expect to see visible damage. Drowning could explain the memory loss too, but there'd have been salt on Cameron's clothes.

"You were likely still alive on Thursday morning. You were raised on Friday night, so the very latest you could have died was sometime early Friday morning. Try really hard: is there anything else you remember? Anything at all that happened Thursday or Friday?"

Cameron stared at the counter, his brows knit.

My phone rang. I swore and scrambled to get it out of my pocket. Maximillian Odu's name flashed on the screen.

Finally. "It took you long enough—"

Max's cool voice came across the line: deep and inflected with the gravelly notes age brings. There was still the distinct touch of New Orleans that he'd never quite been able to shake, despite living in Seattle for over thirty years. "Kincaid, it is good to hear your voice."

Ha. Like hell it was. I covered the mic with my finger. "Cameron, I just have to deal with—" What exactly did I tell Cameron? That I was stepping out to have a conversation with the guy I was pretty sure raised him then ditched him outside a bar? "With someone who'd better have some damn good answers," I said, then ducked into my bedroom and closed the door behind me, waiting until the latch clicked shut before uncovering the mic.

"Max, you son of a bitch, do you have any idea what I've been doing for the last twelve hours? I'll give you some clues: it's something you lost, starts with *z* and ends in *e*."

"Kincaid, I know you must be upset—"

"That doesn't even *begin* to cover it—"

"There was an accident," Max interrupted.

"What kind of 'accident' results in you leaving a zombie outside my local bar?" I balanced the phone between my ear and neck as I grabbed jeans and one of Nate's old concert Ts out of my cleanish-clothes pile.

There was a pause on Max's end. "You found Mr. Wight at Catamaran's?"

Jesus, he hadn't even known where his zombie had got to. I'd assumed he'd sent Cameron there for a reason.

I took a deep, slow breath. Berating Max over the phone wouldn't rile him up one bit. I was remembering exactly why I'd cut short my apprenticeship. No one could get a rise out of me like he could, except maybe my mother.

"Yes, Max. Catamaran's." I lowered my voice so Cameron could not possibly hear. "Not to drill home the point here, but you owe Randall one hell of an apology after we get this sorted. He did *not* have to call me." I knew for a fact that Randall had Aaron's number on speed-dial. Catamaran's wasn't too far from Seattle's main drain-pipes, the ones that carried sewage and rainwater into the harbour. You'd be amazed what crawls out of those things every now and again. "More to the point, besides owing me serious favours for babysitting him all night, you owe me five hundred for brains—Mork upped his price—and on top of that, I had to deal with Mork!" Max knew Mork gave me the creeps.

There was another pause on Max's end. If it hadn't been for the cough, from years of smoking cigars, I might have thought he'd dropped the call.

"How closely have you looked at Cameron?" Max finally asked.

I snorted. "Close enough to know you made a fully anchored zombie. Unconventional with those damn head bindings, though. I still haven't figured out what the hell they're there for, or why his memory is still partly shot. I expect you to enlighten me." Lee's advice from last night reared its head. "Max, he's *stable*, isn't he?"

Officially, we aren't allowed to bind a ghost *permanently* to a body anymore, in the way Lee was bound, for example. But there was no law against temporarily tangling a ghost up in a net of Otherside bindings. Provided it was done right, the zombie was animated just long enough to answer a couple of questions. Once the bindings destabilized, it turned into a harmless, inanimate corpse. But Cameron wasn't one of those; Max had done something different.

"He should be quite safe," Max said. "I only wish you had not taken the initiative to acquire Mork's services."

I couldn't believe it. He was offended that I'd helped Cameron out without waiting to consult him. It was like the time I'd added Nordic runes to stabilize the zombie we were having trouble raising for a court case without asking first. It hadn't mattered that I'd been right. "You're welcome for my cleaning up your mess," I said.

Max let out a laboured breath. "I'm sorry, Kincaid. I do not mean to sound ungrateful. I've been under a great deal of stress this last week."

"Where the hell were you, anyway?"

"I was indisposed, but I'm better now," he said. "We need to speak in person. How soon can you meet me?"

"Max, I still have your zombie on my hands. I can't just come running."

"I know how this looks, but you must trust me when I say it is not as it seems. There are details I cannot discuss over the phone. Meet me at Salida's in thirty minutes."

I sighed. Max wasn't young anymore. If Cameron was a sign he was losing his touch, it was only a matter of time before something went really wrong. I'd hate to turn him in, but I had my own skin to worry about. And he knew it.

"Kincaid, can you do that for me? Please?"

Max had actually said *please*.

I checked the time: 9:30. "All right, I'll be at Salida's by ten. What do you want me to do with Cameron?"

"It is best if Mr. Wight is not with you, for his own safety."

"Max, you're starting to scare me."

"Then you are beginning to grasp the seriousness of the situation. Leave the zombie and do not be late."

The line went dead.

I thought about hitting Redial, then sighed loudly and went back to the kitchen. "Hey, Cameron, I need to step out for about an hour. Will you be okay here?"

He nodded. He'd filled the kitchen sink with soapy water and was halfway through the dishes. "I wanted something to do," he explained when he saw my expression.

I didn't like taking advantage of zombies . . . but he was cleaning my kitchen.

"I remembered one more thing," he said. "Thursday early morning, maybe 2 a.m., I met with one other person."

"Great. Who?"

Cameron dried off his hands on one of my dirty dishtowels. "Ah, well, it's a little—It's not recreational, but when I'm working—"

I frowned as he stumbled over the words. "Cameron, I don't have time for this. Out with it."

"I was meeting a dealer I use, at Club 9. Then I remember heading home, but nothing after that."

Drug overdose. Could it really be that simple? I knew Max was pressed for cash; it wouldn't be the first or last time someone raised a zombie to cover up an accidental overdose. It wouldn't explain the memory loss, but it did explain why Cameron didn't know how he was raised. Because he wouldn't have been the one who arranged it.

Tread carefully, Kincaid. That's what Max had always said. Shame he couldn't follow his own goddamn advice.

"Cameron, I still have no idea what's going on with your memory, or your bindings, or how you ended up a zombie, but I'm hoping to have some answers by the time I get back. Okay?"

He nodded. "One hour?"

"One hour." I was about to go find Nate when I had another idea—one that might cheer Cameron up while he waited. "Give me your hand."

He extended it, warily. "Why?"

I rolled up his sleeve and began probing his arm. "I want to see if it's okay for you to take a shower yet."

His muscles were malleable, with no sign of the zombie rigor mortis you sometimes see. His skin was elastic and didn't tear or peel back, and the colour returned less than five seconds after I pressed down. Not bad. I moved on to the nails, none of which were loose. Fingers and hands are the worst on zombies. The skin tends to peel like an onion in the first few days and the bones turn brittle. The dishwater hadn't harmed them, not even where the pads of his fingers were burned.

I dropped his hand and motioned for him to turn. I reached up and gave a quick tug to see if his hair was loose. Only a few strands came away.

"You're good to go," I told him. "Wait here."

I headed back into my room and dug out track pants and a T-shirt from the very bottom of my drawer. More of Aaron's stuff he hadn't bothered to pick up yet. Cameron was taller but roughly the same build. I bundled the clothes under my arm and handed them to Cameron.

"Ditch your old clothes in the laundry bin. Towels are in the bottom cabinet. If Nate starts talking to you again, either hold up your side of the conversation or tell him to go away. Whatever you do, don't take any more of his advice."

Soon enough, I heard the water running.

Before grabbing my bike and heading out the door, I opened the laptop and went to AnimateMed, like PubMed but for practitioners. Once I was logged on, I ran a search for "memory loss" and "clock-work bindings." Other than a paper on advanced Alzheimer's and zombieism, there was nothing.

Great. Not even the practitioner research community had any ideas to offer up as to why Cameron's memory had holes in it.

I shut the browser down and rifled through the closet for a rein-forced shopping bag, which I shoved into my backpack. If I was going to get by the barrier at Marjorie's, I'd need fresh supplies from the fishmongers. I grabbed my helmet and bike, and headed out the door.

CHAPTER 8

MAXIMILLIAN ODU

I stashed my bike at the bottom of the Pike Place Market, a tiered collection of shops and stalls that resembled a barn built on a steep hillside—a cornerstone of the Seattle waterfront since the early 1900s. All three levels were now filled with restaurants, crafts stores and produce stalls. There was even a touristy practitioner shop that claimed to sell set mirrors. I'd never been in and doubted very much that they worked. Too much liability. The last thing the owners needed was for a ghost to flash someone's kid. Don't laugh, I've seen it happen. Like I said, impulse control goes out the window when you become a ghost.

I spotted Max as soon as I reached the top of the first set of stairs. He was sitting in the corner coffee shop that jutted out of the building, claiming the only grassy spot near the market. Salida's was run by a Mexican couple who were neither unfamiliar with the world of the dead nor put off by it. I thank Cinco de Mayo for that; Mexicans know how to respect their dead. That and they can spot a *brujo*—their term for a practitioner—a mile away.

Max was sitting at the same wrought iron garden table he always chose, the one under the crabapple tree. It was a miracle the tree hadn't been deemed a health hazard yet, to the buildings or people. One of these days a branch was going to break or a crabapple was going to knock someone unconscious. Coconuts do it all the time. He didn't look up from his morning paper as I sat down opposite him.

He presented himself as a throwback to old New Orleans. I'd never caught him outside without his hat, a button-down shirt, sports jacket and polished shoes. Not exactly what you'd expect from a highly regarded voodoo priest, though the jacket and hat were looking more worn than they had the last time we'd met, three months earlier.

Max took his time finishing whatever he was reading before looking up from his paper. "You're late."

"If time was of the essence, you should have picked the Starbucks by the docks."

"I like the coffee here and they remember my name," he said, giving me a hint of a smile.

At that moment an overripe crabapple fell on the table, making a noise that reminded me of a rock ringing a bell.

"And because they serve coffee you like, I have to risk getting pummelled with crabapples?"

He shrugged, but his smile widened, showing a perfect set of teeth. A damn miracle since they were real and he had to be close to seventy. "It's quiet here. And Starbucks are like beacons to the Otherside—something familiar the new dead remember. I can't get a moment's peace in one of them." He stirred more sugar into his coffee. Like most Southerners I'd met, Max liked it sweet. "God knows I've tried other places, Kincaid. But the family here knows how to respect the dead, meaning I can have my coffee without every new ghost falling over themselves to speak to me."

I didn't know quite what to say to this uncharacteristic revelation. Max wasn't one to share unless he had to. He preferred to make his students work for every morsel. More often than not it was a waste of time, and this had become another point of contention between us during my apprenticeship.

"Don't look so surprised, Kincaid. I haven't been your teacher in a long while. What's the point of having a colleague if I can't complain about work every now and then? You prefer your coffee black, no?"

I nodded and he raised two fingers to the teenaged girl behind the counter. Probably the owner's daughter.

Max had aged since I'd seen him last, and the look of him resurfaced my earlier misgivings about his abilities. I have an average affinity for the Otherside, and it took me years of staring into mirrors to get so I could work with it. But Max was a medium; he'd been born to it. The academics still argue over who qualifies as a true medium, and there are a lot of grey areas. The one defining characteristic everyone can agree on is that a medium doesn't need a mirror to contact ghosts; the medium *is* the mirror, a living, breathing, glowing beacon for anything on the Otherside. It had never occurred to me that Max couldn't shut it off. I'd always assumed he had control over it.

I clenched my teeth, tapped the Otherside and let in just enough to form a ghost-grey film over my eyes, and looked his way. Max shone like a gold beacon through grey fog. In contrast, my hands were ghost grey with just a tinge of gold dust. Past Max, the ghosts who pressed themselves against the barrier reminded me of seagulls fighting over breadcrumbs in the water . . . except Max was the breadcrumb and they couldn't get to him. I shuddered and let the Otherside go.

"It is about as fun as it looks," Max said with a faint smile.

I nodded to where the greatest concentration of ghosts had been. "Are they always like that?"

"Always. Wherever I go."

The teenaged girl brought us our coffees, along with a side of cream and sugar that Max proceeded to empty into his second cup. He caught me frowning.

This time he gave me a grin. "At a certain age, you stop caring about your health. It's very liberating." He savoured a sip of his sugary coffee. "Tell me, how is your friend Mr. Nathan Cade these days?"

"Fine, I guess."

Max cupped his mug of coffee in his hands, took another sip and stared at me from under his salt-and-pepper eyebrows.

"He couldn't pay his bar tab to Lee Ling last night, so I did. Again."

"Ahhh, Miss Lee Ling Xhao," he drawled. "Give her my regards the next time you see her. And tell Mr. Cade to keep himself out of trouble."

I snorted. "I'd be happy if he could manage paying the rent on time. I won't hold my breath."

"Anything else of interest in your neck of the woods?" he said.

I shook my head. I knew better than to rush Max through the pleasantries. Most old-school voodoo practitioners like to take their time. I've never got a straight answer as to why, but maybe it comes from dealing so much with the dead. They love to waste my time too.

Max nodded to where I'd seen the ghosts congregating. "They seem to think there is."

What could the ghosts—?

"The mirror," I said. I'd almost forgotten. I gave Max the short version of the ghost trap I'd found in my apartment lobby.

Max shook his head when I was done, and I noticed that his face had taken on a gaunt and ashy hue.

"Stop staring at me and drink your coffee," he said. "I need a vacation, is all. I've been under a great deal of stress the past few weeks."

"Would my lost and found have anything to do with that?"

Something akin to sadness flickered across his face. "In part. I take it you wish for some answers?"

"Yeah, Max. That's putting it mildly."

When he didn't volunteer anything more, I said, "Why don't you start with what the hell is going on?"

Max stared down at his mug. Finally, he offered, "A word of advice, Kincaid. Do not get old—it is not worth the trouble. Nothing works as it should anymore. There was an accident."

"What kind of accident?"

He was still looking down at his mug. By the time he looked up, the face I was used to, hardened from years of dealing with the dead, was back. "Yes, Kincaid. An accident."

"Forgetting to shut the gas stove off, that's an accident. Screwing up a zombie—"

"No irreversible damage was done," Max insisted, his eyes taking on a dark edge.

I stuffed the first response that came into my head, which was that ghosts weren't the only things that couldn't learn from their mistakes. . . . Max had too much pride to listen to someone less than half his age, even when he damn well knew I was right. When faced with change, he just pushed tradition even harder. Like cramming a size-seven foot into a size-six shoe.

"Max, I'm not an idiot—"

"I never said you were."

"You might as well have."

"*Let* me finish." Max glowered at me. Why did getting information out of him always turn into an argument?

"No, *you* let *me* finish," I said, and checked to make sure no passersby were near us on the stairway. I lowered my voice. "You're just lucky he wandered into Catamaran's instead of the neighbourhood McDonald's. If the cops had found him first, they'd have rounded us up, thrown us in jail, then maybe tried to figure out who was responsible."

"Me rounded up by the police? Certainly. You?" He snorted. "I don't see your friends letting anything happen to you."

Funny, that's almost exactly what Lee had said. "They aren't my friends anymore."

Max placed his mug back on the saucer and fixed me with his gold-brown eyes. "I believe you have something that's mine."

I sat back. "Fine. If you won't tell me about the accident, then tell me about those bindings. They aren't like anything I've ever seen. I know you're up to something, and I know it's not legal."

Max shrugged. "I'm sorry, Kincaid. I will tell you what I can, but I make no promises to give you all the answers you want. This story is not mine to tell, and there are serious extenuating circumstances."

I'd take what I could get at this point. "All right, I'm game. Shoot."

"Cameron is a client of mine, a particularly challenging case. How familiar are you with diseases of the mind?"

Anyone raising zombies has to have a basic understanding of the human body. In my spare time I'd flipped through medical texts and taken a couple of night classes in physiology. Diseases of the mind, though . . . well, let's just say that, typically, any organ that fails during life will still pose a problem in death. The brain is just another organ. It was one of the reasons I used to insist on full medical records from clients, back when five-line, permanent zombies were still legal—or technically not illegal. "So Cameron had a disease of the mind? Neurodegenerative? Depression?"

Max nodded when I hit at depression. "Cameron suffered from debilitating manic depression and a resulting addiction."

What was the saying one of my old high school teachers used? There is a fine line between genius and madness?

"When he came to me, Cameron was working on a number of pieces. But he was having great difficulty completing them without substantial chemical assistance. It was taking a drastic toll on his body."

"He's not the first artist who's drowned himself in a shallow pool of alcohol and drugs," I said. "And you know as well as I do that zombieism won't fix any of that. Dead and depressed isn't a solution to alive and depressed."

"Not everything is about zombies, Kincaid. I do have other talents."

Voodoo. I chewed that one over. Voodoo is the subtle manipulation of the natural order of the living world through channelling Otherside. What I did—raising zombies and talking to ghosts—also channelled Otherside, but using the energy of the dead to manipulate the dead isn't such a stretch. Using Otherside to warp the living world? What Max suggested wasn't beyond his capabilities.

"You've said it yourself a hundred times at least: voodoo is a last resort, not a treatment." Voodoo wasn't like an antipsychotic medication. It was fickle and unpredictable.

"This *was* a last resort. Medication helped control his bipolar disorder but was ruining his work. The self-medicating, as you so aptly described it, had also ceased to work." Max broke eye contact and looked down at his empty mug. "I found a way to help him without the use of medications."

Someone once told me if you can't learn to read between the lines, you won't last long. Come to think of it, it was Max. "I'm figuring things weren't quite that simple."

He glanced up from his mug, the sun catching the yellow flecks in his eye. "Everything comes with a price. You know that."

And sometimes the steepest price isn't monetary. What had Cameron had to pay?

As if reading my thoughts, Max added, "All you need know is we reached a mutually beneficial arrangement."

Yeah, I'll just bet. "And the fact that your services could gain you some publicity and validation was nothing to you?"

That got me a smile. "I may not be an art connoisseur, but I can read numbers and reviews. His work was garnering national attention. It was thought to be only a matter of time before he reached the international market. There was significant money to be made if my services could help Cameron reach his goals."

And when it came out that Max had had a hand in restoring Cameron's health, other business would filter his way.

"All right, but you still haven't explained where zombieism fits in."

Max pursed his lips. "That is where a conflict of interest affects my ability to discuss this case."

"You can tell me you used voodoo as an alternative to psychiatry but not how he ended up a zombie?"

Max lifted a hand to stop me. "What I can say is that Mr. Wight's greatest fear was dying before finishing his work."

The pieces slid into place. "You arranged for him to become a zombie if he died before his work was done."

Max nodded. "Part of our agreement was for Cameron to be reanimated in the event of his untimely death. My methods were working, but he still had slip-ups. The unusual bindings are so Cameron would be animated at death—temporarily, I might add—so he could finish his work."

So Cameron hadn't wanted to be a zombie forever—that I believed. Not everyone does. But how had Max managed to lose Cameron? "Jesus Christ, Max. You figured out a way to raise him remotely."

Max frowned. "I really wish you would stop swearing. Your vocabulary cannot be that limited."

I started counting off my questions on my fingers. "All right, fine. First off, how on earth do you manage a remote binding? Second, even if you can raise him remotely, what's the point? The dead can't create anything. Third, if he's temporary, why the"—I stopped myself from saying *hell*—"does he have permanent five-line bindings?"

Max didn't answer.

"All right. Did Cameron know what he was getting into?"

"Kincaid, I swear to you, he knew all the risks."

I let out a deep breath. I knew Max wouldn't lie about that. "Why can't he remember anything? About the animation, about you?"

"I cannot say. He was somewhat of a guinea pig."

The whole thing was crazy enough to be true. "All right. How do we go about getting Cameron back to you?" Services rendered for bringing someone back as a zombie don't end at raising. Teaching someone how to integrate into society as a zombie takes time. Because of the memory loss and the sheer strangeness of Cameron's bindings, I wasn't willing to take on the job.

Max shook his head. "It would be better if you kept him a few more days. It will give me time to research what went wrong."

"Yeah, no. Your zombie—you keep him with you while you do the research."

"Things will go faster and better for Cameron if he is not with me. Take him to his own home if you do not wish him to stay with you. Is he cognizant enough to function despite his amnesia?"

"No! Of course he's not. Jesus, Max, have you been listening? I told you what happened when I probed him with Otherside. *You* take him."

"I can pay you," Max said.

No, Kincaid, don't even consider it. "How much?" I asked.

The gold glint was back in his eyes. "Two thousand for three days' work. Just keep watch for three days, that's all I ask."

"You owe me five hundred more for the brains."

"I will reimburse you for that too."

Three days, two grand, just to watch him. "You said yourself, the bindings are experimental. What if—"

"If they have not fallen apart yet, they will hold three more days." All of a sudden Max looked like a tired old man. "I'm sorry I'm asking you to do this, Kincaid, but I will be able to help Cameron sooner if I am left to research what has gone wrong."

I mulled it over. Best case, it was an easy two grand. Worst case . . .

"Kincaid, please. I am asking this as a favour."

Goddamnit. I needed to stop granting people favours. "You've got three days, Max, that's it. And if anything—*anything*—goes wrong, I will swear it's all your fault."

He nodded, spit on his hand and extended it. It was a voodoo thing. We shook and then he rose from his seat and gathered his hat. "Now if you'll excuse me, I need to attend to another client." He left money on the table and turned to go.

As I stood up and grabbed my bag, Max stopped halfway down the steps. "Did you hear about Marjorie?" he asked.

"Heard about it from Lee last night. Saw the police there, too."

He nodded and the dark look was back. If he suspected or knew Lee had asked me to look into things, he didn't let on. "A parting word of advice?"

"Knock yourself out."

"Tread carefully with that mirror you found in your building. I've seen such ghost traps before. Powerful, and dangerous, especially when the wrong ghost falls prey."

"Like I said, I shut it down."

Max shook his head. "It's not the mirror itself that worries me, but the person who put it there. A person who uses a ghost trap is not someone I would want to meet in a dark alley."

Goosebumps ran up my arms and I opened my mouth to ask another question, but Max stopped me. "Do not ask me for any more details. I am neither inclined nor interested in giving them." He stared into a window while he said it, and I wondered if he was looking at his own reflection or something else. "Sometimes knowledge is not worth the headache it brings."

I crossed my arms. No, that wasn't cryptic at all.

Max continued down the steps. "And stop with the parlour tricks, they are beneath you."

"Parlour tricks" meaning my seances with Nate up at the university. The ones that paid my bills. "Nice seeing you too, Max. And you're welcome."

He waved without looking back, and a moment later he'd disappeared from view.

Cameron, Marjorie and now this. I sat there wondering how the hell I had let Max talk me into watching Cameron for three days. Two thousand dollars, that's how. I checked my phone: 10:30 a.m. I still had half an hour before I told Cameron I'd be back.

I pulled my glass cleaner out of my purse and ducked into the coffee shop washroom to see if I could get hold of Nate.

Thankfully, the mirror was already set. *Nate?* I wrote.

YEAH—WHAT? scrawled back a moment later, followed by Nate's face forming out of the fog.

I was the only person in the bathroom, and talking would be a lot faster than writing. "I need you to do me a favour."

I'M BUSY.

"No you're not—you're stalking your ex. This is important. Go check on Cameron."

OKAY, OKAY.

"Now, Nate."

I SAID I'D DO IT.

"Awesome, I'll wait."

Nate grumbled something inaudible before disappearing behind the fog. Less than a minute later, he returned: *HE'S FINE. ANYTHING ELSE, O GREAT MISTRISS?*

"Yeah. I'll be home in half an hour. Keep an eye on Cameron. The computer's on—text me if there's an emergency. And don't forget the gig at the university library tonight at seven."

ON MY CALANDAR, K.

I got the distinct impression Nate had tuned out. "I'm serious, Nate."
I'M NOT GOING TO FORGET. ALRIGHT?

"Fine. Just stay with Cameron until I get back." I cleaned the lipliner off the mirror and stowed my tools in my purse.

I left my bike at the lower market entrance and took the stairs through Pike Place to the upper floors, where the fishmongers hawked their wares. My route happened to take me right by the tourist practitioner shop. I did a double take. Behind the counter was the neon-haired girl from my building. The one I'd run into last night in Pioneer Square.

I thought back to the set mirror in the lobby. One hell of a coincidence that there'd been a ghost trap mirror in my building last night and one of the tenants just happened to work in the only practitioner shop outside the underground city.

I don't believe in coincidences.

I've also never been a big believer in subtlety either. I was low on sage; it wouldn't hurt to stock up.

I stepped inside the shop. Neon didn't even glance up as the doorbell chimed.

I leaned over the counter. Still nothing. Apparently whatever was on her phone was really interesting.

"Excuse me," I said.

She jumped, and her eyes widened as recognition flooded her face. I smiled. "Hi there. Didn't mean to scare you."

Her bleached blond eyebrows knit together. "Don't I know you?"

I extended my hand. "We live in the same building."

She didn't take it, just stared at it with deep disapproval. I picked up a twig of wrapped sage from the counter basket instead. I'd get better and cheaper sage in the underground, but this would do for now. "I'll take four of these."

"Anything else?"

Definitely not friendly. I feigned browsing, as I checked for anything that might be a set mirror. Hard to tell with the way stuff was packed in here . . . Oh, what the hell. I tapped the Otherside, bit back the nausea and took a quick peek.

Not one thing in the shop had an ounce of Otherside in it. I turned to Neon. "Got any set mirrors for sale?"

I got the distinct impression she was insulted I would ask. "Those are special order. And we don't sell them to just anyone. They can be dangerous."

Yeah, maybe if you had a deadly fear of flashing ghosts.

I threw her my best innocent look. "I'm actually looking for something very specific," I said. "I recently saw this awesome art installation. It was a mirror, but instead of one ghost, there were like twenty. I'd really like to buy one for my mom, you know, for the hallway when people walk in. I'm thinking of naming it *Lament of Tortured Souls*."

Her transition from surprise, to anger, to something I could only describe as indignation was priceless. "Is this some kind of joke?"

I arched an eyebrow. I stopped myself from calling her Neon and checked her name tag. "Morgan. I found one in our lobby last night. How about you tell me?"

I searched her face. I'd thrown her, but if the mirror was hers, she wasn't exactly giving it away. Then again, most practitioners would at least feign shock on hearing about something like that. All she did was ring up the four sticks of sage and put them in a paper bag. "Will that be all? We've got some good beginner books for starting practitioners on sale."

I smiled at her. She'd have to come up with something a lot smarter to get a rise out of me. "Maybe next time." I took my change and left.

I thought about her reaction as I climbed towards the top floor of the markets and the fishmongers. Awfully hostile for a minimum-wage cashier. No question I'd spooked her. If the mirror was hers, though, why stick it in the lobby? Could she be so green she hadn't known what she was doing?

My phone buzzed. Aaron again. Damn it.

CHAPTER 9

COFFEE AND MURDER

I took the last flight of steps to the fish market two at a time. Max might be old and someone I more or less considered a friend, but he was as slick as Lee Ling when it came to holding cards close; he'd had to be to survive growing up in the Deep South voodoo community. "Competitive" doesn't begin to describe the politics between the families. Only world I know of where it's considered business as usual to curse your competitors. Or marry them to make a more powerful family bond. Max had hinted that was why he'd left for Seattle so many years ago: to avoid a voodoo wedding.

The thing I kept coming back to was Cameron's missing memories. Normally that kind of detail would interest Max, as an unforeseen puzzle to unwind, but he'd skimmed over it, chalking it up to the intricacy of the bindings. I didn't buy that for a second. Max had too much pride in his voodoo to let something like that slide. The Max I apprenticed with would have had me drawing the binding patterns I'd seen and then been cross-referencing texts faster than you can say gris-gris. Or more likely he'd have had me referencing them while he sipped his sugared coffee, occasionally piping up to tell me what I was doing wrong. As much as I liked him as a person, a huge weight had lifted off my shoulders the day I'd quit.

Or maybe it was just that Max's pride was hurt because something had gone wrong with one of his raisings, experimental or not. Max's biggest failing in this world was pride.

The telltale smell of fish on ice hit me before I saw the first fishmonger stall. I headed for the one run by a fellow named Edward, who nodded when he spotted me coming. He was lifting a crate onto the table. I wondered why he didn't hire someone with a better back to do the lifting.

"The usual, Ms. Strange?" he asked, a hair shy of friendly but still pleasant. I was a repeat customer, after all.

I nodded and Edward removed a shallow plastic tray, roughly the size of a small coffee table, from a saltwater tank tucked underneath the table. He set it in front of me so I could examine the assortment of spiny, purple sea urchins.

I pulled the reinforced shopping bag from my backpack and handed it to Edward and began pointing out the sea urchins I wanted: large and roughly matching in weight and size. He picked them up with a canvas glove, giving each one the cautious respect it deserved as he placed them in the spike-proof bag. Not a bad analogy for the way he treated me.

A man who'd been perusing the adjacent salmon slabs was watching my purchase with interest. From the suit jacket over tailored jeans and manicured hands, I guessed lawyer doing his weekend shopping.

He gave me a big smile when he caught my glance.

"Sushi?" He nodded at the tray of sea urchins.

I was acutely aware that Edward had tensed. I had a sinking feeling Edward had figured out I didn't buy the sea urchins for sushi. Practitioning wasn't illegal, but it was definitely considered a fringe activity. Also, most people thought that practitioners would make a ghost or poltergeist haunt them if they looked at us the wrong way. Shows what most people know. Getting a ghost, let alone a poltergeist, to do anything useful is like herding cats.

"Best sea urchins in town," I said.

The man's smile widened, and he headed on his way.

Edward narrowed his eyes at me.

"Edward, I'm not about to ruin your business."

He stared at me skeptically as he took the two twenties I passed him and worked on getting change out of his apron.

"You sell the best sea urchins in Seattle. I need you to stay in business."

He handed me my change and the bag of urchins. "That I'll believe." He waved me away and moved on to another customer.

I headed back down the three flights of steps to where I'd left my bike. I hopped on, headed up to First Street and took a right towards old Seattle. The sun disappeared behind a cloud and I tucked my hair under my hood.

At night, old Seattle had the charm of an Old West frontier town complete with the antique lights, narrow cobbled streets and old storefronts. In daylight, however, it was a different matter. I love Pioneer Square, but I'd be lying if I said it fit. It was as if old Seattle was a wrong piece that had been forced into the puzzle slot that was Seattle.

When I reached Marjorie's, I took a lap around the square, stopping at a new artisan coffee shop to splurge on a second—no, make that third—coffee. The takeout cup helped me fit in with everyone else out for a Saturday morning. I took slow sips and pretended to window-shop as I cased Marjorie's storefront from a distance across the square. Eventually I settled on an empty bench.

The red awnings and glass windows set in uneven stone—which had to be the original building material or a very good restoration—gave Marjorie's an authentic feel that was missing from so many of the other buildings. Now that I knew Marjorie herself had been an old zombie, it made a different kind of sense.

She'd seemed like a pretty, middle-aged woman of Nordic descent, with blond hair and a no-nonsense manner. Ten years I'd been going there for coffee, and it'd never once occurred to me to tap the barrier and check. Murphy's Law: every time you think you know something, the universe will prove you wrong.

I watched the place for fifteen minutes while I sipped my coffee. The constant trickle of Marjorie's regular clientele and Saturday morning shoppers stopped at the door to check inside, presumably hoping to catch sight of Marjorie, who'd lived upstairs. A few even knocked.

This many people wouldn't have missed the morning news, so the police hadn't yet reported Marjorie's death. And Aaron had to be involved in that delay. Maybe I should have thrown something at him out my window last night.

I dropped my cup in a bin, grabbed my sea urchins and headed across the park. I walked straight up to the window the way I'd seen her other customers do and peered inside. Everything looked to be in order except for a toppled canister of coffee on the wood counter and a puddle of water on the floor near the sink. Maybe she'd had the water running when she was killed and it overflowed onto the floor before one of the cops shut it off.

If there had been a struggle, all signs had been swept away and any blood cleaned up.

I tapped the barrier and pulled a globe. I'd crammed enough caffeine into my brain that the Otherside didn't sting nearly as much as it could have. Once the globe was stable, I opened my eyes and tried to look through the window. Just like last night, I hit a wall. I took a step back and checked the sill, locating the symbols holding the Otherside barrier in place.

I watched three girls pass behind me in the reflection on the window, students if the backpacks were any indication. I waited until the nearby ring of a door chime told me they'd disappeared inside the adjacent shop before wrapping my hand in the sleeve of my leather jacket to pull out the first sea urchin and place it on the sill.

The barrier around Marjorie's window worked on the same principle as zombie bindings and set mirrors, with symbols that brought Otherside to an object in this world. Instead of animating a body or providing an access route, though, this barrier repelled Otherside. Setting mirrors and dead bodies is not what I'd call a piece of cake, but both already have an affinity for the Otherside. But binding a living person, even a plant, or the wood of Marjorie's windowsill to create a ward? This barrier would have been almost impossible to break when it had been set. I was lucky that it had suffered a few decades of wear and tear.

I placed the first sea urchin over the first corner anchoring symbol, making certain I'd lined it up. I took a knife out of my purse and held it over the urchin. "Sorry, Marjorie," I said, before cutting it down the middle. As Otherside collected around the urchin, I funnelled it into my globe. A bit of nausea, but nothing I couldn't handle. When it passed, I threw the sea urchin's life force into the symbol in one big, overloading shot. The symbol wavered, once, twice, then disappeared. I lined up the second sea urchin at the next corner, checked the reflection in the window to make sure the coast was clear, then cut a second time, bracing for the shot of Otherside. As soon as my knife broke the second sea urchin's shell, I funnelled its Otherside at the barrier, which wavered then snapped up like a blind before collapsing into nothingness.

I scraped the sea urchin bits into a plastic bag and cleared my head. Here went nothing. I loosened the hold on my globe and sent the first pulse through the window. This time I met with no resistance. The inside of the coffee shop was soon bathed in grey.

Given that a zombie had been killed here, and the bindings and Otherside holding her together had to go somewhere, I expected to see solid traces.

I didn't expect to see this.

It was as if someone had taken a brush and drunkenly splattered paint all over the room. I caught a flicker on a chair near the window—a larger piece of Otherside, what looked like half a rune symbol. . . .

"Shit." The thick antique glass reflected my shaking voice back at me. Marjorie's zombie bindings hadn't just been broken, they'd been obliterated, as if a bomb had gone off. Like what slicing my sea urchins did to the windowsill wards, only multiplied by a hundred. I cringed just thinking how much that would have hurt.

I took a deep breath and closed my eyes for a moment. I didn't really want to take a closer look, but if I didn't, I'd have wasted two perfectly good sea urchins. I refocused my globe and forced myself to look back through the window, acutely aware of my breath misting the glass.

The coffee bar and shelf behind it had taken the brunt of Otherside shrapnel; fragmented gold threads covered the bar and the aluminum canisters of coffee, including the one that had spilled over. If I had to guess, I'd bet Marjorie had been standing behind the counter when it happened. Whoever had done this to Marjorie hadn't just wanted to kill a zombie, they'd wanted to punish it. But I'd never heard of an Otherside explosion. Was there even such a thing?

I ran through other possible scenarios in my head, but none of them fit. I kept coming back to the idea that someone or something had attacked Marjorie with Otherside while she was behind the counter, resulting in no physical damage to her place but turning her bindings into shrapnel.

Without the body, there was no way to figure it out. I committed three of the most complete runes I could see to memory, including the partial on the back of the chair closest to the window, then dropped my globe. As I did, I caught a flicker in the shop window. I could have sworn I'd seen the trace of a ghost-grey face—the same face I'd seen in the set mirror and outside my apartment last night. But this wasn't a set mirror, and I'd already dropped my globe . . .

I stood there for a long moment to see if I'd glimpse it again. Surely I was imagining things. Ghosts can't pop into unset windows. It was a figment of my imagination fuelled by too much Otherside, not enough sleep and lots of caffeine.

But why the hell couldn't I shake the feeling that someone was watching me?

I got on my bike and sped home. I was at my apartment's back entrance when I realized my phone was ringing.

Aaron. I checked the time: 11:50. I took a deep breath and did my best to clear my head, then answered. "Aaron."

"You were supposed to call me back before noon."

"It's 11:50."

"My watch says noon."

"Mine says 11:50, and it's set by a satellite, so I win."

"Look, Kincaid, can we talk?"

"About?"

"Seriously?"

"Aaron, there is nothing to talk about. You said you needed a break, I said fine. Nowhere in 'I need a break' is it specified I have to wait for you."

"If I had known you were going to take it this badly—"

"We would still be together, you'd be miserable and making me miserable in the process."

Aaron didn't have anything to say to that.

I said, "Look, we both knew it wasn't working—it's better this way."

"Kincaid, I needed space, but it had nothing to do with us. I thought we were clear on that. You never once told me taking a break meant it was over. It's not fair to do that to me."

Yeah, well, life's not fair, Aaron. "Maybe that's one of our bigger problems, Aaron. I shouldn't have had to say it."

"You're blaming me for what happened at the station."

"You and me and the station are two completely separate issues."

"Bullshit."

I didn't respond. Aaron could keep thinking whatever the hell he wanted.

"Kincaid, we're not done talking about this, but at the moment I need your help with something."

I was not helping Aaron. "*No.*"

"There's no one left on staff who knows a damn thing about the paranormal, and I'm at my wits' end."

I sighed. "I left textbooks in your office. Consult those."

"As you've pointed out more times than I care to count, I can't see Otherside worth shit. I'm useless at a crime scene."

"So tell your boss you need a consultant and hire one."

"You know as well as I do I can't do that. No more paranormal consultants on the books. End of story. Kincaid, I can pay you myself."

I knew how much Aaron made—he really needed my help. I was going to regret this. "So what is the case? Short version."

"I think you know exactly which case I'm talking about, since you were hanging around the scene last night. I'm going to hazard a guess that the great Lee Ling sent you." Aaron had never met Lee Ling or seen the underground city; very few people had. But he knew who the players were.

"I didn't think anyone was investigating," I countered.

"I am," he said.

"They're letting you?" I said, and by *they* I meant the recently appointed captain, Marks—the new PD boss who'd helped usher in the new paranormal laws and made a point of having my contract let go before he set foot in Seattle. I'd never met the man, but by all accounts he was as bigoted and unpleasant about the preternatural as I'd pictured.

"I made a persuasive argument."

I snorted. Would have loved to be a fly on the wall for that.

Since Lee was already paying me to look into Marjorie's death, I wouldn't be working for Aaron for free. And he and Sarah were good investigators. In the long run, as much as I hated to admit it, we'd be better off pooling our resources. "Aaron, *hypothetically*, if Lee had asked me to look into this, I'd have to report in to her first, because she's the one *paying* me. And I'd need the okay from her to share with you."

"How soon can you let me know?"

If I hurried, I could make the underground city before the seance on campus. "I'll let you know tomorrow. But if it is a go, that means you need to pony up everything you've got on the case so far. And there's one other big condition: you've got to get me in to see Marjorie's body."

"Deal."

That was good enough for me. Aaron would keep his end of the bargain. "Fine, I've got to go. I've got Nate up at the university tonight."

"Roger's on patrol up there, I think. I'll give him a heads-up so he can run interference with any of the new hires."

That made me pause. "Since when have seances become illegal?"

"They're not, but to Marks seances and zombies are one and the same. . . ." There was a pause as Aaron decided whether to say more. "He considers seances grounds for a search."

I laughed, but Aaron didn't join in. "You're serious?"

"You think you're having a bad time? It hasn't exactly been a walk in the park over here. If he makes us search another magic shop looking for zombies . . ." He trailed off. "He's not going to give up on finding the city."

"The underground city doesn't exist," I said, more coldly than I meant. "Not the one he thinks."

"Kincaid, I'm not asking, just so you're aware." Aaron sounded fed up, and for once it wasn't with me. I knew he cared about me, but his break from our relationship had an uncanny correlation with the new captain being hired. "Let me know as soon as you can, about whether you can help with Marjorie. And Kincaid? We're not done with the other issue yet."

I hung up.

CHAPTER 10

SMOKE AND MIRRORS

I jiggled the key in my apartment door's warped lock for the third time. Why the hell wouldn't it give? Maybe I should have let Aaron replace the lock, though having a door that was impossible to open didn't seem like the security problem he made it out to be.

At last it popped open.

"Cameron?" I called.

No answer.

I dropped the bag of sea urchins on the kitchen counter and listened. Nothing.

Moving as quietly as I could in boots, I slid a knife out of the block. I palmed it along the sleeve of my jacket and tried one last time. "Cameron?"

No answer. Stable my ass, I thought. And where the hell was Nate?

I thought about pulling a globe, but if the nausea knocked me out before I found Cameron's hiding spot, he might get the jump on me. The knife was a better bet for now. I turned my cellphone off so the chime wouldn't alert him.

My bedroom was closest, so I headed there first. I checked under the bed and in the closet. In order to immobilize Cameron, I'd have to be fast; eyes were best, but severing the tendons on his hands would be easier—he'd come at me with his hands first.

The bathroom was next. I made sure not to open the door any wider than I had to since it had a tendency to creak. I slid through. No one. I threw back the shower curtain to be sure.

All right, last place left was the spare bedroom. The door was closed, and I eased it open, sliding through, knife first.

Cameron was there all right . . . sitting at the desk. With my head-phones on and a pack of pencil crayons and sketch paper I kept for tracing symbols, engrossed in whatever he was drawing.

"Cameron," I yelled, and tapped him on the shoulder, hard.

He dropped his pencil and sat up straight, pulling the head-phones off.

"Kincaid," he said. "When did you get back?"

"Just now." I glanced around the room. "Where's Nate? He's supposed to be watching you."

Cameron glanced down at his sheet, which he'd hidden from my view, and shook his head. "I saw him ten, twenty minutes ago maybe?"

"Well, which is it—ten or twenty?"

"I'm not sure. I was busy." He nodded at the sheet. "He said he'd be back soon."

Figured. I crossed my arms and leaned against the door frame.

"How did it go?" Cameron asked. I didn't miss the hopeful look on his face.

"Well, that depends."

"On?"

"On whether you 'forgot' you were manic depressive with a serious substance abuse problem or just decided to omit that small detail during our conversation this morning."

The great thing about being able to read people is I usually know they're lying before they even open their mouth. "It's not what it looks like—" Cameron said.

"Oh, for god's sake. How is that not important? That's how you know Max."

His eyes narrowed. "I am bipolar—or manic depressive, if you like. The doctors keep changing what they call it. The substance abuse is nowhere near what it used to be. I regulate it with my work."

I snorted. No one regulates their own substance abuse.

Cameron frowned at me. "I've felt more together in the last three hours than I can remember in years. I'm not about to go on a bender—I don't do those anymore." There was no self-loathing in his voice, just acceptance.

But it did raise a question: what happened when you animated someone with a mental illness? The mind is a delicate thing, and the way a zombie is bound to its body—well, not everyone handles animation well. And that was without the added complication of bipolar highs and lows. For all I knew, his disorder was affecting his memory. What if the blank spots were related to episodes he'd had when he was still alive? I could have screamed at Cameron.

"You want to know why I didn't say anything?" Cameron said. "Look at your reaction. One detail changes the way you see me entirely."

"That's not true—"

"Now who's lying?" He turned his attention back to his drawing. "Besides, the only crazy thoughts I've had is thinking I'm a zombie and seeing ghosts, and apparently that's true."

"Okay, I get it. I probably wouldn't wear it on my sleeve either," I said. "So I have good news and bad news: yes, Max is responsible for raising you, but you're going to be stuck with me for three more days." Then I gave him an edited version of my conversation with Max.

"So basically, I'm to sit around for the next three days and hope at the end of it he can fix me?"

I nodded. "That about sums it up. Max needs time to figure out what went wrong."

"I'm a zombie, not an idiot. I don't even remember Max. At all. How do I know you both aren't lying?"

I shrugged. "You don't. But if it counts, I don't think Max would lie about something like this."

He didn't look convinced.

"Cameron, it's the best I can do. As much as I sympathize, you're Max's client. I have to let him call the shots."

Cameron glanced down at his hand. His fingernails were waxy and white now without the blood flow. "I don't have much of a choice, do I?"

I shrugged. "Technically, you could call the police, but I don't think you'd like where that ends."

He ran his hands through his hair and closed his eyes. The policy on what to do with stray and feral zombies was automatic cremation.

"Fine, I'll give it three days," he said.

"I'll take you to your apartment later so you can pick up anything you need." I fumbled for something else to say. Zombie counselling was not in my repertoire. "Is there someone you want me to call? Friends? Family? We can come up with something to tell them."

He shook his head again. "For now, no one will notice I'm gone."

It made me wonder how many people would notice if I disappeared. "At least soon you can start getting your life back together." Or what was left of it. I hadn't had the heart to mention the temporary clause in his agreement with Max. It'd be like kicking someone after hitting them with a baseball bat.

"So you trust this Max?" Cameron asked.

"You trusted him," I said, sidestepping that issue.

Cameron gave a wry smile. "My judgment is suspect at the best of times."

I couldn't argue with that.

As I turned to head back to the kitchen, I caught a glimpse of what Cameron had been working on. It was a sketch of Nate, an uncanny reproduction of the ghost grey I saw when I tapped the Otherside, with an added layer of shading overtop. Only one part of the overlaid image was complete: a pair of sunken, shaded eyes.

Cameron covered the picture with his hand. "It's not finished yet," he said. "I try not to let people see my work until it's finished."

"I've never seen Nate like that."

He shrugged. "Drawing helps me deal with things."

I'd always assumed that to zombies ghosts looked like horror movie extras. Apparently they didn't—or at least Nate didn't. He looked more like a sad victim, the angles and hollows of his face reminding me of people who'd lived on the streets too long. I don't know what it was—maybe just the glimpse into Cameron's new world—but it struck me that I didn't have a good reason not to take a closer look at Cameron's bindings, even research some of the symbols. Max would never know.

"Come on, Cameron," I said, and headed for the kitchen.

"Kincaid?" he said, but then I heard him fall in step behind me.

"There's something we can do while we wait for Max." I pulled out a kitchen chair for him. "Sit."

He did as I asked. "Why do I get the distinct impression I'm not going to enjoy this?"

"I'm going to take a quick look at your bindings—just a look this time. It should only tingle a bit and I'll be as fast as I can. You okay with that?"

He frowned. "I don't remember much from last night, but I distinctly remember not liking that. But if you think it might help."

I was more worried about the effect on me than on Cameron. I wouldn't risk a full globe, but even so my Otherside hangover hadn't quite tailed off yet. If I went easy, just peeked, didn't tweak the lines, I should be fine.

I was not ready for the huge wave of nausea that flooded me. I forced it back, opened my eyes and looked at Cameron.

His bindings reverberated under my scrutiny like strings on a piano, and he winced.

I frowned. He shouldn't be feeling a thing.

"This isn't what I had in mind when I said I didn't want to sit around and wait for three days," he said through clenched teeth. He grabbed the table.

"Just sit still, will you?" I said. "It'll go faster."

He froze in place. I ignored the four main anchor symbols in his body—I already recognized those—and focused instead on the six unfamiliar gear-like symbols in his head. Without looking away, I grabbed a piece of paper and pen from my kitchen desk and began making a map of the gear symbols, capturing as much detail as I could.

I pushed back a second wave of nausea. As soon as I'd copied the symbols, I gave the lines a cursory look. Last night I'd been worried they were fragile, but today they looked stable enough. Maybe Max was right. . . . Hey, wait just a minute. Was it me or had the bindings shifted? I could have sworn one of the gears had turned clockwise a few degrees.

"Kincaid, are you done yet?" Cameron said. He was gripping the chair arms now.

I stared, and then there it was again. The highest gear was turning, slowly and clockwise. Then the gear beside it turned, slower and not as far.

Were they supposed to turn? "Cameron, what are you thinking? Right now?"

"Besides the fact that this blows? Nothing," he said, his face taut. The two gears turned again and Cameron's arm twitched.

"You can't be thinking of nothing. Come on, try harder. This is important."

"I—I was just thinking about a painting I'm working on. It's hard to concentrate on anything, though, with that humming."

"What humming? Explain it to me," I said, none too gently, as I pushed another wave of nausea back. The gears kept turning in slow rotation and one of the thin anchor lines leading to Cameron's heart began to tighten along its length. That couldn't be good.

"The last piece I was working on was a water scene." A third gear began to turn.

"Like what? Boats in the harbour?" I blinked as a bead of sweat ran into my eye. What the—? I shouldn't be sweating. I never sweat when I tap the barrier. . . .

The gears stopped turning and Cameron's eyelids drooped shut. "Cameron!" I yelled.

His eyes snapped back open. He stood and shook his head before they could drift shut again. "No, not boats—more what it would be like diving into murky water without a mask and opening your eyes."

A fourth gear began to rotate, this one counter-clockwise. I watched as the fifth anchor line, the one to Cameron's head, began to tighten.

His eyes rolled back into his head and his legs gave out underneath him. He dropped to his knees.

"Cameron!" I yelled. Damn it, none of the Otherside should even be reaching him.

More sweat dripped into my eyes. Whatever was going on with Cameron's bindings, I needed to stop it before the whole thing unravelled. I dropped my barrier tap. Cameron didn't move and his eyes didn't open.

Shit. If taking away Otherside didn't work, maybe overloading the lines would.

Before the sane, self-preserving part of my mind had a chance to talk me out of it, I tapped the Otherside again. The four gears were still turning and the anchor lines now wavered the way they had last night. I pulled a globe and gathered as much Otherside as I could, hanging on to the edge of the table to stop myself from collapsing. I'd broken out in a full sweat. Not sure that was a good sign. I threw the entire globe at Cameron.

The gears stopped turning. I dropped my globe and breathed a sigh of relief.

Cameron collapsed like a rag doll.

Thank god he was already on his knees, otherwise he might have done some serious damage.

I managed to haul him back into the chair. His eyes fluttered open.

"Cameron, I'm so sorry. It shouldn't have had that effect."

He groaned. "Whatever you just did? Next time, don't." He hunched over the kitchen table. "Did you get what you needed?"

"I think I know where we can start." I opened my laptop and logged back into the Seattle PD's missing persons reports. Still no mention of Cameron. Good.

Next, I entered his name into the Google search window. A slew of images of paintings and snapshots of Cameron at various clubs and art openings came up. A regular Warhol Silver Factory–style prodigy, if the photo catalogue of his night at the Gallery 6 open house was any indication.

But that wasn't what I was looking for. I already knew Cameron had been a spectacular wreck. What I wanted popped up two search results down, thumbnailed with a smiling headshot of Cameron.

His Facebook page.

Cameron hadn't bothered to put any filters in place, so everything was public. The sheer volume of paintings posted told me he wasn't shy about self-promotion. Friends, clients, buyers, fans—a gaggle of models, one or two of whom I thought might be ex-girlfriends. Come to think of it, they might be Nate's ex-girlfriends. . . .

A snapshot of a redhead caught my attention, a selfie posted of her and Cameron dated Wednesday night. That had to be the girl-friend he'd mentioned. The tag said her name was Sybil.

There was no mention of family anywhere. In this day and age, that was unusual. A lot of people wanted to hide some part of their family; most people have some uncle, brother, sister, parent, in-law they'd like to forget. But in the digital universe, the people you wanted to distance yourself from the most were the ones who made it next to impossible. I'd had to change my last name to distance myself from mine. . . . Or maybe Cameron had no family—always a possibility.

Cameron had come up behind me and was peering over my shoulder at his page. "Would you be offended if I told you I found this a bit creepy?"

I raised my eyebrows. "You want to drive? Be my guest." I slid out of the chair so he could sit. "I need you to search for any posts you might have made in the last few days, especially during the nights you can't remember. In fact, look through the posts you made over the past month. My guess is your zombie condition took at least that long to plan."

"That could take a while. I post a few times a day."

I nodded. That's what I was counting on. The more he'd posted, the easier it'd be to pinpoint the gaps in his memory and fill them in. I handed him a pad of paper and pen from my desk pile. "Once you finish with this week, go back through September and August. Make a note of every entry you can't remember posting."

He nodded.

"Remember you told me there were three people you saw this week? I want you to contact all of them: your art dealer, your girl-friend and your drug dealer. Contact them all the way you normally would—e-mail, FB, phone—just do it and ask to meet."

"You think one of them was involved?"

I shrugged. "Probably not, but maybe they can fill in some more blank spots."

Cameron stared at the screen. "Samuel, my art dealer, won't be a problem. But the other two?" He glanced up at me. "I'll do my best."

I headed into the bedroom to grab clean clothes then ducked into the shower, locking the door behind me. No more zombie interruptions.

I hung a towel over the mirror and stripped off my sweat-soaked clothes. While I waited for the water to heat up, my hands began to shake. That was new too. It took me five minutes under the hot water to warm myself up. After I'd stepped out of the shower and dried off, I held out my hands. There was still a slight tremble.

Come on, Kincaid, snap out of it. The problem isn't Otherside—it's that you need a serious vacation.

I got dressed, then checked the time on my cellphone. I had to hit the underground city and touch base with Lee. Hell, she might even pay me what she owed me for looking into Marjorie's. And then to Catamaran's, if I had time: Randall would appreciate an update. I wrote a note for Nate on the mirror: *Heading out—need to see Lee and stop in at Catamaran's. Can you check in on Cameron every hour till 7?*

It took less than a minute for Nate to respond. *SURE, K— EVERYTHING OKAY?*

That was almost laughable. *As well as can be expected. Will fill you in tonight. Brains are in the metal cooler—still has plenty of dry ice so will leave on counter.* Otherwise Nate would have to waste energy opening the fridge—not something I wanted if there was an emergency. *If something goes wrong before 7, message or Skype me.*

AT THE RISK OF SOUNDING OBVIOUS, WHAT HAPENS IF THERES AN EMERGENCY AFTER 7?

Good question. *We hope to hell there isn't one? I'll lock the doors and windows and leave Cameron with instructions to call me.* I'd also leave him with Aaron's number, and explicit instructions to use it only in an extreme emergency, but Nate didn't need to know that right now.

YOUR THE BOSS—SEE YOU AT THE LIBARY AT 7.

I grabbed my jacket off the rack in the hall and headed into the kitchen. "Any luck?" I asked Cameron.

He nodded. "Sybil will be at Club 9 tomorrow night."

Club 9. An upscale club in which I'd stick out like a sore thumb. "Something less ritzy, maybe?"

Cameron shook his head. "You said not to make it obvious. She's planning on going anyways, so I put us on the list. It's the best I could do. She's leaving town Monday for a shoot."

I nodded and slid the cooler out of the fridge and dropped it on the kitchen counter. "The other two?"

"No answer yet. That's not unusual, though—it's the weekend."

"Any pets, or people who might notice you're not home?"

"Already thought of that." He showed me the screen. He'd written a new post saying he was taking it easy this weekend and would see people at Club 9 Sunday. "The doorman at my condo might notice that I haven't been home, but that isn't exactly outside my realm of normal behaviour."

I wasn't sure if I should be thrilled or depressed at that revelation about his life. "We'll go through the list when I get back and see if we can figure out where your memory tailspun."

I motioned for Cameron to give me his arm. The skin and nails were still holding up. Next I checked his eyes. Lighter, but the irises were still a living shade of green. In theory he'd be good for another day without brains, but I wasn't willing to take that chance. I opened the cooler and pulled out one of the packets.

"Look, I'm heading out again. I should be back by midnight, but in case something happens, we're going over ground rules. Write this down."

Cameron nodded and reached for a fresh piece of paper.

I tapped the cooler. "Eat a pack now, and another at seven or eight tonight. If I get delayed, I'll send Nate back to you. Worst-case scenario and neither of us shows up by tomorrow morning, eat a third pack and call Lee Ling." I took the sheet of paper and wrote down Lee's number. "She'll know what to do. If she can't get a hold of me, she'll make arrangements for you to get to the underground city." I paused before making my last point, then said, "If you don't hear anything from me by late Sunday afternoon, call this man." I pulled Aaron's crumpled card out of my drawer and gave it to Cameron.

Cameron picked up the card. "Detective Baal? A cop?"

"Trust me, if you find yourself in a position where you need to call Detective Baal, the fact he's a cop will be the least of your worries.

"Don't let anyone in and don't go outside, and you should be fine. Draw some pictures, watch some TV—try to relax. And remember to eat more brains tonight."

"You told me that already."

"It bears repeating."

Cameron pinned the sheet of instructions and Aaron's card to my bulletin board.

I gave him a last once-over before grabbing my bike and ducking out of the apartment.

One thing Max had said at coffee stuck in my head as I pulled the Hawk out of the lift.

Tread carefully, Kincaid.

CHAPTER 11

FLOTSAM

Midday on a Saturday, Pioneer Square was crowded and the alleys bright in the midday light. Good thing there was more than one entrance to the underground city. I took the Alaskan viaduct along the piers until I reached a spot on the shoreline where one of Seattle's rain sewers emptied through a wide pipe. I eased down one of the old boat ramps and drove right inside. Two hundred yards in, I reached my goal: a circular metal door to a tunnel that had once been used to control runoff. Now it was fitted with a wheel handle covered in etched symbols, much like the entrance off Pioneer Square.

I tapped the barrier, only pulling enough Otherside to see the symbols. After I lined up the arrow and turned it through the right combination, the hinge clicked open and damp, stale air filtered out. I ditched my bike just inside the door behind a stack of old barrels. Ten minutes later, I earned stares from the afternoon crowd as I walked into Damaged Goods. It's rare for me to show up in the middle of the day.

Lee arched an eyebrow at me as I took a seat at the bar. "You are back sooner than anticipated," she said, and held up an empty glass.

I shook my head. "Not with this Otherside hangover. And I thought you were paying me to be fast."

"I do not recall that being one of my conditions."

"Okay, so it's one of mine. Besides, I found something." I took paper and a pencil crayon out of my jacket pocket and began to sketch Marjorie's café, indicating where the Otherside fragments had landed. On a second sheet I drew the three partial symbols I'd been able to make out, the remnants of Marjorie's bindings. I numbered each of the partials and indicated on the coffee shop map where I'd seen them, then slid the two sheets across the bar. With the tip of a lacquered white fingernail covered in red blossoms, she drew them closer. A frown touched her face.

"What are these, Kincaid?"

"As far as I can tell, all that's left of Marjorie's bindings. They look Celtic to me. I had to break wards protecting her window."

Lee's frown deepened. "If I had known about the barrier, I would have told you, Kincaid." She pointed to the largest, most complete rune, then tapped it. Her manicure matched the decor. So did her dress, for that matter. "Why do you assume this is a Celtic rune?" she asked.

"Because Celtic knots were used on the windowsill to anchor the barrier. Look at the edges." The symbol exhibited dashes and loops characteristic of Celtic runes.

Lee shook her head. "This is most definitely not a Celtic rune, nor a remnant of Marjorie's bindings."

"Lee—"

But she'd turned and disappeared into her office. She came back with an old, heavy leather-bound tome as long as my arm and thick with hand-bound pages that looked as though it belonged in a museum or on the shelf of a rare-book shop. She laid it on the bar and flipped through until she found the spread she wanted. Then she turned the book to face me.

"These are Celtic runes. Look at the way they finish on the sides and are joined together in a larger picture. *These*," she said, pointing to the images I had transcribed, "do not look like they were joined to any other runes. They are individual characters." She glanced up at me, dark eyes intent. "Unless you were sloppy in transcribing them?"

I glared back. "No, Lee, that's exactly what they looked like."

"That is what I thought," she said, and flipped to the next page. "I believe they belong to this set, which are ancient Arabic."

These pages were covered in cursive symbols with smoother, more flourished outlines. Nowhere on the page were the symbols linked together; they were always written as individual characters.

"I didn't know there were Arabic incantations for binding Otherside," I said. Though it made sense. Almost every culture on the planet had figured out how to work Otherside, even before the turn of the century, when the barrier thinned. . . .

"The use of Arabic symbols faded in the Middle East during the Dark Ages.

"It was one of the few regions that succeeded in purging itself of practitioners. A few books survived the purge, but they're rare. My brother acquired the only copy we knew of that existed in Shanghai. Lou was one of the few people who studied Arabic bindings. They are quite dangerous. Are you familiar with the legends of the Jinn?"

I nodded. *"One Thousand and One Nights*, right?"

Lee pursed her lips, and the web of scars stood out. "Not exactly. Ancient Arabic inscriptions were used to bind spirits, not to a corpse, but to an element: air, water, fire, earth. An undead entity that is both corporeal and non-corporeal at the same time."

Corporeal and non-corporeal. "All the strengths, and none of the weaknesses," I said. "Surprised it hasn't been picked back up."

Lee made a face. "Jinn were powerful, but to make one was to induce a form of undead slavery. The spirits involved could not be willing, otherwise it would not work."

I didn't want to imagine raising an unwilling zombie.

"Lou said that the early Arabic inscriptions were adapted to act as a leash on the Jinns' power and ability to wreak vengeance. The leashes were often tied to items such as jewellery or lamps, so they would not unwind if the practitioner was mortally wounded."

"Max sure as hell never showed me anything like this," I said.

"He may not know about them. As I said, very few accounts of the ancient Arabic bindings exist. It is possible he's never encountered one."

"So Marjorie was some vengeful Jinn living in Seattle and running a coffee shop?"

Lee clicked her tongue, irritated. "Marjorie was a zombie, like me. These days the Jinn only exist as legends and bedtime stories. The complete bindings and techniques were lost over a thousand years ago. Even these here are only remnants transcribed and lost, then transcribed again. They will not ever be able to raise a Jinn." She pointed to my drawings again. "These were not part of her bindings."

"Then what the hell were they doing at the coffee shop?"

"That is a very good question, and one I'd like answered."

A chill ran down my spine. Just because it takes years to teach yourself how to work Otherside doesn't mean you gain magical wisdom by it. People do stupid things with Otherside all the time. Case in point: six months ago a murderer had raised a victim to throw off the time of death, and rushed it. . . . The zombie strangled two people as a result, including the murderer himself.

"Did Lou ever run into a practitioner who tried to raise a Jinn?"

Sometimes when the light hits Lee's face a certain way, the scars take on an eerie life of their own, like ripples on water. This was one of those moments. "Yes," she said carefully, then rushed to add, "but the victims in those cases were all living and killed in a very specific fashion. Since Marjorie was a zombie, we can't assume . . ."

"Bullshit we can't."

"Kincaid, those murders occurred over one hundred years ago, and the perpetrator was killed in the great fire."

"What if his ghost passed those methods on? You know as well as I do how much ghosts gossip. Who's to say a chain of ghosts haven't traded field notes to a practitioner? Or what if he left a notebook?" Practitioners were always looking for old notebooks that might contain a new set of bindings or symbols.

"*Kincaid.*"

I was trying Lee's patience now, but this was stupid. Any information she had was relevant. "Did it make the paper? Did a practitioner like me ever question the local ghosts? What about the victims—did anyone try contacting them?"

"*Kincaid!*" Half the bar looked up at the sound of Lee's voice. "*Please stop.* I've already told you more than I should."

"You seriously can't expect me to leave it at that—Hey!" I said, as Lee retreated into her office. "You can't walk away in the middle of a discussion, Lee! I don't care if you are dead. . . ."

She reappeared carrying a white envelope sealed with red and gold wax. "Kincaid, I am grateful to you for looking into Marjorie's shop, but I don't wish you to be involved any further." She handed me the envelope.

I stared at it. "You're dismissing me?"

Lee didn't say anything.

"Un-fucking-believable."

On the one hand, I got it: this was zombie business. Lee and the other zombies would want to deal with a zombie killer themselves, and if I was involved, they'd risk drawing attention from the surface. Even so . . .

I shook my head. One minute Lee was begging me to take a look at Marjorie's murder, the next she was warning me off. I wondered if I should even bother mentioning Aaron. If Lee was cutting me out now, there wasn't a hope in hell she'd work with Aaron. Stupid. Aaron would have access to details she wouldn't.

"Lee, you should know Aaron's looking into this too. He wants to pool resources."

Lee's face was unreadable as she regarded me. "I would need to carefully weigh the benefits and disadvantages of his proposal."

I snorted. "In other words, no."

Lee glared at me. I'd overstepped one of our invisible rules of etiquette.

"Look, the only disadvantage I can see to joining forces with Aaron is having to argue with him over who gets to deal with the bad guy—or girl."

Lee's face darkened and the scars on her face once again rippled under the lamplight. "Then you are very short-sighted. There are always unforeseen complications when the Otherside is involved, Kincaid. You would be wise to remember that."

I checked the time on my phone: 3:00. I still wanted to swing by Catamaran's before the seance. When I glanced up, Lee was frowning at me.

"Are you well?" she asked.

"You tell me. Are cold sweats and trembling normal side effects of pulling a globe?"

"Please explain."

"Some new symptoms I'm experiencing when I tap the barrier. It's worse when I pull a globe."

"How much Otherside have you been using over the last few weeks, Kincaid?"

I shrugged. "The same as always."

"Any differences in your activities? Even small?"

I thought it over. "The last twenty-four hours I know I've tapped the barrier too many times—" Lee interrupted me with a derisive noise and I glared at her. "I've been pulling a globe here and there to get more seances in, for sure, but I haven't done a zombie raising in three months, not even a four-line—"

Lee stopped me. "Whether or not you've been raising zombies is not the point. The issue is how often you are contacting the Otherside. The Otherside is where the dead live, and it is as much a part of the dead as anything can be. Do you think there is no consequence to touching it?"

"Max does it all the time." I racked my brain. Besides this fiasco with Cameron in the last twenty-four hours, had I been using more Otherside lately? I'd had the odd Otherside hangover, but nothing I couldn't handle.

"Max is a medium, and the consequences are different for someone like him. You are simply . . ." Lee bit her lower lip, searching for the right word. "Stubborn," she settled on.

"Thanks."

She shrugged. "Kincaid, I strongly suggest you take a break from seances, just for a while. A few weeks. A month at most."

I glowered at her.

Lee continued to study me. "Besides the sweats, has anything else out of the ordinary occurred?"

"Like?"

"Visions? Bad dreams? You tell me."

I flashed to the ghost I kept seeing. . . . But no, that had to be my overactive imagination. I shook my head. "No."

I wasn't convinced she believed me, but she let it go.

I got up. "I'll let Aaron know you're not interested in playing." He wouldn't be happy, but I wasn't going to push. For all I knew, it might end up better for everyone if the zombies handled it on their own.

I was at the door when Lee called out, "Kincaid?"

I turned to face her.

"The sweats, the shakes and the headaches? That is something I've seen before, and it is not a good sign. Please consider my recommendation to take a break."

I nodded. "I will. And let me know if you change your mind about Aaron," I said, and left. Get the seance done, get rent, deliver Cameron to Max and then get some damn sleep. Then I could take a break.

I glided into Catamaran's parking lot. Three guys loitering out front and smoking—early twenties—stared at me and my bike as I rode in, and upgraded to outright gawking once the helmet came off. I ignored them.

Catamaran's wasn't as crowded as last night, but it was still busy. A few people I recognized as regulars. One I was even friendly enough with to exchange nods.

The TVs were all broadcasting different sports, but the majority of people were crowded around the largest screen above the pool tables—the only area where the widescreen fit. The baseball game between the Oakland A's and Toronto Blue Jays was on. I had to dodge a few of the guys stepping back as one of the A's hit a home run. I wasn't sure if they were yelling for or against the A's. Always hard to tell with the non–home team games. I looked around for Randall and spotted him pouring beer and getting an order of fries ready. He waved me over.

"How's that kid doing?" Randall asked, passing me a full glass of water. "Drink the damn water before you tell me. You look like you closed my bar last night. What's wrong with you?"

I complied. When I set the glass back down, I said, "He's not exactly what I'd call a kid."

Randall snorted. "Anyone your age or younger is a kid in my books. How's he doing?"

"I've seen better, I've seen worse."

Randall's brow furrowed, so I rushed to add, "He'll be okay. He's stable and no danger to anyone—I'm making sure of that." Courtesy of deadbolts and Nate. "It's good you called me when you did, though. I don't think he would have lasted much longer. Probably saved me from having the cops show up on my doorstep."

Randall refilled my glass before he delivered the fries and beer to a waiting table. I drank it all down. Maybe I was overdoing the caffeine. . . .

"That's not the whole truth, though, is it?" Randall said when he came back.

It was my turn to frown. "Why do you say that?"

"I used to run bets for Filipino bookies, remember? I know when someone is trying to hide something." Randall used to drive me home after babysitting, and once he'd let slip that this was how he'd spent his teen years in the Philippines—in total rebellion against the family practitioning business.

I shrugged. "I'm still not sure how the hell he got where he is, and not knowing bugs me."

"A problem a lot of people have."

I rolled my eyes.

"Learning to accept things you can't change or know is part of growing up."

In my books, that just meant you hadn't tried hard enough. "How are the kids?"

Randall glanced down at the bar. "Lisa's still at her mom's in California. She hates it. Keeps threatening to come up here."

Randall loved his kids and hated his ex, but that's how it goes. I was amazed he hadn't sent Lisa plane fare yet. Unlike my parents, Randall went out of his way to help his kids. My folks, and my mother especially, had always been more of the "What could you do to make other people like you more?" flavour of parents. I'd never understood the pressure girls were under to be pleasant all the time, as if it was a trait boys were exempt from. According to my mother, I wasn't a pleasant little girl.

"Sixteen-year-olds," he added. "If she were with me, she'd be begging to go to her mom's. Michael's still in the Philippines, visiting his grandmother."

Michael was eighteen now. Good, polite kid, or had been when he was ten. "I didn't know you still had family there." Hell, I hadn't known Randall still had a mom. "Getting to know her better?"

"Something like that," Randall countered.

Something in his voice, maybe just missing his kids, made me drop the subject.

Randall finished loading the last dirty glass into the dishwasher. "Out with it, Kincaid."

I held my hands up in mock defence.

He leaned across the counter. "Somehow I don't think this is entirely a social call."

I chewed my lip, figuring out how to phrase it. I hate broaching touchy subjects about as much as I hate it when four-line zombies try to have deep philosophical discussions with me. Four-line zombies aren't known for their conversational skills, but that doesn't mean they don't try. And it *was* a delicate subject, at least for Randall. Catamaran's wasn't a criminal destination, but it was a sports bar that sold cheep beer, so it attracted a certain clientele. . . .

"Don't take this the wrong way, but has anyone been bragging about, I don't know, knocking a zombie off?"

From the look on Randall's face, the question had gone over about as well as the police showing up to do a random capacity and ID check. "Even if they were, Kincaid, you know I wouldn't say anything about it. Word gets out."

"Randall, I swear it won't go further than Aaron, promise." I couldn't believe I was vouching for Aaron.

"It's true?" he asked.

"Is what true?" Had Randall already heard through the grapevine about Marjorie?

He gave me a level stare. "Rumour has it the new captain told one of his detectives he could keep his job or his weekend-witch girlfriend. Not both."

I tried my damnedest not to let my face or voice betray me. "When did you hear that?"

"About the time Aaron stopped coming in with you."

I thought daggers at Aaron while I held on to my composure as Randall watched me closely.

"Aaron never struck me as the type to go with something like that," he said, "so I didn't give the rumour much credence. From the look on your face, though, I'd say there's at least some truth in there. For what it's worth, I'm sorry."

"Aaron's . . . got things to sort out."

Randall shook his head. "If you were my kid, I'd have shown him the business end of my baseball bat by now." From Randall, that wasn't an exaggeration. Filipino fathers took slights to their daughters seriously. A year back, when Lisa had been helping him out behind the bar, a patron had hit on her. He'd been shown the not-so-nice way out. Good thing he hadn't been a regular.

Randall headed back out to the floor to clear a now-emptied table. When he returned, I said, "Not that I'm petty or anything"— Randall snorted at that—"but I think the captain demoted him anyways." I offered up a small smirk.

"Ditched the girl and still got screwed? Can't say he doesn't deserve it. So why are you still helping him out?"

This time I was able to look Randall straight in the eye. "I'm not.

I'm helping out a dead woman who used to smile, remember my name and make me coffee every Saturday."

Randall held my stare for a minute then looked down at the bar. "So this goes no further than us?"

I nodded. Aaron would want to know where I'd got the information, but as far as I was concerned, he could screw himself. He'd get what I decided to give him.

"Last weekend, a university-aged crowd comes in. They seemed young, so I ID'd them. Figured they were new intake at Washington State. Turns out they were from out of town. Kept going on about how they'd never seen a zombie before and were talking about getting themselves one."

"I get phone calls asking me for that at least once a week," I told him.

"Yeah, but one of them started going on about how he knew how to stop one. With Otherside."

"Interesting. Know where I could find them?"

He shook his head. "I remember that two of them were from California, the third was from New York. I can give you a shout if I see them again, but other than that . . ."

I nodded. Likely guys trying to impress each other. Still, it was a lead.

"Thanks, Randall. Say hi to Lisa and Mike for me."

"Sure thing," he said, and again I thought I saw real sadness in his eyes. Damn, he must miss his kids. I'll bet Mike had never been that far away before. Lucky kids, to have a father like him.

"I'll keep my ears open for any talk of zombies," he added. "You just remember that the kind of folks who go looking for trouble with zombies won't think twice about hurting some practitioner who gets in the way."

"Thanks, Randall, I will." I hauled my sorry self off the bar stool and headed out the door.

*

I had a forty-five-minute ride to campus, which meant I'd have almost two hours to kill before the seance. If Lee didn't want to tell me about Jinn, that was perfectly fine. There were other places to get information.

I ditched my bike outside the library and headed to the fifth floor, where they housed the paranormal collection. The woman at the desk glanced up at me when I stepped out of the elevator. Late thirties, early forties, a few stray grey hairs, but still attractive in a librarian kind of way.

"Can I help you?" she said, and nodded to the sign behind her desk that said Restricted Access in bright red block letters.

I smiled and pulled out my police consultant ID card. It had given me access not only to crime scenes but also to the university and downtown libraries' paranormal collections.

She glanced at my card then typed something into her computer. I waited five slow seconds. . . . Don't tell me they'd finally got around to cancelling my access.

Just when I'd resigned myself to being dragged out by security, the librarian pulled an electronic key card out of her drawer and pushed it across the desk towards me. "Here you go, Ms. Strange. We close at seven this evening. Let me know if you need any help finding anything."

"Thank you," I said, and buzzed myself through the double doors. I headed straight to the Middle Eastern section and did a cursory search on the computer for texts concerning ancient Arabic and Otherside. No luck. Lee was right, it didn't appear that any existed. I widened my search to include paranormal and the Middle East, and added Jinn to the mix.

One title caught my eye. It was a translation of an account of King Solomon's Jinn, written a little over a thousand years ago. I retrieved it from the shelf along with two other interesting texts on the legends of Jinn and headed to the study table situated by the glass doors.

I opened up a bottle of water I'd grabbed on my way in, took a big swig and began to read. Despite what Lee and Randall thought, I did listen to decent advice . . . most of the time.

CHAPTER 12

SEANCE

Saying King Solomon was a bit of an asshole would be putting it mildly.

At one point in his rule, he had over a hundred enslaved Jinn at his beck and call. On paper it said they'd been bound as guards for the king and his councillors, but considering how many Ifrit, or fire-wielding Jinn, he'd created, I got the distinct impression they were less guards than jailors. I'd come across Fire, Air and Earth Jinn by the time I was halfway through the text, but still no Manids, or Water Jinn. You'd think, living in a desert, those might have come in handy.

There was no mention of the inscriptions or bindings used to create Jinn, not even a reference to another text. The only hint was an entry on an Ifrit named Assam, who had been punished for burning one of the cooks: "His disobedience has been carved into his soul for all eternity." I figured that meant they'd added another layer of bindings to prevent him from torturing any more kitchen staff. It was more interesting to note that eternity hadn't been all that long for Assam, given the Jinn hadn't survived.

I leaned back in the library chair, stretched and yawned. I checked the time: 6:15. I closed my eyes to give them a break. . . .

Something buzzed in my pocket and I sat up with a start. I pulled my phone out to see *Jawbreaker 29* flashing on the digital call programme. Nate. Had something happened with Cameron? Then I noticed the time: 6:50. Shit.

I answered. "Nate?"

"Jesus Christ, K. Where the hell are you?"

"I'm sorry, I fell asleep, I'll be right down and grab you."

"Whoa, hold on a sec. *You* fell asleep?"

I closed the books. "Yes, Nate, I fell asleep. It happens to the living, remember?"

"Are you telling me I'm the responsible one this time?"

I threw my jacket on and picked up my backpack.

"I mean, there's hell freezing over, pigs flying, and then there's me and responsibility."

"Nate, get off my computer and back into the mirror. You can ridicule me later."

He sighed. "Fine. See you." The line went dead.

I glanced down at the pile of books. Hmmm, I wonder . . . I carried Solomon and a text on the paranormal history of the Middle East to the front desk.

"I don't suppose I can take these with me?" I said to the librarian.

She glanced up from the computer. "I'm not sure. Let me check."

I passed the books over and she scanned each bar code then stared at her screen. "Not a problem, Ms. Strange. We'll need them back by Friday."

I couldn't believe my luck. "Friday it is. Thanks." I shoved the books into my backpack and headed downstairs to grab Nate before she realized her mistake.

Then I discovered that the elevator was already locked down for the night, so I headed back to the desk to ask for a key card.

There was no one there. I looked around, but it was as if the librarian had vanished into thin air. . . . Then I noticed a sign that I'd missed on my way in: Closed for Weekends until Further Notice.

I rolled my eyes. Goddamnit, I hate ghosts. Never know when to stay on their side of the barrier. The ghost librarian had probably worked here while she'd been alive and was taking advantage of the staffing shortage.

The exit stairwell was just around the corner, but when I tried the door, it caught. I jiggled it again and still it wouldn't give.

I was just about to head back to the desk to do a thorough search for the elevator key card when I caught the reflection in the door's port window: the ghost from the mirror. It flashed me what I could only describe as a vicious smile before vanishing. The air around me chilled and letters began to scroll in the fog on the window.

We need to talk.

I took a step back. This was impossible: ghosts can't set their own windows and mirrors.

Unless I was dealing with a poltergeist.

But poltergeists don't write notes on glass; they throw any heavy object they can find.

Another message began to etch its way across the window.

This is a warning, Kincaid. I'm not to be trifled with. I believe you have something of mine.

The only ghost I knew who owned anything was Nate, and his hold on the PlayStation was tentative at best. I remembered the books in my bag; could they be what he was talking about? Not likely. He'd been following me around since last night.

The words in the window vanished, followed by the chill in the air. I tried the door again and jumped when it opened. The stairwell was empty.

I shook my head. Setting windows, locking doors, writing on glass . . . I don't scare that easy. The best way to handle problem ghosts is not to feed into their cycle. I gave my reflection in the window the most bored expression I could muster. "Is that all you got?" I said, then shrugged. "Not impressed."

There was no answer.

Still, I took the stairs two at a time. When I reached the main

floor, I ducked into the washroom to grab Nate. I had a seance
to worry about, not a crazier-than-average ghost.

University parties were not my favourite gig, but the students weren't
done blowing their student loans yet and I couldn't afford to be
picky. October would be dead until Halloween, when the requests
flooded in—theme parties, spooky graveyard visits, the obvious
stuff. Then there would be another dry spell until the end of
November, when the Thanksgiving and Christmas seances
kicked in, or the season of guilt as I liked to call it—guilt over not
spending more time with the relatives you couldn't be bothered
talking to while they were still alive. I drink more whisky sours
than I care to admit during Christmas. I used to make my real
money raising zombies—not "Please clarify that you really did
mean to leave everything to the cat/mistress/maid/fish" but "Bring
me back as eternal living dead."

I glided my bike into the residential area of campus. Now where
was that street? It had to be around here somewhere.

"Nate, not now," I said for the second time. Why the hell had I
agreed to let Nate ride along? I could just as easily have pulled him
out of a mirror at the frat house.

"What? What did I say?" Nate asked for the third time since we'd
left the library.

I didn't respond, hoping he'd take the hint.

"No, seriously? All I said was, 'What would it take for you to
consider getting back together with Aaron?' I mean, I know you're
pissed at him, but he keeps calling you. Clearly he's still into you."

Birch Street, Oak, Elm—

"Okay, I'll go first: I hate Mindy, but I'd consider getting back
together with her if she pushed my ex-drummer off the back of my
yacht. There. See? Easy. Your turn."

Vine Street—that was it! I turned left. The frat kids had said to
keep going until I reached the end, so that's what I did.

"Look, Nate, I don't want to play this particular game right now."

"Come on. It'll help you get closure, which, by the way, you suck at."

I took a deep breath. There was no point explaining why I was upset to Nate. Finding out from Randall that Aaron really had been given an ultimatum by the department was one thing, but to know that Aaron had taken them up on the offer . . .

I spotted the house: 2135 Vine. "Nate, let's just get through tonight, okay?"

"*Fine.*"

I shook my head. Ghosts.

I parked my bike at the side of the house where it was out of the way and locked it. I trust drunken university students around my Hawk about as much as I trust Nate in the Sony online shop. I took my helmet off and headed to the front door.

Nineties grunge music filtered out to the street and coed voices carried from around back. Beta Kappa Phi was a mansion-sized, colonial-styled white house with a decent-sized lawn and a backyard that eased onto the university green space. It was what you'd expect from a frat house: not in fantastic shape, but not ready to be condemned either. One of the windows had been broken and taped up and the house needed a good coat of paint. At least the lawn was free of beer cans and bottles.

"Time to make rent, Nate," I whispered.

As I stepped up to the front door, I hoped these guys had remembered to get the right stuff. Nate was a princess when it came to guitars. Before knocking, I said, "All right, Nate, you know the drill?"

"Yeah, Kincaid, just like the last time."

I frowned. The last time had been almost a month ago. Ghost short-term memory isn't foolproof. They don't form new memories well, though they think they do, which leads to its own special set of problems.

"If you forget something, *ask* this time."

"What's that supposed to mean?"

"It means if you feel the need to play beer-keg funnel or to streak around the block, or anything else in that realm of behaviour, ask me first."

Nate snorted. "It's called a beer bong." Then, after a pause, he asked, "Did I really streak around the block last time?"

"No, you disappeared all your clothes and jumped into the neighbour's pool."

"Hunh . . . Figured I'd remember something that fun."

There was a note taped to the front door with my name on it. I read it out, mostly for Nate's benefit. "'Come around back. We'll be on the porch. Ask for Kelvin.'"

"Kelvin? What kind of name is Kelvin?" Nate said.

I shook my head and walked around the house, following the noise. "Nate, you've got five seconds to stop talking."

"Don't you think you're misleading them a bit? You aren't actually summoning me."

"I do summon you, I just don't summon you here."

"Slippery slope, K."

I reached the eight-foot wood fence, the kind that's near-impossible to climb unless you are a varsity athlete. Now where the hell was the catch to open the gate? I felt along the edge and found it.

"You know what I think? I think . . ." Nate trailed off as the gate opened into the backyard. For once, he was speechless.

I just stared at the scene in front of me. "Holy shit," I said finally.

"I think they've got Woodstock back here."

"Not Woodstock . . . just . . ." I shook my head.

This was not a frat keg party with a hundred or so students. Yes, the backyard backed onto the university green space, but between the backyard and the campus forest was a sports field. No back fence. The food and beer tables were set up by the back porch, but the crowd stretched all the way to the tree line.

"Damn, there has to be over five hundred kids here."

"Twice that. Easy."

"I should have asked for more money."

"No shit. Sweet Jesus and happy birthday to me—do you see the stage?"

Past the swimming pool and hot tub was a decent-sized stage with sound equipment set up and ready to go. Three guys hovered over the guitars.

"Nate, I think that's supposed to be your band." One of Nate's rules for working frat parties was no bands and no concerts.

Nate was still absorbing. He hadn't seen a crowd this size since he'd been alive.

"Nate, I'm sorry. They told me it was a keg party." I glanced around. No one was paying me any mind. "Look, Nate, we can sneak out, no one will be any the wiser—"

"Are you kidding, K? I forbid you to leave this party."

"I thought you said no concerts. Not ever, no way—"

"Yeah, but this is different. It's not commercial—it's just a crazy, out-of-control house party. Seriously out of control. *This* is what I started out doing."

For a second I debated mentioning that if he played here, film would probably end up on the Internet, and then his old bandmates would come sniffing around Seattle. . . .

But then a lanky student wearing a Hawaiian print shirt and khakis standing behind the nearest beer table began jumping and waving in my general direction. He had a mop of brown hair reminiscent of Nate's. Damn.

"Nate, are you absolutely sure you want to do this?" I whispered out of the corner of my mouth.

"Stop me if I climb up on the roof and start screaming 'I'm a golden god.' No, scrap that. I could totally do that since I can't die or squash anyone."

Hawaiian Shirt bounded up to me with a big grin, hand extended. "Hi, you must be Kincaid Strange. I'm Kelvin. We spoke on the phone?"

I shook the outstretched hand. I didn't have much of a choice. "Yeah, Kelvin, hi. Quite the party you've got going here."

"Yeah, awesome turnout. Amazing what you can do with social media. Well, that and Nathan Cade." I didn't think his grin could widen any more than it already had. I was wrong.

I glanced at the stage and Kelvin jumped in before I could say a word. "Look, I know you said no band, no big productions, but I had a really great group of guys from the student centre volunteer—*huge* Nathan Cade fans—and then word got out." He ducked an empty beer cup that sailed overhead. "You know how it goes."

I crossed my arms and stared him down. "So you expect me to believe this turned into a concert bowl by *accident*?"

Kelvin's smile didn't falter for a second. His phone buzzed with a text message and he glanced down at it. "Whoa, can you wait just a sec? Problems with the lighting. I'll be right back, Kincaid. Just don't go anywhere. I promise you we'll sort this out." He bounded off towards the stage.

"Nate, I'm getting us the hell out of here."

"Come on, K. It'll be fun."

"Nate! He conned us into a concert."

"You got to give him props for that—you're tough to pull a fast one on. Come on, *please*, can we stay for the concert?"

I ran my fingers through my hair. We *were* already here and we needed the cash. . . . Wait a minute, was I actually considering this? It was only a matter of time before the cops shut it down. There was no way this was legal by any stretch of the imagination.

There was a bang from the stage, followed by shouting. Like everyone else, I glanced over to see what the commotion was about.

"Oh, hell. No."

The faulty lights Kelvin had run off to check were a set of neon-pink LEDs in the shape of a pentagram on the floor of the stage. They were bright. Very bright. Hard-to-miss-from-across-campus bright.

I'd told Kelvin I needed enough space to draw a five-by-five pentagram. He'd taken matters into his own hands and done one with neon-pink lights. On a stage. In front of a thousand kids.

"Shit. Nate, they expect me to do the seance onstage." I turned towards the exit.

"K, wait! It'll be fine. Just turn it into a show."

"Nate, you're the performer. I'm not. *I* sit on the floor in a living room and draw a stupid pentagram on the floor. How the *hell* am I going to make that work for a thousand people?"

An icy blast hit me, stopping me in my tracks. The damn ghost had gone right through me. "Nate, I told you never to do that."

"Then stop panicking, will you? I'll walk you through it, promise."

Beer cups being launched at the stage came to mind. . . . Shit. Kelvin was on his way back.

"Nate, I've got a bad feeling about this much exposure—"

"You think I don't get nervous every time I play? You have to trust me. I'll walk you through it."

I thought about it. Again, objects being launched at the stage came to mind.

"This is the one and only thing on the planet I do well," Nate said. "I'm calling it and we stay. Just trust me this once, will you?"

Kelvin pushed through the beer line and shouted, "Kincaid, got the lights working."

I gritted my teeth and hissed, "Nate, so help me god, if you're wrong about this—"

"K, this is going to be awesome."

Kelvin bounded up to me, flashing another grin. "What do you think? We're ready whenever you want to start."

I swear this kid had to be a business major.

Nate whispered in my ear. "Make sure you ask him for more money. He's totally trying to screw us."

"So, a couple of things, Kelvin. First, you're screwing us."

Kelvin held up his hands. "I know the show got out of hand, but it's not my fault—"

I stopped Kelvin in mid-protest. "I'm not saying I won't do the gig."

Nate added in my ear, "Ask for two grand, K. Settle for fifteen, minimum."

"But this is a two-thousand-dollar gig, not a five-hundred one."

Kelvin's face fell. "Look, Ms. Strange, I don't have that kind of cash."

"He's bluffing," Nate whispered. "I bet you fifty bucks he has it in his back pocket."

"Look, Kelvin, I know you're trying to screw me here. I'm not that desperate, and neither is Nathan Cade. You're charging for the beer and a cover. We need two thousand, cash, up front." I nodded at the crowd. "Unless you *want* to tell them there's no Nathan Cade and give them their money back."

"*And free beer,*" Nate added.

What the hell? "And also, we want free beer."

For a second I thought Kelvin was going to argue, but then he flashed me his salesman grin. "You strike a hard bargain, Strange. What the hell." Nate was right: he had the cash in his back pocket. He handed over the two thousand without another whimper. "Stage is all yours," he said, and bounded away.

I shook my head and Nate said, "Should have asked for three."

I headed for the stage, back to wondering how the hell I was going to pull this off. "Let's get this over with."

I'm not sure if it was remnants of my Otherside hangover or my nerves, but my legs were unsteady as I took the first step onto the stage. It was sturdier than I'd expected, though I guess it doesn't pay to end up being sued if you're charging all one thousand of your close and personal Facebook friends for an illegal concert ticket. I hoped Aaron would make sure no cops went out of their way to patrol the campus tonight. Even though he dumped me to keep his job, I didn't think he wanted to see me arrested.

I looked out at the audience. To say the crowd was eclectic would be an understatement, but I guess that's what the college cohort is like nowadays. How the hell did everyone in this demographic end up into zombies and the afterlife? Used to be a grunge and goth thing.

Kelvin climbed onto the stage to test the mic.

I checked myself in my compact, actually a set mirror I kept around for emergencies. My hair was a frizzy mess of black curls, not surprising considering the weather we'd been having. As I did my best to smooth the worst of it down, four foggy words scribbled across it.

Working hard, I see?

"Nate, not funny. Quit screwing around," I whispered.

"Don't look at me, Kincaid. I'm still this side of the barrier," Nate said.

A shiver travelled up my spine. The mirror was set specifically for him.

The first note fogged off and was replaced by a second.

This is my second and last warning.

I felt a brush of cold across my shoulders as the fog that was Nate curled around me to take a peek at the compact. "What the hell is that about?"

I mumbled, "Just a ghost on the far side of crazy."

Well? the mirror demanded.

Normally I wouldn't bother responding; talking to a self-important ghost is like yelling at a telemarketer. But the thing was proving persistent. I wetted the tip of my finger and scrawled back, *I'm only going to tell you this once, so turn your long-term memory on for a sec. SCREW OFF.*

You're stubborn, Kincaid.

"Are you guys ready for a show?" Kelvin yelled into the mic.

Oh, you haven't seen anything yet, I scribbled back as the crowd roared in response. I slammed the compact shut before the ghost could write anything else.

"Here she is, Kincaid Strange. Our very own seance provider, brought to you by KelvinMayer.com. Remember to grab a T-shirt . . ."

Damn, the pop psychologists weren't kidding when they said kids these days were brand entrepreneurs. Guess they had to be, given the planet and economy they were inheriting. Claw your foothold now and hold on like hell.

Kelvin was holding out the microphone to me.

I forced my legs to move in his direction.

Nate whispered, "K, I've got your back. I'll walk you through it. See that guy holding my guitar?"

I gave a slight nod.

"Walk towards him. You're going to take the guitar and stick it in the centre of the stupid pentagram."

I forced a smile and picked up the guitar. Okay.

"Now, these guys are expecting one hell of an entrance. Get as much sage burning as possible: I need a lot of smoke. When there's enough, I'll let you know. Then you count to three, and on three I'll appear. If they're smart, they'll hit me with the floodlights."

Simple. I could do this. I strode to the centre of the stage and took the microphone from Kelvin, to a renewed round of clapping and cheers, and carried the guitar to the centre of the pentagram and set it down.

"See that shot of tequila sitting all lonesome on the speaker?" Nate whispered. "Down it. You're shaking like a fucking leaf."

No way was I adding tequila to the mix. I ignored Nate as I pulled the six bundles of sage I'd prepped out of my bag. I placed one at each of the pentagram points and the last in the middle beside the guitar. Sage is one of those strange plants that retains a portion of its life into death, just like pine needles do. Hitting it with Otherside is like dropping a cat on a hot tin roof: it reacts. Nate could channel the sage smoke into his ghostly body, mixing it with Otherside to give him more substance, which he'd need to hoist the guitar.

I didn't need to draw anything over the pentagram; the symbols we needed were already inscribed on the sage. I closed my eyes, drew in a breath and tapped the barrier. I was so nervous I didn't even notice the nausea.

"No! Not yet," Nate said.

I stopped just short of pulling a globe.

"You've got to say something first. Introduce yourself—"

I turned my back to the audience. "Seriously?"

"Don't be shy, just put yourself out there, like, 'How's it going, Seattle?'"

What the hell. You only live once. I turned back towards the crowd. . . .

So many people. I tapped the mic and cleared my throat. "Hi, I'm Kincaid Strange. . . ." It was as if the mic took uncertainty and magnified it by a hundred. Did I seriously sound like that?

"Okay, now get them pumped," Nate whispered. "Stop being scared—they can smell fear."

Not helping. I unclenched my jaw and took another good look at the sea of students waiting for me to do something.

I froze.

"Ahh, K, not to push, but you seriously need to say something."

Nate tried to feed me lines, but I didn't hear any of it on account of the adrenalin buzzing in my ears. A few people in the front rows started looking at each other. . . . Kelvin, standing off to the side of the stage, had dropped his smile. Well, maybe that would teach him not to trick someone.

Nate swore in my ear. "K? You need to snap out of it. They're getting restless, come on."

I knew how Nate used to handle audiences, but I couldn't do what Nate did. That wasn't me.

Then what the hell was me?

"For the love of god, at least start the seance so I can get onstage."

I pulled my globe, flooding it into the pentagram. The symbols I'd etched on the sage flared gold as everything else faded into the background, including the audience. There were a few gasps, and the snickering stopped. Thank god. The crowd couldn't see the symbols, but in the low stage lights they'd see the grey smoke of the Otherside surround me. My nerves calmed. I was back in familiar territory—Otherside and symbols. That gave me an idea. . . .

"Thank god, K. You totally froze," Nate said.

I tuned him out. Before I lost my nerve, I lowered my head and gave the crowd a slow smile—not a selly Kelvin grin, but the kind you give people before you tell a ghost story around a campfire. My kind of smile. I heard the band fidgeting behind me. I turned and mouthed, "Wait for my signal," and held up three fingers. Then I glanced over at the lighting guy and did the same thing, but also pointed to where I was standing, hoping he got the message.

Then I focused on the audience again. "You ready for some ghosts?" I called, as the sage flared, releasing more Otherside into the pentagram. Clapping and cheers told me that yes they were.

I filled my globe up to the brim and raised my arms over my head.

"*One*," I said into the mic, and let loose a second wave of Otherside into the pentagram. It sought out the sage like a homing beacon and the bundles of herb flared a beautiful, glowing gold. The students saw plumes of grey light flare around the pentagram, mixing with the neon pink. I heard someone bark a command backstage—maybe Kelvin—and in response the neon LEDs shut down, leaving only the ghostly grey Otherside framed by the dimmed floodlights. Had to hand it to the kid: it made for just the right amount of spooky dark.

"*Two*," I said, and let loose the third round of Otherside.

The sage caught fire and the warm green scent filled my senses. Smoke flooded into the pentagram, bound somewhere between this world and the Otherside. It swirled around me, and I waited until it obscured me in a thick fog. The crowd fell silent.

I felt the cold fog that was Nate unravel and peel off my shoulders. He slid into the centre of the pentagram, hidden from the audience. Through my globe I watched as he pulled in the glittering sage smoke. When he had enough, he gave me a nod.

"*Three*," I screamed at the top of my lungs, and released the last bit of Otherside into the pentagram. The sage exploded into a coil of black smoke, neither in this world nor the next.

Then the lights hit the centre of the pentagram and Nate hit a chord on the guitar.

The crowd went nuts as I got the hell offstage.

Nate stepped up to the mic and smiled. "I'm Nathan Cade," was all he said, then launched into "Manhunt," the band taking the cue.

I made a beeline for the beer table, my hands shaking. One of the guys manning the bar was staring at me. In fact, the whole line was staring at me. I decided to use it to my advantage for once and pushed to the front of the line. "Whisky sour," I said, hoping they were serving something stronger than beer.

Mouth still open, he nodded and made me one.

I downed it in one gulp and retreated to an uninhabited spot by the fence underneath a string of dragonfly garden lights. I let out a breath and hoped to hell my nerves calmed down enough so I could ride my bike home when Nate was done.

✳

I checked my watch: forty-five minutes and eight songs in. The wind had picked up, sending more than a few people running to catch the tablecloths before they took flight. I wasn't sure how much longer Nate would hold out, and I'd have to figure out some way to get him out of here before he dropped the damn guitar. It cost more than we'd been paid.

I don't know if it was the band, the crowd of students or just the strange spontaneity of it all, but Nate was playing better than he had in a long time. . . . As song nine ended, he glanced over and arched an eyebrow at me. I gave him a thumbs-up, then tapped my watch and held up two fingers. Two more songs.

He nodded, and went to talk to the band, taking a moment to down another beer. Had to be his fourth or fifth, not that I was worried; ghosts don't get drunk like the living.

"That was awesome."

I turned to see Kelvin beside me, holding two drinks.

"Nathan? Yeah, he's a pro—"

Kelvin shook his head. "Nathan's great, but I meant you."

"Wait—what, me?"

"I've never seen someone do a seance like that," he said, and reached up to bat away the string of lights the wind had knocked into his face. "I've seen them done with a ton of shaking, yelling, calling all spirits. But that," he said pointing to the stage, "was awesome. Can you do Halloween? You could bring Nathan again, or call a bunch of other ghosts."

I stared at the kid, dumbfounded.

"Look, you don't have to answer now. Just think about it." Kelvin patted my shoulder, then pressed one of the drinks into my hand and darted off again before I could refuse it.

I sniffed. Whisky sour. Credit where credit was due, the kid was astute. I settled back into my spot and nursed my new drink.

Nate started into the first chord of "Just Enough Rope." Not one of his hits, but one of his better pieces.

"What the—? Ow!" I'd reached into my jacket pocket and pulled my hand out fast: my compact was burning. I wrapped my hand in my sleeve and reached back in before the plastic melted into the leather. I dropped the compact to the grass and it popped open. I could just make out the foggy script as it scrawled across the mirror.

Don't say I didn't warn you.

Good thing I don't believe in the whole seven years of bad luck thing. I raised my boot to break the mirror.

"I really wouldn't do that if I were you," a deep, male, slightly accented voice said. Nordic or Dutch maybe?

I jumped, dropping my whisky sour.

"You might need it to negotiate a ceasefire," the voice said, clearly amused.

"Yeah, well, you want to talk, call my office," I said, and crushed the compact under my heel.

I covered my ears as a grating laugh echoed around my skull. A massive wave of nausea hit me and I grabbed the fence to stop myself from falling over.

"Still don't want to play nice?" the voice said.

"Go to hell," I said, not really caring who heard me.

"Suit yourself, Kincaid Strange," the voice said.

And just like that, the voice was gone from my head, and the pain too, leaving me with the question of how the hell the ghost had pulled it off. A ghost talking without a mirror was a poltergeist trick . . . but I didn't get a chance to mull over the answer.

The wind picked up, rustling the leaves of the trees. The canopy over the bar tables started to flap, and so did the bamboo blinds covering the screen doors. Chilled air carried the scent of burning sage mixed with burnt hair. Something struck the back of my head—the string of dragonfly lights.

The hairs along the back of my neck stood up—it felt like one by one. Regardless of what ghosts were supposed to be able to do, this one broke the mould.

Nate was mid-song, but he was staring straight at me, trying to get my attention. He nodded and I turned to see what he was worried about.

On the frat house porch, two different wind chimes were swaying violently . . . in opposite directions. I swore and glanced up at the nearby library tower. The flags at the top were dead still. Any lingering hope that this wind was simply the weather vanished.

I made a slashing motion across my throat at Nate, and looked around for Kelvin. Where had I seen him last? The porch. I caught sight of the guy he'd been talking to, a frat boy sporting an impressive beard and the start of a beer gut, who'd been serving.

I ducked around the crowds converging on the beer tables to reach him. "Where's Kelvin?" I must have turned up the don't-mess-with-me vibe, because he stumbled back into a pile of empty kegs.

"I don't know. He went out front to talk to some guys—" He glanced nervously back at the house.

I headed for the screen door. When I stuck my head inside, I caught the tail end of a heated debate between Kelvin and someone I didn't recognize coming from deeper in the house.

I turned back to the beer keg with a beard, who stood there fiddling with the taps. "You know what I do for a living? Spill. Now."

His eyes went wide. "Okay, fine. Some cops showed up to ask some questions about the noise. Kelvin's handling it."

Cops. Here. "They'll want to come in and check for underage drinking."

The guy shrugged. "They always want to check for underage drinking. Kelvin will get them to go away. He always does. Besides, this is Beta Kappa property. They need a warrant to come in."

I snorted. I remembered being in university and thinking that too. Why was it university students were always so damn sure the cops couldn't stroll into their parties on campus?

Beard guy leaned over to grab his backpack.

"If you're so sure the cops can't come in, why are you getting ready to bolt?"

"If Kelvin's wrong and the cops do come in, my parents will drag me back to Alaska."

Not as clueless as he looked. I let the kid go and headed over to the gate. Peering through the gap in the slats, I noted only one cop car in the driveway, and the lights weren't even going, probably so they didn't cause a panic. A thousand drunken students fleeing a party were multitudes more dangerous than any underage drinking that was going on.

I ran back to the screen door and into the kitchen, creeping silently towards the front hall.

"Look, you can't come in without a warrant," Kelvin said.

"You're selling event tickets and booze. Out of our way."

Definitely not a voice I recognized.

I headed back outside. The wind was now so strong it was picking up discarded hoodies. I shielded my head against a string of dragonfly lights that had come loose. They bounced off and skidded across the beer table before wrapping around two girls, who squealed as they tried to untangle themselves. The sooner I was out of here, the sooner the crazy ghost would leave, without hurting anyone.

I waved to get Nate's attention and tapped my wrist.

He held up his pinky finger with a pleading look on his face. One more song.

I shook my head and mouthed the word, "Cops."

Two more strings of dragonfly lights came loose from the fence and launched themselves like rabid sea snakes into the crowd.

I tapped the Otherside. Sure enough, the lights took on a ghost-grey shimmer.

I heard the scream just in time to duck as a lawn chair sailed over my head and crashed into a table, upending it and sending drinks flying.

Someone yelled, "Tornado," as another yelled, "Cyclone." Great, panic was setting in.

The wind picked my hair up and whipped it into my eyes. I tied it back in a messy ponytail and ran for the stage. The band had stopped playing and were dodging beer-cup projectiles. Nate was staring blankly at the unfolding chaos as if hypnotized.

"Nate!"

He looked around, trying to pinpoint me. The Otherside unleashed in the backyard was disorienting him. He couldn't tell the sky from the floor anymore.

I leapt onto the stage as another lawn chair sailed overhead. People were screaming now, which meant the cops wouldn't be far behind.

The chair went straight through Nate before crashing into the drum set. I waved my hand under his nose. "Nate, here!" I yelled.

He blinked twice then managed to focus on me. "What the fuck? It's like the Otherside is bleeding through."

I glanced at what was left of the party. A table lifted this time, chasing a group of students. Shit. I was going to have to figure out a way to shut this down before someone got really hurt.

"I'll explain later. Right now I need something big and reflective." Just then, the drum set crashed over and one of the cymbals rolled across the stage, spinning until it collapsed in a slow circle. Bingo.

"Nate—cymbal, now!"

He blinked at me, then scrambled out of the pentagram and grabbed it for me. I flinched as he fumbled it. He was fading, but this was an emergency.

People were running for the gate and forest now, trying to get the hell away from what they thought was a flash windstorm. If I could funnel the Otherside fuelling this freak show back across the barrier, I could stop this mess.

I knelt down by the back of the stage where there was some shelter from the wind. I could smell burnt hair over the sage now—the scent of unfiltered Otherside. And it was getting stronger as more of it flooded through. I started polishing the cymbal with the hem of my concert T. When it was as shiny as I was going to get it, I pulled a black china marker from my bag and drew the first symbol I needed along its edge. Nate came up beside me.

"K, what can I do?"

"How much juice do you have left?"

"Not much. Ten minutes, maybe?"

"The best thing you can do is go get my bike and bring it around back of the stage."

Nate stared at the grey fog filling the backyard.

"But only if you think you won't get lost in that fog."

"It's not me I'm worried about."

That was doubtful. Nate was all about self-preservation.

"I mean, what if you get hit by something?"

"That's why I need this," I said, pointing to the cymbal.

He glanced down at it, now half covered with china marker, and frowned. "Shit, K, how many globes have you pulled in the last couple of days?"

"Not now, Nate. Besides, I'm not doing anything fancy," I lied. "Just sending the Otherside fuelling this disaster back where it came from, that's all."

"How stupid do I look?"

"Just go get my bike. If that fails . . . I don't know, stall the cops so I have enough time to fix this."

Nate looked far from convinced but dissolved into fog.

I focused on the cymbal, scribbling with the marker to create a reversed mirror.

I heard Kelvin shout, "Dude, you can't come in! This is a private party!"

He was still trying to save his ass, which might save mine.

I finished, then double-checked my work. I'd exorcised enough poltergeists while working with the PD to know what I was doing. I just hoped it worked on this Otherside wind.

I mentally crossed my fingers and pulled a globe, bracing for the nausea that hit me full force. At least I didn't pass out.

Before I could siphon Otherside into the cymbal to catalyze my inscriptions, the cymbal fogged up, and across it scrawled:

Had enough yet?

Smug bastard. I wiped the message off with my sleeve and replied with the marker.

Yup.

Students were either fleeing or using the tables as windbreaks. No one was looking at the stage. Good. I crawled to the centre of the pentagram, carrying the cymbal. There was still some Otherside left from burning the sage, and I used it to stabilize my globe.

Crouching in the pentagram, I held the cymbal over my head and flooded the inscriptions with Otherside. The entire cymbal flared gold and the ghost-grey wind shifted course, rushing towards me.

Shit.

I braced myself against the cold as Otherside shocked through me. I held on to my globe for dear life as more and more Otherside rushed into the cymbal turned portal. It hurt like a son of a bitch, but it worked; the wind began to die down.

I just had to last long enough as impromptu conductor to get rid of the wind. I forced a second wave of Otherside into the cymbal, hoping to speed things up. The funnel picked up speed and more Otherside wind rushed towards the pentagram, along with a chill that went straight to my bones and set my teeth chattering. A smarter person would have let go, but I have a stubborn streak. Sharp pain built up in the space behind my eyes as unfiltered Otherside filled my head.

Okay, maybe faster wasn't such a great idea. . . .

I screamed as the pain behind my eyes thrummed through my whole skull.

"*This is getting us nowhere.*" The ghost's voice was in my head.

"Speak for yourself."

"*Look, I've been dead a long time, but I'm fairly certain it's not a pleasant experience. You're getting dangerously close to the end of the road.*"

I fought to keep the siphon going. "Let me guess. I wipe off the china marker and you give me a running start? No deal."

I thought I heard the ghost sigh. "*Fine. Have it your way.*"

And just like that, it was gone. Again.

I didn't have time to celebrate, though, as a string of dragonfly lights whipped towards my head. I almost dropped the cymbal as I ducked out of the way.

Then another set wrapped around my throat. I managed to wedge my free hand between my neck and the cord, giving myself a little breathing room. I clenched my teeth and held on to the cymbal for dear life. A few more seconds . . .

The cord tightened, cutting off the circulation in my fingers. My vision clouded. If the ghost kept this up much longer . . .

Like hell was I going to be killed by a ghost.

Miraculously, I hadn't dropped my globe yet, and with a last burst of adrenalin I threw every ounce of Otherside I had left into the cymbal.

Nausea overran all my senses and the funnel kicked into overdrive. All I could do was sink to my knees and keep a death grip on my consciousness. At last the cord loosened, and I pulled it free and tossed it across the stage. I pushed myself back up to standing and gasped as I surveyed the backyard. Though the place looked as if a tornado had touched down, all traces of the Otherside-fuelled storm were gone.

Score one for me against the crazy ghost.

There was a tug at my globe. I glanced down at the cymbal in my hand. It was still trying to funnel Otherside. When I attempted to turn it off, the cymbal just pulled harder at my globe. Shit. In all Max's drawn-out lectures and lessons on how to corral Otherside into bindings and back through to the barrier, he'd never said a damn thing about people being dragged through with it. And he used to wonder why I kept pushing for answers. Exactly because of situations like this!

As the last trace of my globe was siphoned off, the funnel latched on to me. It stripped life force, energy, whatever the hell you want to call it, off me in thin, painful layers.

I started to panic.

"Gotten yourself into trouble, I see?"

The damned ghost in my head again.

"Fuck off."

A hollow sigh sounded in my mind for the second time that night. *"Unfortunately, you're no good to me dead."*

The pressure stopped just like that. It felt as though a dozen elastics snapped against my brain as things resettled. I managed to get over to the side of the stage before I threw up.

Once my stomach was done revolting, I sat down on the edge of the stage and took an unfiltered look at the destruction from the ghost storm.

People started to emerge from under tables and other objects they'd hidden behind and look around at the garbage-strewn waste-land that had once been the backyard. I rubbed my neck and pulled my fingers away as they hit the tender parts. The dragonflies had left a mark. Well, it could have been worse. There could have been bodies wrapped around the mangled lawn chairs. . . . Now, where the hell was Nate with my bike?

A megaphone cut through the quiet. "This is the Seattle police. Everyone remain calm—"

The announcement had about the effect you'd predict. The few hundred people who were left went into full panic mode. It was as though we'd been in the eye of the storm and the police raid was the other side. The remaining beer table, loaded down with kegs, upended as people jumped over it in their rush to get away.

Idiots. People were going to get injured in the stampede out of here. Either the cop with the megaphone had no idea just how many people had been packed into the field or he wanted to be a jerk. I figured it was fifty-fifty.

"We need to detain everyone for questioning," the voice on the megaphone announced.

Like hell was I sticking around for that. I forced myself to stand in spite of my head pounding away.

"You, up on the stage, remain where you are."

Since I was the only person left on the stage, he must mean me. I spotted a decent-sized pack of people cramming along the side of the stage, the kind of group I'd be easily lost in. I'd like to say I jumped down gracefully, but the fact is I looked more like a walrus rolling off rocks into water. Blame it on my Otherside hangover.

The crowd bottlenecked as people headed for the forest and the neighbouring backyards. I wasn't getting past them, so I dove under a table that was still standing against a row of dense bushes, its plas-tic tablecloth still in place.

I smacked headfirst into someone already hiding under the table. "Oww!" I grabbed my forehead and so did the other guy. I glanced up. "Kelvin?"

"Hey, Kincaid. Don't worry, you keep this table, I'll find something else."

Must have lost himself in the crowd when the cops started the stampede. I grabbed him by the sleeve of his Hawaiian shirt before he could disappear. I pulled out half the cash he'd given me and shoved it into his hand. "Kelvin, I'm real sorry about this. Usually cops don't raid a seance and, well—" I pointed towards the destroyed backyard.

"No way, dude, *that* was awesome!" He shoved the money back at me. "A Nathan Cade concert bowl that ends in a cop raid? Talk about an authentic experience. That's, what, once in a lifetime? You're free for Halloween, right?"

Part of me wanted to express how unwise it was to try for a repeat of tonight. Instead, I nodded and pocketed the cash.

I felt the brush of cold on my left just before Nate appeared beside me under the table.

"K, cop with the megaphone is closing in."

I peeked under the tablecloth and swore. Four cops, including the one with the megaphone, were heading our way. Time to make our exit.

"Loved the show, Nathan, and I loved your last album," Kelvin said.

I cut off a badly timed super-fan moment. "Where there's four, there'll be more. Nate, where's my bike?"

"I pushed it under there," he said, pointing at a group of bushes nearby. "And I don't think we'll be dealing with any more cops," he continued. "Managed to get on the radio. Pretty sure I diverted them."

Leave it to Nate to find a stupidly illegal way to get us out of a jam. *He* was dead and couldn't go to jail. Me, on the other hand . . .

"I'll buy you some time to get out of here. My parents are lawyers," Kelvin said, and started to crawl out into the open. I heard shouting and something garbled over the megaphone. Probably aimed at Kelvin.

I might have stalled another second or three to watch the outcome, but Nate was already dragging me towards my bike. Give a ghost a corporeal body for a couple of hours and they forget they're dead.

"Get on the back," Nate said.

Like hell I was getting on back. "Nate, you haven't ridden a bike in fifteen years!"

"I've still got ten minutes of juice left. Come on, we'll switch at the 7-Eleven down the hill."

"You said that ten minutes ago!"

"But which of the two of us has more experience outrunning cops?"

That I couldn't argue with. I climbed on the back. "One scratch, Nate, one scratch," I warned. "And as soon as we get off campus, we're switch—"

Nate gunned the engine, cutting me off.

One thing kept running through my mind as we rode away: my stalker ghost was well past parlour tricks.

CHAPTER 13

NO GOOD DEED...

Nate miraculously didn't crash my bike on the way to the 7-Eleven. His hands were barely corporeal when he handed it over, and he dissolved back to the Otherside without so much as a word. He'd overdone it. I felt bad I hadn't stopped him from driving the bike, but by the time I reached the front door to my apartment, the number one question doing laps in my head was what the hell my stalker ghost wanted. What could I possibly have that belonged to him? A close second was, Where had he accumulated his extensive bag of tricks?

Projecting thoughts? Sure, every now and then a ghost or poltergeist manages to pull that off. Localized weather disasters, throwing things around a room? Usually the work of poltergeists, but it happens all the time. Ghosts setting their own mirrors? That shouldn't be possible: the barrier only works one way.

My crazy stalker ghost wasn't the only thing frustrating me; it took me three tries to jiggle the front lock open this time.

"Cameron?" I yelled as I stepped inside.

He ducked his head around the spare room door.

"Everything all right?" I asked.

He nodded, then frowned. "Yes, and you?"

He came towards me, and I watched him for a misstep, something that might betray neurological failure. He looked fine. Still, I reached for his hand.

"I remembered to eat the damn brains," he said, frowning when I pried at one of his fingernails. He was fine, totally fine. The front loading on the brains seemed to have helped.

"You're fine and I'm fine too, Cameron. Go back to whatever you were doing. Just scream if anything strange happens."

He gave me an odd look. "Like what?"

"Trust me, you'll know it when you see it."

Tea, that's what I needed, and ice for my neck. . . . I dropped my bag on the desk in the kitchen. I pulled the textbooks out and placed them beside my laptop. Somehow King Solomon's Jinn didn't seem so important anymore, not with my ghost stalker disaster.

"Seriously, go back to whatever you were doing," I said when I realized Cameron was still hovering.

He said, "I finished with the list—the missing parts of my memory. I left it on your laptop," then headed back into the spare room.

Yet another thing I had to worry about: getting Cameron's life back on track. Maybe I could hit two birds with one stone. . . . I grabbed my phone after I turned on the kettle and dialed Max. Straight to voice mail. "Max, call me back. This is important. Ghost trying to kill me is able to set own mirror." Max didn't appreciate long-drawn-out messages. I dialed Lee next. Maybe she'd know about ghosts that could pull those kinds of stunts.

Lee didn't answer either, and I left another message.

I had a hard time believing that neither Lee nor Max had any inkling there was a very powerful and psychotic ghost in the area. It pissed me off they hadn't bothered to warn me. But then again, that was the paranormal community. Everyone worked on a need-to-know basis.

I switched on the ringer on the phone and left it on top of King Solomon's Jinn so I'd be sure to hear it if Lee or Max called back.

I was too cold to take my boots or jacket off yet. I checked the heater, but it was on, and why hadn't my water boiled yet?

"Hey K, you made it."

I scowled as Nate floated out of the bathroom back to his normal non-corporeal self. He didn't look too worse for wear, except maybe a little more transparent, though looks can be deceiving when it comes to ghosts.

"A damn miracle considering you barely got my bike into the 7-Eleven parking lot before it fell on its side." I glared at him until the kettle whistled. I couldn't get to the hot water fast enough. I poured myself a cup of tea and wrapped my hands around it. It barely warmed the skin on my palms. Son of a bitch.

I grabbed a wool sweater from the closet and dug out a pair of slippers. I thought I had a hot water bottle stashed somewhere too. I headed into my room to find it, checking the dresser mirror for any signs of my stalker ghost before searching under the bed. Maybe I'd be lucky and the concert was the last I'd see of him. Doubted it, but one can hope.

"What's with you?" Nate asked as I re-emerged from my room bundled up and began filling the water bottle with what was left in the kettle.

"I've never been this cold from Otherside before. It's like it seeped into my bones this time."

"Are you okay, though?"

I gave Nate points for trying; he actually sounded *and* looked concerned. A feat for him, since he usually only managed one or the other.

"I'm fine, Nate. I just need to warm up." My god, I was freezing.

Nate watched me with something resembling concern as he settled on the couch, only bothering to keep his face in focus as the rest of him faded into a hazy mix of yellow and blue.

I didn't know why I was so grumpy with him—he was only being Nate. I gave myself a mental shake and started over. "You ghosts are a gossip factory. Have you ever heard of a ghost who could do any of what happened back there?"

His face greyed, in colour and expression. "Serious questions get you serious answers, Kincaid. Trust me, no ghost on my side of the barrier wants that."

I took another sip of tea as I mulled his cryptic answer and how best to board my place up against any more ghost attacks. Sage smoke might be enough for a jerry-rigged barrier. Adding Otherside would work better, but like hell was I doing that—not for another day at least.

A knock sounded at the door.

"Are you expecting anyone?" Nate said.

I shook my head.

Nate floated over to the door and peeked through the fish eye. He turned to me and mouthed, "Aaron," at roughly the same time as Aaron called, "Kincaid, it's me. Open up." He didn't sound happy.

Nate began making gestures for me not to open the door.

I shook my head. Aaron would just stand there and keep yelling until I did. He'd done it before. "Go warn Cameron to stay in the spare bedroom," I whispered.

"Kincaid, open up now or I'll drag you down to the station," Aaron said.

"He only ever threatens to arrest you when he's really pissed," Nate said.

"Yup," I said, and yelled, "Coming!" Nate disappeared through the closed bedroom door.

I took a deep breath, straightened my sweater and turned the knob.

Aaron was in jeans and a red hooded jacket that doubled as a raincoat. Aaron kept his hair short, and it was still damp, meaning he'd probably just showered and driven over. My heart skipped a beat and I told it in no uncertain terms to stop.

I put my best scowl forward. "Don't you think it's a little late?"

He shrugged and walked past me into the living room. "I'm here on business."

"That's one way to describe it, but please, by all means, come right on in."

Aaron ignored me and headed straight for the kitchen. I hung back by the doorway as he opened the fridge and helped himself to a beer. He chugged half of it then put the bottle on the counter and pulled his phone out of his pocket.

"Great couple of shots of you up at the university tonight," he said, and turned the screen so it was facing me. "Looks like they documented it from start to finish. This one's a particularly good angle for you—"

I covered the distance between us and snatched the phone from him. Sure enough, there I was up onstage looking scared out of my mind. Then summoning Nate. I winced. I figured someone would put it up on YouTube, just not so soon. "Shit."

"I guess that's one word to describe it," Aaron said.

I fast-forwarded to see where it cut off. Whoever the camera belonged to had abandoned filming the moment the wind picked up. No one had linked the "storm" to my seance.

"Well?"

"There's not much to tell. Me and Nate had a gig up at the university. It paid, we did the show, I now have rent money."

Aaron finished off the beer. "You knew the party was illegal as soon as you walked in. Not *one* permit."

"Not my job to check permits, Aaron. I was hired as the entertainment."

He held up his phone again. "Yeah, I know. Which is the only reason no one is going to charge you—this time. Consider it your 'Get out of jail free' card. Any more gigs up at the university, you have to ask for permits and prove you asked."

Was he nuts? None of these kids had permits. *No one* got permits for events on campus. "Aaron, that's not fair! I won't be able to work up at the university if I have to check for permits. That's not my job, it's the cops' job—"

"Well, maybe you shouldn't have agreed to work a concert bowl. Nathan Cade is famous on YouTube right now, which is quite the accomplishment since YouTube wasn't invented when he was still alive. The department was screening calls about the noise all evening. Explain to me why I don't arrest you now?"

"You wouldn't dare."

"Watch me."

I took a big breath and shoved down the anger. "Aaron, I won't be able to work, which means I won't be able to eat. Besides, you knew I was going to be up there!"

He held up another shot of the concert, this one taken from the stage. "I repeat, you said seance, not concert bowl. And how is this going to affect Nate? If you thought people were hounding you before . . ." He shook his head.

To be honest, I'd thought about that, but not nearly as much as I should have with Nate egging me on. Aaron was right, I'd have ghost binders looking for Nate in no time.

"What the hell has gotten into you? Three months ago you'd never have even considered doing something like this." He knew he'd made a mistake as soon as that last part left his mouth.

Before I could explode, he rushed to say, "I don't want to fight with you. That's not what I came for. I just wish you'd thought this through. You already had a target on your back."

"Causing more problems for you."

"What's tonight got to do with me?"

I probably should have stopped there, but three months' worth of pent-up anger was not to be restrained. "Aaron, listen real good before I throw you out."

"I said I was sorry—"

"Sorry doesn't cut it. I lost my job—a job I *loved*—where I was able to make a difference. All gone overnight because of some lousy new boss of yours who hates practitioners. And you have the gall to criticize me for how I make ends meet now?"

"I'm not blaming you—"

"But you have no problem judging my choices. I haven't done anything wrong!"

Aaron did something I didn't expect. His face softened and he leaned against the wall, letting out a sigh. "Kincaid, you're not listening to me—"

Because I didn't want to. I didn't have to.

"I know I haven't handled things as well as I should. God knows I'm not perfect, but I've been trying to talk to you the last three months and you won't let me—"

"You really want to know why I didn't call you tonight? Why I try never to call you? Because you can't get it through your thick skull that I don't want to see you anymore."

Aaron was staring at the almost-empty beer bottle now, not me. "You don't mean that."

"You want to know something else? I knew that concert was a stupid idea. I stuck around because that is the only work I can get right now, and now it looks like you're going to make sure I can't even do that either—"

Aaron put the bottle on the counter. His eyes were calm and there was no trace of answering frustration. "You could move out of here and come stay with me," he said.

"What—?"

"It's better than you killing yourself trying to pay your bills. If I thought for a minute you were in this kind of a situation—"

I froze. "What kind of situation?"

"Forget it."

"No. What kind of situation?"

Aaron glanced down at the linoleum floor and ran a hand through his hair before meeting my eyes. "Take a good look at yourself in the mirror. You look like you haven't had a good night's sleep in weeks."

I pulled my sweater tight around me. Son of a bitch. He felt sorry for me—*me*. That's why he was asking me to move in with him—he felt responsible. "So do you."

Aaron's face contorted in anger again. "That's because I *haven't* slept. None of us have, because of Captain Marks's stupid policies. Our paranormal response has become a joke." His voice rose. "The difference between you and me is I can admit there's a problem. You? You can't bring yourself to say you might need help because then you'd be admitting you weren't in control of every facet of your life."

I walked out of the kitchen, eyes on the floor.

Aaron followed me into the living room. "Kincaid, please. I really didn't come over to fight. There's been another murder—" He stopped mid-sentence. "Who the hell are you?"

I glanced over my shoulder. The spare bedroom door was open

and all six feet of Cameron leaned against the doorway, relaxed and composed. The exact opposite of Aaron as he sized Cameron up.

"Aaron, it's not what you think—" How many people had uttered those exact words over the centuries, and they sounded just as idiotic every time. But why the hell was I defending myself? It wasn't any of Aaron's business if there was a man in my apartment.

Cameron extended his hand, seemingly oblivious to the tension between me and Aaron. "I'm Cameron Wight. And you are?"

Aaron just stared at him standing there . . . in Aaron's clothes.

Cameron put both his hands back in Aaron's sweatshirt pockets. Either he had the best timing in the world or the worst.

I cleared my throat. "Cameron, meet Detective Baal, a friend of mine. Aaron, Cameron is—"

"The artist. I know." Aaron continued to size Cameron up.

Come on, brain, work out a reason for Cameron to be here. "Cameron is a client of mine, Max's actually—"

"Sober companion," Cameron interrupted.

Sober companion? I did my best not to make eye contact with Aaron, but shot Cameron a look meant to convey that if he weren't already dead I'd kill him.

Aaron wasn't buying it either. The man knew me.

Cameron trudged deeper into the lie. "Maximillian Odu has been treating me for the last few months. I'm just in the last stretch, getting back to my day-to-day life, that sort of thing."

Aaron gave me a sideways glance.

Oh, what the hell. "Uh, yeah. Max suggested it as a way to pay my bills and branch out. Voodoo seems to work as an alternative for treating addiction. That's legal, isn't it?"

"But why is he dressed in my track suit?" Aaron said.

Cameron jumped in before I ruined the tentative verbal ceasefire. "It was pouring earlier tonight. I was having a rough time, so I headed over, but I wasn't thinking straight and didn't grab an umbrella or rain gear." Cameron nodded to the spare bedroom. "My clothes are still in the dryer and this was all that Kincaid had available in my size."

An awkward silence fell. Cameron broke it with, "I'm sleeping in the spare."

I almost laughed out loud at the blunt statement, but chimed in. "Cameron's having trouble disassociating his apartment and his art from his addiction. Max had another case to work this weekend, so he asked me to fill in and provide a place for him to stay if he needed it."

Aaron's jaw was still tight. "I would think you'd need a more experienced companion," he said to Cameron.

"Maximillian highly recommended Kincaid. I'm mostly on the mend."

Aaron turned back to me. "But you don't have any experience with counselling or addiction."

"You could count wrangling Nathan."

"And you aren't exactly patient with people."

"So sue me for trying something new."

"Kincaid, can we talk in private?" Aaron said, glancing at Cameron.

"Sure thing." I shot Cameron a relieved look and grabbed Aaron by the sleeve of his coat and led him out into the apartment hallway.

The hallway was deserted. I closed the door and leaned against the opposite wall, a few feet from Aaron, ignoring the chipped blue paint. I wasn't worried about anyone hearing us; on a Saturday night, most people wouldn't start stumbling back for another few hours. Dear god, I'm twenty-seven and live in a dorm. . . .

"A sober companion?" Aaron asked.

I nodded. "Max is working on a—system." The best lies are grounded in truth. "Aaron, I don't want to fight with you anymore." What was I supposed to say? I was too hurt? I was too pissed off? I still cared? All of the above? I settled for changing the topic. "What about this murder you mentioned? Another zombie?"

He shook his head. "Ah, no, a practitioner this time."

"Who was it?" I said.

"Her name was Rachel McCay. Did you know her? Early thirties, single, no children, lived in a house in Northgate."

"Aaron, you just described half the hobby practitioners in Seattle." Georgetown was a popular hangout for the artistically inclined hobbyists, Capitol Hill and Fremont for the richer variety. "I don't keep track of hobbyists, though Max might."

"It happened this morning. The scene was the same as in the café—no physical marks, no obvious signs of forced entry except an overturned chair in her kitchen."

"That in itself doesn't link this murder to Marjorie's. How do you know she didn't just have a heart attack?"

"Come out and take a look at the scene tomorrow and I'll tell you."

Lee had vetoed an open sharing of information, but she hadn't said anything about trading. "You want to trade? My eyes on the scene for your coroner's reports?"

Aaron nodded. "I'll do one better. I'll get you in to see the bodies."

"All right."

He let out a breath.

"You guys must be really desperate for a practitioner," I said.

"You don't know the half of it." His phone buzzed, and he frowned as he checked the message. "I have to get back to the crime scene. I'll have Sarah pick you up tomorrow and bring you out. Do you still have her number?"

I nodded.

Aaron started towards the elevator. I was about to head back inside the apartment when he turned around and covered the distance between us in three steps. He leaned in close, close enough I could feel his breath on my face and pick up traces of the cologne that smelled like amber.

Shit. I'd forgotten about that.

He placed a warm hand on the side of my face, which, considering how damn cold I still was . . .

So I did something stupid.

I kissed him.

He slid his arms around me and pulled me closer. My hands found their way to the back of his neck. . . .

And then I pushed him away, gently. I stepped back, keeping my eyes on the worn blue hallway carpet.

We stood for a long moment.

"Kincaid?"

I glanced up.

"Please don't push me away out of spite," he said.

I'd be lying if I didn't admit to myself that I missed him, and this.

"I need more time," I said.

"Why?"

"To be angry, to get my life back on track, to be angry." I took a step towards my door.

"You said 'angry' twice."

"It bears mentioning twice."

"You're the one who kissed me."

"But this isn't something we can fix with a kiss, Aaron."

He forced a smile. "Friends for now, then?"

I nodded. "Friends."

He headed for the elevator and I turned back to my apartment door and all the fantastic, messed-up problems that were looming behind it. I turned the doorknob.

"By the way?"

I glanced back. Aaron was standing in the freight elevator, but the door hadn't shut yet.

"You eventually have to return those library books." He winked. The elevator gate closed.

I leaned against the door and pinched the bridge of my nose. Of course Aaron had noticed the books.

Cameron was leaning in the spare room doorway again.

"When I say don't come out, you know I mean it, right?"

Cameron inclined his head towards the front door. "Your boyfriend is a cop?"

"Ummm, not the answer to my question. Homicide detective, actually. He's just a friend—sort of. We used to work together. *And* I was handling it."

He shrugged. "You weren't defusing the situation, you were throwing lighter fluid on it."

"Funny," I said, and headed past him into the kitchen to boil water for more tea.

"Seriously, if I was a hostage and you were the negotiator, I'd throw myself at the guys with the guns. Better survival rate," Cameron called after me. "And get on Nathan's case, not mine. He was the one who told me to intervene."

I filled the kettle for a second time and turned it on.

"Look, Cameron, I appreciate the thought. And I hate to throw this at you, but Nate and I have a minor problem with a ghost."

"He already filled me in. It doesn't sound minor."

"I'm handling it."

"Like you handled him?" Cameron shook his head. "Somehow that doesn't give me much comfort."

"Look, if I decide I need a zombie's help with my love life, you'll be the first one I ask."

He raised both hands in defence. "Not my fault you're fighting with your boyfriend. Just a zombie, remember?"

I ducked past him into the spare bedroom and grabbed the compact mirror.

Nate, do you think you can watch the place for a couple hours? I scrawled onto the glass.

SURE K BUT I'M OUT OF GAS TIL TOMORROW AT LEAST. WON'T BE ABLE TO DO MUCH EXCEPT WATCH. SORRY, Nate scrolled back.

Just keep your eyes out.

I dug through my backpack for the plastic bag I kept the sage in. I had four bundles left. I couldn't pull a globe, but I could put up a smokescreen—literally.

I grabbed four metal plates from the kitchen and placed one on the stove, one in the living room, one on the office desk and lastly one on my bedroom dresser, lighting a bundle of sage in each.

"Cameron, if anything happens—blinds start blowing, footsteps—"

He nodded. "I'll yell. Loud," he said, and closed the door.

I turned the deadbolt. "Good night, Cameron."

✳

I was still freezing. It was time for that shower. I grabbed a pair of clean pyjamas and turned the hot water up. I tossed a towel over the shower door and waited until the steam poured out of the stall before peeling off my clothes. I stepped in and let the water run over me until the heat reached my bones. It must have been ten minutes before the scale between cold and fatigue finally tipped in exhaustion's favour. With a big yawn, I reached for the towel I'd hung over the door.

It wasn't there.

I could have sworn I'd put it there before stepping in. I'd picked out that exact one because it was the thickest towel I owned.

I opened the shower door and peeked around the steam-filled bathroom. "Nate?" I said. No answer. I reached for my pyjamas on the stool and wrapped the top tight around me before stepping out of the shower. I felt something hard underneath my feet where the bath mat should have been.

I reached down and picked up my hair dryer. What the hell was it doing out of the drawer? I hadn't left it out. . . .

As I remembered the dragonfly lights and the bruises still fresh around my neck, the black hair dryer flared to life in my hands, shooting out cold air instead of hot. I dropped it and jumped back. It wasn't plugged in.

Shit. The steam from my shower had created a stress point in the sage. . . .

Otherside hit me like a bucket of ice water. I slipped on the floor and smacked my chin on the sink. I fell and the side of my face hit the floor, and I stayed down while my brain reorganized itself through the ringing. I tested my jaw. It wasn't broken, as far as I could tell.

I staggered to my feet and reached for the door handle, but it wouldn't turn. I abandoned the door. No sense calling Cameron since I'd locked him in the office. I grabbed my lipliner out of the toothbrush holder and struggled to get the lid off. Sink meeting chin does not equal hand-eye coordination. At last the cap flew off. The steam was condensing on the mirror and walls and it was getting colder. I was really starting to hate this ghost. . . .

I wiped down the mirror with my sleeve and wrote: *Nate!—GHOST!* I hoped to hell he was paying attention.

To my relief, his face floated into foggy focus. "Kincaid? I can barely see you."

"Nate, he's here in the bathroom. Get Cameron." The condensation collecting on the walls and sink was turning to frost.

"K, I don't know what I can do—" His eyes widened at something behind me. "Watch out!" A swirl of black smoke flooded the mirror and Nate vanished.

Something akin to a frozen hand clasped my shoulder. I turned slowly to see what was behind me.

The hair dryer cord flew at me and wrapped around my neck, twice, just like the damn dragonfly lights had. I grabbed at the cord, but I couldn't even wedge my fingers under it. I opened my mouth to scream, but cold air cut me off. I couldn't make a sound. I couldn't breathe either, and I tore at the dryer cord in panic. I needed it off now!

As if I was on a leash, the cord pulled me around until I was once again facing the mirror. And the stalker ghost.

As I met his eyes, he loosened the cord enough for me to draw in a breath. I tried to steady myself; fear and panic are like drugs to ghosts, and the worst thing I could do was show him I was scared. "What the hell do you want?" I croaked.

He smiled and the ghost-grey eyes glittered black. "You're a hard person to corner, Kincaid Strange."

I swallowed. "You have my full, undivided attention."

CHAPTER 14

GIDEON LAWRENCE

"I don't believe we've been properly introduced," the ghost said. He disappeared from the mirror and fog coalesced in the room until he stood before me, exactly as he had looked in the mirror, with his close-cropped blond hair and eighteenth-century clothing, all of him tinged with a ghost-grey sheen. The air temperature around me dropped another few degrees at the ghost's proximity.

"I'm Gideon Lawrence." He bared his teeth at me in something approximating a smile. "I believe you have something of mine."

The hair dryer floated up between us and pointed at my face, though the cord stayed loose enough for me to talk.

"I don't know who you think I am, but you've got the wrong person."

Gideon lowered his head like a large cat about to pounce. "Wrong answer," he said. He inclined his head at the door. "Nice try with the sage. Might even have kept me out for another hour. Now *where* is it?"

I cut my eyes at the door, wondering if the ghost could keep the hair dryer animated and the door locked at the same time. "I don't know what the hell you're talking about," I said, sinking to the floor. I wrapped my hand around the metal wastepaper basket behind me. An object thrown at ghosts won't hurt them, but it usually makes them look. I launched it and lurched for the door.

Before I could get the door open, the cord tightened around my neck and pulled me back. I swore.

"Bad idea." Gideon *tsk*ed as I struggled to wedge my hand under the cord. "Now let's try this again. You met with Maximillian Odu earlier today. What did he give you?"

The cord loosened enough for me to get a handful of words out. "I—He didn't give me anything!"

A translucent hand shot out and gripped my throat. Ice shot through me at his touch. His hand was so cold the muscles in my throat only shuddered: I couldn't scream. I thrashed, but my arms and legs only passed through him, suffering more unpleasant shocks of cold.

"I'm out of patience," the ghost hissed. Ice travelled up my throat, sending my teeth chattering. "What did Maximillian want with you?"

"Nothing! I was the one who called Max. I needed help with a zombie problem."

Gideon's eyes turned dark. "Wrong answer."

Desperate, I tapped the Otherside.

When it flooded into my head, I shrieked. There are different kinds of pain—dull, aching, acute—depending on what kind of damage your nerves are receiving. This was all three.

"You're either much better at your practice or more reckless than I thought," Gideon said, an edge of wariness creeping into his voice.

I needed all my concentration to hold the globe but still managed to say, "Both."

Gideon squeezed harder. "You need to stop this before I do something you'll regret."

As my globe settled and I could focus, I realized the ghost was covered in bindings. Thin gold ribbons of inscriptions whirled around him amidst an Otherside haze, criss-crossing his shoulders in tight, orbiting loops. I recognized a handful of the symbols, runes mixed with Latin, but they moved too fast for me to read.

I snared the closest ribbon, reeling it towards me the way I would unravel a zombie binding.

Gideon winced but hung on. I went for another loop, tugging it so that it collided with another in a flash of gold Otherside. The hair dryer cord loosened.

Gideon clenched his ghost teeth. "I mean it, Kincaid, stop that now."

"What? Or you'll strangle me?"

Gideon's eyes glittered black. "No, you'll kill yourself."

"Says the ghost trying to kill me." My lips were suddenly dry and cracking. . . . Odd.

Despite his discomfort, Gideon smiled. "Parched throat and lips? It's the Otherside starting to burn you up like frostbite. How long do you really think you can hold on?"

Another crack split my lip and I wondered for a moment if the ghost was telling the truth. I ignored the thirst creeping up my throat and the beads of sweat running down my forehead.

Gideon's body flickered grey. He didn't let go, but the hair dryer unravelled and crashed to the floor. "Drop the globe and we can talk," he said.

"No deal. You'll just kill me anyways."

Gideon's lip curled up in a cruel smile. "Oh, you're killing yourself just fine on your own. The Otherside is stealing the very water out of your blood. That's what happens when you've used too much—or do they not bother to teach that anymore?"

My focus blurred. He was lying, had to be. One of the remaining inscriptions slowed as it wrapped around the ghost's waist. I snagged it. What is it they say? Third time's a charm?

Funny how things don't always go according to plan.

The ribbon of Otherside stuck to the surface of my globe and twisted in on itself until it resembled a corkscrew. Then it began to burrow through my globe.

I tried shaking it off, but it kept burrowing. I tried dropping my globe, but the corkscrew held it in place.

"Don't say I didn't warn you," came Gideon's voice.

Shit. I shunted as much Otherside as I could in front of the cork-screw, and it slowed.

"Interesting technique, if completely lacking in finesse. And it won't work."

"Go to hell." More sweat ran down my face, a bead of it collecting on my lip. It had a metallic, acrid taste to it.

"I had a sinking suspicion you'd say that." As the words left the ghost's mouth, the corkscrew broke into three pieces. For a second I thought I'd won. Then the other two pieces began to burrow at two other sites.

I concentrated on reinforcing not one but three places. More metallic-tasting sweat stung my cracked lips.

"Look, I admire your persistence, but you really don't want to see what happens when they break through," he said.

Surely the threads couldn't turn forever. If I could just hang on for a few more seconds, marshal just a little more Otherside . . .

I gave him the finger.

Gideon sighed. "I guess we do this the hard way, then." The three corkscrews split into six.

A high-pitched noise escaped me as I tried to fend them off. I needed more Otherside, so I pulled at the barrier and shunted a new influx of Otherside straight into my globe. I couldn't remember ever using this much before. Another drop of cold sweat ran down my face and dropped to the floor.

Not sweat. Blood.

That wasn't supposed to happen.

Fine cracks shot from the spots where the Otherside corkscrews were burrowing. The cracks spread, and soon covered the entire globe, reminding me of the black lines that ran over Lee's face.

Then it shattered into a thousand pieces, as if someone had stepped on a light bulb. I think I screamed. I know I passed out.

✳

When I came to, I was frozen and sore everywhere, and thirsty— so thirsty.

I was lying on the bathroom floor, and when I sat up, I saw a small puddle of blood where my face had been. I felt my face and my fingertips came back covered in blood. I don't think I'd ever had a nosebleed in my life. . . .

"That was getting us nowhere."

The ghost. Shit. My hand flew to my throat to check for the hair dryer cord.

Gideon said, "I thought for the moment that I'd put the hair dryer away and you could shelve your death wish."

I turned in the direction of his voice—a little too fast, apparently, as nausea coursed through me. He was sitting on the floor, as much as any ghost "sits." There was a glass of water within my reach. It took all my willpower not to grab it.

He stared at me, eyes glittering like a cat's. "How about we try a civilized conversation? I may have overreacted, and for that, I apologize."

I snorted.

Gideon indicated my head. "I'd advise against accessing the Otherside any time soon. I've never seen a practitioner foolhardy enough to block an attack like that. Especially when they had no idea what they were doing."

I reached for a washcloth and wiped the blood off my face. "Look, Gideon, if your plan is to ridicule me before killing me, just skip to the killing part. I have a really bad headache."

"I've decided you're more useful to me alive."

I leaned my head against the cabinet while I tried to decide whether that was a good thing or bad. "Look, whatever beef you've got going with Max, I'm not part of it—"

Gideon raised a translucent hand. "Save your breath. I'm starting to believe you."

It was my turn to look skeptical.

"Let me put it this way. If you had any idea what was actually going on, you would have given me what I wanted. Unless you're completely mad."

"So you believe me because you think I'm an idiot." Not sure how I felt about that.

"Something like that. A talented idiot, if that makes you feel any better." A corner of Gideon's mouth turned up and the smile spread its way to his eyes. "It's a novel situation for me—a practitioner telling the truth."

"So what do you want?" I said.

"People from your time so dislike the art of conversation. But fair enough." Gideon fell silent for a moment, then said, "I had an arrangement with Maximillian Odu, one that was mutually beneficial. I have completed my part in full, but Max has not seen fit to deliver my payment."

"What is it? Your payment."

One corner of his mouth twitched up again. "An item of great value to me, as you might have gathered."

"And you assumed, because I'd met with Max, he'd given it to me?" I shook my head, and immediately regretted it. Holding on to my temple, I said, "You clearly don't know Max."

"As his old apprentice, you were one of many possible leads I was pursuing."

Something clicked. "That's why you were in the ghost trap downstairs. You weren't caught, you were checking me out."

The ghost-grey eyes glittered black again, but this time Gideon didn't answer.

Maybe it was the headache, but I still didn't see why he was chasing me. Why didn't he stake out Max's house? He had to come out eventually. Then I remembered the coffee shop. Max had even stronger wards around his place. I bet they were strong enough to keep a ghost as powerful as Gideon out.

"You can't get past Max's barrier, can you? That's why you're bothering with me."

Gideon *tsk*ed. "Max's refusal to speak to me makes me suspect he has no intention of paying. And this particular payment has a time limit on it."

I could see Max taking his sweet time paying, but not dodging a payment entirely. "You still haven't told me what it is you expect me to do."

"I need you to deliver a message to him. Tell him I require payment, and if he delivers, there will be no consequences."

"And why would I do that?"

Gideon glanced at the hair dryer and lifted his hand. It rose. He levelled his hand at me and pointed. The hair dryer turned and floated my way, the cord trailing. "I believe this could be considered motivation. You deliver my message to Max and I will refrain from killing you."

I tried to scramble back, but I was already up against the cabinet. "I thought you said I was worth more to you alive?"

He glanced around the small bathroom as if bored. "Only if you deliver my message. Otherwise, I might as well kill you."

"So I deliver the message to Max and you'll leave me alone? That's it? No more strangulation by hair dryer cords, dragonfly lights, or any other form of torture and murder?"

Gideon nodded.

"And you'll stop popping in uninvited?"

That same partial smile touched his face. "I might need you to relay another message. Especially if Max chooses to be . . . difficult. Do we have a deal?" Gideon extended a translucent hand towards me.

What did I have to lose? I extended my arm, and shivered as his hand passed through mine.

"What's the message?" I said.

"Simply what I already said. Tell Max that Gideon Lawrence expects payment, and if he pays up, there will be no consequences."

"That's it?"

"That's it." Gideon began to fade into fog just like any other ghost.

"Wait!" It tumbled out before the intelligent side of my brain could stop it.

Gideon ceased disappearing, but did not look happy about it.

"How did you come through my mirror?" I blurted. "And what did you do to my globe?"

Gideon regarded me. "That is the kind of information people

pay me for. And as lovely as you are, you have nothing I need." He vanished into ghost fog.

I lay down on the floor to let my brain readjust. Then Nate's dissociated voice cut through the thrumming in my brain.

"K? Aw shit."

"Nate, I'm fine," I said, not bothering to sit up. My own voice hurt my head. "Just had a run-in with a homicidal ghost. We're good now, though." I briefly related the events of the last few minutes, including the tentative truce with Gideon.

Nate swore. "Look, I'll come out. You need help."

"I'll be fine. I just need to stay here on this nice floor for the next few hours."

"When I saw you in here, I went to get Cameron to help, but he's collapsed in the guest room."

Shit. The sheer volume of Otherside Gideon had needed to bypass the sage smoke and animate the hair dryer could easily have spilled into the rest of the apartment, and then I'd tapped a huge amount too. Considering what had happened the two times Cameron had got close to Otherside . . .

"Coming," I said. I downed the glass of water Gideon had left for me. Hanging on to the sink, I pulled myself up to a crouch, waited until the head rush passed, then stood. Shaky. I reached for the door handle, missed and crashed into it.

"K, you really don't look so hot. I'm coming out—"

"Nate, don't waste your energy now. When I see what's up with Cameron, I really might need your help." This time I got the door open and made my way to the spare room, leaning on the wall.

I tapped at the office door. "Cameron?" No answer.

I headed into the kitchen for my tools, but before I grabbed them, I poured myself a second glass of water. I was still thirsty after I'd downed it, but I couldn't take time for another. I opened the bottom drawer and sifted through my zombie raising tools to find a heavy leather roll that contained my version of a last resort. I carefully undid the string and rolled out the assortment of antique Civil War surgeon's tools. Anything and everything you'd need to saw off limbs and sew people back up *circa* 1861. I removed the six-inch amputation blade. Thin enough to slide through the ribs, long enough to reach the heart. Without pulling a globe and disrupting the bindings, there's only one way to stop a zombie: take out the major anchor point, its heart. If Cameron had gone feral, that's exactly what I'd have to do.

I unlocked the office door and edged myself inside, blade first.

Cameron was on the floor near the desk, drawings scattered around him.

"Cameron?" No movement, not even a twitch.

I spotted one of my spare "set" compacts amongst the drawings. I stepped around Cameron, keeping an eye on him and making sure I had a good grip on my amputation knife, to retrieve the mirror.

I cracked it open and Nate's face materialized in the mirror. "One second we were talking, then you screamed, and next he lurched out of the chair and collapsed," he said.

"Did he move afterwards? Make any noise?"

"Naw, nothing far as I could see, but I was in here, so I couldn't see how he fell."

I crouched close to Cameron, doing my best to ignore my headache, and waited to see if his reflexes kicked in. Live dinner and all. I counted to ten, but he still didn't move.

"I'm going to roll him," I told Nate, and heaved Cameron's lifeless body over onto its back. His eyes were open but not focused. I squeezed his wrist. Not even an eye flicker. If I didn't know better, I'd guess he was just another corpse.

"K, is he, like . . . dead?"

I frowned at Nate's face in the compact.

"Oh, come on, you know what I mean," he said.

"Honestly? I don't know. I've never seen a zombie do this. In the last twenty-four hours I've seen a hell of a lot I'd never seen before, and your guess is as good as mine."

Unfortunately, there was only one way to check if Cameron was still a zombie. I shook my head and aimed the amputation knife between two of his ribs. My hands were shaking so much I had to anchor the knife tip in the skin to make sure it wouldn't veer off. I drew in three even breaths, braced myself and tapped the barrier.

Gideon wasn't kidding. The Otherside wasn't cold—it burned.

"K? What the hell is going on with you?"

I couldn't spare the energy to reply as I tried to keep the knife steady. Once I had enough Otherside, I forced my eyes open. It stung, like getting an eyeful of sand and bright sun all at once.

As always, his anchors showed up first, followed by the finer lines. Finally, the clockwork bindings appeared.

"Shit."

"K? For fuck's sake, I can't see anything. Talk to me," Nate said in a panicked voice.

All six of the gears were rotating, tugging at the anchor lines like tiny fishing reels. I peered at the lines more closely, wondering if I should chance it and try to stop one. . . . It'd be so easy, just keep pulling Otherside until I had a globe, then reach out and stop one.

"K, watch it!" Nate's voice pierced the fog filling my head.

I shook off the Otherside, glad to be rid of the burning sensation, and glanced at him in the mirror.

"K, what the hell's wrong with you? Don't look at me, look at Cameron!"

Cameron was sitting up, his green eyes focused on me. Even before his mouth curled into a snarl, I knew from his blank, white-green stare that Cameron wasn't in there anymore.

He reached for the hand still holding the knife.

I yelped and tried to scramble away, tripping over my bathrobe. Cameron grabbed my wrist and squeezed. Do you have any idea how much pressure a human hand can exert? Especially when there isn't anybody driving to register the damage he might be causing to his own hand or me.

"I'm really sorry about this, Cameron," I said, and drove the knife towards his heart. He jerked away and the blade slid off his rib cage and into his abdomen.

Shit, I'd have to stab him again.

But before I could use the blade again, Cameron's eyes went wide and the vacant zombie stare, well, vacated. "Goddamnit, that hurt!" he yelled.

"Cameron?" His grip on my wrist loosened and I put distance between us.

He glanced down at the amputating knife sticking out of his flesh, then back at me and back at the knife. "You *stabbed* me? With a knife?"

"Yeah, ah, sorry about that."

He stared at the antique wooden handle sticking out of him, then reached around to feel his back. He brought back blood on his fingers. He frowned at me. "It went all the way through." His expression shifted from shock to anger. "Do you have any idea how much that hurts?"

"I had to. You were zombieing out. Besides, it didn't do any real damage."

His frown deepened and he held up his bloodstained fingers.

I made a face. "All right, so it pierced your kidney, maybe your liver, neither of which you're using. We'll get some more brains in you and it'll heal up in no time." I crouched down to examine the wound. Narrow, barely any blood . . . I grabbed the handle and pulled fast.

"Ow!" Cameron screamed.

I wrapped a towel around the entrance and exit wounds. Not that there was much blood flow, but I didn't need it dripping all over the apartment.

"You could have warned me," Cameron said, wincing as he laid a hand on his abdomen.

His skin had taken on a clammy grey appearance and his eyes were whiter. I tried one of his fingernails and almost peeled it right off. He was degrading fast. Again. Whether it was a direct result of the gears turning or just a side effect of passing out, I couldn't be sure. I also didn't want the blood pooling in his abdomen. I made him stand and led him into the kitchen. I dumped the knife in a bucket under the sink with bleach and washed my hands before handing another brain packet to him. "Just get it down—we don't have time to cook it. Cameron, when did you last eat?"

"Ten," he said between bites.

I checked the garbage and there was the empty packet. It was just past midnight now. Two packets in less than three hours.

Just what the hell was I supposed to do with a broken zombie I had no way of fixing?

My phone rang and I managed to get it out of my jacket by the front door before whoever was trying to get a hold of me hung up. It was Lee.

"Kincaid?"

I didn't let her get further. "Who the hell is Gideon Lawrence?"

The silence on the other end lasted five whole seconds. "I'm not sure where you heard that name—"

"He introduced himself after he crashed my seance and tried to strangle me. *Twice*."

She didn't respond. I took that as a cue to keep going. "Did you know he can set his own mirrors and bypass sage smoke?"

"Kincaid, I think you should come see me right now."

"Seriously? That's your answer? You've got to do better than that."

"There's been another zombie murder. This time in the underground city."

CHAPTER 15

DEAD AND BURIED

Lee slid my second double whisky sour across the bar. She'd changed the colour scheme of the bar's paper lanterns again. They were now a pale pink that reminded me of cherry blossoms, and decorated with red script. At least she hadn't decided to repaint the chairs and walls. That smell with this headache?

I swirled the ice in my glass. I wasn't convinced double whisky sours were the best cure for Otherside hangovers, but Lee seemed to think they worked. I took another sip.

"Better?" she asked.

"Lee, I don't think anything short of a coma or a bullet will make this headache any better."

Cameron snorted. He was sitting beside me, still working on the first concoction Lee had brought him, one that looked oddly like a margarita on the rocks, complete with green food colouring and what smelled like lime juice. There was no way I was leaving him alone at my apartment, even with Nate standing watch.

We'd both needed a drink after seeing the body. Lee had left the

zombie where she'd found her, face down in a shallow pool of rainwater in the runoff sewer I'd used to enter the city just yesterday.
The similarities between this zombie's death and Marjorie's were
uncanny, from the Otherside shrapnel strewn around the tunnel to
the traces of ancient Arabic symbols. But the body showed not a
trace of trauma anywhere; she'd either known the person who
attacked her or thought she had nothing to fear.

"Any idea what time she was killed, Lee?"

She nodded. "After midnight. She was collecting shells, seaweed
and whatever trace of sand she could find on the low tide last night,
but no one noticed she was missing until past midnight."

Both sand and seaweed were in high demand in the underground, the dried seaweed for various crafts and the sand to help
curb dampness and erosion. Sand was in such short supply on the
west coast, a lot of zombies had taken to collecting shells and crush-
ing them in old jerry-rigged grist mills.

"Did anyone see her down by the water?"

Lee shook her head.

I took a second sip of my whisky sour and winced. "Lee, her
Otherside bindings were ripped right off of her."

Lee kept her eyes on the glasses lining the bar, maybe checking
for dust. It was pointless: everything was always covered in a layer of
dust. A hazard of the underground.

"I think someone is trying to make a Jinn, Lee."

She stepped away from me and began preparing her version of a
Bellini for a table of four zombies, pouring the first pink-coloured
layer into each of the funnelled glasses.

"Come on, Lee, why the hell ask me to come if you don't want
my opinion? You can see Otherside shrapnel just as well as I can."

But Lee had already loaded the tray of glasses and was heading
for the table.

"Goddamnit, Lee, get back here."

"Want to know what I think?" Cameron said.

I glanced at him as he took a careful sip from the margarita concoction and grimaced.

"I think you're asking a lot of questions she really doesn't want to answer."

"No, if she really didn't want to answer, she'd have kicked us out by now. She'll answer when she's good and ready."

A few minutes later, she ducked back behind the bar. "Are you certain it was not a poltergeist that attacked you?"

"My ghost problem can wait. Aaron's got a murdered practitioner he thinks is linked to Marjorie's death, and with the one tonight that makes three. Tell me what you know about the Jinn and those Arabic symbols—"

Lee hissed as she raised her hand to silence me. "I asked you a question, Kincaid. Please show me some patience and respect." Her scars shifted like shadows. "Are you certain your attacker was not a poltergeist?"

I stuffed down my own anger. "No, it wasn't a poltergeist. Nowhere near angry or crazy enough."

She pursed her lips. "With respect, Kincaid, the ghost did attack you, unprovoked, twice."

"Oh, he's evil, all right. But he had a plan. Poltergeists never have a plan; they just throw things around until someone gets hurt."

She nodded. "I have never had the misfortune to meet Gideon Lawrence, but I am familiar with his name and reputation. He is a trader of sorts, mostly of information. He is very powerful and dangerous."

I pointed to the bruises around my neck. "I could have told you that."

She frowned. "Gideon is the ghost of a powerful sorcerer."

"Sorcerer? Don't you mean practitioner?"

Lee shook her head. "Practitioners such as yourself use Otherside to communicate with the dead. Sorcery is an old practice that involves manipulating Otherside."

"Like protective barriers? Or designing the locks that protect the city?"

Lee nodded. "Those are simple manipulations, little more than channelling Otherside into inscriptions, like setting a mirror or binding a zombie. A sorcerer's spells break the natural order, warping Otherside into something that no longer belongs in this realm or the other."

I'd always been taught that the defining feature of Otherside is that it doesn't belong on the living side of the barrier. That is the trick of working with it: the Otherside is always fighting you, pulling back, hence the need for inscriptions and bindings. If you could warp it, make it stop fighting . . .

As if reading my thoughts, Lee added, "Sorcery carries much more risk than simple channelling. When things do not go as planned, the consequences are dire. Once Otherside has been warped, the barrier no longer recognizes it. When a sorcerer's spell fails, the energy becomes trapped between this world and the next, and it is very unstable."

"So what happens? It explodes?"

Lee pursed her lips, considering. "I suppose it does. When Otherside is released from the confines of a sorcerer's spell, it searches for somewhere to lodge itself. Anything can happen, from starting a fire to striking someone dead."

"To tearing inscriptions right off a zombie," I added. "That's what you think happened with the murders, don't you? Someone's trying to make a Jinn and the spells are backfiring."

She nodded. "My brother always suspected that Jinn bindings required a mixture of Otherside and sorcery to work. Which is why I ask about the sorcerer's ghost."

Yet she'd withheld the information . . . I stopped myself. No sense getting upset about Lee's cagey nature at this point. "You think Gideon is behind the murders?"

She shook her head. "No. A sorcerer's ghost retains only a fraction of his power and spells. These inscriptions would be well beyond Gideon's capabilities. But he may have traded the information to a human practitioner, maybe knowing their intentions or maybe not."

Gideon was in the middle of an argument with Max over payment. "Max isn't involved in the murders, Lee, he can't be," I protested.

She nodded. "I agree that Maximillian is not behind this. I'm merely pointing out the coincidence of the sorcerer's ghost appearing in Seattle and the murders. It would be wise to question Gideon about the Jinn if and when the opportunity presents itself."

"I thought you wanted me to stay the hell out of it?"

"As you so eloquently put it, with three victims the circumstances have changed."

Lee ducked into her office and returned carrying two large volumes, one under each arm. She dropped them on the bar and tapped the leather cover of the larger, scrapbook-sized book. "I believe these are the references you wished to consult."

I carefully flipped it open. The first yellowed page was a collection of newspaper clippings, glued down and wrapped in Cellophane. The earliest was dated 1888 and was a short report of the deaths of a dozen or so crib girls, struck by a sudden illness. The article was little more than a warning: "Stay away! Sick people!" Crib girls were about the lowest form of prostitute there was, Chinese slaves who lived and died in wooden shacks, or cribs, down by the docks, in easy reach of passing sailors. Death by disease wasn't an uncommon fate.

Beside the report were handwritten notes, in both Chinese and English, listing dates and numbers. Below those were four detailed drawings of female torsos, with cut marks and black Xs over the organs, each diagram marked with a number that corresponded to a note above. Shit, these were autopsy reports. The crib girls hadn't died of disease—they'd been murdered, and horribly so. Three binding symbols were noted in the margin.

"These are your brother's notes, aren't they?"

Lee nodded. "But please continue. You will see why I did not immediately consider these relevant."

I flipped to the next set of clippings, spread over two pages, decorated with newsworthy headlines of murder. The first was dated May 23 of the same year, right after the crib girls' deaths had been reported. It detailed the murder of a seamstress. In the Seattle of that era, a seamstress was often also a prostitute. According to the tax rolls, there were more seamstresses living in Seattle than on the rest of the west coast combined, San Francisco excluded.

I flipped to the next page and was faced with anatomical diagrams and notes detailing where each girl had been found, with an X marking where each of the bodies had been mutilated. I checked the Xs against the original victims. Each had been mutilated differently and had had different parts excised: tongue, eyes, heart, kidneys. The list read like a bad horror film. More symbols had been annotated; some were Arabic, and others I recognized as Celtic runes and voodoo symbols. All of them were used in creating zombies.

Lee turned the page to the next set of clippings. The headline WHITECHAPEL COPYCAT stared up at me in stark black print from the otherwise yellowed page. The Jack the Ripper Whitechapel murders had been committed over almost three years, spanning April 1888 to February 1891. Though the killings in London had just started, the news had had plenty of time to reach America. In my world, even now, people loved to speculate as to the nature of the killings, the most popular theory being zombie experimentation using fresh volunteers.

This was the first article in the book that was accompanied by a photograph, a flattering black-and-white headshot of a pretty woman with classic blond corkscrew curls and a porcelain-doll face. The caption read "Anna Bell, June 18, 1870–June 18, 1888." Her eighteenth birthday. Her murder diverged from the pattern of the crib girls' deaths in that it did not occur at the docks but where Anna had lived.

"Either the killer knew her or that was one hell of a coincidence," I said to Lee. Then I noticed the story mentioned Louise Graham, the high-end madam whom Lee had worked for, and at the same time too. "You knew her?" I said, pointing to the portrait of Anna Bell.

"We worked together, briefly. She had been in Seattle two years longer than I and had done well on her own, and even better once Madame Graham recruited her. We were not friends, but we tolerated each other as well as could be expected. Before Madame Louise opened her brothel, Anna Bell had run a lucrative side business out of the Oriental Hotel as a body dealer."

I let out a low whistle. Back in Seattle's early days, the university was always looking for cadavers for the med students to dissect. They were hard to come by, so the faculty offered ten dollars a cadaver—a lot of money back then. The university quickly had to add a couple of rules: no knife marks, ligature marks or signs of strangulation. The odd man or woman with no family, no friends, just passing through Seattle, would end up drowned under the pier after a night of hard drinking; the university rules said nothing about drowning. Turn-of-the-century Seattle had attracted a damnable mix of creative folk.

Lee leaned over and pointed to a paragraph three-quarters of the way down the article, her white nail with painted pink cherry blossoms striking the Cellophane with a soft tap.

"The reporters and police were used to bar brawls and muggings. They were at a loss when it came to dealing with a sophisticated killer. For example, they never noticed that all the women were killed on Thursday nights, almost always by the docks."

I flipped back to double-check. Sure enough, every girl had died on a Thursday night. "Lou did, though, didn't he?"

Lee turned the page, revealing another of her brother's annotated anatomical drawings. This one had many more notes on it, and showed more detailed bindings on the body. His sketch of the murder site included eight of the Arabic symbols drawn in sequential order.

"Since this murder happened in my own backyard," Lee said, "I was able to sneak Lou in while the police and coroner argued over how to move the pieces." She flipped the page over to another torso diagram, this one of Anna. "There were similarities among the bodies, the types of cut marks, the tools, zombie symbols . . . The selection of organs removed was always different, as my brother also noted and the police and coroner failed to catch. But this," she said, flipping the page once more, "was what truly concerned Lou about Anna Bell's murder. Something he had not been in time to catch at the previous scenes."

Lee opened the second book, which was the one she'd shown me before with the Jinn references. She pointed to a series of symbols labelled by Lou as incomplete Jinn bindings. I looked back and forth from it to Lou's sketch of the scene. The third one from the top was identical to the ones found at the site of Anna Bell's murder.

I glanced up at her. "Whoever killed those women really was trying to make a Jinn."

"That is what my brother strongly suspected."

"Lee, you knew—"

"I knew nothing except that the Jinn symbols and the explosion pattern at Marjorie's were similar to the ones Lou found on these murder victims over a hundred years ago. I did not wish to elicit a panic." She shook her head and scowled, not at me but at the situation. "With three murders in two days, that now seems unavoidable."

Marjorie had been killed on Friday night, and Aaron had come to me after my disastrous seance tonight to tell me about the death of the practitioner. None of the victims had been cut up, and two of them were zombies. The only true similarities to the old crimes were the Jinn symbols.

"You had a suspect in mind, didn't you?" I said.

Lee worded her answer carefully. "I *still* have a very dangerous suspect in mind, Kincaid. A ghoul, the same one Lou suspected a hundred years ago. Unfortunately, I have not yet pinpointed his whereabouts—"

"Bullshit, Lee. You know where every undead in the underground city is!"

Her eyes narrowed. "That may be true, but finding this one is not a simple task."

I laughed. "No, you want to keep the fact that a serial killer emerged from the underground city under wraps. In these times especially."

Lee drew in breath, something she rarely did. "It will take me time to extract him. He is holed up in the third-level docks."

My anger dissipated. Lee might run the place, but even she stopped short of the caverns on the third level. Everyone with a grain of sanity did, zombies included. Until the early 1930s, the underground docks had held a black market where the paranormal communities had traded with boats coming in from the surface, but that traffic had fallen out of use in favour of more subtle routes. Since that time, they'd become a slum of a sort where the feral zombies and ghouls were sent along with the sane ones who could no longer pay their bills. It was not a safe place.

"I have not been complacent. I've had the lower docks quarantined ever since you brought me the details from Marjorie's. No one has entered or left."

A few more things clicked into place. "So even if this ghoul is responsible for Marjorie's murder, he couldn't have killed the practitioner or your zombie."

She made a sharp clucking sound in disagreement. "I suspect he has an access route to the surface—"

"Or we're dealing with an accomplice."

Lee levelled me with a stare. "That is the only way I see him being able to evade all my agents." She sighed. "As much as I'd like to keep this private, excluding you and Aaron at this juncture would only hasten the possibility of exposure and failure."

Translation: leaving me and Aaron in the dark would only help the killer, meaning there was a greater chance more murders would occur and that someone on the surface would put two and two together and make the paranormal connection. If that happened . . . well, a mob armed with torches from Home Depot, anyone?

"Believe me, Kincaid, neither of us wants a Jinn loose in the city."

Or under the control of someone who didn't care how they made one. I needed to see the bodies. . . .

I reached for the books, but Lee put her hands on top of them. "On one condition."

"What's that?"

"You will be employed and paid by me while working with Aaron, and you will bring me everything and anything you find. A thousand dollars a day until we find the culprit, ten thousand if you apprehend the accomplice."

This was uncharacteristically generous. "What's the catch?"

"Under no circumstances are you to try to contact the ghoul."

"What if the killer strikes again on the surface, and it is your ghoul?" Cameron said.

Lee and I turned to stare at him, Lee in irritation and me in surprise. I'd thought Cameron was still totally zoned out.

"Well? What if Kincaid runs into the ghoul on the surface?" Cameron challenged. "What is she supposed to do? Stand there?"

Lee shook her head. "I do not believe the ghoul will risk the surface, not while I am searching for him. It would be safer for him to use his accomplice."

"A lot of ifs," Cameron said. "And not much leeway."

Lee glared at him, but despite her displeasure, she considered the point he'd made. At last she turned to me. "Fine. If you come across the ghoul in Seattle, be my guest, but my restriction about contacting him still stands. Do I make myself clear?"

I thought it over. "All right. I promise I won't contact the ghoul."

Lee ran her finger once more along her brother's notes. "Be careful, Kincaid. Any person living or dead who is willing to raise a Jinn is not to be trifled with."

I took the books and nodded to Cameron. He downed the last of his concoction and climbed off his stool. We turned to go.

"Kincaid?"

I glanced over my shoulder at Lee.

"My advice concerning the sorcerer's ghost? Deliver the message for him and try to determine if he knows anything of Jinn being raised in the city, then forget you ever had the misfortune to hear the name Gideon Lawrence. He has a reputation for offering people things they cannot refuse."

We wound our way along the boardwalk towards the main underground city entrance, weaving between zombies and the odd ghoul. It was 5 a.m. and still dark above ground, so I had no qualms about us crawling out into the alley in Pioneer Square.

I held up the books. "Do you have any idea how much detail is in these?"

Cameron fell into step beside me. "I think she's holding back. She knows more about the murders than she's letting on. I know when people are hiding details—I've had enough experience at hiding stuff over the years." He was referring, no doubt, to his attempts to hide his mental illness.

"You already suspected the murderer might be a zombie," Cameron continued.

"*And* I was wrong," I said.

Cameron shrugged. "Same difference. Both are living dead who eat brains."

"Ah, now that's where you're wrong."

We were passing by the market, which never closed, and I scanned for the right stall. . . . There it was. I spotted the regular pocket of Polish ghouls, one of which specialized in ghoul delicacies. That the ghouls in the city were almost exclusively eastern Europeans wasn't a surprise. Becoming a ghoul was the preferred method of living past death in that part of the world, despite the gruesome appearance.

I stopped Cameron and pointed towards the stall. "There, that stall with the grey and black things hanging from the rafters."

Cameron followed my finger, then crinkled his nose. "Are those—? It can't be."

"Rotten cuts of meat of unknown origins? Exactly. Ghoul food."

One of the ghouls sensed the scrutiny and swivelled his head in our direction. The market gas lamps weren't nearly as bright as the electric sodium fixtures lighting the boardwalk, but we still got a good look. The ghoul wore a thick leather apron over a sailor's sweater and black canvas dock pants, as well as a leather hat that matched the texture, if not the colour, of his face. His skin had been cured to a deep brown leather and the flesh drawn taut over his bones. Any stores of fat were long gone, along with most of his nose. Leaving the socket exposed. When he turned his face, I noticed a patch of yellowed, exposed bone on his chin where the skin had worn off. Cameron only partly succeeded in not making a face.

"Most ghouls wear hats: they only keep their hair for a year or two before it starts falling out. The skin goes leathery and wrinkled like that fast. And don't ask me how they get the meat to rot quite like that without falling apart. Some secrets are best left unknown."

Cameron couldn't take his eyes off the ghoul. "Why would anyone—"

"Live like that? It does come with benefits. Zombies like you and Lee can see Otherside, but you can't warp it. Ghouls can—something about the body still decaying. A lot of people in the paranormal community think it's a decent trade-off. The older a ghoul gets, the stronger it gets as well."

As if sensing they were the subject of my impromptu ghoul-versus-zombie lesson, two more ghouls turned and narrowed their eyes at us. Then one yelled our way in Polish.

Cameron stiffened. "What did he say?"

"I'm assuming, 'What the hell are you looking at?' I never bothered learning Polish. They don't exactly like being the centre of—" I shut up as all three ghouls lifted their noses to sniff the air. Shit . . .

"What are they doing?"

"They're hard-wired to smell rotting meat."

The ghouls made a point of sniffing a little longer as they kept their yellow gazes on us. Then one of them grunted something in Polish and they all turned their backs to us.

"Here, Cameron, hold these," I said, handing him the books.

He took them, looking warily at me.

I lifted his shirt to check the knife wound.

"Hey!" Cameron said as I peeled back the bandage.

The skin around the wound was oozing yellow fluids now tinged with green. It wasn't healing. I replaced the bandage and pulled his shirt—Aaron's shirt—back down.

"It's not good, is it?"

Well, it wasn't great. "Your wound here got their taste buds going," I said. "You're not decaying, but you're not exactly healing either. You've had two packets of brains, three if you count the drink Lee gave you, in the past seven hours—" I was about to tell him my theory about his bindings limiting how much he could heal, but then thought better of it. Instead, I said, "A normal zombie would have healed an hour ago. But you're not a normal zombie."

"A one-of-a-kind zombie," Cameron said. "Somehow that feels like it should be ironic or something."

"At least you've kept your sense of humour."

When we reached the bottom of the great staircase, Cameron asked, "Where to next?"

"Well, it's coming up on morning now. I figure it's high time to swing by your place. I'm hoping we'll find a clue there as to what Max did to you, or what went wrong."

He frowned. "Someone is killing zombies, and practitioners are trying to raise an undead myth, and we're going to rummage around my apartment?"

"I figured, from all those drawings on my desk, you'd want to see your paintings, make sure they were okay."

Cameron shot me a sideways glance. "No offence, but catching a serial killer strikes me as a higher priority."

I smiled. "Don't worry, I'm not leaving you there alone."

We kept walking in silence until Cameron finally asked, "So you're really not going to contact the ghoul?"

"Nope."

Cameron shot me a sideways glance. "I barely know you, and don't figure you for the type who'd back off from a lead like that."

"Who said anything about backing off?"

"You just said you weren't going to contact Lee's suspect."

I shot Cameron my best Cheshire cat grin. "Who said anything about contacting the ghoul? I'm contacting his victims."

CHAPTER 16

YOU CAN'T TAKE IT WITH YOU

A good view can make just about any city look pretty, even on a rainy morning right before the sun comes up, when the sky is the greyest and ugliest. It's the shine of the street and car lights, and the fact that there is still enough darkness to cloak the things you don't want to see. Having said that, the view of Seattle harbour from Cameron's apartment would blow the postcard pictures away any day, rain or sun.

It turned out that he lived in an exclusive building complete with concierge and front desk. No one had a place here unless they had a lot of money to blow. The concierge had given me a suspicious once-over when we'd entered the building. Apparently Cameron coming home at 6 in the morning with a female companion was not out of the norm, just not one with frizzy hair and clad in leather.

But Cameron's studio itself was about as pared down as you could get. The walls had been reduced to brick facade, between drywall where his paintings hung. The floors were concrete with a few rugs to soften them. With the exception of a partitioned-off bedroom, it was open plan, with canvases occupying most of the space in lieu of the usual furniture and TV.

I tore my eyes off the city view and headed back to the two books, which I'd left lying open on Cameron's kitchen table. Though I'd taken a quick nap when we got here, it didn't feel as though it had put any dent in my Otherside hangover. Thank god Cameron had coffee, and speaking of which . . . I stifled a yawn and got up to refill my empty mug, stealing a glance at Cameron to see how he was holding up. The trip back here was clearly long overdue: Cameron had been standing in front of the same canvas for more than an hour. I thought more of it was covered in paint now, but it was hard to be sure.

I'd already found Cameron's address and appointment book and flipped through it. He was one of those people who preferred to keep his agenda on paper. He'd noted three appointments leading up to Thursday, and it was the third one I wanted to broach with Cameron, but not until he finished working on his painting. I figured I'd give him that.

The chapter staring up at me dealt with Ifrit, or Fire Jinn. Compared with the accounts I'd read of King Solomon's Jinn, Lee's text lacked storytelling but made up for it with detail. There wasn't just one set of binding symbols and inscriptions for each type of Jinn, there were many, though all of them were incomplete. As Lou had pointed out in his notes, most were a mash of old pre-Islamic Semitic symbols, a seemingly haphazard mix of Arabic, Aramaic and Canaanite.

I turned another page to confront three more sets of Ifrit bindings, these ones with red Xs as placeholders where the missing symbols might go. Each set of bindings was more convoluted and contradictory than the previous. No wonder a Jinn hadn't been made in a thousand years: no one could sift through all these bindings.

One of the symbols matched a partial I'd found at Marjorie's. According to the book, it was ancient Aramaic. I checked my drawings of the other partial symbol from Marjorie's. I found it on the same page but in a different group. This one was supposedly

Canaanite. I marked the page with a sticky note and flipped to the next spread. The two symbols appeared twice more, both in incomplete bindings.

I leaned my head against the back of the chair and closed my eyes. So what the hell did it mean? Did whoever was trying to raise Jinn have an actual set of bindings to work off, or was it trial and error?

Something metal struck the concrete floor behind me. As I turned to see what it was, I knocked my coffee mug over. A paint can rolled by my feet and under the table, leaving a trail of thick pink paint.

I swore and pulled the books out of harm's way; Lee would kill me if I got coffee on the pages. I glared at Cameron as I took a roll of paper towels to the paint spill.

"Sorry," he said without moving his eyes from the canvas. Whoever coined the phrase "You can't take it with you" did so without having met a zombie or a ghost. Taking their shit with them is the first thing the dead try to do.

Case in point: as soon as we'd stepped into the apartment, Cameron had been fixated on his artwork at the expense of everything else. They were done in multiple mediums—pencil, charcoal, watercolour, chalk, oil—and were mostly abstract, though in some there were figures and images hidden beneath the swaths of colour. Were they any good? They had a certain artistic integrity, though I'm the first to admit I wouldn't know artistic integrity if it bit me.

"Are you done rifling through my personal accounts yet?" Cameron asked.

I'd made him hand over his laptop and cellphone and all the passwords. I wanted to make sure I didn't miss any clues. When I got fed up with the bindings and murder accounts, I switched to sifting through those, though as of yet I hadn't turned up anything I didn't already know or suspect.

"Well?" he said, still not tearing his eyes off his painting.

"Not even close."

There was another pause, then, "What do you really think happened to me?"

"Honestly?"

At that, he turned to me and I waved him over to the table. I flipped the appointment book around to show him the meeting I'd found—with his drug dealer late Thursday afternoon, right before he'd died. "I think you accidentally overdosed, just like you and Max were afraid you would."

Cameron stared at the entry. There was no surprise or resistance on his face, just acceptance. "Then why didn't Max's binding work the way it should?"

"Well, when I worked for the PD, we had a couple of instances where someone died of an overdose and the drug dealers panicked. They paid hacks to raise the victims so no one could prove time or place of death. If you accidentally died and someone paid a practitioner to raise you, Max's bindings would have got messed up." I shrugged. "Or maybe Max didn't really know what he was doing and your memory tanked just because."

Cameron greeted that with silence, then turned and went back to his work. I tried to focus on the Jinn book.

"When are we going to talk to the ghosts?" Cameron said at last.

"*We* aren't talking to the ghosts, *I'm* talking to the ghosts. *After* I go to look at Aaron's new victim. *You're* staying right here."

He frowned at me. "Is it the best idea for me to stay here?"

"Your wound's not healing, true, but otherwise you've been stable since we went to see Lee. To be honest, I'm more concerned about someone figuring out you're a zombie than you zombieing out again." Considering the zip code, I highly doubted anyone would pull a globe in his vicinity if he stayed here. If I was wrong, and the worst happened . . . well, better off here than while I had my back to him chatting with ghosts.

"I meant, is it safe for you?" he said. When I looked confused, he added, "You collapsed the last time you did the Otherside thing, and you don't exactly look like a picture of health right now."

The zombie had a point. "To talk to these guys, I need to channel Otherside—"

"And being near you when you do that might be enough for me to lose it?"

I nodded.

He went back to painting.

"Cameron, what would you rather do? Stay here working or come see dead bodies and murdered ghosts?"

He snorted.

"If it makes you feel any better, these are not the kind of upstanding ghosts you want to meet." Not that Nate was upstanding, but Nate had only drowned when he'd died. Not pretty, but child's play compared with murder victims. "I'll leave you a cellphone. If something goes wrong, if you even *think* something is going wrong—"

"I'll call," Cameron said.

I stifled another involuntary yawn. "Look, if you want to do something useful, convince your art dealer to meet us at Club 9 tonight too." That was where we were supposed to meet Cameron's girlfriend Sybil. With any luck, we'd run into Cameron's drug dealer as well. That was one person I wanted to be watching when he saw Cameron.

"If you're so certain I overdosed, why bother?"

"Because I'm not a hundred percent certain you did. I'd like to rule out every other possibility. *This*," I said, pointing to the appointment book entry again, "is coincidence. It doesn't prove anything."

Cameron looked away from the canvas, out the window. A little light was seeping through the grey morning sky. Might even get sun later today. "I was trying really hard. Whatever Max was doing was working for me," he said.

What was I supposed to say in response to that?

I checked the time on Cameron's clock: 9 a.m. now. If I left at 9:30, I'd have enough time to get to Pioneer Square and meet Sarah, Aaron's partner, by ten. I had a half-hour to kill and tried to focus on Lee's Jinn text, but my eyelids began to droop. Son of a bitch. At this rate I'd be useless when I got to the crime scene. Maybe dousing my face with cold water would help me stay awake. I headed to the washroom.

I turned the faucet and waited for the water to grow icy before splashing it over my face. Three handfuls later, I couldn't feel the tip of my nose, but I'd stopped yawning. I dried myself off, straightened and stretched. Then I pulled down my collar to check the blue bruises on my neck in the mirror.

"Son of a bitch—" I stumbled back into the towel rack as my reflection vanished, replaced by Gideon's face.

He frowned at me, not homicidally but more as if he was frustrated and impatient. "You haven't delivered my message yet," he said.

I forced my heart rate down and pushed myself off the towel rack. Never let a ghost see you scared. I walked up to the mirror and said, "Yes, I did. I left a message on Max's answering machine."

Gideon's lip twitched. "Perhaps I wasn't specific enough."

"I can't *make* Max call me back."

"If I was willing to wait for Maximillian to contact me, I wouldn't have involved you."

So the ghost was involving me? "I thought you were coercing me?"

He gave a noncommittal shrug. "Different time, different definitions. My message?"

I sighed. I did not have the time or the brainpower for this. "Look, I'm going to see Max in person tomorrow morning." Gideon looked as if he was going to object, so I added, "I can't just barge into Max's house." I may be a practitioner, but Max was voodoo. You don't intrude onto a voodoo priest's property without an invitation—not unless you want to spend money on removing the resulting curse.

Gideon's brow furrowed in the mirror and I could tell he wasn't impressed.

"Take it or leave it," I said.

He stared at me with those cold black eyes and the temperature in the room dropped. Great, round two with the sorcerer's ghost. I checked the room for any ropes or wires.

Then Gideon rolled his eyes. "Have it your way, practitioner. Until tomorrow. In the meantime? Get some sleep. You look like you've been dragged through the Otherside one too many times."

I snorted. "I'll remember that the next time I run into a flying hair dryer cord. Would probably help if I didn't have to pull a globe twice a day to look at bindings."

Gideon stopped his fade into the ghost-grey fog. "Why on earth would you need to touch the Otherside for something as simple as looking at bindings?" He stared at me as if I was an idiot.

Stupid, self-absorbed ghosts. Dead for a few decades and they forget the living can't see Otherside . . . "Umm, because otherwise I'd never see bindings?"

I didn't know what the hell I'd said, but Gideon regarded me with renewed interest. "Is it possible you don't know? Don't bother answering, I can see from your face that you don't."

"Know what?"

"I suppose it makes sense that Maximillian wouldn't bother teaching you how to do it, since he's a medium. So you 'pull a globe,' as you say, every time you need to see Otherside?"

I think I preferred the pissed-off, homicidal Gideon. "All right, spit it out. What the hell has you so interested all of a sudden?"

He lowered his head and looked at me as if I were prey. "Just that there's a much easier way."

I frowned. Why wouldn't Max have taught me that?

"You might even be able to persuade me to show you. I'm sure you have something you could trade."

Lee's warning came back with a vengeance. *He has a reputation for offering people things they cannot refuse.* "Not interested."

"Surely you don't think you can keep going like this? Let me guess—nausea comes and goes now, accompanied by sweats and thirst? No matter how much you sleep, you're always tired? Don't bother answering, I see it written across your face." His eyes glittered black-grey. "I can help you with that."

"Get out," I said.

"How much longer do you think you'll last? A month? A week?" His eyes narrowed. "I'd wager you can't stop yourself anymore—"

"*Now.*"

He shrugged. "Live, die? Makes no difference to me. Let me know if you change your mind."

He vanished into the fog.

I grabbed a towel and launched it at the mirror. Gideon was wrong. All I needed was a vacation, a few days off from tapping the Otherside.

And just how long did I plan to keep telling myself that?

"What the hell was that, K?" Nate's voice was followed by his face materializing in my compact, like a normal ghost, one that I'd *actually* called.

"Just my stalker ghost trying to sell me snake oil." I filled Nate in on the day's plans, including that I needed him to keep an eye on Cameron over the next few hours.

"And don't get attached to anything," I said. Nate'd had a bit of a shoplifting problem as a kid . . . and as an adult . . . and as a rock star. Don't ask. You'd think being a ghost and having difficulty picking things up would have fixed the problem, but it hadn't. He could only go after tiny, relatively light stuff, like coins and cigarettes, but still. Lee'd resorted to threats to make him bring back all the glasses he'd lifted from Damaged Goods.

Nate ignored me and floated into the studio. "Hey, Cameron, what's up? You're looking better—Hey, what's this?" he said, hovering in front of a painting.

"Cameron, watch your wallet and small paintings." I stowed Lee's two texts in my backpack in case I needed them for reference at the crime scene. "Cameron?"

"I know—don't let anyone in and if I remember anything, write it down?" He looked up from the canvas. "What else should I do?"

"I don't know, Cameron. Reminisce? Do whatever you used to do at home?" He just stared at me, bleakly. "Tell you what, your job is to sort through your stuff, pack some clothes and come up with plausible reasons for us to see your art dealer, got it?"

He looked as if he was about to argue with me.

"Come on, you're a creative guy."

"You want me to lie through my teeth?"

"If that's what it takes. Nate can help you—"

"K, fuck off—" Nate said.

Cameron drew in a deep breath. "I'll call and tell him I have a new piece." He frowned at me and glanced back at his painting. "Granted, I'll have to finish it first."

I grabbed my jacket and headed for the door. "I have faith in you. Back by noonish. Call if you have any problems, and keep the door locked."

"Hey, Kincaid?"

I glanced back over my shoulder, expecting another argument.

"Just . . . good luck with everything. I hope you figure out who's killing these people."

Well, that was unexpected. But kind of nice.

I kept my eyes on the floor as I rode the elevator down. Why do expensive buildings always cover the walls with mirrors? Do rich people actually like looking at themselves?

I stepped into the lobby and noted the new concierge at the front desk. I kept my head down and focused on the floor as I walked past him. I do not have the best of luck with security guards in places like this. Apparently I arouse suspicion. In the reflection of the window I saw that he stared at my back for my entire trip across the lobby.

I was about to push through the glass doors when I caught sight of someone sitting on a white leather chair in a small waiting area beside the doors. A tuft of neon-pink hair peeked over the top of a fashion magazine she was reading.

I strode over and planted myself in front of her. She didn't look up. I cleared my throat.

Slowly she raised her face from the pages, then lifted an eyebrow as if in surprise. "My god, they let you in this building? Dressed like *that*?"

I smiled. Amateur. "You'll have to be a hell of a lot more creative to get a rise out of me."

She frowned, sat up straighter and crossed her legs, exposing a pair of spike heels I could only imagine teetering in. "Can I help you with something?" she said.

"Cut the crap. What are you doing here?"

Her eyes dropped to my muddy leather boots and lingered longer than I cared for.

"I have an appointment with a client this morning," she finally said. "What are *you* doing here?"

"None of your business—"

The concierge straightened in his chair. "Is there a problem here?" he called.

Oh, for Christ's sake. *I'd* actually come out of the elevator. I wasn't slumming in the lobby reading a magazine. . . .

Unfortunately, Neon fit in. I didn't. Wealthy people concerned about the afterlife blow a lot of money on practitioners. Not the real ones like me, mind you. The whitewashed models, like Neon. Chances are good you don't really want to know what your parents, deceased spouse or jilted friends actually have to say about you. Amazing what people will pay for someone to lie to them . . .

I also didn't have any *proof* she was following me or had any other nefarious schemes cooked up.

I smiled apologetically towards the concierge. I've had practice over the years. "Sorry, sir, just catching up with an old friend."

"This is a private building. Take your conversation outside," he said, nodding at the door.

Neon smirked. I turned my back on her and managed a steady walk until I was around the corner and out of visual range. I took a deep breath to calm my temper and pulled out my phone. I don't believe in coincidences. The fact that Neon was hanging out around Cameron's building spooked me. Time to see if Max was answering his phone.

He wasn't, so I left another message. "Max, it's me. Things are getting awfully crowded this side of the barrier. Just get back to me before I have to knock down your door, will you?"

CHAPTER 17

THE LIVING AND THE DEAD

While Aaron made sure the coast was clear at the crime scene, I'd arranged to meet Sarah at the only coffee shop on Pioneer Square that still made a decent Americano. It's harder than it looks. It's not just adding hot water to espresso, there's technique involved. I tugged my hood up before I headed inside.

I got in line and looked around for Sarah. I was at the cash register when I spotted her . . . on account of the fedora, leather trench coat and newspaper.

I shook my head. Why did I even bother trying to be inconspicuous?

As soon as my coffee was up on the bar, I headed to her corner and slid into the seat opposite. "You look ridiculous."

Sarah lifted her head out of her newspaper wearing a big grin. "Oh, come on, Kincaid. Where's your sense of fun?"

"I don't know, Sarah. I just haven't been having all that good a time recently."

She was about to make a crack, then paused, taking in my pallor, the bags under my eyes, all the signs of wear and tear connected to too much Otherside. She just nodded.

Aaron's partner was definitely the more senior of the pair. If she hadn't crossed the forty threshold yet, she was close. Her red hair had begun to fade and she either couldn't be bothered or didn't see the point of remedying it with dye. Still attractive, just maybe not in a conventional way. Her most striking feature, though, was her size. She'd been an Olympic weightlifter in her youth, and she still had the physique. She easily outmuscled the majority of men on the force. Scratch that—she outmuscled most of the men in Seattle. Witnesses and suspects alike were so shocked by Sarah's physical presence they spent the first minute or so in her custody stammering in an attempt not to spill what they knew. By the time Aaron stepped in, suspects were too intimidated to lie. Or lie well, at least.

I'd missed Sarah. We weren't friends; the age difference and the fact she had a couple of kids meant we didn't have much in common. But she was one of those people in a perpetually good mood, and I enjoyed her sense of humour.

The fact that Aaron, unlike the other men on the force, had never had a problem with Sarah had earned him a lot of brownie points with me when we first met.

Sarah stood up, came around my side of the table and wrapped me in a bear hug. "Kincaid, you've got no idea how happy I am to see you."

This was well outside my realm of comfortable. I gave her an awkward pat on the back. "Uh, yeah. Nice to see you too—"

She released me and slid back into her chair like a cat. You'd think a woman her size would be awkward, but then she'd had to dodge all those barbells on their way down. I think the un-nimble weightlifters get weeded out.

"Is it that bad at work?" I said.

She snorted. "You never met Captain Marks, did you?"

I shook my head. "Seen him on TV and in the paper, though."

Sarah's face turned serious, an expression she usually reserved for the more gruesome murder cases. "The man's an idiot, Kincaid. He wants us to ignore all paranormal cases."

"He's not an Orthodox Realist, is he? The ones convinced ghosts are a hoax?" Since the barrier was thinnest along the ocean coast and near the Great Lakes, if you lived near them, you were used to the odd ghost. But if you grew up in the Midwest and the Prairies? No water, hence fewer ghosts. Orthodox Realists weren't the first religious faction to claim there was no such thing as ghosts, but they were the most vocal. "This is Seattle. I mean, he has to have seen a ghost by now. Eventually he's got to walk by the water at night. Just drag him down to the square in the rain and make him stand under the Pergola, problem solved."

Sarah shook her head. "Naw, that's not it. He believes in ghosts just fine." She gave me a measured look. "His problem is with encouraging people like you to contact them."

But that was just . . . stupid. Ghosts were just there. Whether people could contact them was beside the point. Charlatans had been conning people for centuries. At least I offered the real deal. "I'm guessing he's never had to settle a will dispute. You have any idea how much time and money a zombie saves?"

"Preaching to the converted, Kincaid. He's got this notion that if people just ignore the ghosts, they'll go away."

"Fat chance."

"He's a fanatic," Sarah said. "He likened having paranormal consultants on staff to keeping drug dealers and whores around for information. Not that I've ever had a drug dealer or whore tell me where a dead body was buried that they *hadn't* shot, but hey, there's a first time for everything." She blew on and then sipped her coffee. "He's taking it upon himself to clean up the paranormal underbelly of the city." She levelled her grey eyes at me. "He called you a paranormal terrorist."

Great. Solve a bunch of unsolvable murders, and what does that make you? A terrorist. No point in calling it crazy, though. Crazy and stupid have one thing in common: they never listen. "How the hell did this guy get hired? *In Seattle?*"

Sarah laughed. "Trust me, Aaron and I asked the same question. He had enough pull to get the job despite his stance on the paranormal. His wife is the mayor's sister."

The wheels in my head churned. "Why haven't I seen any of this in the newspaper? This is Seattle. Ghost and zombie mischief is relentless. The first set of parents that go on TV whose kid is missing and they have to wait for the FBI to bring in a medium? It'll be a media bloodbath."

"Politics. The mayor's trying to keep the captain's attitude quiet, at least until he can figure out a way to shift public opinion in his favour over the hire."

"Good luck shifting public opinion when the seasonal poltergeist calls start coming in." Thanksgiving and Christmas bring out poltergeist rage like nothing else. "What is he going to do? Read the poltergeists the riot act? I mean, the zombie laws are bad enough, but this is just—"

"He's not thinking, Kincaid. No one is. They figure they can sway public opinion by insisting that people who get poltergeists bring it upon themselves. Marks really believes if you ignore the ghosts and outlaw practitioners, it'll all go away. Nothing Aaron and I've said has made a difference. Except he won't let us near the paranormal cases anymore, and has told us the paranormal community is off limits too."

"Just make sure you're on vacation in November, Sarah. Preferably somewhere warm with a good poltergeist squad."

She grinned. "I've got a few weeks of vacation time banked. Maybe I'll take the kids to Hawaii."

"If you and Aaron both take off for poltergeist season, that could make for some great entertainment." They were the only two cops I'd trust on-scene with a poltergeist. "So how does Marks feel about you two looking into a zombie murder?"

Sarah just about choked on her coffee. "Oh, no. Marks has no idea Marjorie was a zombie." She turkeyed her neck and fixed me with a glare. She dropped her voice an octave and, in a bad Midwestern accent, said, "No such thing as the living dead."

"Love to hear him say that to Lee Ling's face," I said. I downed the last of my Americano. "So you have some sort of crime scene for me?"

She waved her phone and stood up. "Got the all-clear from Aaron. Let's go."

I ditched the mug in the washtub and followed her out.

"Try to be civil to Aaron—for my sake if no one else's?"

"I'll try."

"Let me guess. No promises?"

I smiled back and pulled my hood up to ward off the rain. "Sarah, you know me well."

✳

I followed Sarah across the street to where she'd parked the dark blue sedan.

On the drive, Sarah made small talk to pass the time. "Nathan Cade still squatting at your place?"

I nodded.

"Heard you had a new job."

Again I nodded.

Silence stretched between us. "Sober companion? Seriously?"

I shrugged. "Just trying it out, as a favour to Max."

Sarah glanced sideways at me. "Aaron had a few choice words about the guy you're helping."

That surprised me. I wouldn't have thought Aaron told that kind of thing to Sarah.

"He's fine," I said. "Just an artist who got in over his head. What do you two want me to look for?"

"I think we'd rather just get your unbiased opinion on this one."

"Fair enough."

After a twenty-minute drive, we pulled off the highway into Northgate, a suburb popular with paranormal practitioners and university students. We parked in front of an older townhouse, not old enough to qualify as heritage but old enough to be a place your parents grew up in. From the chip-rock covered walls, cement porch with black wrought iron railing and yellowed grass, I guessed rental. The other homes on the block had been renovated and were surrounded with manicured gardens.

I also noted that the cops were gone or really well hidden.

Before I got out of the car, I took a deep breath and discreetly tapped the barrier, pulling in only enough Otherside to see with. Better to get it over now while I was still sitting down. To my relief, the nausea wasn't too bad. I stepped out of the car. I spotted nothing strange in the front yard or porch. No barriers, no symbols—just a normal-looking house. I let Sarah go through the front door first, then followed.

The front hallway looked completely normal. No sign of Aaron, either. Might be canvassing neighbours or out back.

"Knock yourself out," Sarah said as I began to look around.

I saw no lingering Otherside bindings or binding paraphernalia. In the kitchen I pulled open the cupboards to see if there was anything stashed out of sight. I even checked for sage in the spice cupboard. Nope.

The bathroom was plain, painted white, with a grey and black raindrop shower curtain. The mirror wasn't set. I checked the last room off the hall, which was the bedroom. A double bed, with decent box-store sheets and duvet. The antique dresser was the only piece out of place in the modern decor, but its mirror was normal. Propped on it was a picture of a woman with short brown hair. I imagined it was the victim, Rachel McCay.

I headed back out into the hall. Sarah was leaning against the front door, regarding me patiently.

"So the victim lived here?" I asked.

Sarah nodded.

"And you're *sure* she was a practitioner? Not someone who just dabbled?"

She nodded again.

I chewed my lip and stared around me. It wasn't outside the box for practitioners to hide their work stuff, especially if they had family, friends or landlords who disapproved. So maybe there was another room here. A hidden closet, part of the basement? Unless . . .

Pulling a globe and stuffing the resulting headache, I scanned the hallway ceiling. Bingo. I caught the corner edges of the wards before I saw the blurred outline of an attic door. A barrier, but more basic than the one at Marjorie's. This barrier only caused the Otherside to bend the light, encouraging your eyes to register the attic door edges as cracks in the ceiling. After a few seconds of searching, I found the latch release recessed into the wall, also warded. I pulled it and had to dodge out of the way as a set of stairs dropped down.

Sarah had a wide grin on her face and was already on the phone. "She found it," she said.

A moment later Aaron stepped in from the backyard. He gave me a quick nod before glancing up at the attic. "I've been searching outside for a way to a basement or root cellar for an hour now."

I crossed my arms. "So yet again I pass the is-she-or-isn't-she-a-real-practitioner test. Either of you want to fill me in?"

Aaron stepped past me to test the stairs. "Our victim was found in the backyard. We confirmed she was involved in the paranormal community, but when we searched the house, there was no sign of any paraphernalia. Remember the White case last winter?"

Unfortunately, I did. A hobby practitioner named Simon White tried teaching himself zombie raising off a website. Hadn't gone well for the test subject, especially when White decided the bindings weren't working so he should carve them in with a knife. The instructional DVD he'd ordered had glossed over the section where your zombie was supposed to be dead *first*. The DVD had done a much better job instructing White how to hide the evidence in a drawer using Otherside, which is where we found the knife and DVD.

Aaron started climbing.

"We're hoping whatever's up here will tell us why our victim was killed," Sarah said.

I followed him up the stairs, Sarah behind me.

The attic was little more than a crawl space for hiding boxes, of which there were plenty. Thick black marker designated them as kitchen supplies, books or other. There was one with *Christmas* written across the side, in red and green. Cute. The things you can learn about a person by rifling through their stuff.

My headache was getting worse, but I managed to hold my globe as I scanned the attic. I was starting to think it was a bust when I caught an edge of Otherside trailing out of a small open box, only big enough to store a handful of paperbacks. "The corner," I said, and pointed.

Aaron was closest, so he was the one who picked it up and peered inside.

"Well?" Sarah said after a few seconds had passed.

Aaron tilted the box so we could both see the contents. "Books, incense, one china marker, a mirror and this," he said, pointing to a stick of bound sage.

"Let me see," I said, motioning for Aaron to bring me the box while Sarah passed me a pair of latex gloves.

Rachel had had a decent basic Otherside binding text and two others on contacting ghosts, but nothing special. The mirror was set, and I checked the bindings on it. Simple, clean, nice work. I flipped it over and noted a red stamp on the back naming the store where it had been purchased: the Pike Market paranormal shop. Besides the fact that she'd overpaid, there was nothing strange about that. There was also nothing about Jinn or references to ancient Arabic bindings. Not even a history of the practitioner's art.

I looked up at Aaron. "Nothing out of the ordinary and nothing that would link her to Marjorie. The texts are basic, the mirror is good. She was a decent practitioner." I handed him the box. "All this says is she knew what she was doing."

Sarah and Aaron exchanged a glance, and all of a sudden the attic felt claustrophobic.

"You said she was found outside. Can I have a look?"

Another glance between them.

"Trust me, if you think this is connected to the zombie murder, you want me to take a look."

Sarah broke out in a smile. "God, do I miss working with someone who knows what the fuck they're doing. Lead the way, Kincaid."

My globe started to waver partway down the stairs. I held it in place but slipped on one of the rungs. Aaron caught my arm before I could slide the rest of the way and land on my ass.

When we were all at the bottom, Sarah frowned at me. "Take a break, Kincaid. I've got to make a couple calls." She nodded at Aaron. "I'll meet you two out back."

Sarah went out to the front porch while I leaned against the wall. My headache was worse, but I couldn't let my globe down. If I did, I knew I wouldn't be able to tap the Otherside for hours.

Aaron waited until Sarah closed the front door behind her. "Kincaid, what is going on?"

I remembered I hadn't had a chance to tell Aaron about what I'd found at Marjorie's since Lee had given me the okay. "Sorry, Aaron. I forgot I hadn't told you about the partial bindings I found at Marjorie's. I need to see where this victim was killed. If it's the same perpetrator, there'll be distinct traces of Otherside left—"

Aaron shook his head. "No, not that. What the hell is going on with *you*?" He cupped my chin gently and studied my face the way he'd done at my apartment. "You look worse than you did yesterday. It's not just lack of sleep, is it?"

"I had a few later nights than normal. It'd make anyone look bad."

"I was right, wasn't I? You are having trouble with the Otherside."

I ducked around him into the kitchen, but he still made it to the screen door first, blocking my exit to the backyard. "What happened?"

My first instinct was to yell at him to get out of the way, but if there's one thing I've learned over the years, it's when you're caught—really caught—there's no sense trying to lie your way out.

"I may have been using too much Otherside lately. So I'm only using it when I have to. And don't worry—as soon as this is over, I'm taking a break."

Aaron didn't look convinced, and he didn't move out of my way. "You're talking about Otherside hangovers?" When I didn't respond, he added, "Kincaid, you only ever used to get those when you were really overbooked, once every few months maybe."

Wait . . . what? It hadn't been that infrequently, had it?

"How often are you getting them now?"

Try every time I tapped the Otherside. "Aaron, it's not a big deal, I'm just stretched a little thin. I'm going to fix it."

"'Going to fix it' is not the same as fixing it, Kincaid. How long has this been going on?"

I sighed. I knew this interrogator side of Aaron well. If I didn't answer, I'd never hear the end of it. . . .

"Just a week or two. *Honest*," I added when he didn't let up the scrutiny. If Lee had a suspect in her sights, it couldn't take longer than that, could it?

Aaron shook his head but held the screen door open for me. "You're the paranormal expert, not me."

I stepped past him into the backyard. Technically this was a win, but it sure didn't feel like one. Worry about it later, Kincaid.

The backyard turned out to be an improvement over the front. Bordered on all three sides by a wood fence tall enough to keep prying neighbours from prying, it was a private oasis. In the centre was a decent-sized cherry tree whose limbs formed a canopy over most of the backyard. Three large winding flower beds helped mould a path out of the bright green grass. There it was. I strode over to the closest bed and picked some fresh sage, holding it up for Aaron.

"I thought it had to be dried?"

I shook my head. "Old wives' tale. Just easier to buy and store it that way. So where was she killed?"

"You tell me."

I sighed and scanned the garden through my globe. I was about to give up when I caught the first trace of shrapnel on the trunk of the cherry tree. I pulled more Otherside into my globe to get a better look and bit back another wave of nausea. I squatted to study the trunk.

Sheared pieces of Otherside covered the tree's north side, which was facing away from the house. I stood and took a step back, extending my search to the grass and tree branches. More Otherside traces filtered into view, like splatters from a paint bomb. Just like at Marjorie's.

"She was found here, wasn't she?" I said to Aaron, pointing.

"How do you know?" Aaron said.

"Remember I said I found something at Marjorie's? Well, the same kind of thing is here. It looks as if someone played Otherside paintball with the tree and the tree lost. Marjorie's shop was covered with the same kind of splatter."

I motioned for him to bring my backpack to me. "Here," I said, "I'll show you." I pulled out the map I'd made of Marjorie's and laid it out for him on the grass. "Most of what's here is just shrapnel, but there are a few pieces that were intact." I pointed them out.

Aaron's phone rang, and when I glanced at him, he was staring at it as it continued to ring. Captain, I was guessing.

"Look, Aaron, take the call. I'll come get you if I find something." I pulled out a fresh sheet of paper and started to sketch the shrapnel on the tree. What I wouldn't give for a camera that could capture Otherside.

Aaron nodded. Probably wondering how to explain a paranormal killing spree to his boss. "Don't touch anything you don't have to. Forensics needs to come through here again."

I frowned at him, but he'd already turned away. I knew not to touch anything. It hadn't been that long since I'd worked a crime scene.

As soon as I heard the back door close, I went back to scanning the yard. It took me less than a minute to find an intact symbol lodged on one of the lower cherry tree branches. I spotted a second intact symbol burned into the grass. The ground was still wet. Was she out here watering the tree and garden maybe? Waste of water with all the rain we'd been having.

I pulled out Lee's Jinn textbook and flipped to the Ifrit pages I'd flagged, then on to a section on Manids, Water Jinn. I found the symbols from the cherry tree on the second incomplete ring, along with one of the ones I'd found at Marjorie's, and another I recognized from the zombie's murder in the tunnels. The water found near all three victims was starting to make sense. . . .

"Shit." Someone was trying to create a Water Jinn, the most powerful and dangerous of the lot. And whoever it was had just graduated to live subjects.

I stood up, stuffing another wave of nausea.

My phone buzzed in my pocket. I got it out and checked the ID, then dropped my globe.

Max.

I don't think I've ever answered a phone that fast in my life. "Max, you lying son of a bitch."

"Kincaid, please, you're loud enough to wake the dead."

"Who the hell is Gideon Lawrence?"

After a moment, Max said, "An evil, troubled spirit."

"Troubled? Try homicidal. And by the way, he wants to be paid for whatever the hell you bought from him." I proceeded to fill Max in on my run-in with Gideon, then told him about Cameron's binding instability. "Anyone pulls a globe in Cameron's vicinity, he drops like a rag doll. You were almost out a zombie last night. Again."

"Tomorrow morning at sunrise. Bring Cameron to me then."

"Not tomorrow—*now*."

I heard a sharp intake of breath. If I hadn't been so pissed off, I might have toned it down.

"I'm sorry, Kincaid, but I can't take him now. I have my reasons—"

"Max, you've never messed up a zombie like this. Hell, you've never messed *anything* up like this." I glanced at the kitchen window. "I've got a good mind to tell Aaron."

"No! Kincaid, you mustn't—"

"Then give me a non-bullshit reason."

He took another sharp breath. "Kincaid, I think I know what went wrong, why Cameron's bindings are not right. . . ."

"I'm waiting."

"I believe Cameron's death was not accidental."

I just about choked. "He was murdered?" Shit. If Cameron had been murdered, someone out there knew he was dead. What if that someone had seen me with Cameron and put two and two together about the fact he was a zombie?

Max interrupted my panic. "I've been consulting with ghosts, trying to track down one who might have seen something. It has been very draining, which is why I am only now returning your calls."

"In what universe did I not need to know about Cameron being *murdered*? Someone could be looking for him. They could be looking for *me*."

"I didn't want to worry you unduly with an old man's suspicions. If I had known sooner . . ."

"Max, have you ever played a game of dominoes? You line these carefully balanced rectangles up until they *all fall over*. You should try it sometime."

"Kincaid, these events have been beyond my control."

I sighed. Yelling would make me feel a hell of a lot better, but it wouldn't get me closer to a fix. "All right, so who murdered him? Maybe I can figure out a way to broach this with Aaron so that neither of us ends up in jail."

"The ghosts are foggy on the details. Whether by coercion or otherwise, I am not sure. I need more time."

"Not what I want to hear!"

"I do not know what Cameron's killer wants, but I do know that he or she has not exposed Cameron's death."

Yet being the operative word.

Max hurried on. "It is possible they do not understand what Cameron has become. I doubt the killer will show himself to you—there are always people around you. But I live in the middle of nowhere. Cameron is safest with you."

That made sense, but now I was covering up a murder. "I never thought I'd say this, Max, but you need to call Aaron. We'll tell him—I don't know what we'll tell him, but we need to fill him in."

"Give me until tomorrow morning, please."

"*No*, you need police protection—I need police protection."

"Kincaid?"

I turned to see Aaron standing on the back porch, frowning at me.

I swore under my breath. "Look, Max, I need to go. But we are going to talk about this."

"Tomorrow morning, sunrise," he said.

"No fucking way—" The line clicked. "Max?" The dial tone cut in. He'd hung up on me. Again. Like hell was I letting him get away with this. I hit Redial.

"Something wrong?"

I hit End Call, took a deep breath and turned around. Aaron was a few feet away, studying me.

"That depends," I said. I shoved the phone back into my pocket.

"On?" Aaron said.

I pointed to the tree. "On what you think about a serial killer using Otherside to try to make an undead mythical monster."

I edged closer to the door as the coroner pulled a second body out of the cooler. I figured Dr. Heathcliff Blanc had to be in his late thirties to early forties. He was tall, almost as tall as Cameron, but carried himself awkwardly, as if he'd never quite caught up with his teenage growth spurt. He tended to hunch over everything, which made him appear more quirky than he really was. He'd been with the Seattle coroner's office well before I'd started, but I'd for the most part managed to avoid him. Dr. Blanc had an unsettling interest in the undead.

I shouldn't be one to talk. I work with the dead, I talk to the dead, I raise the dead—hell, I even hang out with the dead. You'd think a coroner would be right up my alley.

Think again.

I swear it's the smell of formaldehyde and bleach. I felt like a pet going into the vet's office. And Dr. Blanc wouldn't stop talking. . . . Aaron and Sarah had both ducked out. Damn them.

"Huh?" I'd missed whatever it was Dr. Blanc had said.

"I was saying this is a fascinating case, Ms. Strange."

He opened two metal fridge doors and slid out two bodies: Marjorie, whom I'd known, and the person whose home I'd just been in, a paler and older version of the woman in the picture. The only obvious marks on either body were from the autopsy cuts.

Okay, a zombie dying, sure, unique. But *fascinating*?

The doctor continued. "This woman—the zombie—beautiful preservation by the way, a completely intact and functioning nervous system. Not something I see every day, and I consider myself somewhat of an animated-dead expert. Her cause of death is unique—"

"I'm sorry, did you just call yourself an animated-dead expert?"

He broke into a smile. "Yes. My research thesis was on the effects of long-term animation on the body." He turned back to Marjorie, pointing. "You can see where she was restrained, here and here."

I peered at the white depressions on Marjorie's wrists and ankles.

"She'd been running the coffee house for years, no one ever the wiser she was a zombie, a seamless integration. In fact, when the police did some checking, they found she'd owned the place since 1898. She disappeared every few decades, left a family member in charge. She kept in close contact with her nieces and nephews. They had to be aware of her condition. I wonder how many families have a similar relationship with an undead relative?"

And people wonder why the undead stay hidden? "Marjorie," I said.

He gave me a blank stare.

"The zombie on the table? Her name was Marjorie."

The realization hit, but maybe not the right one. "You'll have to forgive me. The detectives mentioned you were acquainted with the victim." Dr. Blanc moved around the table and carried on. "On first inspection, although the zombie and human victims were both restrained, there is no other superficial trauma."

I knew I shouldn't tap Otherside again so soon, but I was impatient. I tapped the barrier and focused through the nausea until traces of hazy Otherside gold appeared on Marjorie's body. Her bindings hadn't been removed, they'd been massacred; not even a single gold thread remained intact. I glanced at the human victim, Rachel McCay. Even though there'd been no bindings to undo, the same hazy Otherside glow encompassed her as well.

Dr. Blanc was watching me intently. I dropped my globe and nodded at the bodies. "Marjorie died because her bindings were ripped off. The same method seems to have been used on the human victim as well."

He inclined his head. "I will defer to your expertise on the zombie—I mean, on Marjorie. But I'm afraid I have to disagree with you on cause of death of the second victim. She was most definitely drowned."

Dr. Blanc brought over a metal tray and showed me two lungs, not pink, as they would be in a living person, but an in-between white. They were filled with water.

"When I determined Ms. McCay had been drowned and considered the similarities between both scenes, I moved Marjorie's autopsy up on my list of priority cases. Though I doubt that was the cause of her ceased animation, she too had been submerged long enough for her lungs to fill with water."

Had Lou overlooked drowning in his thirteen victims, all found near water?

"Ms. Kincaid?"

I glanced up from Marjorie's lungs to Dr. Blanc. "Otherside might not have killed her," I said, nodding at Rachel McCay, "but whoever killed her used the same Otherside signature that was used on Marjorie. Thanks for your time, doctor."

I turned to leave, but Dr. Blanc stopped me. "Ms. Kincaid?"

I turned to face him.

"Don't mistake my enthusiasm for what I discovered in the autopsy as an insult to Marjorie. My profession is the dead, and I take it very seriously. If I don't know my zombies and ghouls, what kind of a doctor of the dead am I? Too many people come through here too young, too sick or having been caught in the wrong place at the wrong time." He shook his head. "I'd be happy to see all of them get up and walk off these tables."

"Has anyone ever told you that you come off a little creepy?"

He smiled. "Frequently."

Before he could say anything more, Aaron came in to retrieve me.

"You ditched me in there on purpose," I said as we exited the morgue through the side entrance, the one that led into the hidden back parking lot. There was no sign of Sarah.

"You should have seen how excited he was when I said I was bringing you in."

I snorted. "Yeah, I'll bet. At least Sarah had the good sense not to come back. You, on the other hand, forget I know exactly how you work."

"Really?"

I smiled. "Along the lines of 'I'll bring the practitioner in to see you if you move my zombie autopsy up.'"

"Is that how it is?"

"Yup," I said, and headed for the car.

Aaron grabbed my hand and spun me around until I faced him.

"Aaron," I warned.

"I thought you knew exactly how I worked."

The heat rose in my face as I realized we were alone for the first time since my apartment. . . . A familiar smile played on Aaron's face, his hand warm as it held mine.

My body responded in spite of myself. Just the two of us here right now, with no one else in the world watching or judging . . .

I wrapped my hands around Aaron's neck and pulled his face down to mine.

He kissed me with the ferocity I'd forgotten. His hands slid under my jacket and I sighed as their warmth radiated up my back and along the skin under my breasts. My god, I needed the warmth. I had been so cold the last three months. . . .

Aaron's mouth moved on to my throat, finally settling on the spot below my ear. He bit it lightly, making me gasp. I was the one who kissed him this time, then pushed him back against the wall, keeping him at arm's-length. Aaron waited for what would or would not happen next, watching me, his expression unguarded, full of longing.

It had been so long, and I wanted, no, *needed* this. . . .

"Aaron, take me back to your place before I change my mind."

CHAPTER 18

GHOSTS

I edged myself down the gravel path, grabbing the wet grass to stop myself sliding down to the beach . . . well, rocks more than beach . . . Why can't the ghosts I need to talk to ever hang out in easy-to-reach places? Like an old bar, or the park? No, they hang out in condemned buildings and under the pier. The lengths I'd go to solve a murder worried me.

One hour with Aaron had turned into two. I guess that's what happens when you avoid someone you are physically attracted to for three months. Why is it that brief moments of weakness always lead to the big mistakes? . . . Or was it a mistake? That was maybe the part I couldn't wrap my head around. Aaron hadn't pressured me for anything afterwards. I'd told him what I knew about the Jinn, and what I thought our killer was trying to do. When I'd asked him to drop me off in the square, he hadn't even argued. Then again, I hadn't told him what I planned to do next.

The fact that a fine drizzle had made everything slippery wasn't helping. I probably could have gone straight to the docks and climbed down one of the ladders, since very few people were out in this weather.

But better safe than sorry when contacting ghosts. . . . The last thing they need is an audience—derails the conversation too much.

First I'd tried the ruins of the Oriental Hotel in the underground city, but it had been a complete bust. That area smelled bad; it was full of rats and who knew what else after dark. . . . I'd made contact with one of the crib girls and one of the three murdered prostitutes. After I'd flashed a bottle of laudanum, which I keep handy for dealing with turn-of-the-century ghosts, they'd been more than happy to tell me what they remembered. Unfortunately, it wasn't much, only a handful of images seared into their minds right before they died. But they both mentioned the same smell: a chemical odour that had burned their noses and throats.

Chloroform? Formaldehyde? I couldn't imagine a situation where they'd be exposed to enough of that without suffering burns on their skin. Ether? More questions than answers.

There was no way I was going to contact Anna Bell, the whore Lee had worked with. Rumour was she'd become a poltergeist. Lou had noted a witness to two of the murders in his notes—luckily for me, someone who had died shortly afterwards of drowning. For whatever reason, drowning ups the chance you become a ghost—something about the act of dying in water. Anyway, that's who I was hoping to contact: one Tom Jones.

Shit. Loose gravel slid out from under my feet and I started to slide down the beach. . . . I grabbed for a low-growing shrub and only managed to uproot it. I hit the high-tide mark of shale, broken shells and barnacles ass first. I scrambled up and grabbed my backpack, which had rolled a few feet away, and started to walk towards the piers, where the old city dock used to be before the fire. I worked my way across a patch of beach that was more mud and seaweed than shale, and finally reached relative shelter under the pier.

I strained my ears, but the drizzle and wind drowned out any voices from above. Which meant no one was going to hear me either. The air temperature dropped and I froze.

The fog coalesced beside me and Nate appeared. I'd forgotten that this close to the ocean he could pop through the barrier easily, especially in the rain. "Nate, what the hell? You're supposed to be watching Cameron."

"K, calling ghosts here is dangerous."

"I call up ghosts all the time. Thieves, scam artists, murderers— *you*."

He ignored the jibe. "This place is different." He lowered his voice. "What if she hears you? It's fucking poltergeist territory, for Christ's sake."

"I'm not calling *her* directly, I'm calling a witness."

"To ask about someone who killed *her*."

"Trust me, I'll be fine."

"K, she was a body dealer who killed people, *here*, and you're calling up someone who could easily have been one of her victims to ask about the killer who got *her*. If this isn't stupid, I don't know what is."

I frowned. "Nate! Stop it. That's the part I'm trying very hard to forget right now."

That Anna Bell became a poltergeist when she died shocked absolutely no one. Poltergeists by definition are malevolent spirits, but from there it's a sliding scale. Doing something really horrible while you're alive doesn't guarantee you'll end up a poltergeist; it's the complete lack of empathy and conscience that nets you that kind of power in the afterlife. Anna Bell was a breed all on her own. She'd killed a lot of people in the body-dealing trade, and she'd liked it.

"Nate, if you have a problem with me being here, go back to watching Cameron, which is what you're supposed to be doing."

"He's fine. No one's getting in his building. Come on, K, let's get out of here. This place gives me the creeps."

I shook my head. "The docks give you the creeps—what kind of ghost are you?"

"A smart one who doesn't fuck around with poltergeists!" He wrapped his arms around his body in a very alive gesture and glanced around. "Besides, it's weird around here. If I lose my concentration for a sec, I start to slip back through."

"Look, just stand over there and keep quiet."

Nate muttered something less than complimentary but moved a few feet away.

I pulled out my waterproof china marker. I'd had too many errant waves wash away my painstakingly drawn symbols to mess around. Out here you didn't need a mirror; drawing a symbol on wood or metal then placing it under water worked just as well, if not better.

I sketched the first symbol, an Egyptian one, on the sheet of metal I carried around in my backpack for just such occasions. The old Egyptian symbol for broadcasting someone's name worked best in water and was easy to draw, too: a basket with an ibis on either side. Above the basket I wrote *Tom Jones*, hoping the ghost could read, and then walked to the water's edge and held the sheet just under the surface.

I took a deep breath then tapped the Otherside and pushed it into the metal sheet. It charged fast, draining Otherside through me like a funnel. Hot damn, I'd forgotten just how effective salt water is as a catalyst. Yes it hurt, but there was a rush laced through it. It was as if a beacon shot out through the water and all of a sudden I became the centre of attention for a thousand and one eyes.

I cleared my throat. "Tom Jones, died 1888 by drowning. Are you out there?"

A minute passed. . . .

"Tom? You out there?" I called again, and felt the submerged metal reverberate through the Otherside.

A few breaths later, a grey fog coalesced above the water in front of me into a figure. . . . No, wait, make that three figures, in varying stages of undress.

The ghost on the left had managed to form a pair of suspenders and boots, and that was it. The middle ghost had done a better job, achieving a cowboy hat and flannel shirt. The last ghost wore a pair of red long johns. That could have been what he died in.

None of them had well-defined facial features; think of a blurred composite through a shaky camera. Ghosts from the turn of the century, unless they'd been very vain and/or upper-class, don't have a good grasp of their own facial features. It's the ghost's memory that has to do that work, after all, manifesting what they figured they looked like.

I felt the touch of cold again at my shoulder and ear. "*Nate*! I said back off."

"Didn't want to miss this. Jackpot, K. You got three."

"Shut up," I said out of the corner of my mouth. Then I addressed the ghosts. "You can't all possibly be Tom Jones."

They looked at each other, then back at me, and all three gave a slow nod.

"Who died in Seattle, 1888, by drowning?"

Again, the three ghosts nodded.

Nate snorted with laughter.

I shot him a dirty look. "Not helping." I looked back up at my trio of ghosts. "Okay, which one of you was murdered, probably tied to the pier while you were unconscious? Raise your hand if that was you."

Slowly but surely, all three raised a hand.

Nate howled with laughter.

"All right, so who died in June? Come on, guys, the beginning of summer?"

All three hands stayed up.

"Oh, for crying out loud . . ."

Nate couldn't stop snickering.

"*Nate*, knock it off—"

"Oh, come on, Kincaid. You can't tell me this isn't funny. I mean, what are the odds?"

"What happened to being scared of poltergeists?"

He sighed. "Fine." He vanished.

I turned back to my shambling lineup of Tom Joneses. "So, just so we're all clear, all *three* of you are named Tom Jones and were drugged and tied to the pier and drowned in the month of June, 1888?"

Again, all three nodded, floating over the water with their feet trailing on the glass surface. I'd never run into this problem before: multiple ghosts who fit the same description—or claimed to.

"All right, boys. Since you all claim to be Tom Jones, I need to know which one of you witnessed a murder—"

The ghost in suspenders spoke. "This man, called himself Dr. Green, said he wanted to be my friend and bought me a drink."

Why oh why hadn't Lee's brother written down a middle name?

"Not your *own* murder. I'm interested in information about the killing of two girls, prostitutes, who were found cut up on the beach."

"That's not very nice," the ghost in long johns piped up.

"What? That they were prostitutes or were cut up?"

"My mother cared about my murder," the ghost in suspenders continued.

This is why I hate working with ghosts who are over a hundred. At fifty, most of them start going a little screwy.

I sighed. "Look, I'm sorry, but *maybe* you shouldn't have been taking drinks from strangers?"

Suspenders ghost said, "That's not fair. I hadn't had a drink in months, and I had no money, and here's this nice doctor . . ."

"Look, you're right. What happened to you was horrible, but so was what happened to these girls."

"I thought you just said they were prostitutes?" the long john–wearing ghost said. "Sounds like they got what they deserved."

I squelched my temper. I still needed to know who killed them.

I pulled a black-and-white photo of one of the girls out of my backpack. "All right, let's try it this way. Raise your hand if you remember seeing two women murdered around the time you died, on this very beach." I held up the old black-and-white photo.

All three ghosts raised their hands.

"Do any of you *actually* remember anything?"

Tom Jones with the hat lifted it and scratched what was left of his hair, or at least what he remembered had been left of his hair. "We're pretty sure we remember Tom Jones."

The other two nodded.

"We're just not sure which one of us might be him."

I closed my eyes. "And the women?"

"We're pretty sure we've heard of them murders. . . ."

"Let me guess—you can't remember which one of you saw them?" I shook my head. "Why did you answer my summoning?"

The ghost with the suspenders said, "We don't get to talk to people too much. No one ever calls us and it gets awful boring."

"All right, think, guys, or try to think. These woman would have been badly cut up—face, body, fingers."

Only one ghost spoke up this time, the one wearing the cowboy hat. "There were two girls killed like that, but I only really saw the one killed. I found the other one. Stumbled over her while I was alive, I think. Neither one of them were the one in your picture, though." His face scrunched up. "That Chinaman, the one with the sister, he asked me all sorts of questions, made me look at the body. I never saw anything like it." He shook his head. "He kept asking if the cuts had all been there when I'd stumbled across her. Made me sick to my stomach to look, but he paid me well. I took my money to the bar afterwards. . . ." His voice trailed off as he looked towards the pier, not the one he'd died under but the modern one that had replaced it. "That's how I ended up here, I think." He dropped his chin. "No good deed, eh?"

Yeah, I'll say. "Look, do you remember seeing anything else strange that night? Under or around the docks? Something or someone?"

He shook his head. "That Chinaman asked me the same thing. It was dark and, whatever it was, it kept its head covered."

"It?"

The ghost nodded. "It ran out into the water, and I never saw it come back up—some kind of devil or sea monster."

No such thing as devils and sea monsters. More likely a ghoul. Salt water doesn't ruin their skin the way it does with zombies. He could just grab a rock and sink, no need to breathe.

I noticed the water was now lapping around the soles of my boots. I'd been so focused on keeping my ghosts wrangled, I'd missed the tide coming in. The drizzle had let up, too, and sun now peeked out from behind the grey clouds, lighting up spots on the beach. People would be venturing onto the dock and the beach soon: time to get out of here.

I pulled out my remaining bottle of laudanum and offered it to the three of them. "Look, guys, it's been fun," I said.

"Keep it. Next time, bring us some whisky," Suspenders said, grumpily. And with that, all three ghosts vanished.

I extracted my boots from the mud and turned to head back up the shore.

All the warning I had was chilled air brushing the back of my neck.

I glanced behind me to catch sight of a dark, solid object sailing towards me. It clocked me on the side of the head.

"Damn it—" I slipped on the seaweed and wet rocks, and hit the shallows face first, getting a good mouthful of salt water. I pushed myself back up until I was standing again. My god, did my ears ring.

A raspy laugh pierced the ringing in my ears. I glanced around the shale and shadows under the pier.

"You know, I heard you weren't the brightest knife in the drawer, but I never thought you'd come down here all by your lonesome."

It was a woman's voice, and raspy. Another flash of ice ran down the back of my neck as the sun ebbed in and out of the clouds. The ghost of Anna Bell floated above me. Large blond ringlets curled around her face and shoulders, and she was barefoot, her small feet pointed like a jewellery-box dancer's and dangling under the hem of a cinched blue dress. Resting on her shoulder like a parasol was a piece of broken, waterlogged two-by-four.

What could I use to defend myself against a poltergeist except Otherside? But it was fifty-fifty that I'd pass out if I tapped the barrier again. I'd have to run for it. I gauged the distance to the pier's ladder.

Anna Bell's eyes flashed red and a smile spread across her face.

The two-by-four came down on my head again.

CHAPTER 19

DROWNING

I coughed up cold salt water. My throat burned from it. I was bone chilled, soaking wet, and my ears rang like after a seance, when I'd been standing too close to Nate's speaker.

Anna. The last thing I remembered was the poltergeist. . . .

My eyes fell on the rope wrapped around my waist and chest. Thick rope, the kind you find washed up onshore, pinned me to one of the pier's pillars. I was sitting with my back against the pillar in a shallow pool of water, my hands bound behind my back. If my pounding headache was an indication, Anna must have knocked me out and tied me up. The sun had disappeared and the rain had picked up again. The lights on the pier had been switched on, bathing the shallow water around me in yellow light. If I had to guess, I'd say I'd been out for an hour or so. She must have hit me hard with the two-by-four.

I shook my head, trying to clear it, but all I managed was to get wet hair in my face and up the level of pounding in my head. I was so numb, I heard more than felt the water lapping against me. The tide was coming in. Not good. It was a wonder I didn't already have hypothermia.

I needed to get a hold of Nate.

I tried to curl my legs underneath me and push up. It was no use. The ropes tying me to the pier might be wet, but they held tight.

I tried getting my hands loose next, but my fingers were so cold I could only fumble. No way I could slide my set compact out of my back pocket.

A small wave struck me, shooting water into my face.

"Nate?" I yelled. No answer.

"Anyone?" Maybe someone on the docks might hear me.

A grating laugh drifted towards me, as if through a hollow tin can. The poltergeist . . .

I scanned the water around me for my sheet of metal and china marker. I spotted them tied to my backpack, which was hung on a rusty nail. Just out of reach, but where I'd be sure to see them.

"Goddamnit, I hate poltergeists."

The irritating laugh stopped. "I'd be more careful of what I said, Miss Kincaid, considering your position. . . ." The mist and fog coalesced in front of me and Anna Bell appeared. She floated closer to me, until the cold emanating off her chilled me even more. Anna Bell's features were clear and crisp. She must have spent a lot of time looking at herself in the mirror.

As she stared at me, her eyes deepened from a bright blue to a pure glossy black.

Yup. Definitely knew the effect an appearance could have . . .

"I'd heard someone was looking into the murders," she said. "Heard chatter about it from some girls I used to know. Had to investigate for myself." She smiled, showing rows of sharpened teeth, like a shark's. "But I have to say, the apprentice of the great Maximillian Odu does not impress."

"Why don't you give me my marker and sheet metal and we'll see how much I impress you?"

She actually sighed. "I haven't tied someone to the pier in years. Used to get ten dollars a body." She came closer and ran a finger down the side of my face, leaving a trail of ice.

"No one pays ten dollars for bodies anymore, Anna."

She gave me another slow smile. "Who said I ever cared about money?" The ropes tightened around me, and I gasped.

"So how's Lee doing these days? Still got all those scars?"

I closed my eyes. Why the hell hadn't I listened to Nate?

"Now Miss Strange, why don't you tell me what you think you know about these murders."

There is a method to dealing with a ghost you know is going to hit you regardless of what you say. "Go to hell."

Anna Bell flashed me a smile that would have been vicious even without the teeth. "Why don't you tell me about mine and we'll go from there?"

I rolled my eyes. "So if I tell you everything you want to know, you'll let me go? You seriously expect a practitioner to fall for that? I'm not an idiot, Anna Bell. You're a poltergeist. You guys lie, cheat and steal. *If* I told you everything, you'd still torture and kill me for kicks. Where's the incentive?" I gave her the most nonchalant shrug I could muster.

Her features rippled with shock and outrage.

I took the chance and slowly, carefully tapped the Otherside, hoping she wouldn't notice. Since my ears were already ringing and my head ached, I barely noticed the nausea.

Anna was clearly used to the screaming-in-fear variety of victim. Unsettled, she rasped, "If you don't tell me what I want to know, I'll definitely torture and kill you. If you do, I might let you go. Some chance is better than no chance."

I just laughed. "I'm much better off not telling you. At least then I won't look like an idiot before I drown."

I'm not sure what pissed her off more, that I was calling her bluff or laughing at her, but she hissed, "Remember what I said about never selling a body with marks? It was more of a guideline." Her hand shot out, morphing into a fog-like ribbon that wrapped around my neck, freezing the skin where it touched me. Great, another ghost who liked strangling people.

Every inch of me wanted to panic, but I forced myself to look into her black eyes. Another few minutes siphoning Otherside was all I needed. . . .

I sucked in a breath. "You know what, Anna Bell?" I forced out. "I dare you to knock me out right now, before the tide comes in, so the only thing you'll be able to do is sit there and watch—"

"Be quiet, I'm trying to think," Anna screamed, losing her tentative grasp on her temper. She'd probably never dealt with a victim who talked back. Well, this could be a learning experience.

Her hand tightened and I almost lost my hold on the Otherside. "What kind of amateur poltergeist are you?" I challenged. My throat seized from the cold and I coughed. "Don't tell me you've never dealt with a practitioner before."

"I said *shut* up—"

Coughing relentlessly now from the ice in my throat, I managed to say, "Shut up? Seriously? Come on, I expect a little more—"

"*Shut up!*" she screeched. The two-by-four shot out of the water and into the air then slammed into my leg. Sharp pain shot up my thigh, and I screamed. There'd been a nail on the end of it and she'd driven it into my leg.

Anna Bell laughed, and her face relaxed as if she were taking the first sip of wine at the end of a long day. Her icy hands slipped from my throat and I gasped in air.

"Now *that's* more like it," she said.

I shut my eyes and tuned her out. Must not drop globe, Kincaid, must not drop globe. I held on through the pain.

Satiated for the moment, Anna floated down until her face was inches from mine, the cold rolling off her. I braced myself for another assault. But she didn't attack. Either she couldn't feel me pulling a globe with the barrier this thin or she was too busy drinking in my pain. There was a serene look on her face I didn't like. When an entity as violent and psychopathic as a poltergeist is at peace, I'm far from it.

"You have no idea what you're looking for, do you, Miss Kincaid?" she said in honeyed tones.

The water was at my chest now. If I didn't pass out from the pain of the nail in my leg, I'd drown soon enough.

Anna's nose twitched and she sniffed the air around us. Had she noticed what I was doing? I tried to distract her. "What is it to you if

I am looking for a serial killer? Hell, it's the one who took you out. I'd have figured you'd want a piece of him yourself."

Anna let loose a high-pitched laugh. "Oh no, Miss Kincaid, the others were victims, not me. I helped pick them." She floated so close I could see her eyes burning black. Her lip curled. "But not me. I was to be made a *god*."

So Anna Bell had been a volunteer.

"You lured those girls, didn't you? You were an accomplice." I kept my voice as steady as I could. "No offence, Anna, but you got shafted on the deal. Did you know your boss was a ghoul from the start, or did you only figure that out after?" A wave splashed my face, and I sputtered. The water was up to my collarbones now.

"Be careful what you say, Miss Kincaid. My master is someone much greater than you or me." Her smile spread. "He doesn't take kindly to people taking an interest in his business. Ask Lee Ling. He thought the merchant's wife did a lovely job of cutting up her pretty face and taking the eyes. Served the Chinaman right for poking his nose into the murders. Lucky for him, my friend didn't want to work with men. Only me."

"That's not a friend, Anna Bell, that's a pimp." I spit out a mouthful of salt water as another wave hit my face. "You're awfully slow on the uptake."

Another laugh, but there was no missing the vicious tone. "You're funny. Most of my victims weren't very funny. They tend to sleep through it. Or scream. I preferred the screaming."

"It's a real fucking shame I don't have a piece of chalk." I was almost there. I just had to keep her talking for . . .

"Why Thursdays?" I said.

She stared at me, frowning.

"All the murders were on Thursday. Why?"

The light went on and Anna laughed. "Because Thursday was my night off from Madame Louise's."

I shut my eyes. Of all the stupid patterns for me to have fixated on . . .

Anna stroked a ghost fingernail across my cheek so cold it burned.

"How about this, Miss Strange. You start screaming and I'll tell you all about my friend. That way we both get what we want."

A wave broke over my head. Whether I had enough Otherside or not, I had to try now.

"Fuck off, Anna," I said, staring into the black pits that passed for her eyes, and I threw every last bit of Otherside I'd siphoned straight at her.

She froze mid-air. She knew something was amiss, but with the barrier so thin, she was unable to see the golden cage of Otherside coalescing around her. Recognizing her as one of its own, the Otherside dust began to twine itself into a free-form net, the endgame being a collapse back beyond the barrier, dragging Anna with it.

The water was at my neck now. I had to wait for the Otherside surrounding Anna to collapse and I'd be home free. . . .

She reached out a tentative hand, snatching it back as a spark of Otherside flared at her touch. Anna screamed, her face contorted in rage. "You'll wish you hadn't done this," she threatened, and raked her fingernails down the length of her cage. Small tears opened in their wake. Ignoring the sparks of Otherside eating at her flesh, she raised her hand to rip at her cage again. The entire time, her eyes were fixated on me, her target.

I didn't think, I just tapped the Otherside and siphoned as much as I could, throwing it at the cage. The tears began to seal, but not fast enough as Anna raged and tore.

I strained to pull more Otherside through . . . and the cold realization hit me. If I planned on surviving, I needed even more Otherside. A lot more.

Going against every instinct, I dropped my globe and let pure, unfiltered Otherside flood my skull. For a moment I thought my heart had stopped, and fire coursed through my blood and brain. I probably screamed.

But I managed to throw all of it at Anna.

"No!" she screeched as the cage collapsed around her, dragging her back across the barrier in a flash of gold.

I felt like I was on fire. My throat was dry and my vision blurred. There was too much coming through, but then it stopped. I took a deep breath and opened my eyes. I was alive . . . and there was sea water up to the bottom of my chin.

I fumbled at the ropes again. I don't know if it was luck or the adrenalin, but this time I found the edge of the first knot, though I had trouble feeling its strands.

My fingers slipped. I swore and tried to find the knot again. Come on, Kincaid, you beat a poltergeist and now you're going to drown in water shallow enough to stand in?

"Nate?" I screamed on the off chance he was listening. When there was no answer, I screamed again, hoping someone on the pier above might hear me. I took a gulp of air and submerged my face, trying to get a better grip on the rope. No use. All I could hear was my heart beating, begging me to get out.

More sea water made its way into my mouth.

Cold Otherside brushed my face.

"Nate, am I ever glad to see you," I said as a ghostly grey form coalesced beside me.

It wasn't Nate. It was Gideon, sitting cross-legged above the water. He smiled at me. "It strikes me that you're in a bit of a fix."

"I'm kind of busy here, ghost. What do you want?"

"Interesting way to banish a poltergeist," Gideon continued. "But after sending Anna back, how exactly did you intend to untie yourself?"

I glared at him. "I delivered your message to Max." The knot slipped through my fingers again. I swore.

"It's a tough knot to untie, not to mention the hypothermia setting in." He glanced around the pier. "I suppose you could scream some more. Someone might hear you and care. If you hadn't overdone the Otherside when you banished Anna, your attempt to call your ghost might have worked better."

"Spit it out," I growled.

"I appear to be the single being on this beach who can help you."

Another small wave hit me and I swallowed salt water. "What do you want to untie me?"

His smile widened.

"I'm about to drown here."

He shrugged, still smiling.

Water lapped to my lips. I tilted my head up.

"I do believe you've lost your window to scream for help," Gideon said. "Not unless you want to fill your lungs with water. Are you going to hear my offer or not?"

I nodded. What felt like ice-cold breath hit my face as Gideon leaned closer to me.

"You don't even have to accept," he whispered. "I'll still untie you. All you have to do is agree to listen. That's *all*."

I nodded again.

Gideon grabbed me by the front of my jacket and lifted me as high out of the water as the ropes allowed. I took a deep breath.

"My deal is this: I'll teach you how to see Otherside *without* linking through the barrier. No more nausea, no more Otherside hangovers, no sweats. In return, all you need to do is run the odd errand for me."

"What kind of errand?"

"The odd message, picking up the odd payment. Nothing that would contradict your laws above ground or underground."

I noted he didn't say his errands wouldn't contradict my morals.

"Besides," he added, "I'm sick and tired of watching you stumble through any and every situation tapping the Otherside. It borders on obscene. I'm amazed you're still standing."

I took another deep breath as Gideon waited for my answer. I can't say I wasn't tempted. But frankly, drowning right now would be better than being indebted to a monster. I shook my head. "No deal. Now let me go."

I expected rage. Gideon only shrugged. "Well, I can't say I'm not disappointed, but a deal is a deal."

The ropes loosened. I tried to stand, but my legs were too cold and numb to feel the bottom. I slipped under the water.

Gideon grabbed the front of my jacket and hauled me back up so I could breathe. "One thing you'll learn about me, Kincaid, is that I *never* break my word."

He towed me by the collar of my jacket—none too gently, I might add—out of the water and onto the beach.

When he let go, I rolled onto my stomach and heaved up the sea water I'd swallowed.

Gideon's voice floated to me. "I remember the living being a lot harder to kill. You're all right?"

I nodded.

"Good. Let me know when you've changed your mind about my offer, and try not to put yourself in a position to get killed again."

He was gone. I shivered and pushed myself up to a crouch, testing my legs. As I managed to stand, the nail wound started to throb. I hoped my tetanus shot was up to date. My backpack was lying on the beach beside me. Considerate of Gideon. I grabbed it and made for the highway.

I slipped on the shale and broke the heel off my right boot.

Great. How the hell was I going to get home?

Calling Aaron was out. No way was I letting him see me like this. Nate couldn't drive worth a damn, and it was too dangerous for him to bring Cameron.

Where was my phone? I dug it out of my backpack—happily, it was dry—dialed and counted six agonizing rings before he picked up.

"Catamaran's."

"Randall?" I said. "I need one hell of a favour."

I swirled the contents of the coffee mug. Not coffee. Instant chicken noodle soup.

Randall watched me take another few sips before he put a second mug in front of me. Coffee. I settled on alternating sips. Randall had also bandaged my leg and wrapped me in a big towel, but now he started in on me.

"So let me get this straight. You went down to the beach to deal with a couple of ghosts."

"Right. To ask them about a hundred-year-old murder case, one we think is related to three recent killings. Zombie stuff." I'd told him the short version on the way back to the bar.

"And you ran into not one but two poltergeists?"

I shook my head. We'd been over this too. "Only one of them was a poltergeist. The other is a really messed-up ghost."

"Only poltergeists can do that kind of stuff."

I shook my head. "A sorcerer's ghost can too." Randall didn't look as if he was buying it. "What, you think I'd make that up?"

He shook his head and went back to polishing the glasses. There'd been only a few people in the bar when Randall brought me in, slow for a change. They hadn't wanted to know what was going on. Smart people.

"I just never pegged you for someone that unlucky. Or who had pissed off that many ghosts. My mother was one hell of a practitioner, and not in forty years did she ever run into problems. My grandmother never did either."

What could I say to that? "Thanks for the ride. And the soup."

"You mind if I offer you a bit of advice?"

"Can I stop you?"

"Look, kid, in all seriousness, get the hell out of this murder investigation. Let Aaron and Sarah deal with it."

"It's not that simple, Randall. Sarah and Aaron are out of their league and they know it."

Randall frowned and pointed a finger at me. "Not your problem. It's theirs. Tell them it serves them right for firing you. They want you back, they can bloody well pay you."

"I'm a practitioner. It's in my best interests to figure out who the hell's behind these murders."

Randall shook his head. Then he leaned towards me across the bar. In a whisper, he said, "How's he doing, Kincaid? You know. Friday night?"

"Oh, he's doing better." Not a lie.

"Know what happened to him yet? How he ended up in my bar?"

"I'm still trying to figure that out. But I do know that it was only an accident he ended up here."

Relief spread across Randall's face. Had he really been worried someone had sent the zombie here on purpose? Who would have it in for Randall like that?

I shelved that and other thoughts for later. Not that I didn't appreciate the pep talk, but about the only thing I could handle right now was a scorching shower and a gallon of hot tea and my bed.

"Do you think you could make one of these for the road?" I said, holding up my empty cup of soup.

CHAPTER 20

BAGGAGE

I'd had three lousy hours of sleep before Nate kicked me out of bed—*three*. After he had pelted me with half the pennies in my change jar, I gained a groggy understanding that Cameron was not doing well.

"Not doing well" was an understatement. Finding out he'd been murdered hadn't sat right with him. Nate had done the only thing he could under the circumstances: tricked Cameron into the bathroom—the only real room in his apartment—and barricaded the door with a chair. When I finally stepped through the front door an hour later, the first thing my eyes fell on was the ruined canvas left on the studio floor. The one he'd spent the last twelve hours working on . . .

A zombie destroying his obsession? Not good.

And now we were wandering through downtown Seattle at night on our way to Club 9—Cameron pissed off, me running on next to no sleep, and Nate, well, being himself. As the three of us waited on a corner for the walk light, I checked the time on my cell: 11 p.m. Nate wasn't exactly visible, but he could hear me. "I still can't believe you didn't come to check on me, Nate."

His face appeared in front of me. "Whoa—just wait a minute. For the last time, I did *not* ditch you with a poltergeist."

"At what point does me not showing up constitute you starting to worry?"

"Hey, *I* was doing exactly what you told me to do: watch Cameron. I wanted to stay at the pier. But oh no, the great Kincaid Strange can handle herself." He floated close enough to whisper. "And trust me, I had my hands full with Cameron, all right? You couldn't have dragged yourself out of bed any slower, could you?"

The light turned to Walk and Cameron took the lead. He'd been quiet ever since we'd left his studio. I lowered my voice. "I almost drowned. *And* froze. I should still be in bed."

"You know, I hear the whining. . . ."

I sighed. There was only so mad I could be with Nate. He was a ghost. Even if he hadn't been an irresponsible overgrown juvenile when he was alive, asking Nate to be concerned about the passage of an hour or two was like asking a cat to read. Being a good friend is accepting the limits of the people you surround yourself with. . . .

I focused on Cameron. He was fixated on the sidewalk. He hadn't said a word about the painting.

"How are you holding up, Cameron?" I said, catching up.

He glanced at me. "You mean, how am I handling the concept that someone close to me, someone I probably considered a friend, tried to kill me? No, wait—they *did* kill me."

"You don't know it was a friend. It could have been anyone. We still haven't completely ruled out an accident."

"Samuel won't be stopping by tomorrow to see the painting, or any time else."

"I think you're overreacting—"

Cameron whirled on me. "You tell me, Kincaid. You saw the same clips I did."

By "clips," Cameron was referring to an incident last week, one he didn't remember. But whether that was due to his zombie memory loss or his state at the time was anyone's guess. If I hadn't made him call Samuel to ask whether he could show him the new painting, he'd never have found out about the last opening. Fist fight. With a critic. In an art gallery. On YouTube. And he didn't remember a damn thing.

"Why didn't you tell me?" Cameron said.

"Cameron, I asked you to go through your FB and social media so you could find possible triggers or conflicts. What did you think I wanted you to look for? GIFs of cats?"

Cameron stomped ahead, still angry.

"This is what I've been putting up with," Nate whispered. I ignored him and focused back on Cameron.

"So you hit a guy?" I called after him. "It happens. People have bad days and do stupid things all the time. It didn't land you in jail, so apologize, move on and forget about it. And it doesn't mean your art dealer killed you. Your antics might have cost him a client or two, but he also has the most to lose financially from you dying. . . ." I trailed off. What was it I'd read once about artists? Worth more dead than alive?

Cameron had stopped to stare at me.

"Well, he does. You don't have nearly enough finished work to make killing you worth it."

Cameron rolled his eyes at me before turning them back down at the sidewalk. "Remind me never to talk to you when I need cheering up."

"Ditto," Nate added.

Well, at least he was talking again. Albeit snarkily. I sighed. And I still hadn't broached the issue of checking his bindings, not with the state he'd been in when I arrived at the loft. But I needed to see what was happening. "I'd like to check your bindings again when we get back. It will probably hurt—"

"I don't care, Kincaid. Go ahead, wherever and whatever you'd like."

I grabbed his arm and spun him around so he was forced to face me. He wore another look I'd often seen on a zombie's face: despair.

"You can do whatever you want to me after we're finished tonight. All I want to do right now is find out who the hell killed me."

I reached out to grab his shoulder before he could turn away from me again. He caught my wrist before I could touch him. I hissed as his finger bones bit into my flesh. "Cameron, let go—"

He didn't let go. Instead, he pulled me into a side street and with his free hand lifted his shirt, exposing the bandage. I drew in a sharp breath as he gently lifted the cotton pad. The skin around the wound had turned white, making the red and inflamed edges appear all the more angry.

It was getting much worse.

I'd been so set on getting him out of the loft and to the club, I hadn't thought to check the wound.

"Like I said, I really don't think it matters anymore what experiment you run on me."

"Cameron—"

He shook his head and started walking towards the club.

"K, you can't bring him in the club like that," Nate whispered.

Nate was right. If he ended up in a fight, how the hell would I explain exposed knucklebones to a crowd of screaming people?

"Cameron, tell me why you destroyed your painting and locked yourself in the bathroom," I called after him.

He stopped and stood staring at the sidewalk.

"Come on." I leaned against a brick wall. "Might as well get it over with before we need you to talk to people."

His lightened green eyes flicked over me. "Why do you work with Otherside?"

"I don't know," I answered. "Maybe because I have a cast-iron stomach that verges on supernatural?"

"If you're not going to take this seriously, why the hell should I?"

Why the hell did I use Otherside? "Cameron, sometimes you do what you can. I *can* work Otherside, ergo, that seemed a better career option than waiting tables."

Cameron shook his head. "You'd make more money as a coffee jockey. You're avoiding the question. I've seen you, and it's more than just a job. You tell me why you do it and I'll tell you why I destroyed the painting."

I sighed. "I started working with Otherside when I was taking history at college. I was writing a paper on pioneer Seattle before the fire and I decided to interview people who'd lived through it, rather than rely on textbooks." And that bit of initiative had led to its own set of problems. . . .

"But what do you get out of it now?" Cameron said. When I didn't immediately reply, he added, "You live with a ghost who's your best friend. In fact, as far as I can tell, you can count your living associates on one hand."

There were a lot of why questions in my life. Why had I left home? Why had I changed my name? Why had I barely spoken to my parents in ten years? Why did Aaron judging my life choices piss me off so much? Why did I do *anything*? "I got tired of all the lies we tell ourselves to fit the box other people stick us in. I got tired of the box. The dead don't judge your choices. They don't have much interest in what you do with your life."

"You seek the truth." Cameron's voice was barely a whisper.

"I raise zombies and talk to dead people, Cameron. In most countries, that gets you a one-way ticket to jail."

"I paint to express myself," he said. "What I'm feeling, what I see in the world around me. I realized this afternoon that I won't be finishing any of my works."

"I thought finishing was what you wanted to do? That's what you bartered with Max for."

He stayed silent as we crossed the street. I could see the club entrance at the end of the block, if not by the neon sign then by the crowd outside.

Cameron turned to face me, stopping me in my tracks. "Here's some undead truth for you, Kincaid. I was an idiot. It doesn't matter how many paintings I finish, I'll never create anything again. That's why I ruined my painting and why I don't care about what experiments you try on me. I wish I'd never done this to myself."

"You think that now—"

"Don't tell me it'll pass, Kincaid." Cameron shook his head at me. "You realize we're the same? You can't stop using Otherside any more than I could stop painting, even though it's probably killing you too."

I grabbed his arm. "I am *nothing* like you. The only reason I'm using Otherside is to try and help you and find a killer. *That's it.* I don't *need* to use it."

Cameron stared down at me. "You know what I think? I think only half of you hanging out with the dead is a search for truth. I think it's mostly because the dead don't care enough to call you on your bullshit."

Cameron walked over to speak to the bouncer while I stood there racking my brain for a comeback. I didn't have one.

I took a deep breath. Zombies might be perceptive, Kincaid, but that doesn't mean they always have a point. Yeah, keep telling yourself that and you might start believing it. There wasn't anything else to do but follow Cameron into Club 9.

A dark purple neon sign spelling out Club 9 hung over two black doors. On either side of the doors was a bouncer, dressed in black. I scanned the people in the lineups for any reaction to Cameron, but they were too caught up in their own world to care about others.

I caught Cameron giving me the once-over. I didn't miss the small shake of his head. "What?"

"You've more or less got a goth thing going, but you need to blend in. Try not to say much, and look deep and intellectual."

Nate broke into peals of laughter.

I stuffed my temper and followed Cameron inside as the bouncer waved us in.

The club was up a flight of stairs lit with tube LEDs in the same shade of purple as the sign outside. The noise and flickering purple and white lights got more intense with each step. Halfway up I closed my eyes, but there wasn't much relief to be had. The sooner we were out of here, the better.

"So where are we meeting this girlfriend of yours, Cameron?" I shouted over the noise.

"Her name is Sybil. And we'll bump into her eventually."

"I thought you said you called her?"

"Texted. And she didn't get back to me exactly. She'll be here, though," Cameron said.

At the top of the stairs I felt the first bead of sweat run down my neck. There were people, a lot of people spilling out of the doorway and crowding around the landing. Strobe lights mixed with the LEDs, and that somehow made the music louder. How was that even possible? I grabbed a free spot on the wall and closed my eyes as I tried to push the noise back.

I opened my eyes in time to see Cameron duck through the doorway and disappear into the strobe light mess.

Shit. I wiped another bead of cold sweat from my forehead and dove in after him.

The room was packed, and the lights bombarded the dance floor, competing with the music for my attention. A woman brushed up against me and I jumped, startled by the touch.

Cameron was suddenly in front of me. He was saying something. I watched his mouth, trying to focus. I felt hands grab my arms and I gasped again. What was he saying? I stared at him, trying to make out the words.

It was my name. He was calling my name.

Shit . . .

I reached out to grab the sleeves of Cameron's jacket and closed my eyes. It was too much for me, I'd been using so much Otherside I'd burned my senses raw.

The noises got louder, sharper, demanding my attention.

Come on, Kincaid, you've done this before: shut it down. Slowly I began to peel the stimuli off my raw senses.

"What the fuck is going on?" I heard Cameron say, clearly this time.

I opened my eyes. "I'm just really tired. Lights are killer on an Otherside hangover."

Cold air brushed my ear. "Yeah?" Nate whispered. "Then why the hell haven't I ever seen you react this way before, K? I'm starting to think this is a real bad idea."

Cameron let go of me, but he didn't look convinced.

"Seriously, Cameron, I'm okay. The lights and noise caught me off guard, that's all. We'll look for Sybil then get the hell out."

Cameron glanced around the bar and I watched his nostrils flare as he sniffed the air. He stopped when he realized what he was doing. Being in a place this packed with people couldn't be good for him either.

"Find Sybil and get the hell out," he repeated, and began pushing his way towards the bar. I followed close on his heels, acutely aware from the sideways glances just how out of place I was. I zipped up my jacket to hide my Led Zeppelin concert T.

More beads of sweat ran down the small of my back. No wonder I never came to places like this.

"Do you see Sybil?" I asked when we reached the bar, the quietest place in here, thank god.

Cameron shook his head. "Not yet, and she's not answering my texts. We need to walk around."

Yeah, not with my head like this. I scanned the room and spotted a free table with a decent view of the bar on the outskirts of the dance floor. "We can watch for her from there," I said, pointing to the table.

"We won't find her sitting down."

I gritted my teeth. "All right, we'll walk around." I braced my shattered nerves against everything this place offered up, and followed him.

It took two laps for Cameron to finally spot her. "There," he said, pointing to a table set in a private alcove.

Unlike the rest of us, Sybil looked exactly as she did in her photographs. Then again, that's probably why she was a model. She was dressed in a strapless black dress, her blond hair draped over one shoulder. Just looking at the dress made me shiver.

At that moment she turned and spotted Cameron. Disbelief, shock and anger passed across her features before she smiled to mask them. She said something to a friend before getting up and striding towards us.

"I told you she wouldn't be happy to see me," Cameron said. "She doesn't like surprises."

She stopped inches in front of him and planted her hands on her hips. "What the hell are you doing here? I thought we agreed not to see each other anymore."

There'd been nothing in his personal correspondence mentioning a breakup with Sybil. From the look on his face, Cameron had no recollection of it either. He recovered fast, though. "Why the hell didn't you say anything when I texted you that I'd stop by?"

"Because I thought you'd get the hint when I didn't text you back."

Even shooting daggers with her eyes, she was still gorgeous. Hunh—pretty even when you didn't want to be. Somehow that struck me as more of a curse than most people would figure.

"And who the hell is she?" Sybil said, nodding in my direction. She took in my face, hair, outfit—or lack thereof. "If this is some attempt to make me jealous, it's a pitiful one."

Nate chimed in at my ear. "Whoa, that was low. Want me to ice her?"

"Not now, Nate," I said through clenched teeth.

"Sybil—" Cameron started. But she didn't let him finish.

"I'm not sure whether you're trying to make me feel jealous or sorry for you. I mean, *look* at her."

"Um, yeah, ouch," I said. "Don't mind me—I'm just the sober companion."

That got me a second look. Her anger and contempt evaporated.

She turned back to Cameron, and in a softer voice said, "Look, I'm glad if you're getting help, but it doesn't change my mind. I'm still not going to see you." She turned to walk away but shot me one last glance over her shoulder. "Good luck," she said, nodding at Cameron. "You'll need it."

Cameron called after her, "Wait, Sybil. Why?"

Sybil kept walking straight for the bar. Cameron started after her, but I stepped in his way. He just about tripped over me. "Cameron, not a good idea right now."

"I don't remember anything. I never thought there was a problem." His voice carried a cold edge. As I stared up into his face, I could see he was on the edge of a freak-out. A zombie freak-out.

Shit.

Cameron grabbed one of my wrists. "Kincaid, I don't remember. I don't remember anything." His grip tightened and pain shot up my arm.

"Cameron—"

He looked right through me as he searched the faces around us. Anger, despair, fear . . . Okay, he was still here, but he was losing control fast.

Clenching my teeth against the ever-increasing pain in my wrist, I managed, "I can't help you if you don't let go of me."

He glanced down, as if shocked to see he was hanging on so hard. He let go and took a step back.

I rubbed my wrist. Cameron looked shaken. To be honest, so was I; this was the second close call in a very short time frame. Fresh zombies do better with a task to complete. I decided to give Cameron one. "Are you steady enough to go get yourself a water at the other bar and make it back here? To this exact spot?" I didn't need him staring at Sybil while I tried talking to her.

Confusion passed over Cameron's face. I took his hand and gently pinched his skin. It took a full second to settle back. "You're parched. You need water. As soon as you finish a glass, we'll get you the hell out of here."

"What about jogging my memory?" he said, sounding lost.

"It's not worth risking you going off the rails. We'll figure out something tomorrow with Max."

Cameron nodded.

Nate whispered by my ear, "I'll follow him, K, and let you know if things go belly up. Not that it'll help much—you'll probably hear the screaming first."

I nodded. "Try to make sure he doesn't come back while I'm talking to Sybil."

I watched until Cameron was speaking to the bartender, then took a deep breath and headed over to Sybil, the only person in the entire club who knew what the hell Cameron had been doing last Thursday night. She was still at the bar, and still thankfully on her own. I tapped her on the shoulder. "Excuse me. Sybil?"

Surprise flitted across her face, followed closely by irritation. I almost retreated right there and then. Come on, rudimentary social skills, don't fail me now. I said, "Can I have a seat?"

She frowned, but nodded at the adjacent stool. "Cameron should have told you we broke up. To be honest, I'm happy he's finally getting professional help." She took a sip of her drink. "I'm not upset with Cameron, just tired of the bullshit. The drugs, the stupidity, the lies. I only saw him last Thursday to tell him it was over in person. I didn't want to say that sort of thing over the phone."

I don't know what exactly I'd pictured from her photos: mean, nasty, vindictive, acutely aware of the effect her appearance had on people? Composed, calm and sympathetic hadn't made the list. And I'm the one who can't stand people who judge me by my cover.

She didn't even really seem that angry, more disappointed. Kind of the way Aaron had looked at me lately . . .

I decided to go a route I don't normally take: the truth.

"Look, Cameron didn't mean to upset you, either. He's got amnesia: he can't remember a damn thing from last week. As part of his"—shit, what would a real sober companion say?—"therapy," I went with, "I'm trying to help him piece together what happened."

Sybil's face flooded with concern. "I hope he wasn't in an accident."

I shook my head. "We figure it's due to his recreational activities." Nice phrase, Kincaid, very professional. "I was hoping that you could tell me what happened when you saw him the last time. We're trying to piece together what he's missing."

Sybil drained her glass. "Of course I'll help. I just hope it has nothing to do with me calling things off." Not that killers don't lie, but Sybil sure wasn't coming across as the homicidal ex-girlfriend.

"I'm thinking it has more to do with what he was taking."

"I met Cameron twice last week. On Monday night I told him I didn't want to see him anymore. He took it as well as could be expected. We'd already agreed to be seen here together, on Thursday, so we came as planned and had our photographs taken. . . ." She frowned, as if remembering something unpleasant.

"Was there anything odd about that night? How was Cameron behaving?"

Sybil chewed her bottom lip. "I didn't think anything of it at the time, but a woman followed Cameron around for most of the night. I thought it was because we weren't together much, and maybe she picked up on an opportunity. Pretty, dressed nicely. But she was very persistent, and she was about the last person Cameron wanted to talk to. At one point they had words."

"Do you know what they were arguing about?"

Sybil shook her head. "I wasn't close enough to hear, and Cameron left shortly after that."

So Cameron had got into a fight with a groupie.

"Do you remember anything more about what the woman looked like?" If I got a good-enough description, I might be able to get Aaron or Sarah to run a check for me.

She nodded. "She was slim, and wore an expensive dress. Cameron's type. Which was why I was surprised he wasn't interested. Except for the pink hair."

A chill ran down my spine. What were the chances of two pink-haired women being so interested in Cameron?

I thanked Sybil and she gave me her number in case anything else came up. Cameron had really screwed himself over by screwing it up with this woman, not that I'd ever tell him that. . . . Speaking of Cameron, he was still at the other end of the bar, talking to people. Normal. I headed for him, then stopped dead. Was that Aaron sitting at one of the tables? I strained to see past the dancers. It couldn't be Aaron. He didn't hang out at places like this.

I felt a tug at my elbow, and turned.

"Ms. Kincaid Strange, I presume?" It was an older man, late forties or early fifties, with close-cropped white hair and a lean physique. He smiled, showing perfect teeth, but the smile didn't reach his eyes. Samuel Richan, Cameron's art dealer. He wasn't even supposed to be here, and what's more, how did he know who I was?

I got over my shock as fast as my Otherside hangover and frayed nerves allowed. "Mr. Richan—"

The corner of his eye twitched when I addressed him by name. "Samuel is fine," he said, the smile never dropping. He extended a hand and I reluctantly shook it, catching a glimpse of the scars running along the backs of his hands and wrists. It was all I could do not to pull back.

He said, "Pleasure to meet you, Kincaid. May I call you that?"

A shiver travelled up my spine. "I prefer Ms. Strange, if it's all the same to you."

"Indulge me," he said.

Now I knew why Richan had been so damned successful predicting art trends over the years. I'd seen scars like the ones on his wrists only once before: on a soothsayer Max had introduced me to.

Soothsaying sounds pretty harmless, and that's the treatment it gets in popular culture. Trust me, it's about as far from harmless as a shark is from a goldfish. Just like practitioners and mediums, soothsayers bind Otherside and talk to ghosts. It's rare, but every now and then a ghost gets confused and starts jumping through time, a bit like getting on and off the train without knowing your stop. If you could find one of these ghosts and convince it to add direction to the nonsensical time jumps, well, you had one hell of a fortune teller. Provided, that is, you could get the ghost to come back. That's where the scars come in. Soothsayers bind ghosts. It's an unpleasant business that turns the ghosts into little more than vapid shells, one of the reasons Nate tried so hard to stay under the radar. To my mind, soothsaying is the closest thing the paranormal community has to black arts.

Shit, where the hell *was* Nate? He wouldn't be much use to a soothsayer, but he was worth his living weight in gold to his old bandmates and a few record companies.

Richan stepped close and leaned down to my ear. "Please don't tell Cameron I was here. I have no wish to see him. I have a general distaste for the undead." He gave me another wide smile and sent another shiver through me, then added, "I assure you I have no more than a passing interest in you or your ghost. I was just curious."

I glanced down at his scars and chose my next words carefully. "And what would you know about Cameron's new state?"

He shrugged. "One day Cameron was an artist of some renown, the next day he was not. I didn't quite believe Miranda when she told me, as she can be quite scattered. That was why I had to come see for myself."

Miranda must be Richan's ghost. If she'd told him about Cameron, then there was a damn good chance she'd seen him murdered. . . .

"It's a shame, though. He really was quite a talent." Richan checked his watch. "Be a dear and tell him I'll take whatever he has left, will you?"

"Wait. If your ghost told you about Cameron, then you have to know—"

He stopped me with a shake of his head. "I have no interest in becoming involved."

Before he could disappear into the crowd, I grabbed his arm. I slipped and almost fell—would have if I hadn't managed to snag Samuel. I concentrated hard to block the noise and lights that were beating their way back into my head.

"How much money did you make off Cameron over the years? If you know who killed him, you need to tell me. You owe that much to him."

Richan glanced down at my hand restraining him, then glared at me as if I were something distasteful.

"Ms. Strange, I know my limits. I strongly suggest you determine the same. Now let me go or I'll tell you things about your future that will have you jumping off a pier before the end of the night."

The open malice in his voice told me he'd do it, too. I let go.

He straightened his sleeve and slipped back into the crowd. I let out a breath I hadn't realized I was holding. Evil and creepy all rolled into one.

I glanced towards where I thought I'd seen Aaron, but the crowd on the dance floor was in the way. Just then, Cameron turned from the bar and headed for me, carrying an overpriced bottle of water in one hand and what was obviously a drink in the other.

"Cameron, at what point did I say go ahead and order yourself a drink?"

"This?" He held it up. "You said I had to pretend to be normal. Me not ordering a drink is not normal." He started for an empty table. I followed.

"I'm supposed to be your sober companion, which means no booze —" I lowered my voice. "Especially with your oozing chest wound."

"It's not oozing," he said, and slid the drink across the table to me. I lifted it and sniffed. Whisky sour.

"A thank you would be awesome," Cameron said. "I managed to remember what you drink. I don't remember breaking up with my girlfriend, but I remembered your taste in alcohol."

I made a face at him but took a sip. I decided not to tell him about my chat with Samuel for now. Instead, I scanned for Aaron again. No sign of him . . . I shook my head. One afternoon of relapse and I was seeing things. And we needed to get out of here. I shot-gunned my whisky sour and stood up. "Come on, Cameron, time for both of us to go —"

I caught a glimpse of blond hair in one of the booths along the far wall. It was Aaron, and he wasn't alone. A shot of ice raced through me as I realized his companion had pink hair. Neon pink. "Son of a bitch." How the hell dare she come here with my ex-boyfriend? I headed for them.

Cameron stepped in front of me.

"I just spotted Aaron," I said.

"So?"

"He's with someone. Get out of my way, Cameron."

"New girlfriend? Old girlfriend? Co-worker? Kincaid, why do you care?" Cameron said, but he got out of my way.

Aaron's back was to me, but Neon saw me coming. Her eyes went wide and she spilled some of her drink down the front of her dress.

Damn right I should make you nervous.

Aaron glanced over his shoulder to see what was going on. I smiled as his eyes fell on me. I was so angry I ignored the music and lights pinging my senses raw.

"Aaron," I said.

"Kincaid." His voice was even, but I could tell I was about the last person he'd expected to run into here.

I waited for him to introduce me to his date. He didn't. The silence drew out into awkward territory as he made it obvious he wasn't going to explain.

I searched my memory for the name on Neon's name tag. . . . Morgan, that was it. "Morgan, I keep running into you everywhere lately."

Her eyes widened, stagily. "Wow, Strange, you really know how to lower the tone in a place. Did they shut that joint down by the docks or something?"

I stared at Aaron, willing him to defend me. I could have cared less what Neon thought of me. But he just sat there. Neon leaned forward to whisper to him, her eyes never leaving mine. . . .

Three words reached my ears.

Too much Otherside.

She was laughing at me. Worse, Aaron smiled back at her.

After he'd come crawling back, after he'd begged me to help him work the case . . . Randall was right: I wasn't anything to Aaron except a means to an end.

My tentative wall against the sensory overload came down. Lights, music and Neon's laugh pierced me. I needed to get out of here—now. I stumbled as I turned on my heel, managing to grab the edge of the neighbouring table so I didn't fall on my ass.

Now where the hell did I leave Cameron? More noise and lights flooded in. This wasn't good. Steady, Kincaid. Find Cameron, deal with the issue at hand . . .

A strong urge to pull a globe hit me—something, anything, to dull my senses before I exploded. I might pass out, but the Otherside would drown out everything else.

A hand fell on my shoulder. "Kincaid?"

It was Aaron. I refused to turn around. I'd either hit him or burst into tears.

"Kincaid, please look at me." This time he didn't leave me with a choice as he turned me around. I didn't have the strength to stop him.

Concern was etched across his face, but also embarrassment. "What are you doing here?"

That stopped even one tear from falling. "Excuse me? What the hell am I doing here? My job. Making sure Cameron can stay sober for work functions that feature alcohol. Why the hell are you here with her?"

I caught the tick in the corner of his eye. Subtle, barely a twitch, but I knew what to look for. He was couching his answer. "She's another practitioner who's agreed to work with me."

"So you sleep with every one of us?"

His composure dropped. "Of course not! I've been seeking out other practitioners because you said you were overusing Otherside."

"So why did you just blow me off like some piece of trash? You *humiliated* me!" I was yelling and the room was whirling again. I steadied myself against the wall.

"It's not like that," Aaron said. "She said she's got information on the case and she asked to meet me here. That's it. Jesus, Kincaid."

"You think I missed the way she laughed at me? And the way you just went along?"

"Kincaid, she has information I need. It wasn't personal. How many times do I have to say it?"

"Until I believe you! You never once brought me somewhere like this."

"What?"

"Not once, Aaron, the entire time I was seeing you."

It was his turn to act as if he'd been slapped. "Kincaid, I never thought—"

"Never thought what?"

He met my eyes. "Look at yourself. You don't exactly fit in here."

I knew I didn't fit in here, but to hear it said so bluntly . . .

I had to go. I needed to get Cameron out of here, and I wasn't going to last much longer either. I turned to get away from Aaron and staggered. He caught me.

"Kincaid, what the hell are you not telling me?"

"Go back to the practitioner you're not embarrassed to be seen with, Aaron. Ask her for help from now on. I'm done."

"Kincaid, I don't care about her, I care about you—"

"You've got a lousy way of showing it."

"Kincaid?"

Saved by a zombie.

Cameron said, "Is there a problem?" His tone was light, but the look on his face was anything but.

Aaron stared at me hard, then let go. Backing away, he said, "No, no problem. Kincaid just slipped. Might want to start wearing flats. You've been stumbling a lot lately."

Cameron slid his arm around my shoulder. "Washroom then exit," I whispered.

"What the hell happened there?"

"I don't want to talk about it right now."

"Kincaid, whatever he said, it's not your fault—"

I held up my hand to stop him. "You were right, I was wrong."

Cameron frowned. "I said a lot of things tonight I shouldn't have."

"Having Aaron see me like this?" I shook my head. "It wasn't worth it." We reached the restrooms. "Cameron, I need a few minutes on my own."

"I don't think that's such a good idea right now."

"Just stay here. I promise, just a few minutes."

Cameron looked as if he was about to argue, but I didn't wait. Thank god for overpriced hipster-bar single-stall bathrooms. . . .

I turned the faucet on and splashed cold water on my face. I checked my reflection in the mirror. My eyes were rimmed with red and I was really pale. I stuck my hands under the running water.

"You know the whole Aaron thing? It might not be any of my business—"

Nate. I closed my eyes and leaned over the sink. I thought about lecturing him on privacy, but I didn't have the energy. Besides, he'd strategically forget whatever I said. "I take it you were listening?"

Nate took that as an invitation to materialize in front of me. He shrugged. "Voyeur, remember?"

I wiped my eyes. It only made them more red. "And what does your infinite wisdom tell you?"

"He cares," Nate said, settling on the counter. "You called him on something I don't think ever crossed his mind. Let's face it, you aren't exactly a touchy-feely, discuss-your-emotions type. And this isn't exactly your scene."

I drew in a breath, held it for five, then let it out. "I can't really screw things up any more than I already have, can I?"

"Oh, don't get me wrong—Aaron's being a dick. Part guilt because he let you get fired and figured you'd be cool with it because he wasn't an active participant. And then he shows up at a place like this with someone else." He shrugged. "Hard to explain that one away."

"From where I was standing, it looked like he was embarrassed to know me."

"It'll blow over, K. He figured you'd have forgiven him by now, and you haven't. Like I said, he's being a dick."

"What if I don't want it to blow over this time, Nate?"

I couldn't tell what Nate was thinking as he stared at me. Finally, he said, "You push and push and push people away, K. I get it. It's easier that way for people like us."

"What do you mean, 'people like us'?"

"The kind who can't help but self-destruct."

I was about to disagree but then thought about the mess I'd managed to reduce myself to.

"Seriously," Nate asked, "are you going to be okay?"

I nodded. "Okay" might be an overstatement, but I knew what I had to do. "Want to give me a couple minutes alone here? I need to collect my thoughts."

He gave me a sidelong glance.

"Trust me, Nate. I'm about to do something really stupid and you don't want to be here."

For a moment it looked as though he might argue with me. Which would be completely out of character. Finally, he said, "Nothing too stupid?"

"Not off the scale, anyway. But it's something I have to do on my own. It'll only take me a minute. Promise."

I waited until he'd vanished before pulling my china marker out of my purse. The bathroom mirror in here wasn't set, but I didn't think that'd be a problem.

Hand shaking, I wrote *Gideon Lawrence* across the glass. I knew I couldn't keep living like this, and the alternative? I didn't want to think about that right now.

In less than a minute he was there, in the mirror. His expression shifted from mildly pissed to neutral as he took in my appearance. "Somehow I don't think you're calling me to deliver a message from Max," he said.

My mouth was dry and part of me wanted to run screaming.

Gideon's eyes flashed black. "You know, I do have other things on my plate besides answering every practitioner who writes my damned name on glass whenever they happen to swing by a mirror."

Steady, Kincaid, steady. This was the only way. "You said you could show me how to see Otherside without a globe?" I could barely hear my own voice.

"And?"

"Is it true?"

He regarded me, his eyes shifting to a ghost-grey blue. He gave me a slow nod. "I can do that, and a great deal more. Why?"

Come on, Kincaid, not the time for pride. I took a big breath. This was the only way.

"Because I need help," I said.

Gideon watched me as I tried not to shake. "My terms?"

I nodded.

Apparently a nod was enough. Gideon materialized in front of me.

Before I could move back or rethink my course of action, he placed a hand on either side of my head in the kind of grip I'd only thought a poltergeist capable of. I gasped at the cold.

Gideon's eyes glittered black and the barest trace of a smile passed over his lips. "Brace yourself, Kincaid. This is going to hurt."

CHAPTER 21

PERSONAL DEMONS

I'm amazed I walked out of Club 9 on my own two feet. "This is going to hurt" had been an understatement.

"Lousy ghost barely stuck around to see if I was okay," I said, mostly to see if my ears still worked. They did. Whatever Gideon had done to me had blocked out the bar noise. The lights weren't bothering me either. The son of a bitch had kept his word. For some reason, that pissed me off more than the pain he'd inflicted.

Cameron had been watching me closely ever since I stumbled out of the bathroom. I'd refused to tell him what had happened. But Nate had taken it upon himself to do that.

"Of all the stupid, reckless, idiotic stunts," Nate whispered in my ear.

"Be really nice if you'd shut up about now, Nate." Miraculously, he did.

Cameron still wasn't letting me walk unassisted. I focused on seeing the Otherside in the way that Gideon had instructed, and Cameron's bindings flared, showing every little gold thread winding through his skin. I barely had to think about it. Whatever he'd done to me had worked. I could see Otherside without tapping the barrier.

"He might be an evil son of a bitch, but he held up his end of the bargain, Nate," I said.

"Great, just fucking fantastic, K. I hope you remember that real fucking well when he asks you to pay up."

"Will you two stop arguing and tell me where we're going?" Cameron said.

I motioned for him to stop so I could rest awhile against a shop wall. It was a good question. Back to Cameron's? With my luck, I'd run into Neon stalking the lobby. My place? Neon was one of my goddamn neighbours, but at least I'd be back on home turf. Thanks to a lack of funds to fix the deadbolt, I knew my door was un-pickable.

While I stood there trying to decide, Cameron's phone rang. He removed it from his pocket and stared at the screen.

"Who is it?" I asked.

"It's Jayden. My drug dealer." He answered. "Jayden? What's up?" Out of reflex, he stepped towards a nearby alley. I swore and started to follow, but my phone chimed too.

"Don't worry, K. I'll watch him," Nate said, and headed after Cameron into the blind alley as I tried to figure out how to silence the ringer on my phone.

Aaron.

I stared at the screen until Cameron reappeared, a perplexed look on his face. He frowned when he realized it was my phone making all the noise.

"Are you going to get that?" he asked.

"Not a chance," I said. I turned the ringer off and shoved it back in my pocket.

"I want to stop by Jayden's," Cameron said.

I shook my head. "An hour ago I'd have been all for it, but not now. I need some rest, and I'm pretty sure you need more brains."

"But I think something's wrong," he said. "Jayden never calls me — we only ever text. And he never asks me to come over, which he just did." Cameron shook his head. "He seemed eager."

Nate snorted. "Your drug dealer's eager? Big fucking surprise."

Cameron shot Nate a dirty look. "He's never been eager. Ever."

"Cameron, neither of us is in any shape to be dealing with this," I said.

"Can't we just stop in and see if he's okay? It's practically on the way to your place."

Practically? I felt my phone buzz with a text message. "Let me see what the hell Aaron wants while I — I don't know — decide what the hell to do."

Aaron's message was to the point: *Kincaid, please call me back.*

Could he not take a goddamn hint? I called him back.

Aaron picked up on the first ring. "Kincaid." There was relief in his voice. "Where are you?"

"Aaron, what the hell did I tell you?"

"I don't have time for your identity breakdown. We need to talk."

My identity breakdown? "I told you to get yourself another damn practitioner and never call me again." I hung up. Cameron and Nate were both staring at me.

"All right, where the hell does this dealer of yours live?"

Ever get the feeling you made the wrong choice? That's what I was thinking as I followed Cameron up a warehouse stairwell a few blocks and a bad neighbourhood over from where I lived.

I heard scurrying ahead of us, as if large rats were trying to get out of the way. Bubonic plague, anyone?

I almost bowled into Cameron as he stopped in front of me.

"We're here," he said, hand on the second-floor exit door. Given Cameron's deteriorating appearance, I had a sinking suspicion the smell in the stairwell was Cameron, not rats.

I pushed the door open a crack. The hallway, lit by flickering fluorescents, was deserted.

"Just remember, in and out," I said.

Cameron nodded. "First a bar, now a visit to my old drug dealer. You realize this makes you the world's worst sober companion?"

I ignored Cameron and knocked on the door of apartment 251, wondering what the hell I was getting us into.

The door edged open under my knocking. Both the deadbolt and the door handle turn lock had been removed. Anyone could waltz in.

"Does Jayden normally leave the door open?"

Cameron shook his head. "Jayden's paranoid about locking the door. Obsessively paranoid."

"Nate?" I said.

"Ahead of you, K." A grey mist coalesced in front of me and slipped through the crack.

A minute later I felt the cold brush of Nate returning. "K, you'd better get in and see this."

I pushed the door open and motioned for Cameron to stay close behind.

In contrast to the stained yellow carpets and 1970s wallpaper in the hallway, Jayden's apartment was white pine floors and sills; minimalist white furniture added to the appeal. I caught the scent of coffee, not burnt yet but close. And something else, a metallic smell . . .

I stopped in the kitchen doorway, not sure what to make of the violent and visceral sight in front of me. By now I'd seen three Jinn kill sites, but never with the body still fresh.

Cameron swore behind me.

The Otherside had exploded, coating the kitchen walls and linoleum floor. The body was laid out face up with arms and legs spread. He'd probably been knocked unconscious first, considering there were no rope or ligature marks that I could see.

"This one is different from the others," I said.

"It's violent," Nate said, and shook his head. "It looks like it belongs on my side of the barrier."

Using my sleeve, I flipped on the light to get a better look. Jayden was lying in a pool of water that also contained traces of Otherside. Unlike at the other murder scenes, this water had blood in it.

I stepped closer, careful to avoid the water, and crouched down. His grey sweatshirt was soaked with blood. Wrapping my hand in my sleeve, I reached for the hem of his shirt so I could see what had happened to his chest.

Cameron hissed a warning. "There's someone else here."

Nate whispered, "K, I checked, I swear—"

All three of us heard the creak of the floorboards. I made it into the living room in time to see Neon coming out of the bedroom. She frowned when she saw me, then a sneer spread across her face.

"You're a lot faster than I thought."

"I'm running into you everywhere, aren't I?"

Neon bolted for the door.

Athletic I'm not. Never have been. So I fight dirty. I stuck my foot out and she hit the floor face first.

Neon snarled and pushed herself up in one fluid motion, a knife suddenly in her hand. I braced, hoping I could keep her the hell away from Cameron and my own flesh.

Neon torqued her head towards the window as if listening then darted towards me, knife first. I jumped back, but instead of pushing her advantage, she bolted past me and out the apartment door.

"What the—?" She'd had me here, unarmed, yet she'd been more concerned about getting away. I headed to the window. "Nate, Cameron, do you hear anything?"

Nate said, "Alarms in the distance."

This time of night, *not* hearing sirens would have been out of the ordinary. Still . . .

Cameron went back into the kitchen and crouched over Jayden's body. "If we had of gotten here sooner . . ."

I knelt beside him, careful to keep my knees out of the blood-stained water. "He'd still be dead, Cameron. He was dead before she made him call us."

I lifted the sweatshirt. As a general rule I'm not one to ruin a crime scene, but I had to see what had been done to his chest. The

Jinn bindings had been carved straight into his flesh while he was still alive, then flooded with Otherside. From the traces left in the wounds, it looked as though the killer had got further this time; in all the other bodies, the bindings had been reduced to shrapnel. But it made no sense. Cameron's drug dealer hadn't been a practitioner. He hadn't even been part of the paranormal community.

Unless that had never been the point. Maybe the fact that Jayden had been connected to Cameron was the point. The murder wasn't one of the Jinn experiments. It was meant to draw attention to me and Cameron.

I felt the cold before Nate burst into the room. "K, hurry up! Cops out front and coming into the building."

Shit. "Cameron, what's the best way out of here? Cameron?"

He was staring at the carvings on Jayden's chest. I grabbed his arm.

"There is nothing we could have done and there's nothing you can do for him now, especially if the cops find out you're a zombie. We've got to get out of here."

"The bathroom window," he said. "Jayden kept a rope in there for emergencies. It's only a two-storey drop and the alley's out of sight."

"Go. *Now*," I added when he didn't move.

I ran to the bedroom. What had Neon been doing in here?

On the dresser for the world to see was a bag of sage and a mirror. There was even a piece of chalk and a bindings book. The mirror hadn't been set, and the chalk was wrong for using with sage. Even so . . .

I flipped the book open. Rudimentary bindings. On the back was a stamp from the Pike Market practitioners shop.

"What?" Nate said, peering over my shoulder.

I held up the book. "Nate, she planted this. We're being set up."

We both heard the heavy steps coming up the stairwell. Nate swore. "K, get after Cameron."

"Nate, you aren't a poltergeist, you can barely hold a game controller—"

"For once in your goddamn life, will you trust me? Get down that rope and out of the alley fast. Go as far as First at least before doubling back to your place."

"What are you going to do?"

"Lead them on one hell of a goose chase." He picked up the only object on the dresser that had any weight to it, a black eight ball, and hefted it in his hand. "Always wanted to throw one of these," he said.

I winced. I didn't want to think how much Otherside he'd burn through doing that.

"If I burn fuel for nothing, I'm going to haunt you until you go nuts. Get out of here!" he said, and headed towards the front door with the eight ball. "Hey, asshole! Get a load of this!" I heard a crack as the eight ball hit the wall. Yelling and barked orders carried from outside the door as Nate whooped down the hallway.

I ran to the bathroom and lowered myself down the rope.

Cameron wasn't complaining, but he was starting to move with the jerking motions of a zombie going through rigor mortis—basically, starvation. I'd made two calls and left two messages, one for Lee Ling and one for Max, both relating the same thing; "I know who's behind the killings and we have a problem."

I thought about calling Aaron and almost dialed twice. But the last time I'd seen him, he'd been having drinks with the killer. My mind told me there was no way Aaron was involved, that he couldn't know, but my gut wouldn't let me make the call. What was I supposed to tell him? By the way, you know that girl I accosted in front of you at Club 9? Your new informant? Yeah, she just lured me to a Jinn murder scene and fled while I was crouched over the body: she tried to frame me. Even *if* he believed me, Aaron's hands would still be tied.

When we reached the alley behind my building, I let out a sigh of relief. No cop cars, no Aaron . . .

"We've got brains upstairs and I'll see if I can patch up that wound. If I sew it shut until Max can fix it in the morning, you should feel better, at least."

I heard something behind us and stopped. I searched the lamplit stretch, then pushed my Otherside sight—thank you, Gideon—to see if I could pick up a ghost. Nothing.

But there came the scrape again. I motioned for Cameron to stand behind me.

"Nate?" I whispered.

"No, not Nate, it's me." Aaron stepped under the street light.

"Jesus, Aaron, don't sneak up on me like that. How long have you been standing there waiting for me?"

He shrugged. "Awhile. Just wanted to make sure you got home all right. Where's Nate?"

I kept a straight face. "On the Otherside or stalking his ex would be my guess. Want me to call him so you can ask?"

Aaron shook his head.

Neon must have called him . . . and told him what? That she just happened to be walking by a murder scene and saw me run out of a building? Or that she had been standing innocently in a dead man's apartment when I barged in?

"Aaron, I'm tired and I need to get Cameron settled in."

"I told Morgan about your Jinn theory," he said. I bristled, but he carried on. "She disagrees. She thinks it's a practitioner using a ritual to make it easier to use Otherside. To avoid the sweats and nausea."

I didn't know what to say for a moment. Of all the dreamt-up garbage. She probably hadn't known I knew about the Jinn until Aaron told her. All she'd figured I'd known about was Cameron, and how the hell his state played into the Jinn killings was beyond me at this point. Now she'd upped the ante, and it was Aaron's fault. If I hadn't managed to get out of the building, I would have been found at the scene in possession of a zombie. Even *if* Aaron had been on my side, he'd have had to question me. . . .

She was good.

"Aaron, I studied for two years with Maximillian Odu, one of the most respected voodoo priests in North America. I've also probably helped solve more murder cases than any other practitioner in the Northwest, including Canada. Morgan works at a hobby shop. I'm not convinced she can set a mirror properly. You've already got my notes and my analysis. In my professional opinion, Morgan is taking you for an idiot. Is there anything else?"

"She offered information," Aaron said.

"Yeah, and I'd start asking why." I turned away from him and unlocked the back door. Aaron stopped me and I felt Cameron tense beside me. I waved Cameron through. I could still handle this.

"You're not telling me something," Aaron said.

"And you're being a self-righteous asshole." How long had it taken me to go from love interest to suspect? A matter of hours? Less?

"Kincaid, I trust you. I've always trusted you, but you need to help me make sense of what the hell is going on. Please."

That was like a slap in the face, as if he literally had said, *Whatever happens after this is on you, not me.*

But there was a pleading in his eyes and that *please*. I closed my eyes. Did I really want to keep this to myself? How was that turning out for me? Another person was dead by the Jinn killer, that's how. I was out of my depth. When I opened my eyes, I'd just about made up my mind to tell Aaron everything.

And I might have if I hadn't noticed the flash of Otherside in Aaron's sedan. I narrowed my eyes as Neon stepped out.

How had she caught up with him so quickly? How could he be so blind?

"Kincaid?" Aaron hadn't yet realized what I'd seen.

Well, Neon might be an Otherside-wielding criminal mastermind, but timing she didn't have.

I pushed Aaron away. "I don't know anything more than I told you. Believe whatever the hell you want to." I stepped inside.

Cameron was holding the elevator door for me. We rode up in silence, and once inside my apartment I tossed him a pack of brains from the cooler. "Heat it up or blend it, Cameron. But eat it damn quick."

I flipped on the kitchen light but left the living room light off, crouching down by the sill so no one would see me. I heard the frying pan crackle as one of the packets went in.

Aaron and Neon were still below me. It looked as if they were arguing, but I didn't want to risk cracking open the window so I could hear.

I watched them for maybe five more minutes before Aaron finally got back into his car. It was about then I felt the drop in air temperature beside me.

"What the fuck is Murder and Mayhem doing chatting with Aaron?" Nate said.

"Good question." I kept my eyes on Neon as she watched Aaron drive off. She glanced up to my darkened apartment windows before setting off down the alley.

I stood up too fast and accidentally iced myself passing through Nate. I grabbed my jacket.

"Oh, hell no, K."

"Just stay here."

He floated in front of me, blocking my path. "If you go out that door, I'm coming too. K, she'll eat you alive. You saw the shit she did to that kid?"

But Nate was fading. Whatever he'd pulled to distract the police had done him in. "Nate, she's turned me into a suspect. Aaron was here to *question* me. I've got to stop her before she does any more damage."

"Aaron's not that stupid—"

"Aaron might be a lot of things we never suspected."

Nate watched me while I pulled on my boots the way he did when he was about to ignore whatever it was I'd asked him to do.

I stood up. "I'm just going to follow her. I'll hang back. You want to do me a real favour? See if you can find her apartment."

He looked as though he was about to argue again.

"I need to know how good she is. Seriously, I'm giving you the okay to break and enter." That got his attention.

"Anything goes?"

"Anything goes," I said. "Just make sure you're the hell out by the time she gets back." I ran out the door.

✳

Try avoiding puddles in the middle of the night with heeled boots. Maybe I did need to rethink the whole flats things. Amazingly, I managed not to make any noise as I tailed Neon down the alley. Once I figured out she was taking my route—*mine*—to the city entrance, I would have liked nothing more than to jump her. But then I'd never know whom she was working with. And that she was working with someone from the city was a given; Lee knew all the practitioners with access, and Neon wasn't one of them.

I crept along until she reached the storm doors that led into the city. No one was there and she didn't try to open them herself.

I swore under my breath. Neon was going to have to wait, and every minute I waited with her made it more likely I would get caught.

I ducked into a side alley and dialed Lee. Come on, Lee, pick up, pick up . . .

"Yes, Kincaid?" Lee said.

Thank god. "Lee, I know who's behind it—or some of it. Practitioner, pink hair, pretty."

"There is no practitioner by that description who comes to the city, Kincaid. Where are you?"

"By the city entrance in Pioneer Square. She must be waiting for someone. I followed her from my place to the storm doors here, and she's standing there right now, which is why I'd really like to hang up my phone and get out of here."

Lee went silent. Then she said, "You need to get out of there now—"

I would have said I heartily agreed, except for the boot heel that came down on the back of my knee. I buckled and the phone went skidding across the alley.

"You know, Kincaid, you really need to stop thinking about yourself and Max as the only game in town," Neon said. Then she launched a kick that sent me sprawling into a puddle. I scrambled up and put some distance between us.

She smiled. "Right now Aaron thinks you're a liar and an Otherside junkie. You do know that's what you are, right? Maybe the medium who taught you never bothered to mention that risk, seeing how mediums don't have that problem. All the sweats? Nausea?"

I stepped to the side. I remembered the knife she'd used on Cameron's dealer.

"Oh, and Aaron knows you were in the building where the drug dealer lived. He doesn't believe you're behind the murders yet, but I'm working on him."

I caught the glint of metal in her hand.

Well, at least Aaron was just being an idiot. . . .

"Great, so, Aaron will arrest me and you'll go free. Scapegoat successfully deployed and you can go on your merry, murderous way."

A slow smile spread across Neon's face. "That's what my boss wants me to do."

Her boss. She *was* working for someone.

"Except I got an offer I can't refuse."

Offer? For what?

"He hasn't been very interested in the Jinn for at least a hundred years. Said the whole thing bored him. Then you piqued his interest. He said he'll show me all his notes if I deliver you into the city."

Oh shit . . . Kincaid, one of these days you will learn not to stick your nose where it doesn't belong.

If I reached her before she got me with the knife, I could take her. She had an inch or two on me, but I had about ten pounds.

Her eyes shifted to a spot behind me and I realized it wasn't Neon I had to worry about.

"Aaron," I said carefully, and began to turn.

The rope caught me around the neck. I kicked back but didn't connect.

"You didn't think we were done yet, did you?" Anna Bell whispered in my ear.

I'd have laughed at myself for walking straight into a trap, but I blacked out.

CHAPTER 22

MURDER AND MAYHEM

I could hear water . . . or was that just my ears? I think there was a radio as well, playing . . . classical music?

Hard to tell with all the arguing.

"You said I could have them both to play with!" Anna Bell shrieked.

"You can have her. Once I'm done."

The second voice was dry and strained. I'd guess ghoul by the vocal-cord decay. Probably male, but you could never be sure just by the voice. . . . The radio was playing. Definitely classical.

"You promised me!" Anna screamed. The ghoul had her right pissed off.

I tested my hands and found I could move them. She hadn't bothered with restraints, didn't need to if I was right about where they'd brought me. I stretched out my hand and felt damp wood beams under me.

I lifted my head. Well, "lifted" might not be the right description for what I managed; tilted my head to the side in a way that didn't make me pass out is more accurate.

Ambient light from three lanterns strung on the beams of the dock shack filled the room. No windows, no natural light. Only the sound of running water and the radio. Neon and Anna had brought me to the last place in the underground city I wanted to be.

If Anna Bell was arguing with someone down here . . .

"I see you're awake," the grating voice said.

I craned my neck to see my captor. There wasn't enough light for me to make out his clothing, but his face I could see just fine. Male, guessing from the bone structure. By the yellow, leathery appearance of his skin I'd put his age at a little over one hundred, one twenty-five at most.

"I thought all you century ghouls covered your faces?" I said, mostly to see if my own vocal cords were still working.

He crouched down, close enough I could smell the dry rot coming off his skin. "I'm sure I don't need any introduction. What I would like from you, though, is for you to tell me why that whore Lee Ling and everyone else in the city seems to be set on finding me, hmmm?"

How to survive kidnapping by serial killers: figure out what they want and do your damnedest not to give it to them. While they're pissed off, try to get the hell away. "My guess is you did something stupid to piss her off—Ow!"

A rock had hit my shoulder. Hard. I glanced up. Anna Bell floated overhead. She gave me a sweet smile. "Answer his questions or the next one will be in your face."

Did I mention the other part of surviving serial killers is making sure that at no point in the process do you end up dead?

I swallowed. "Someone is trying to make a Jinn. Lee figures it's you, up to your old tricks."

The ghoul sat back on his haunches. "Is that what's causing all the trouble?" He shook his head. "The girl who brought you here didn't know that." He glanced at Anna Bell. "See, Anna, this is why we don't immediately kill every young woman who crosses our path."

Anna shot me a dirty look before dissolving back into whatever corner of the Otherside she'd crawled out of.

The ghoul turned his attention back to me. "It isn't me."

"Bullshit," I said.

The ghoul laughed, and shook his head. "I realize that this might come as a surprise, but Lee Ling does not know everything. Jinn are a pursuit for the young and naive. Not worth the trouble. I satisfy myself with other pursuits now." He flashed me an incomplete set of sharp yellow teeth.

"If you're the ghoul behind the 1888 killings, you were trying to raise a Jinn then. Why the hell would I believe you're not behind it now?"

He let out a raspy laugh. "I will admit I experimented with Jinn. But that was many, many years ago. Isn't that right, Anna?"

She laughed, too close to my ear for comfort.

"More trouble than it's worth," he said, "and a wasteful endeavour. What you might call a pipe dream. Though I did find out something very interesting about myself all those years ago."

"And what was that?" My voice sounded thin, scared.

The ghoul smiled. "I like killing people."

He moved aside, revealing the rest of the shack. There was a large wooden table a few feet away. I heard a moan and saw a thin white hand drop over the side, a red-stained leather strap with a short lead wrapped around it.

Shit. Neon.

"I much prefer it when the victims walk right in. It's satisfying in a way you can't possibly imagine—Zen, even."

Another moan escaped Neon. I hoped to hell she wasn't awake.

"You, on the other hand, don't quite fit my criteria."

"Guess you'll have to let me go," I said.

The ghoul smiled. "As is so often the lesson in life and death, my dear, sometimes we just have to make do." He headed towards the back of the shack and through a side door. Moments later I heard metal strike metal.

I didn't know what he had in store for me when he got back, but I planned to be long gone. The ropes holding my hands were secure but gave me enough latitude that I could prop myself on my elbows to get a better look at Neon.

"Morgan," I hissed.

Not even a moan. I inched my hand towards the rock Anna Bell had thrown at me and when the banging resumed behind the door, I lobbed it at the table.

Neon's head turned my way.

I wish to hell it hadn't. Both her eyes had been removed and her eyelids sewn shut. From the blood around her mouth, I guessed she'd also lost her tongue or teeth—maybe both. . . .

I tried to push myself up, but my muscles wouldn't respond. Fatigue and cramps from lying here for who knew how long.

There should be a tunnel out, or maybe the water was a better bet. It exited into the bay somewhere. Why the hell hadn't I ever studied the sewer maps? Because I knew better than to end up in the docks, that's why.

Neon groaned and pulled against the straps. She was waking. . . .

"And here I thought she was immobilized. How careless of me—I must not have gotten the dose right."

I hadn't heard or seen the side door open, but the ghoul was back, wearing a black leather apron and carrying an antique syringe.

"What did you do to Neon?" I said.

The ghoul smiled. "Neon? Is that what you call her? She claimed her name was Morgan." He glanced sidelong at the radio sitting on a chair. "I prefer the classical stations to the vernacular."

He walked over to Neon and shoved the needle into her neck. Her back arched once before her movements ceased and she slumped on the table.

"Interesting young woman," the ghoul continued. "Very impatient. She came here under the assumption I'd advanced further than she had in my Jinn experiments all those years ago—incorrectly, I might add. She hoped to barter with me by delivering you, behind the back of her current employer." He tsked. "No accounting for loyalty these days, isn't that right, Anna?"

I tried to move, but my muscles didn't respond at all.

"I see the neurotoxin is taking effect. Can't have you running away through the tunnels. What would the others think?"

I collapsed to the dock floor.

The ghoul's eyes glittered black under the lights, reminding me of a ghost I knew. Though this expression had nothing to do with amusement and everything to do with having power over me. That's what Aaron had always said: it's never the act, it's having the power to do it. I shoved that thought away. I really didn't want to think about Aaron right now.

My best bet was to keep him talking. "So who is it?"

The ghoul's right eye spasmed, though if it was an involuntary movement, a degenerative nerve tick or a deliberate attempt at a rarely used facial expression, I couldn't be sure.

"Neon's boss, the one behind the Jinn killings? I'm sure you got it out of her." I raised my voice with a confidence I didn't feel. "You said it yourself: I won't be going anywhere, so why not tell me?"

The ghoul laughed. "How fascinating that you have considered the option that I wasn't involved. I assure you most definitely that Lee Ling has not. Though it could be she's simply chosen this as an excuse to get rid of me. Tell me, whom do you suspect? Maximillian? He is certainly a very talented medium, but he wouldn't dream of orchestrating something like this—Jinn, of all things. I can imagine the distaste rolling off him now. Hmm, I can tell by your face that you never even considered Mr. Odu. Who else, then?"

He was toying with me until he got bored and killed me. Considering how little I knew, how little I could feed him, I wouldn't last long. "I'm not playing this game. You know who's behind the killings and you're not going to tell me. Fine, you win."

The ghoul regarded me with the first sign of displeasure he'd showed me. "Shall we play another game, then? My protege needs another victim. Shall we guess who that might be? That's one of my favourite games, you know, choosing a victim." From the glint in his eyes, I could tell he meant it.

"They have figured out by now that they need to bind a true practitioner, the stronger the better," he continued. "They've exhausted the available zombies, and they've tried enough normal people to know that won't work—they pass out and die before the bindings can set. They need someone with affinity for Otherside. That's why they tried with the zombies first, but then they realized the victim needs to be living. Yes, someone who uses a great deal of Otherside but isn't dead yet. Can you guess why that is?

"No point in trying to nod, Kincaid—you can't. I can see from the way your eyes follow me you have no idea. It has to do with blood sacrifice. Toads and rats won't do. In the case of a Jinn, you need something a little larger," he added, almost wistfully.

Numbness was seeping into my face. I had to make anything I said count.

"So who, then?" he mused. "You are most certainly a candidate. Why didn't Neon lure you to her master? If I was in his shoes, you would have been my prime candidate. So why are you off limits?"

"It's called a scapegoat," I said. "They need me to take the fall for the murders."

"Who else in the city would suffice? Neon herself? I'm not certain the girl is bright enough to have seen that she is both proverbial fox and deer. There are not that many practitioners left in Seattle besides you. Unless . . ." The ghoul placed a bony yellow finger on his lower lip in mock thought. "I have to admit I never thought of using a medium. Your mentor Maximillian is a medium, is he not? A little old for sacrifice, mind you. . ."

Son of a bitch. Max was the strongest Otherside user in the city. If Neon's boss got hold of him . . .

The ghoul's smile fell and was replaced by undisguised malice. He grabbed my chin and studied me. I couldn't move my mouth any longer. All I could do was stare back at the ghoul, unable even to close my eyes.

"You were so busy trying to hide your little zombie, you never considered he was one of the first victims, turned zombie by accident. Misdirecting murder and mayhem—it's the oldest trick in the book. Why do you think I used to cut all those girls up after I was done with them?"

My time as a curiosity was up. The ghoul had got everything out of me he wanted.

"Don't worry yourself too much, dear. You did a sight better than I would have expected a young thing like you to do. Better than that whore Lee." He turned away and busied himself at the table. "Maybe I'll turn you into a zombie? Or a ghoul? Or I have some more theories on poltergeists to test. How would you like to try that? Or maybe I'll just kill you." He advanced on me, eyes glittering as a white cloth came down over my nose and mouth.

I breathed in sweet chloroform.

"Pssst."

I stirred. I was lying on something hard and I could hear a radio, a news channel—no, weather. Something about storms off the coast. But that hadn't been the noise that woke me. It'd been more irritating.

"Pssst—"

There it was again.

"Jesus Christ, K, will you wake the hell up already?"

Nate. What was he doing here, and why was he whispering . . . and why was I so groggy?

My eyes flew open. I could see. I still had my eyes. Face, arms, stomach, heartbeat, lungs: everything was still where it should be, and as far as I could tell it was all working again.

I tried sitting up but hit restraints. I glanced down at my wrist, encircled by the same brown-stained leather straps that had bound Neon.

"I was worried you were going to stay passed out," Nate said. He'd only bothered to form a face. Smart with a poltergeist floating around . . .

"Nate, what are you doing here?"

"When you didn't show up, Cameron and I came looking for you. He followed your scent all the way to the city storm doors."

Shit, Cameron.

"Shhh, K, it's okay, he's fine. He didn't come down here. No zombieing out." He glanced around the dock shed. "*I* don't want to be down here. Let's get you the hell out before that psycho ghoul comes back."

Nate produced a small key for the lock on the restraints. Never let it be said I didn't value Nate's kleptomania.

On the first try he fumbled and the key clinked through his fingers to the floorboards. He cursed, but managed to grab it before it slipped through a crack.

A scream shattered the silence, coming from beyond the closed door. Neon.

Nate swore a blue streak and tried to fit the key in the lock again. His fingers shook. "I've been listening to that on and off the last half-hour. He's coming for you as soon as he's done with her. Come on, you stupid, no-good key, get in the lock."

"Nate, you're doing fine," I said.

Even as the words came out of my mouth, he dropped the key again. It had passed right through his hand. Nate had used up so much energy, he was almost out. Not only was the lock old, it was heavy. Even if he got the key into the lock, how would he turn it?

"It's not your fault, Nate, anyone could have dropped it."

Anger and fear played across his face. "K, shut up before the psychos hear you."

Another ear-piercing scream came from behind the door.

Nate was really shaking and flickering now. He could barely hold the key, so he abandoned it. Instead, he tried to hit the lock with his fist. "Give, you stupid, goddamn lock." It barely rattled as his fist passed right through.

"Nate, we'll think of something else," I tried, keeping my voice calm.

Nate looked at me, almost completely done in. "What the hell good am I if I can't get a stupid goddamn lock open? Huh?" He reached for the wrist restraint. I watched his hand pass right through me.

He stared at it as if it were some kind of cruel trick.

My heart broke watching him. I closed my eyes. "Nate, it's okay, I'll think of something."

He opened his mouth to reply, but he never got a chance before he faded back to the Otherside.

A tear slid down my cheek. At least Nate wouldn't have to watch.

"Now, Miss Kincaid, I'm not the one who went looking for ghouls and serial killers, am I?" The ghoul was back and was still wearing his apron, though now it was covered in blood. "You really have no one but yourself to blame, so no need for tears. I see the neurotoxin has worn off." He searched around the table, then in his apron pocket. "Where did my scalpel go? I used to be a surgeon—did Lee mention that? No, I suppose she didn't." He sighed and headed for the back room. "Anna, dear, do you have my scalpel?"

As soon as the door shut, I tried my restraints. The leather squeaked as it stretched against the board, but it didn't give.

"You know, Kincaid, I don't think you've quite grasped the concept of 'Try not to get yourself killed.'"

I opened my eyes. Gideon stood beside the table holding a silver scalpel in his hand. If he didn't look so pissed off, I'd almost be glad to see him. . . .

"How the hell am I supposed to collect on our bargain if you keep ending up in situations like this? That's, what, twice in one day?"

His voice was loud and I glanced to where the ghoul had disappeared.

"Don't worry, they'll be searching for this scalpel for quite some time. They'll find my distraction first." He frowned at me. "I expected you to be happier to see me."

"I still haven't figured out whose side you're on."

He seemed to think about that. "Fair enough. How far would getting you out go?"

"If you loosen the straps, I'll tell you."

"That won't do you much good if I don't show you a way out. It's a labyrinth down here, and there are an awful lot of zombies and ghouls who are nowhere near as civilized as the ones you're used to in the upper city."

"Will you lay off the sarcasm? Of course I know what the zombies and ghouls down here are like. I'm going to be dead as soon as *that* one finds another scalpel, so get me out."

Gideon frowned. "For someone in your position, I expected you to be more gracious." With a flick of his hand, the straps opened. I rolled off the table, rubbing my wrists, then leaned over to massage my feet. They were still numb from the neurotoxin the ghoul had used.

I eyed Gideon. He didn't strike me as the good-Samaritan type. "Why are you helping me?"

"Because, contrary to what you believe, I don't make a habit of beating up defenceless practitioners. I'm trying to make up for what I did to you. Though considering your attitude towards me, I'll be damned if I know why."

I just stared at him.

He sighed. "All right. How will I get payment if you get cut up by the ghoul? I was serious when I said I needed someone to run errands for me."

This I actually believed. Now for Neon. She needed serious medical attention, but if I could get her out . . . I headed for the side door.

Gideon materialized in front of me. "You can't do anything for her."

I tried to dodge past him, but he only materialized again.

"I can imagine what's going through your head, Kincaid. Allow me to be the bad guy. You don't have time to rescue anyone. They know the tunnels better than you or I do, and there's the small matter of the psychotic poltergeist to deal with."

A scraping noise followed by a howl of pain startled us both.

"I'd start running," Gideon said. "My distraction appears to have arrived early."

"Zombies? Your distraction was zombies?"

Gideon shrugged. "Some ghouls as well. I work best with the tools at hand."

"How many?"

He regarded me. "You really don't want to know the answer to that."

"Then you better hurry up and help me get her out of here!"

Silence.

I swore. "Fine, I'll do it myself." I tried to push past Gideon, but I found myself held in place. I glanced down and saw Otherside bindings wrapping my feet.

"Out of my way, ghost!" I snarled, trying to release myself from the bindings.

We both heard Anna Bell's shriek as she presumably discovered the distraction of ghouls and zombies Gideon had cooked up.

Gideon said, "Take the lefts all the way to the sewer ladder. There's a pressure valve with the combination twelve, ten, thirteen—use the north-pointing arrow. I'll hold off the poltergeist."

"If you can fend off the poltergeist, why can't you help me save the other girl?"

Gideon's eyes grew cold. "Because some people don't deserve saving."

"No one deserves *that*!" I said.

More noise echoed across the water as it lapped against the underground dock. Ghouls and zombies, packs of them. With all the Otherside in the world, I couldn't drop a pack on my own. I stared at the door through which Neon had been taken.

"Take it or leave it," Gideon said. "You try to save the girl and I *will* leave."

Gideon was evil, cruel and probably a hair away from being a poltergeist. He'd do it.

I said a silent "sorry" to Neon, not that she'd care what I thought, but still . . . Then I took off and didn't look back until I'd reached the pressure valve. My hands shook as I went through the Otherside lock, hoping to hell I'd picked the north-pointing arrow—I suck at directions. Thank god I didn't have to pull a globe to do it.

I climbed out on the surface in a waterfront alley. I pulled out my pocket mirror and called Nate as soon as I could hazard it. He might just have enough juice left to show his face. I didn't want him trying to get back to me and getting caught in Gideon and Anna Bell's crossfire.

Nate materialized out of the mirror and threw his arms around me in a weightless bear hug, icing me in the process. "Oh my god, K!"

Not that I didn't appreciate it, but the ice was a bit much.

"Where's Cameron? Were you able to check on him?"

"Waiting at the all-night coffee shop. Brains finally kicked in about an hour ago. He smells a bit, but we used Aaron's old cologne."

I pulled out my phone to dial Max. It was a sheer miracle I still had it on me. Shit—the clock read 5 a.m. I'd been underground a long time. His voice mail picked up. As I started jogging towards the coffee shop, a conversation we'd had many times played in my head.

"Kincaid, you can't use sea urchins," Max had said.

"Why not? They work ten times better than a chicken or a rat, and I don't feel bad about it!"

"That is not the point. You need to learn and master the proper methods before you change them!"

Other things Max had said to me over the years rushed through my head.

"Kincaid! Will you please stop pestering me with questions? Read the textbook. That is what it's for."

"Kincaid, stop forwarding me invitations to these seances! I will not raise the dead for someone's amusement, I do not care what it pays."

"Finally, you replicate my bindings without changing them. This is a momentous occasion that deserves tea."

"I don't care if your way is faster! These slower traditional bindings will teach you patience—which you are sorely lacking."

I clenched my fists and told Nate, "We need to grab Cameron and get to Max's now."

"Whoa, no. *You* need to go home. You can deal with Max later—"

I held up my phone. "Max isn't answering."

"Like he ever answers?"

I shook my head, trying to bite back the tears. Why is it always at moments like this that I remember there are only a handful of people in this world who care enough to put up with my personal brand of bullshit?

"We need to get there now. He's the next victim."

CHAPTER 23

OTHERSIDE BOUND

"Kincaid, this is a really stupid idea," Nate hissed at me for the third time.

Nate was still smarting from failing to rescue me, but he had a very good point.

I had Cameron on the back of my Hawk and Nate yelling in my ear. At least the sun was coming up and for the first time in three days it wasn't raining. . . .

"No one walks in on Maximillian Odu. Not even us ghosts. It isn't done," Nate yelled.

Another brilliantly accurate point. "I'm not walking, I'm riding. Do you have a better idea?"

"Yeah! Go home and call Aaron!"

"Nate, I told you already, I have no idea what Aaron will do. Neon had him convinced I was involved, and I don't think her being missing will help my cause."

"And I told you I'll fucking believe that Aaron wouldn't help you when I see a pig fly!"

"Besides, if Max's in trouble, like I think he is—"

"And what if he's *not*? Am I the only one who thinks about our skins?"

"You don't have a skin."

"I have a PlayStation!"

"That makes *no* sense whatsoever."

"If you had any appreciation for video games, it would," he said.

I shook my head. "Too late—we're here." I pulled up to the curb in front of Max's, which was the only place to park. He had decided years ago to turn the gravel driveway into garden space.

Max's home was not what you would call well-kept, just a cottage set in an overgrown garden. The house was rundown, but the gardens made up for it, including the tangle of potted plants that covered the cracked cement porch.

Wind chimes rustled and I could hear birdsong, but nothing else. I climbed onto the porch and focused on the Otherside until I figured out where Max's famous ghost barrier was, the one that kept them from hounding him day and night. It was still intact. Cameron had followed me up to the porch steps.

"Cameron, it's best if you wait by the bike. The place is surrounded with Otherside. It isn't going to play nice with your bindings. If Max is okay, I'll have him drop the barrier."

He nodded and went back to the bike. I glanced around. The last thing we needed was an anonymous call to the police, so maybe Cameron should wait somewhere else, like in the park down the road.

I called, "Why don't you head to the park and wait for me there? It'll be safer."

He exchanged a glance with Nate before complying. "Shout if you need me," he said.

Nate joined me at the edge of the barrier.

"Ready?" I asked him.

"No," he said, but dissolved back to the Otherside anyway. I stepped through Max's ghost barrier, registering no more than a slight tingle. As soon as I was across, I pulled out my pocket mirror and wrote Nate's name. Easiest way to get him across without setting off an alarm.

When he was back with me, I thought about knocking, but all that might do was alert the killer I was here. I tried the door and it opened.

"K, this is too easy," Nate said. "Why would Max leave his door open?"

"Because the only people who come looking for him are ghosts and he has a barrier for that?"

Nate floated through the door and back out. "Pulling me across was awful easy. Way too fucking easy if you ask me."

"We'll be careful," I said.

The inside of Max's home matched the outside; it was not without its charm but was in need of a fresh coat of paint and some repairs. There was no sign of Max as Nate and I walked through the living room, though his large coffee mug was sitting on the coffee table. It was half full and the milk had begun to curdle. Not like Max to leave something like that lying around. In the kitchen, I noticed that the bird feeder that hung outside the window was down to its last few sunflower seeds.

Max hadn't been avoiding me. The coffee and bird feeder suggested that he'd been gone since he'd come to see me in Pioneer Square. He'd said he had a client to go see.

The spring hinges squeaked as I opened the screen door into the backyard. And there Max was, standing in the vegetable garden with his back to me. One hand rested on the crabapple tree he threatened to cut down each and every year.

"Max?" I said.

He turned and gave me a tired smile. "Took you long enough."

I started down the steps towards him. "Thank god, Max!" I stopped when I caught sight of the symbols soaking through his shirt. I switched my view to Otherside. The lines were everywhere, woven through the garden and anchored to the blood symbols drawn on Max.

"You must be the thickest, most stubborn apprentice I've ever had the pleasure to teach. I expected you to break down my door when Gideon showed up, not call and leave me a message."

Another piece of the puzzle slid into place. "Gideon Lawrence didn't find me by accident. You planned that. That's why you insisted on meeting me for coffee, so that damned ghost would catch sight of me."

"A plan? No. More of a hope. When you called me about Cameron, I saw an opportunity. Though I failed to foresee this happening." He inclined his head towards the lines holding him in place.

Max's client, the one he'd been going to see after meeting me. More pieces fell into place. I shook my head. "If you hadn't played the senile voodoo priest so well, I would have been here two days ago."

Max shrugged, careful not to move from his spot. "If I hadn't been so convincing, I would be long dead. They've been watching me for a while. I needed a good reason to come see you, one my captor would believe and yet would set you on a path to find me." He glanced at the bindings. "Though I didn't expect them to lose their patience with me so . . . drastically."

"Who kidnapped you, Max? Who's trying to raise a Jinn?"

"I believe I am his next test subject."

"Yeah, I know that. But who is it?"

He shook his head. "I cannot speak the name or disrupt these bindings. The consequences would be . . . unwelcome. One thing my captor has succeeded at is re-creating the symbols that force the Jinn into servitude. They work just as well on the living, it would seem."

"How about I guess, Max? If I get it right, all you have to do is nod."

He sighed. "All I can say, Kincaid, is that if they were someone you know, you would never guess it was them."

Aaron. My heart fell. I'd never have suspected him in a thousand years. Though that was before Neon started manipulating the situation.

No time to worry about that now. I needed to get Max free.

I concentrated on the active bindings holding him in place. I recognized a symbol here or there, but the patterns of Otherside lines running through them were foreign to me.

How far were they from raising an actual Jinn?

As if reading my thoughts, Max said, "I believe I am to be the first success."

"Figures. If they could control you, they could control anyone."

The activated bindings had been ravelled so tight I didn't think I'd be able to unwind them. Maybe the unactivated ones.

"Max, if I get rid of the bindings, will I set anything off?"

He gave me a ghost of a smile. "I believe they were in quite a hurry to leave." Not much of a clue there.

I nodded. Now where the hell to start? Max couldn't exactly give me instructions.

"Kincaid, do you remember the game I used to give everyone in my class?"

"Of course." He used to give us incomplete binding puzzles in lieu of written tests. We had to fill in the missing parts of whatever binding pattern he'd laid out. Later, when I'd become his apprentice, and moved from seances to raising zombies, Max had used that same principle, relying on patterns and symbols I already knew to teach me the new ones. An intricate fill-in-the-blank mixed with "one of these things is not like the others."

I could see Max working out what he could say to me. "I believe you were always very good with Egyptian symbols."

Right, Egyptian symbols used for summoning ghosts near water. My favourite anchor for Otherside. I searched the patterns in the bindings until I found the Egyptian anchor symbol. Along with acting as an anchor for the Jinn ring, it held two separate lines of Otherside tied to Max himself.

I swore. Normally I'd just trash the binding with Otherside, but with the inactive Jinn lines so close to the active ones, I didn't want to risk setting off a chain reaction. The old man watched me, his expression giving nothing away.

"I hope you didn't bet too much on me figuring these out," I said. Whoever had trapped Max here would have known to clean his supplies out of the fridge. I headed back towards the house at a run and pulled the loose board off the second step, peering underneath for the small cooler Max kept there. I breathed a sigh of relief: they hadn't found Max's stash. I checked the contents. Sage, sea urchins and a decent knife.

Just being able to see the Otherside wasn't enough for this situation, so I braced myself and pulled a globe. I bit back the head rush and nausea and used the knife on one of the sea urchins to dissolve the first Egyptian symbol. As soon as it faded, the anchored lines snapped and wavered, unstable in their new alignment.

I glanced at Max to see if I'd guessed the first step right.

"You were always adept at reading between the lines, Kincaid," he said.

I spent the next twenty minutes following Max's subtle clues to the various anchors holding the Jinn rings in place, then picking them off one by one with the sea urchins.

I kept asking him in different ways who had trapped him, but to no avail. He couldn't tell me directly who had done this. Still, by answering a mix of yes-and-no and indirect questions, he was able to fill me in on the killings as much as he could.

Someone had been stalking people with Otherside affinity in Seattle for a month or more. Max had spotted Morgan one day leaving Cameron's apartment building. The girl was clearly interested in what Max was up to with Cameron, but she had had very little skill, so Max had not thought much about it. It was not until later he realized his mistake, and by then it was too late to warn anyone.

"So with each victim they've sought more and more Otherside affinity?" I asked, and he nodded. I dealt with the last outer anchors. A Celtic rune. Man, whoever had set this up wanted to make damn sure an amateur couldn't unravel it.

They'd tried a zombie first, but Cameron had inadvertently been the trigger that had set them on a course of practitioners. He was still alive when Neon had mistaken him for a zombie — reasonable considering the number of bindings Max had attached to him. As the ghoul had suggested, Neon hadn't realized her mistake until after she'd killed him. Right, of course: Neon was the one who killed Cameron.

"Why did he lose his memory?" I asked.

Max almost laughed. "An unforeseen complication."

"On her part or yours?"

"Both. I did not anticipate someone attempting to layer bindings on Cameron, and she assumed the existing bindings meant he was already a zombie. An unfortunate mistake."

"Why leave Cameron wandering the city? Why not just finish him off?"

"Simple. Cameron rose as a zombie after they'd killed him in their experiment, and they didn't know how or what they'd done. When they eventually realized it was an accident, they used him as a decoy."

"To keep me busy—the only other practitioner in the city besides you who'd stand a chance of figuring out they were raising a Jinn."

"Though they did not count on your tenacity." His smile fell. "Small comfort to Cameron, I know."

Finally, I was left with the un-stabilized, un-anchored Jinn ring floating precariously between the two active lines still holding Max in place.

"Now what?" I asked.

Max nodded to the ring of Otherside symbols floating above him. "This reminds me of an old voodoo zombie set, do you not think?"

I studied it. Voodoo uses a small ring of symbols suspended above the corpse to act like a switchboard for lines of Otherside. The technique isn't used often anymore, as more stable and efficient anchors are available. A traditional voodoo set ring is too easily disrupted where the lines meet the ring. . . .

I looked for the intersections. I'd be able to unhinge the Jinn ring from Max by tying the lines to something else. If all went well, the Jinn ring would float off and I could work on unravelling the lines still holding Max in place.

I tapped the Otherside through my globe. I should be able to thread the lines bound to Max onto a free symbol left in the tree. I took a deep breath and wove my first thread, careful not to touch the ring itself.

I made conversation to keep his mind off what I was doing. "I've got Cameron stashed in the park. If you could fix up his screwy bindings, that would be useful."

Max was silent. I glanced up to see if he was still okay. He was watching me.

"Kincaid, Cameron's bindings aren't meant to be permanent. Those were his wishes. They were only to last until he finished his paintings. That he was murdered for the Jinn experiments is tragic but does not change his goal."

"No offence, Max, but Cameron got a raw deal." I tied one thread to the tree.

"When I am free from these bindings, we can take a look."

I concentrated on threading the last line.

"I'm sorry for bringing you into all this, Kincaid," Max said. "For not taking Cameron as soon as you found him, for exposing you to entities like Gideon." He shook his head.

"And then both you and Cameron would be dead and there would be a Jinn loose in Seattle. Apologize later. *After* you fix Cameron and buy me a really fantastic bottle of whisky." I threaded the line through the hoop and started to tie it off. Careful, Kincaid.

I let out the breath I was holding as the new anchor set. The Jinn ring dissolved. I'd done it.

Max breathed deeply, as if a great weight had been lifted off his shoulders.

I wiped sweat off my forehead. "All right, Max. Where do you want me to start on your binding lines?"

I caught the first flash of Otherside as it kicked off one of the remaining lines. I swore. I hadn't touched the line yet. So I'd made a mistake and triggered the fail-safe. That Otherside flare rushed along the line like a lit fuse to a stick of dynamite.

"Max! You said these bindings were safe for me to unravel."

He gave me a sad look. "I said that I believed together we could remove the Jinn ring and save me an eternity as a Jinn slave. Saving my life is at this point beyond either of our capabilities."

"Son of a bitch, Max, why the hell didn't you warn me!" The bindings running through Max's chest began to glow. Maybe if I threw enough Otherside at him, I could short-circuit it. . . .

I started siphoning Otherside as fast as I could.

A shadow passed over Max's face. "Kincaid, please do not hurt yourself. There is little point—" His face contorted as smoke began to rise from the ground around him.

Shit, he was going to burn alive.

I threw everything I had at him. It bounced off as if it was a drop of rainwater on a forest fire.

If I doused him with water, I might stop the fire. I looked for the hose, but it had been disconnected. Max had to keep a fire extinguisher somewhere. I ran for the kitchen.

"Kincaid!" Max fell to his knees as more smoke billowed around him.

I was out of time. I turned back to him.

"Tell Gideon I am sorry about not keeping my end of our bargain. Remember he is only to be trusted so far. There may be something in my notes to help with Cameron, though only if the sixth line is still dormant. I'm sorry, Kincaid, I'm sorry for—" His face contorted with pain as more smoke billowed around him. His skin began to peel like paper in a fire. "Time to see what the Otherside is like," he said. He didn't scream, just closed his eyes and evaporated in a plume of smoke and fire.

I stood there, vaguely aware of the air getting cold.

"K, we gotta go! Come on, snap out of it," Nate shouted in my ear.

"He taught me everything I know," I said.

"Yeah, and there are cop cars coming, K, two of them, and Aaron on his way too."

How the hell had they known to come here?

A trap. Nate had been right. I'd been set on getting Max out . . . and the killer had known I would be. Yet again, I'd done exactly what he or she expected me to do. . . .

"Tell Cameron to take off!" I said.

"He's out of sight, hiding in the park."

I started to follow Nate through the back gate. "Shit, Max's notes!" I bolted for the house.

"K, no!"

"They're the only chance Cameron has," I yelled. Now where the hell would Max have put them? I checked the kitchen drawers, the office, his bedroom. Then I remembered Max once telling me where to hide my books if the police ever came by: the oven.

I slid back into the kitchen and opened the oven door. A neat stack of notebooks bound with thread was sitting on the bottom element.

I heard a loud knock at the front door. Followed by, "Police."

I hefted the notebooks. My bike was outside the house and the cops would already have seen it. The door opened and I cursed myself for not having had the foresight to lock it behind us.

I ran for the bathroom and shut the door, locking it.

I heard footsteps in the hall. I wrote *Gideon Lawrence* across the mirror as fast as I could and crossed my fingers he was listening.

He materialized with the first bang on the bathroom door, took in the surroundings and gave me a wary look. I shook my head and shoved the notes at him, whispering, "No time—police. Max is dead and these are his notes, probably even has one on your deal with him. He always wrote everything down."

"What do you want me to do?"

"Hide them, read them, whatever you want, but I need all the notes on bindings and everything to do with a recent zombie named Cameron Wight. Deal?" Someone was trying to force the bathroom door.

Gideon nodded and took the pile before vanishing. Then the door crashed open and two men burst through with guns drawn.

"On the ground, hands behind your head."

By the time Aaron got there, I was in handcuffs. Our eyes met. I couldn't read a damn thing in his. It was probably best that way. We didn't say a word as he led me through the house and stuffed me into the back of his car.

As soon as I was alone, Nate materialized beside me. "K, what the fuck—"

"Find Lee and tell her I've been framed." I remembered what Max had said about the killer being someone I would never suspect. There was only one person who fit that description, however far-fetched it sounded. "I think Aaron is behind this," I said, my voice barely a whisper.

Nate's eyes went wide and he started to say something, but officers were heading my way.

"Just make sure she knows. Get Cameron to call her from the apartment, okay?"

Nate swore, but the cops were almost to the car. He dissolved into fog, leaving me to face whatever the Seattle PD had in store for me.

CHAPTER 24

JAIL

Want to know how to mind-fuck a practitioner? Put them in a room with no windows and mirrors. Trust me, the luxury of having no ghosts to talk to wears off fast. There wasn't even a reflective metal surface in here so I could get hold of Nate and find out what the hell was going on.

Max was dead and I was in jail. I leaned my head against the white wall. "You'd think I'd have learned by now."

I felt the telltale chill in the air. I knew who it was without opening my eyes.

"We really need to work on this whole try-not-to-get-yourself-killed situation."

I opened my eyes. There, lounging on the bench beside me, was Gideon.

"No one wants to kill me. They just want me in jail."

"I fail to see the difference."

"I take it this is where you tell me I'm an idiot?"

"Oh no—I can see why Max took you on as an apprentice." Gideon took in my cell, lingering on the bars. "You know, I'm sure there's some sort of sentiment I should express in situations like this, but after four hundred years it escapes me."

I shook my head. "Do I even want to ask how you got in here?"

He shrugged. "A piece of advice, Kincaid? Stop telling them you're innocent."

I glanced over at my sociopathic ghost. "Why? Because the evidence is stacked against me?"

He shook his head. "No—because they already know you didn't do it."

"They might know I'm innocent, but one thing about the living is what they know and believe tend to be two different things."

"For the moment they've all conceded you probably didn't kill anyone. Since you can't exactly float out of here, I assumed you'd be interested in what's been going on."

"Aaron's not going to let me leave, not if he can help it," I said.

"Right now he's claiming you know more than you'll admit to. He has a point."

Silence passed between us as he let that sink in.

"The world of the living revolves around reasons. Cause and effect, loyalty, why we're on this godforsaken planet," he said, giving me a measured stare. "The unfair nature of life makes people uncomfortable. They'd much rather push logic to the side and find someone to blame. That's the way it was four hundred years ago, and I've seen nothing to convince me anything's changed."

"No offence, but if you're trying to cheer me up, you're doing an abysmal job."

"Because this is an area where I have an unfortunate amount of experience—loyalty, friendship, love even." Gideon shook his head. "They all play a distant second to the quest for a scapegoat. No matter a lack of evidence, no matter what they know in their hearts to be true. At this moment they doubt you've done any wrong, but give them time." Gideon glanced up at me again. "They'll persuade themselves you're guilty, and that's when the fun really begins."

Silence passed between us once again, then Gideon said, "Look, I'm not very good with condolences, but for what it's worth, I'm sorry about Max."

"Is he a ghost?" I asked.

Gideon shook his head. "No, Max made peace with what he was a long time ago. No need to become a ghost."

I nodded, relieved. I didn't think Max would appreciate being a ghost. "I'll need those notebooks back at some point," I said. "If I ever get out of here."

"Stupid business, all this raising of a Jinn. There's a reason no one's succeeded in over five hundred years. They're dangerous." He looked around my cell again. "I've been in worse places than this."

Yeah, right. I ran over Max's words in my head. "Max told me the Jinn killer is someone close, someone I'd never suspect. It has to be Aaron. He's the only one who had contact with Neon."

"*That* one is hard to read," Gideon conceded. "It is within the realm of possibilities he is behind this."

I shook my head. "I still can't believe it."

"Think for a moment, Kincaid. Attempt to use that still-corporeal brain between your ears. What do you know that they don't?"

"I know someone is trying to make a Jinn. Why and how, I don't know—"

"If you ever bothered listening to anyone around you, you'd save yourself a mountain of grief."

"*Fine.* I know that someone is trying to make a Jinn. Not Lee's original murdering ghoul, but someone new."

Gideon closed his eyes. "What else do you know?"

"This is pointless. Why don't you tell me what the fuck I'm missing—"

"If I do, you won't learn. Self-sufficiency is a virtue, Kincaid. So what else?"

"Very few people succeed and no accurate binding set exists. It's considered incredibly dangerous by everyone, including people who are for all intents and purposes already dead."

"Why all the dead bodies?"

"They're experimenting, trying to get it right. They figure they've got the control bindings figured out. After seeing Max, I'd agree. They know their victim needs to have a high degree of affinity for Otherside—"

"I think we can assume there were two people involved, otherwise someone would have been babysitting Max. With the woman dead, there's one left—no doubt a man. He's confident; he thinks they're close." Gideon changed his line of questioning. "What is a Jinn?"

I sighed and recited what I'd read in the text and Lou's notes. "A powerful, enslaved animated dead, one capable of great destruction and great deeds—"

"My god, have you learned nothing from the accounts of King Solomon's Jinn? Capricious, angry, unwilling victims, tortured into an existence of servitude, hell-bent on vengeance if they could only get past those damned control bindings. The *only* thing all accounts agree on is that the Jinn turn on their masters as soon as the opportunity presents itself." He gave me a pointed look. "They're a monster to beat all undead monsters, including me. So what does that tell you about the killer?"

For the next minute all I heard was my own breath. "He's desperate. A person smart enough to make it this far knows how dangerous Jinn are. He really thinks this is his only option."

Gideon nodded. "Desperation. A sentiment you are all too familiar with. I would venture you know the killer better than any of these officers."

"I'm not desperate."

Gideon arched an eyebrow at me. "And I suppose you were just dying to crawl into the proverbial bed with me in exchange for bindings that let you see Otherside without killing yourself?" He snorted. "No, you agreed to my deal out of complete and utter desperation, which is what your killer feels. No one would attempt to create a Jinn without feeling that way."

It slipped out before I could censor myself. "Did you ever try raising a Jinn?"

Gideon's eyes glittered black as he regarded me, reminding me I shouldn't misinterpret tentatively converging goals for friendship. "I didn't live long enough to get that desperate. Then again, when I was alive, you didn't need proof to torch someone, just a passing inclination. Nowadays? Who knows?"

He glanced up at the ceiling and we spent the next few minutes in silence, me with my own thoughts and Gideon with whatever the hell passed for his. Then I heard footsteps.

Gideon regarded me. "Remember what I said about them not caring that you're innocent." He vanished as I heard the far door to the cell wing open.

"Why don't you stop treating me like the enemy?" Aaron said.

I slumped in the metal chair. It was uncomfortable and wasn't helping my mood.

Neither was Aaron. I didn't know what was worse, Aaron pretending he was clueless or the seemingly good cop act. I figure it was fifty-fifty.

"Kincaid, please tell me what you were doing at Max's. I'm on your side—"

Did Aaron really think I was that stupid? Or was it for show? I turned to the one-way mirror and gave it a good long look. I knew it'd make every last one of them squirm.

"How's Morgan doing? You know, your new practitioner? I'd have thought you would have brought her in to question me." Okay, that was low, even for me, but I was near my breaking point.

Aaron hazarded a glance at the mirror. Subtle, but I was watching for it. Did they know she was missing? Or had someone figured out she was involved and Aaron didn't want them to know he was connected to her? "Like I told you, she volunteered information about the case."

"And I have a fantastic bag of magic beans for sale, if you're interested."

There was a rap at the door. Warning number one. Aaron was supposed to keep things professional. Let's see how long we could go before the captain burst in.

"Maybe you can help me with a little bet I have," I said.

Aaron sat back and crossed his arms.

"See, most people bet you dumped me to save your job. Understandable. Nate, on the other hand, figures you're not that bad, but he wouldn't know a normal relationship if it hit him over the head with a guitar."

"Is there a point to this?"

"Not really, but let me finish. I figure the truth is a little more complicated. I figure you just think I'm too stupid to realize when I'm being screwed."

Aaron's hands clenched on the table. "I've tried, I've really tried, Kincaid. I don't deserve this."

Knock number two . . .

Aaron's eyes narrowed as he got his composure back. "There was another murder. Same MO. Two people were seen running from the scene. You wouldn't know anything about that, would you?"

I did my best to look surprised.

The door opened. I watched Aaron bristle as Sarah waved him out. He didn't so much as shoot me a glance as he left.

To my surprise, it wasn't Sarah who came next. It was Captain Marks, carrying a large folder.

I'd never seen the man in person. He was smaller and less intimidating than he seemed on TV. He sat down and watched me for a few moments.

"I'd like to take a look around your place, Ms. Strange," he said at last.

I lifted an eyebrow. "Have a warrant?"

He smiled and I followed suit. "We will. What were you doing at Mr. Odu's home this morning?"

"Max and I were meeting."

"And why would that be?"

"Book club."

"Can you tell me your whereabouts last night?"

Yeah, I was kidnapped by a ghoul and a poltergeist, and forced to hear another practitioner gutted. Oh yeah, and she was trying to kill me too. "Not really."

That caught him off guard.

"An alibi?"

"Lots of them." I glanced at the two-way mirror. "Including Detective Baal. Club 9, the artists' hangout. Ran into him there while I was working with my client as a sober companion."

Marks watched me, reassessing.

"Am I under arrest?"

"You're being detained."

"For what and how long?"

"That's up to my discretion where known necromancers are concerned. That is what you folk call yourself, Ms. Strange? Necromancers?"

I managed to keep the distaste off my face. "'Practitioner' is the correct term, Captain. People think necromancers have something to do with sex and dead people."

His eyes widened. "I'll have to remember that," he said, and turned his attention to the folder. "So can you tell me a bit about being expelled from Washington State University for cheating?"

I felt my face flush. "It was a misunderstanding. They wrote a new rule against using ghosts as a primary resource after I turned my paper in. The expulsion was revoked on appeal." Though I'd never gone back.

"Ah." He looked again at the papers. "And a short while afterwards you were charged with grave desecration? Is that right?"

"That had nothing to do with me. It was a will dispute. The charges were dropped."

The captain glanced up from the file. "Ah. Another misunderstanding." He nodded. "Funny thing, Ms. Strange. One-offs happen to everyone. Wrong place, wrong time." He shrugged. "But when someone ends up with a file this full of misunderstandings, I start wondering what's going on."

I didn't say a word.

"What about raising an unwilling zombie?"

I went cold. "Is there a point to this?"

He didn't reply, just pulled out another set of papers. I caught the Canadian RCMP logo in the top corner. "Born in Vancouver, Canada, dual citizenship through your father. Says here you were involved in the raising of your mother's corpse a few years back. Against your mother's and father's wishes."

Where the hell had he got that?

"I quote: 'The victim'—your mother—'was unwilling to testify. Treated as hostile.'"

I glared at the mirror again, wondering whether any of them cared that this line of questioning was probably illegal. I was going to be having one hell of a phone call with the Vancouver RCMP. After my raising a few dead witnesses for them, you'd think they'd be a little more grateful. The file should have been closed. Except I'd told Aaron about it . . .

For once in your life, Kincaid, don't let it get personal.

Dad was an asshole all his life, and a coward. I'd made my peace with that a long time ago, and also found out that cowards back down once they know you'll make good on a threat. It was my mother who couldn't be bothered to muster up a backbone and stand up to him.

"That was a domestic abuse investigation, Captain. The police suspected the victim—my mother—was thrown down a flight of stairs after being severely beaten. Canada's laws are different when it comes to murder investigations than they are here, and they allow raising victims and witnesses, even hostile ones." And believe me, my mother had been hostile. Thrown down a flight of stairs and from the grave she was still making excuses for him . . . "That file should be sealed."

Captain Marks ignored me. "Case was dismissed, lack of evidence. Your father wasn't very happy with you. Innocent man accused of murdering his own wife. Disowned you afterwards, for being a 'crazy hell-bound devil worshipper.'" He chose that moment to look up at me. "Strong words, Ms. Strange. Suppose that's why you changed your name and moved to Seattle. Can't blame you. I'd be ashamed to show myself around my hometown too if I were in your shoes."

I don't know what the hell else the captain said after that; all I could hear was the blood rushing in my ears. And all I could see was my mother's corpse lying to me, telling me it'd been an accident, he hadn't meant to do it . . . and the only thing I could think about was wringing her insipid neck. Screw anger management. I launched myself at the captain across the metal table. He jumped out of his chair, managing to get himself out of my range.

I was vaguely aware of yelling and the door opening.

Sarah got hold of my waist and dragged me out of the room before I could wrap my hands around the captain's neck. God knows I tried.

He was smiling at me as Sarah dragged me out.

Sarah had me walking towards my cell fast, cursing the entire way. "Assholes. Can't even run an interrogation properly . . ."

Only when I was back behind bars did she turn her ire on me.

"I've seen you do a lot of stupid things, Kincaid, but that tops all of them."

"Did you not hear any of what he said to me?"

"Yeah, and you already knew he was an asshole."

"Sarah, they think I'm a serial killer. If I didn't know better, I'd say you and Aaron figured me as the perpetrator on this. . . ."

She looked at the floor then and it dawned on me.

"How long, Sarah? How long? How long have I been your primary suspect?"

She didn't answer and she didn't look up at me.

"Son of a bitch, was I ever *not* a suspect?"

"How the hell were we not supposed to consider you a suspect? You and Max both, until he turned up dead this morning." She shook her head. "For the record, I don't think you did it, and not because you're a friend, but because there isn't any evidence." Her expression hardened. "Not that your stunt back there helped any. Now get yourself together while I go try to—I don't know—get them to behave like adults?"

"Sarah?"

She turned back at me.

"You never said you thought I wasn't capable of it."

Her face softened. "That was implied."

I sat back down on the bench and closed my eyes.

*

"Ms. Strange?"

I lifted my head. My neck was sore, my mouth was dry, and I was damn tired. The young officer who'd retrieved me from my cell for my interrogation was outside the cell.

"Someone asking to see you." He cleared his throat. "Your lawyer?" It should have been a statement, but it ended up sounding like a question.

I heard two distinct sets of footsteps coming my way, someone in runners and another person in heels.

"Cameron," I said as he appeared behind the officer. Thank god, not looking worse for wear. When the second person came into view, my jaw dropped.

Lee Ling.

She'd covered her face with enough makeup to hide her scars and was dressed in an impeccable black suit. She allowed me a fraction of a smile. "Ms. Kincaid," she said. "This lovely gentleman will be letting you out."

The officer unlocked the door and the next thing I knew I was following Lee and Cameron towards the exit. No sign of Aaron or Sarah. I'd probably slug Aaron if I saw him. Shit, spoke too soon. I swore and earned an elbow jab from Cameron.

"Watch how you use that thing," I said. "You realize it's liable to fall off?"

"I won't use my elbow if you stop looking like you're about to attack a cop."

"Fantastic, tell that to *them*."

Aaron and the captain were bearing down on us. The captain reached me first. "This isn't over. As soon as we find evidence—"

"You won't," Lee said, stepping in front of me.

The look on his face told me everything I needed to know. He could care less about a few practitioners getting killed, probably thought someone was doing the city a favour; he just wanted me locked up.

Marks looked as though he wanted a piece of Lee too, but Aaron stepped in his way. The captain might be an asshole, but he wasn't stupid. Not wanting to risk an altercation with a lawyer, he left us at the front desk. Aaron hovered while Lee filled out paperwork and I collected my effects.

"Kincaid," Aaron tried.

I ignored him, but when I turned to go, he blocked my way. He leaned in close and whispered, "Whoever is behind these killings, Kincaid, is running out of practitioners. Stop involving yourself."

"Is that a threat?"

"A warning."

I pushed past Aaron and followed Lee and Cameron out the door. To my relief, my Hawk was waiting for me.

"How the hell did you pull that off?" I said to Lee once we were out of earshot.

"You need evidence to charge someone," she said.

"But the body? There were charred remains—"

"Dealt with," Lee said.

"All they can do is fine you for an illegal bonfire," Cameron added.

I stopped to stare at him. "You're serious?" I knew Lee had crews to handle surface-side zombie mishap cleanup, but Max's place had been crawling with cops. Forensics must have picked up some remains.

Lee gripped my arm. "I have no intention of discussing the details. Keep walking," she hissed.

"Lee, I need to know who's left practitioner-wise in Seattle."

Lee and Cameron exchanged a glance. She said, "That meet the killer's specifications? You are it."

Why did I even ask?

CHAPTER 25

THE DEVIL'S IN THE DETAILS

Gideon had left Max's notebooks on my bathroom counter, except for one. There was a message left in Manhunt red lipliner on the mirror.

I took the notes on clients, Gideon wrote. *I need those to see if I can piece together wherever the hell my payment got to.*

I frowned. That lipliner was exclusively for summoning Nate. It wasn't cheap. And I'd wanted to consult the client accounts specifically for the notes on Cameron, along with what the hell Max's arrangement with Gideon had been. I should have said something back at Max's.

I collected what was there and headed to the desk in the guest room. I'd have to settle for reading Max's technical accounts, where he recorded all the bindings and modifications he'd used. I found the ones on Cameron near the back of the notebook, and there wasn't one page but many. . . . What the hell had Max done?

The gear-like symbols were both the problem and the solution. Thinking of them like clock bindings was accurate, because that's exactly what they were: a clock meant to count down a set number of days until Cameron was finished his paintings. Once that time was up, the sixth and last gear would start to turn and unravel the rest of the bindings. It was an ingenious system: remotely raise a client at the time of death, guaranteeing there'd be minimal damage, and then create a fail-safe that would drop Cameron back to a corpse a week later. I had to assume Cameron and Max had discussed time frames and Cameron had thought a week would be enough . . . or all that was feasible within the bounds of Otherside.

The problem was that nothing like this had ever been tried before. I figured out in no time that the bindings in Max's notebook were incomplete since I could see lines on Cameron that had never reached the page. Either Max had still been adding to them or he was interrupted before he could write the final arrangements down. He'd never finished testing for side effects and complications. He hadn't discovered the Otherside resonance issue, or the lack of healing, or he didn't think those things were problems if Cameron was a zombie for only a week.

Which presented an entirely different can of rotting worms. Cameron was down to the fifth gear. In theory, if I could keep the sixth gear from triggering, I might give myself enough time to fix the rest of the bindings so that Cameron would start repairing like a normal zombie. Or he might just go feral. Like I said, one big can of zombiefied worms . . .

I felt the warning brush of cold before Nate slid into the chair beside me.

"Nate, please say you found something good in Neon's apartment." He'd located it two floors up and one over.

He shook his head. "Nothing. Not even a creepy serial killer journal."

"There's got to be something. Souvenirs, phone numbers, Post-it notes—"

"K, if she's got anything, it's hidden somewhere good. Are we even sure this chick really understood what was going on?"

I remembered the look on Neon's face before the poltergeist knocked me out. "Nate, she was obsessed with getting her hands on a Jinn. There's got to be something—a list, a set of instructions. It might not be obvious. Get creative. Pretend you were the one hiding it."

Nate sighed. "All right, I'll keep looking." He dissolved.

I looked down at the notebooks and tried wrapping my mind around the fact that Max was gone. I failed. I stood up and headed into the kitchen.

Cameron was lying on my kitchen table as Lee sutured his wound. She'd abandoned the suit for a red silk dress covered in white flowers and had removed the thick layer of makeup. I picked up the sweet smell of formaldehyde as Lee tied off the last stitch then wiped blood from her fingers with a kitchen towel. She pursed her lips when she saw me, and after taking a sip of a brain concoction that vaguely resembled a pink cosmo and exchanging a soft word with Cameron, she came over to me.

I didn't think I had martini glasses . . . or food colouring . . .

"How is he?" I asked.

"Not good. I've done what I can for the wound itself. The formaldehyde-and-ether soak I embalmed it with should halt further deterioration, but Cameron is not well."

"How are the brains working on him?"

Lee shrugged. "The wound isn't healing and he is showing signs of internal decay."

I closed my eyes. In short order he'd no longer pass as a human. "How long until he has to move into the city?"

"I'm not sure I would allow him anywhere but the docks. You've said it yourself: Otherside makes him too unpredictable. Did you find anything useful in Max's notes?"

I sighed. "Cameron was meant to be temporary. I might be able to diffuse the Otherside fail-safe Max loaded into his bindings. If I can figure out how to do that before it goes off and unravels the rest of his bindings, I should be able to fix him."

"That sounds like a yes, not a maybe."

"He was only supposed to last a week—just enough time to finish whatever paintings he was working on. That was the deal."

"I see."

"I'm a prime suspect in four murders, my zombie is broken, and your response is 'I see'? Great."

Lee tilted her head. "I would be sorely surprised if Aaron was behind this, Kincaid."

"Were you listening?"

"I was. If Aaron were behind this, you would never have left that station."

I started to object.

"Think, Kincaid," Lee said. "With Maximillian gone, and no access to my city, you are the practitioner within his reach who meets the criteria. He would simply have planted evidence at the drug dealer's murder scene." She shook her head. "The more I think on this, the more I believe he is a pawn, like Max was."

"You didn't see how he looked at me, Lee."

Lee cleared her throat. "Be that as it may, I think it more likely your own prejudices are colouring your judgment. In any event, even if he is involved, Aaron is not in charge."

"You said it yourself: there are other practitioners, underground."

"And that is where you should be until we identify the killer."

I shook my head. "That just concentrates the pool of available victims." Like herding sardines into a net . . .

Lee's eyes darkened. "No one leaves or enters the city without my permission."

Lee might be ruthless and resourceful, but she didn't understand serial killers. "The only reason he hasn't breached your defences is that he's had easier pickings up here and on the outskirts of the underground city. If I head down there, we'll just be giving him a reason to try his luck."

Lee looked about as happy with that assessment as I figured she'd be.

My phone buzzed in my pocket. Randall. What could he want?

"Lee, I need to answer this."

I'd barely said hello when he cut me off. "Kincaid, you still looking for people who have a grudge against zombies and practitioners?"

In all the turmoil of the last two days, I'd completely forgotten I'd asked Randall to put his feelers out. "Yeah, but whoever's behind the murders is a lot more dangerous than I thought. Stop looking right now, Randall. Don't ask any questions. Anyone asks you what you know, especially Aaron—"

"Too late for that, Kincaid. Besides, I know how to be subtle. Got it into my head to tap some of my family's old community connections. Heard something you definitely need to know."

I didn't want to be responsible for Randall being pulled into this mess. I covered the mic and glanced back towards the kitchen. Lee was working on Cameron again. No one would miss me if I made a quick pit stop at Randall's to find out what he knew. I checked the time as I ducked into the bedroom. It was just before noon. The bar wouldn't be open yet.

"Look, Randall, I'm coming over. Can you keep the place closed for another half-hour?" The last thing I needed was someone overhearing us.

"Sure, kid."

I grabbed my jacket and checked outside the bedroom window. No sign of Aaron or his sedan. "I'll be there in ten." I hung up.

"Where do you think you're going?" Lee was standing in my bedroom doorway.

I filled her in. She was even less enthused than I'd expected. "Don't go, Kincaid. You are taking an unnecessary risk."

"Your objection has been duly noted." I grabbed my bag and bike helmet.

"At least take Cameron with you," she said.

"You just told me he wasn't stable!"

"Around Otherside. I believe he should be fine to go with you to the bar. Anyone would think twice before attacking two individuals."

"All right, I'll take him. Watch for Nate, and let me know if he finds anything at Morgan's. Call if anything disastrous happens, like Aaron showing up with a warrant." I slid my jacket on and headed into the kitchen to wrangle my zombie.

"Kincaid?" Lee said in a tentative tone I wasn't used to from her.

I glanced back.

"It has come to my attention you are still in contact with the sorcerer's ghost." She held up her hand before I could say anything. "I do not wish to argue. Just be wary of those who mask their intentions by offering assistance."

She looked so serious, I could only nod.

"And please be careful," she called after me.

I smiled to myself. "You only say that because you've never seen Randall's baseball bat collection."

I'd decided to take the back alleys in case anyone from the PD was following me. The smell of formaldehyde carried off Cameron and I was worried, if we got pulled over, the cops would pick up on it.

"Bring back memories?" I asked as we pulled into Catamaran's.

He shrugged and shifted uncomfortably. "It looks strange in the daylight. Dirtier."

"Cameron, if you ever find a bar that doesn't look seedy in the daytime, run for your afterlife, because there's something wrong."

He snorted and slid off the bike before I edged it into my hiding spot behind the green Dumpster. I grabbed the back screen door then stopped, scanning the area.

"What's wrong?" Cameron said. He'd picked up on the change in my scent from the rush of adrenalin in my blood.

I scrutinized the back of the bar, then resigned myself to the fact I was paranoid. "Nothing," I said. "I'm just used to Randall's damn cat taking a swipe at me."

My phone rang. Aaron. I didn't answer.

It rang again. This was the last thing I needed.

"Just a sec, Cameron," I said.

"Before you hang up, I know you aren't behind the killings," Aaron said.

I closed my eyes. "Yeah, because arresting and interrogating me is really the way to get that message across."

"You were standing at a fucking crime scene—"

"What's the deal with Neon?"

It took a second for him to clue in. "Morgan? She's another suspect, one who's missing, but I suppose you wouldn't know anything about that?" Aaron hadn't lost his touch. "Kincaid, I didn't know you were a potential target. Where are you?"

"I wasn't a target? Aaron, just how many practitioners do you think there are in Seattle? And it's none of your damn business where I am!" I hung up.

"What did that accomplish?" Cameron said.

"Either way, it should send him to Neon's. If he was involved, he'll know what to look for and where."

"And if he wasn't?"

"He'll get a warrant and rip the place apart. Either way, it'll help Nate."

I pulled out my pocket mirror and scrawled, *Nate, heads-up for Aaron.*

"Come on," I said to Cameron, and headed inside.

Randall was nowhere to be seen. "Randall?"

"Just a sec, kid," I heard Randall call from the cellar where he stored the kegs. The only time he could haul them up was when the bar was empty. Why he wouldn't hire more staff . . .

He appeared a moment later in the doorway behind the bar well, the one that led to the basement. "Hey, kid, let me just grab you the names—" He stopped when he saw Cameron and his easy smile fell.

"He's okay," I told him. "All fixed up."

Randall didn't look convinced, but he didn't argue either. He also didn't take his eyes off Cameron as he stepped behind the bar and held up a beer mug with a questioning tilt of his head. "How are things holding up?" he said.

I shook my head. The last thing I needed was a drink, and the less Randall knew about the whole disastrous mess the better. My conscience didn't need anyone else turning up dead. "Let's just say you were right, Randall—I need to learn when to quit."

He nodded but still couldn't seem to pull his eyes off Cameron. Finally, he said, "You mind if the zombie stays outside? No offence—"

I glanced at Cameron, who shrugged and started walking towards the back.

"I'll be out in a few," I said, and waited until I heard the back screen door swing shut.

Randall was still fiddling with glasses behind the bar. "You know anything more about the killer?"

"Well, I know there was more than one. Trust me, that's all you need to know."

He ducked down behind the bar to tap the kegs. "Kid, I got no problem saying this world keeps getting weirder and weirder. Get out while the going is good, come back when things blow over."

"Yeah, well, too late for that. Don't think I'd make it past the city limits."

My phone buzzed. Nate. Before I could answer, I heard a scuffle from the front of the bar.

"Randall, did you hear that?"

"Probably your zombie," he said. He was still kneeling behind the bar.

"It came from the front." My phone rang again. "Randall, give me a sec, I need to get this."

I headed over to where the pool tables were, in an alcove where I'd have a bit of privacy.

"Nate, what's up?" I said.

"K, you alone?"

"I'm with Randall. Cameron's stepped outside because he makes Randall nervous."

"K, whatever you do, don't look at Randall. I found something at Neon's—a coaster from Catamaran's with numbers written on it, including Cameron's and the other victims'."

"Nate, it's a sports bar. A lot of people meet—"

"Yeah, but it didn't seem like her kind of place. Remember she called you on slumming it there? Don't answer me and don't look at him, but did you know Randall's kid died a few weeks back? Car accident, a bad one in the Philippines?"

"No," I said, struggling to keep my voice conversational. "That never came up." In fact I remembered Randall saying that Michael was coming home in the next week or so. . . .

"K, be careful," Nate said, but a noise, like a chair scraping across the floor, demanded my attention.

I craned around the alcove to see three men at the front entrance. I couldn't see their faces, but there was something about their movements that bothered me. Then they stepped under the light.

One of the men was wearing a red baseball hat and lumberjack jacket, while the other two wore jeans and flannel shirts. All three wore heavy workboots. It took me a moment, but I recognized them. They were the same men Randall had scared off the night I'd come to pick up Cameron, the ones who'd accosted me. They hadn't been dead long, but the decay was obvious. Randall, oblivious behind the bar, dropped something and all three zombies turned their attention towards him. I focused on seeing the Otherside to check their bindings: all three were four-lines.

Shit. I put the phone back up to my ear. "Nate, call Aaron and tell him where I am." Whether the zombies picked up my scent or heard my voice I don't know, but all three turned their attention to me.

"Got to go, Nate," I said, keeping the three zombies in view.

Randall swore. He was standing now, staring at the zombies as they dragged themselves across the floor towards me.

"Damn phones," he said. "That's the one thing I could never figure out: how to get a four-line zombie to ignore the damn phone."

I swallowed hard as I backed into the pool table. "Randall, whatever they've offered you, whatever they've threatened you with, it's not worth it."

Randall didn't look at me. "Well, you were right about one thing, kid. You never did know when to quit."

I realized why Randall had his hands below the bar: to hide the aluminum bat.

"You were supposed to be in jail, kid, not able to walk into my bar."

"Morgan set me up for that murder. . . ." I trailed off. Hold on, I hadn't told Randall about the last two murders, or my hours spent in jail.

Randall shook his head. "When Morgan didn't show up, I figured she'd run into trouble. Should have gotten rid of her myself after the whole Cameron fiasco. Shows up in my bar with a fucking zombie." He muttered in Filipino under his breath. "Couldn't spot trick bindings from real zombie bindings to save her life. Messed up that ghost trap mirror I gave her to stick in your lobby. Was supposed to keep you busy looking for your ghost and out of my hair. Ought to thank that ghoul for taking care of her, though on the other hand, it's yet another practitioner gone. You'd have been safe in jail, kid. I'd have found someone else. . . ."

Keeping my eyes on Randall and the bat in his hands, I inched my fingers along my phone's call screen.

"Don't do it, kid. I'm old, but I'm still fast," he said, pointing the bat at the phone.

I slid my phone back in my pocket, gauging how far the back door was from me.

I took a step, trying to wrap my head around everything. Randall's family were practitioners, but as far as I knew, he'd never been. "You're not even a practitioner," I said.

"I'm better than most of you, kid," he said. "I know how to hide it."

Randall vaulted over the bar with ease and strode towards me. Like hell was I taking on Randall; I'd seen him break up too many bar fights with that bat.

"I really wish it hadn't been you, Kincaid." He barked a command at the three zombies and they stilled their advance.

Shit . . .

I ducked as the bat hit a wooden beam close enough for me to feel the air stir. I didn't get a chance to be relieved as Randall readied for another swing. I pushed a chair in his way and dove under the pool table as the bat came down. The chair shattered. I smacked the top of my head against the underside of the table as I scrambled out of reach.

Randall frowned at having missed. I was running out of pool table.

"I was gunning for Max, you know. Wouldn't have had a problem killing him. Or Morgan, for that matter." Randall readied the bat over his shoulder. "You? I'm going to feel bad about you."

Small fucking comfort . . . Randall edged around the pool table towards me.

"If there's one thing I've learned the last few weeks, it's that kids never listen. That's why we're both here, isn't it? Mike never listened to a thing I said about speeding, and what happens? He races a bike off a bridge and kills himself. That's what kids do, though. You should have taken my advice and stayed the hell out of this. Just remember whose fault this is."

"I know exactly whose fault all this is, Randall. Yours."

Randall's feet were less than a foot away. "I always liked you, Kincaid," he said. "You were a good kid. I really hate to do this."

Now.

I tried not to picture my skull cracking under the bat and bolted for an oak table closer to the door. I scrambled under as the bat came down. Randall barked another command and the three zombies rushed to block the back door.

"No one is getting in or out of here until we're done, Kincaid," Randall said, edging around the table.

I crawled towards the middle of the table, hoping he couldn't reach me. I focused on the zombies. Definitely four-lines, as I'd thought, but good, strong ones.

I tapped as much Otherside as I dared and pulled a globe. Randall would notice the drop in temperature, so I'd have to move fast. I focused on the nearest zombie's bindings, the one with the baseball cap, and threw as much Otherside at him as I could, biting back the nausea.

The zombie stumbled, but before I could exploit the opening, other bindings filled in for the one I'd damaged. The zombie regained his footing.

Shit, Randall really was good.

The baseball bat cracked against the table and the legs groaned.

"No Otherside!" Randall yelled.

"You can't bring your son back as a Jinn. It'd be living torture," I yelled at him, half hoping Cameron had heard us. He wouldn't stand a chance against three zombies, but maybe he'd have a stroke of brilliance and call Aaron or Lee. . . . "Besides, you don't even know if it'll work. The ghoul couldn't even hazard a guess, and he killed way more people trying than you have."

I took a deep breath and eyed the neighbouring tables, trying to map an escape route to the back door. "I'd watch that bat, Randall. It'd really suck if you killed me by accident," I yelled, and dove for the next table.

Not fast enough.

I screamed as the bat hit the back of my thigh. Whether it was the angle or just luck, the bone didn't break and I managed to scramble out of his range again. One more table and I'd be close enough to the back door to make a break for it. . . .

My hand slid out from under me as I hit something wet and slick. Blood. Why would there be blood? Then I noticed the trace of Otherside and followed it to the motionless orange form. Now I knew what had happened to Randall's alley cat. I may have hated the damn thing, but I only used sea urchins, for Christ's sake. Then it dawned on me that Randall hadn't been trying to catch me with the bat and the zombies. He'd been corralling me. Here.

The back door was to my right, but Randall and the zombies were now in the way. I had a clear route to the front door. Run on three, Kincaid. One, two, *three*—nothing. I threw myself forward again, and again was held fast. I scanned the bindings. They were eerily similar to the ones I'd found on Max. I'd triggered them when I'd touched the blood. He'd hidden the binding trap under the table so I wouldn't see the blood sacrifice.

"Always said it was worthwhile feeding that cat," Randall said as I struggled. "I learned from Max. Those bindings won't let you move or tap Otherside. I never thought the crazy old man would trigger the fire wards like he did."

"All right, Randall, you win," I said. "There's no need to practise on me. Hell, I'll help you raise Michael as a Jinn if it means that much to you." Not if I could help it, but I was out of options here.

Randall squatted down so he was eye level with me. "Who said anything about raising my kid as a Jinn?"

"Why the hell else would you be . . ." I trailed off as I remembered a passage I'd stumbled over in King Solomon's text: "Bound in torment but granted power over life and death." I'd assumed it referred to weapons, but that wasn't the only interpretation. Randall must think it meant a Jinn could bring back the dead. He was further off the deep end than I'd thought.

"For god's sake, this isn't a genie, it's an undead. Jinn kill things on demand, they don't grant wishes." But I could see in his eyes that there was no point arguing. "I'm going to be really pissed off if you turn me into a Jinn for nothing."

A voice said, "I'd put down the bat."

Cameron. I craned my neck. I couldn't see him, but all three zombies were on the floor, necks broken. Randall had been so busy with me, he'd somehow missed Cameron getting rid of his wrecking crew. We both had. One drawback to Otherside? It's easier to get the drop on a practitioner when he is using it.

Randall smiled before standing up to face Cameron. "I'm the one with the bat, zombie."

Cameron nodded. "But you're forgetting I'm already dead, and much taller than you. Harder to reach my head. Do you really want to take the chance I'll get to you before you can kill me? I'm pretty hungry." Cameron flashed Randall a feral grin.

I couldn't look as I heard the crack of the bat meeting bone, but it was Randall who yelled. Despite likely breaking all the bones in his hand, Cameron had caught the bat and tugged it out of Randall's grasp.

"Now, let Kincaid go," Cameron said.

Randall didn't have much choice. I felt the bindings start to give as he peeled the layers away. We were actually going to walk out of here. . . .

But then he turned to face Cameron. "Seems I remember something about you feeling lousy around Otherside."

"Wait!" I screamed. "Randall, you made your point. I won't fight if you promise to let him go." Even as I said it, I knew how stupid it sounded. Of course Randall wouldn't let Cameron go. Why the hell would he? He'd be an idiot to leave a witness.

"No," Cameron said. "It's me who will do whatever you want if you let Kincaid go."

That got my attention—and Randall's.

"Seriously, raise me as a Jinn. I volunteer. That's the right term, isn't it?"

"I need someone who's alive," Randall said, but I could see his mind turning. I hadn't been his first choice, just his last resort.

"How about this, zombie boy," Randall said. "If it works on you, I'll let Kincaid go."

"And if it doesn't work?" Cameron said.

Randall shrugged. "Then Kincaid will be next. You won't care, though, because you'll be dead."

"Set her free of those bindings and we have a deal," Cameron said.

The bindings tightened as if to remind me that Randall knew as well as I did that he wasn't going to let me walk out of here, even if he managed to turn a zombie into a Jinn. Randall walked back to the table and hauled me around until I was half in, half out of the binding circle. I could clench my hands, but my legs wouldn't move.

"Half now, half later. Stand there, Cameron, back against the wall. And keep your hands where I can see them," Randall said, pointing a cue at a spot behind the pool tables.

With effort I scanned the room. Only one other person besides Lee would have known to take Randall's zombies out by the neck. I'd taught that to Cameron since he couldn't use Otherside worth a damn. Time to buy time.

"Did you at least *try* to call someone?" I called to Cameron.

"Didn't seem much point," he said.

The back door was closed and I caught no moving shadows under the fluorescent lights.

"That's enough out of both of you," Randall said.

I winced as the bindings on my legs cinched tighter. Come on, Kincaid, front door, you can do it. It was still ajar.

Randall crouched in front of Cameron and began tracing the symbols on the floor. Once he flooded them with Otherside, I wouldn't be able to do a damn thing for Cameron.

"Randall's going to kill us, both of us," I yelled.

The bindings tightened so much around my waist, they knocked the wind out of me. "One more word, Kincaid, and so help me—"

Cameron caught my eye then glanced at the bindings at his feet. "Someone once told me you suck at patience, Kincaid," he said.

I'll bet they did. I didn't know if Aaron was on the way, but I was damned if I was going to let these cards fall. I couldn't pull a globe, not in this trap, but the beauty of such a trap was that the bindings were real specific. Hoping Randall had underestimated how reckless I was, I tapped the Otherside without a filter. And with that, I flooded pure, unadulterated Otherside into the bindings holding me. I don't know if I was more shocked that it worked or by the pain that seared through my head.

First I screamed. Then, when I felt the last of Randall's work burn off, I cut my tap. I heard Cameron yelling followed by the crack of a gun sounding through the bar. Not that it mattered to me—I was doing my best not to pass out.

When I was able to look up, Aaron was standing over Randall's still form, holding his arm, blood seeping through his shirt. How the hell had a gun ended up in this equation? But there it was, in Randall's hand.

"I thought you were supposed to be the one with the gun?" I said to Aaron.

"He already had his drawn," he said, nodding at Randall. "I told you I didn't think you were the killer."

With Aaron and Cameron's help, I crawled away from the trap and stood. "That. Was. Stupid," I said.

Aaron almost smiled. "Agreed. Could you stop trying to get yourself almost killed?"

"I wasn't trying to get myself killed, I was trying to stop a killer."

"You were doing both."

I closed my eyes. I couldn't believe it: two seconds and we were already arguing.

"You were doing so well until you started talking," I said.

I opened my eyes as the corner of Aaron's mouth turned up.

I glanced down at Randall to make sure he was still unconscious, and noticed his chest wasn't moving.

"Shit." I crouched down beside him then looked up at Aaron and Cameron.

Randall was dead.

✳

We settled on arson.

I know how odd that sounds coming from a cop and a practitioner wanting to stay out of jail, but in the end it was the only solution we could think of.

With Randall dead, I'd spend the next few months explaining to rooms full of skeptical police officers what a Jinn was and why a respected bar owner and supposed non-practitioner was trying to raise one. Even with Aaron backing me up, no one would believe me, but no one would be able to prove me wrong: two circumstances cops hate. Then there was the small issue of Cameron being a zombie. . . . Since Max was gone, I'd probably end up charged for both Cameron's raising and Randall's manslaughter, and Aaron would lose his job.

Much easier to throw the four bodies in the cellar, light the place on fire, and leave.

Besides, it was almost the start of poltergeist season, and everyone knows a poltergeist loves a fire.

I sent Aaron away after he helped us drag the bodies into the cellar. The bullet had only grazed him, but he still had to get the wound cleaned up.

"Cameron, get yourself upstairs," I said as I dumped whisky over the bodies. I knew somewhere I should feel bad, but I just couldn't bring myself to.

"All this over a Jinn fairy tale," I said to Randall's corpse.

I felt a brush of cold behind me.

Gideon.

"How much did you hear and see, ghost?" I said.

He shrugged. "Enough." He examined my pyre in the making. "Interesting streaks of bad luck seem to follow the living everywhere nowadays."

Max, Randall, his kid, Marjorie, the two other victims—all for some mystical monster no one had seen in five hundred years? I grabbed the igniter fluid and added that to the mix, though the whisky should cover it. My foray into arson was the kitchen-sink edition.

"We need to talk," Gideon said.

"I'm a little busy. Later."

"Now. It's about your zombie friend upstairs."

I glanced at Gideon, who was perched on the pile of bodies. Well, not really, but it looked like it. There was something in his expression that brought Lee's and Max's warnings back to me.

"I'm very sorry, Kincaid," he said.

I backed up towards the cellar stairs, not that it would do me any good if Gideon attacked.

"Max was very good," he said. "I don't think I would have believed it if I hadn't read the client accounts you found for me."

My throat was dry as Gideon continued to regard me. "Believed what?"

He nodded up towards the bar. "That my payment was hidden right under my nose. Intricate binding layered over intricate binding so I couldn't recognize what he was. Brilliant on Max's part."

"What about Cameron?" I said.

Gideon's eyes never left mine. "Cameron is my payment from Maximillian Odu. A body I could inhabit."

I took another step towards the cellar stairs.

"I wouldn't do that," Gideon said. "We had a deal, Kincaid, one all parties had agreed upon, including Cameron."

"Gideon, he doesn't remember any deal."

"He can't remember anything."

I licked my lips. "There has to be another way."

"You have nothing I wish to trade for."

Maybe if I screamed . . .

"Kincaid," Gideon warned, and I felt ice lash against my skin. "You know what I can do. Don't think for a moment I won't hurt you."

I knew not only what Gideon could do to me, but Sarah, Aaron, Lee . . .

"So call Cameron. Nicely. Now." He sent another wave of ice towards me.

"Cameron, could you come down here for a moment." I glared at Gideon as I heard Cameron's footsteps. "You don't have to do this," I said. "He's damaged and I don't know if he can be fixed. Find someone else."

For a second I thought maybe, just maybe, Gideon might change his mind. I really did. Then he shook his head.

I couldn't let it happen.

"Cameron, run!" I screamed. "It's a trap."

The Otherside blast hit me and I dropped to my knees.

"Kincaid?" I heard Cameron's footsteps on the stairs as Gideon knelt beside me.

"I'm feeling very generous, so I won't kill you, Kincaid. But I'll be taking Cameron."

"Fuck you," I said. "I'd rather be dead than hand him over to a mad ghost like you."

Gideon's face showed something close to disappointment before his mask of indifference returned. "I can arrange that."

Cold fingers wrapped around my throat as he lifted me off the floor, and I gasped. Cameron's footsteps halted at the bottom of the stairs. Damn it, I'd told him to run. Now or never, Kincaid.

"Stop fighting me and I'll teach you anything you want to know," Gideon said.

"I don't want anything from you."

Gideon's eyes shifted from ghost grey to black. "Last chance, Kincaid. I'm not above killing you."

I shot a glance at the stairs. Cameron stood at the bottom, perfectly still. I flicked the lighter. Cameron saw it.

"Kincaid," he warned, taking a step forward. "I heard. It's okay, I'm fine with this."

"Finally, one of you shows an ounce of sense," Gideon said, and dropped me on the pile of bodies. I couldn't light them now, not while I was lying on the accelerant.

"If I hand myself over, she can go, right?" Cameron said, taking another step.

I swear the damn ghost rolled his eyes. "That's exactly what I've been proposing."

"Cameron," I warned, "the last thing I want is *him* walking around this side with a body."

Gideon glared at me. I couldn't have cared less.

Cameron was within arm's reach, close enough he'd feel the edge of Otherside gathered around Gideon. "This will be easier, Kincaid. You even said it. I'm a ticking time bomb." He looked away from the ghost for one moment and met my eyes. "You know, I never got the chance to thank you."

In another time and place I would have laughed at the absurdity of Cameron thanking me. "For what?"

"Giving a damn what happened to me. I mean it, it meant a lot."

I realized too late what Cameron planned to do.

"You want me?" he said to Gideon. "Here I am." Cameron's hand shot into the Otherside that was Gideon. His bindings cracked and whistled like a string of firecrackers.

The sixth gear in Cameron's bindings started to turn and his body convulsed.

I searched for a way to stop the unreeling—an anchor, a binding point—but it was as if a fuse had been lit. I couldn't do anything as the bindings burned away.

Cameron leaned against the cellar wall then slid to the dirt floor. I've always said, you know when a zombie's gone. It's in their eyes.

I watched as what had just happened dawned on Gideon.

"What the hell has he done?" Gideon snarled.

I couldn't tear my eyes off Cameron's empty corpse.

"Do you have any idea how much it will cost to salvage this?" Gideon shouted at me, examining Cameron's body as the bindings dissipated. All I could think was that Cameron deserved better than this. . . .

Somewhere in the commotion I'd dropped the lighter, and now I spotted it by Randall's feet. I picked it up and with shaky hands lit it before dropping it on the pile of bodies. The accelerant caught and flames shot straight up to the low ceiling. Heat singed my face and eyes as smoke filled the cellar and choked the air.

Gideon swore.

The flames hadn't touched Cameron's body yet. Maybe I could reanimate him with Max's notes. . . . The sane part of my brain stuffed that idea. Cameron had made his call.

Sleeve over my mouth, I crawled up the steps. The door wouldn't budge.

I didn't see Gideon through the smoke, only felt the icy grip on my foot before I slid back down the steps. I tried to free myself, but I was stuck, the Otherside ice reaching through the fire's heat, tethering my ankle to the cellar floor.

"You have got to be kidding me—" I sputtered, hit by a coughing fit. I covered my mouth with the sleeve of my jacket, hoping to filter out some of the smoke. "Gideon, I don't have time for this. Open the fucking door!"

His face coalesced over me and cold pressure came down on my chest.

"I've killed *kings* for less than this," he said.

"So go ahead and get it over with. I hope you enjoy watching me burn."

Gideon swore, but the pressure eased off my chest.

I didn't know how much it helped, as more smoke filled my lungs. I glanced up at the door. I could still make it out but soon it would be obscured by smoke. All I had to do was crawl up and then across the bar to the back door. . . . I grabbed a step and pulled myself up. Gideon made no move to stop me.

A few more steps, Kincaid, come on, that's all you have to do.

I heard Gideon swear and then felt him grab the collar of my jacket. Everything went ice-cold. Excruciatingly cold. No air, no feeling, no sound. Just cold.

And then I was gasping, and burning, and choking all at the same time as noise pierced the air. Otherside . . . so much Otherside . . .

I opened bleary eyes to Gideon's face, twisted in a snarl. "I have no idea why the hell I keep saving you. Do you have any idea how much trouble you've caused me? Don't think for one minute this is over, Kincaid. You owe me one hell of a favour. And this changes nothing of our deal. In fact, consider yourself in penalty."

Then I heard him say, "This is your problem," and I didn't think he was talking to me. "Send someone to put out that damned fire before Seattle burns. Again."

Gideon vanished and then Lee's scarred face came into view. I was lying in her backyard underneath the canopy of white Christmas lights. Huh. Gideon hadn't tried to strangle me with them. Go figure.

"Kincaid?" Lee said.

I noticed the new lanterns interspersed among the lights, dark red with gold letters this time. "Do you ever get tired of redecorating this place?" I said, in between coughing fits.

I felt her cool hands on my face. "What happened to you?" she asked.

I couldn't bring myself to say anything about Cameron's fate.

"I found the killer, Lee," I said, though that felt like cold comfort. "And you owe me ten grand." I passed out.

I woke up in bed. At home. Alive. No Otherside hangover, no sorcerer's ghost trying to kill me. I crawled out of bed, prompted largely by my stomach, and headed for the kitchen.

I didn't make it past the doorway. There was a covered easel sitting in my living room with a delivery receipt attached. Aaron or Lee must have let them in.

Somehow Cameron had known he wasn't coming back with me. Or maybe he just decided he'd had enough? I'd never know. I stood there staring at the easel until I got up the courage to pull the cover off. It was one of the pieces I'd seen in his apartment. Less abstract than most of his work and done in grey and gold, reminding me of Otherside and bindings.

I stared at the canvas for a few minutes before going to the kitchen and turning on the coffee. In the bathroom there was no sign of Nate, but there was a single sentence scrawled across the bathroom mirror in Gideon's tight script.

You owe me.

*

For the next few days I kept my head down and tried to recover my balance. So many losses: Max, Cameron, even Randall.

I made coffee, ordered pizza, spent a little time with Aaron in a platonic truce I had no desire to break. I knew he had questions I didn't want to answer, and we were not all right, not by a long shot. But he let me have a respite. Most of the time I was on the couch in my pyjamas watching TV.

And Nate left me alone. He needed the rest too.

When I finally succumbed to the urge to check in on the murder investigation, the Seattle PD was back to calling Aaron the head of the paranormal unit. Poltergeists and fire will do that.

I was interrupted by a knock at the door, which soon turned to loud banging.

"I'm coming," I shouted, though I wasn't too crazy about opening the door to just anyone in my pyjamas.

I stood on my toes to check through the dusty peephole, figuring I'd see Aaron or maybe a reporter.

A grey sweatshirt hood. A head of shoulder-length red hair. How could it be?

I swung the door open and pulled Cameron inside. He staggered out of my reach without any of his usual grace or coordination.

"K, it's me," Cameron said.

I frowned. Cameron didn't call me K. And he tended to stand

up straight, not slouch. I sought out his eyes, which were unfocused, shifting. . . .

Only one person ever called me K. I reached out to steady myself against the wall.

"K, I really think I might have messed up."

"*Nate?*"

He nodded, attempting to give me a grin. Shit. Where Gideon had failed, Nate had succeeded. He'd stolen Cameron's body.

"Nate, what the hell have you done?"

ACKNOWLEDGEMENTS

Thanks to my husband, Steve, and my friends Leanne Tremblay, Tristan Brand and Mary Gilbert, who read each and every chapter. I don't know if I would have finished this book, or any book, without their feedback and encouragement. Also thanks to my awesome co-host at *Adventures in Sci-Fi Publishing* podcast, Brent Bowen, and his family. Hosting the show every week reminds me why I love writing so much.

I also want to thank my agent, Carolyn Forde, who picked my first manuscript out of the slush pile and perked up when I described this new project. Also my amazing editor, Anne Collins, at Random House Canada for fixing up this scientist's prose and making the novel so much more than it would have been otherwise. I will never forget the day Anne admitted she "liked" my novel, with its voodoo and zombies.

There are many other people who have mentored and encouraged me in my writing career over the past few years—thanks to all of you!

Kincaid Strange,
not your average voodoo practitioner,
is back in the freshly imagined and
hugely entertaining second installment
of Kristi Charish's urban fantasy series.

READ ON FOR A SNEAK PEEK OF

LIPSTICK VOODOO

Arriving January 2019 from Vintage Canada

CHAPTER 1

LIPSTICK SEANCE

I tapped my foot on grass crunchy with frost, let out my breath and watched it condense into white fog around my face. This cold already for mid-October was not a good sign for my perpetually chilled state. I'd planned on spending my Thursday night wrapped in a blanket in front of the TV, not standing in a graveyard beside a marble tombstone easily worth about four months' rent. The soil in front of it was freshly turned, and the grass surrounding the gravesite sparkled under the overhead sodium lamps. Though, I had to admit, the layer of frost made the graveyard look a lot prettier than it had any right to be—except for all the mud around the recently dug-up grave, that is, and the current company.

I let out another breath and watched the air condense. *Concentrate on the job, Kincaid.* "Look, Mr. Graeme—" I started again.

"Ah—now what did I say?" The eighty-five-year-old man standing in front of me frowned and wagged his finger. He was dressed in a suit that probably also cost a few months' rent.

"I always get pretty girls like you to call me Michael," he said. He smiled, or tried to—only the left side of his mouth turned up and a week's worth of desiccation in the grave meant his lips stretched into a thin grimace. "And where'd you get such pretty, curly black hair like that? You Irish?" He leaned in and added in a whisper, "Or part black maybe? I know that's a lot more common nowadays."

I shot a glance over my shoulder at my client for the evening, Cody Banks, a young lawyer who'd contacted me two days ago with an urgent job. He'd offered more money than I usually demanded for expedited will cases, and I needed the cash, so it had been impossible to say no.

He gave me a fake smile, but his eyes communicated something very different: *Get the job done.*

That was my first mistake: taking this job. I turned back to Mr. Graeme and squeezed my arms, wishing to god I'd worn something warmer than my leather jacket—my second mistake.

"Okay, let's try this again, *Mr. Graeme.* You aren't alive anymore." There, I'd said it. Again. Here's hoping this time it stuck. Zombies usually remember how they died, why the hell this one was being so stubborn about admitting it. . . .

Michael Graeme, a.k.a. tonight's zombie of the hour, furrowed his brow . . . which contorted unevenly due to the paralysis from the stroke that had killed him.

"You know what I think?" the late Mr. Graeme said. "I think this is all a hoax. Jonathan's idea of a bad joke." He raised his arm and jabbed a pale finger in the direction of the sixty-year-old woman dressed in a tasteful black suit and veil standing to the left of my pentagram. "Bertha, are you and your brother behind this?" he shouted.

The recently widowed Mrs. Graeme clutched at Cody's jacket and launched into a fresh round of sobs—though considering her serene state before I performed Mr. Graeme's raising, I had trouble believing the grief was genuine.

Cody cleared his throat—loudly.

I sighed. "Wait right here, Mr. Graeme," I said, though it wasn't like he had a choice. I'd raised him and set the limits so he couldn't step outside my summoning ring, regardless of whether or not he believed he was dead.

With effort Cody detached himself from the widow and headed for my pentagram. I met him at the edge, sage smoke and gold Otherside billowing between us—though I was the only one of us who could see the Otherside. All Cody would see was smoke.

As soon as his back was turned on his clients, he dropped the smile. "You said this would be fast," he hissed.

Cody was a lawyer and, from my experience, they were to be treated as carefully as you would the devil himself. "Normally, yes, but he is refusing to acknowledge the fact that he is dead."

"I thought all zombies knew they were dead."

"That doesn't mean they don't try to lie to themselves."

"How the hell can he lie to himself? I mean, it's obvious he's a zombie, look at him."

I clenched my fists, trying not to lose my temper. Damn it, I wished I'd pushed harder for cash up front. I hate being desperate for work. "I don't see why it's so surprising. People do it to themselves all the time."

Cody held up his hand. "Look, I don't care how you do it. Just get him to sign the paperwork."

I watched Cody stalk back to his clients, shook my head and turned my attention back to the deceased Mr. Graeme. He was staring at the small collection of lawyers and family gathered ten feet away, only the left half of his face frowning in concern for a wholly unpleasant effect.

How were the people gathered outside the pentagram handling tonight's entertainment? Well, depended on who you were watching. Mrs. Graeme—the deceased's wife—her two sons and their wives were weeping and clinging to each other. Cody was comforting them and sneaking acid looks at me. The tall, thirty-something redhead keeping her distance from them—Samantha Diamond, professional entertainer, was how she'd introduced herself—was shaken up but otherwise composed and huddled with her own lawyer. And why shouldn't she be composed? Mr. Graeme had left her all his liquid cash.

Man, what I wouldn't give to be anywhere else but here. . . .

I checked my phone. A quarter to twelve. I was running out of time to get the papers signed by midnight. Time to employ more direct measures. I pulled my compact mirror out of my pocket and held it up to Mr. Graeme.

"Michael, you are most certainly dead. You died one week ago of a massive stroke." I'd read the full examiner's report before agreeing to the raising to make certain there'd been no other mitigating factors. Before raising a zombie—even a four-line like Mr. Graeme—you need to do some fancy footwork with Otherside lines to repair the damage. Otherwise, when I activated the temporary zombie bindings, Mr. Graeme would only have stood, looked at the crowd surrounding his grave and collapsed from a stroke all over again. Talk about misfortunes repeating themselves.

I'd used some new bindings—better artery reinforcement in the head but took more Otherside and didn't last as long. Still, I'd thought it would leave me plenty of time to get this damned will sorted out.

I glanced back at Cody, who had his arm around Mrs. Graeme and was still staring daggers at me. I sighed and turned back to the late Mr. Graeme, who was examining his face in my compact, probing the paralyzed side with shrivelled fingers.

"Your doctors have been warning you about your blood pressure for the last thirty years." I took back my compact and retrieved a folder from my backpack: his medical files—the pared-down version, mind you, with the important details, namely, his doctor's bitching about Graeme's refusal to take his blood pressure medication.

Graeme squinted at the folder and I held out his glasses, which I'd had tucked in my jacket pocket. According to his wife, he needed them to see just about anything.

He sniffed at the air—a common reaction for any zombie on account of the subconscious parts of their brain picking up familiar scents. Probably his wife, or the girlfriend, or even faint traces of his old life.

He hesitated for a moment then snatched the glasses from my fingers, placing them on his face and motioning for me to fork over the folder.

"Knock yourself out." I crossed my arms and watched as he flipped through the pages. For a slim man, his blood pressure had been obscenely high. It was a miracle he'd made it to eighty, let alone eighty-five. . . .

He snorted and looked up, jabbing at the last page. "Says here I'm dead," he said. "Can't be dead, I'm standing here talking to you."

Bingo. I opened my mouth to explain, but I was interrupted by a tug at the sleeve of my jacket and turned to find Cody at my shoulder. "You gave him the autopsy report? Are you nuts?"

"Trust me, it moves things along. And you're supposed to stay the hell outside of my pentagram."

Cody ignored me. "If by moving things along you mean making the zombie angry—didn't you see the New Mexico case?"

This time I couldn't stop myself from rolling my eyes. The marshals had shot down the White Picket Fence killer, a.k.a. Martin Dane, two weeks ago. He'd targeted families in California living behind—you guessed it—white picket fences. He stabbed and strangled the sleeping family and after everyone save one was dead, he dressed their corpses in 1950s clothes. The survivor, usually a girl, was taken hostage. Martin would kill her after he had chosen the next family and leave her body in the new hostage's home, a sick and twisted game of "musical corpses." With over a dozen murders in three years, he'd terrified suburban Americans chasing the middle-class dream. Luckily for suburbia, he'd been identified courtesy of a hidden nanny camera and shot by the police at a New Mexico gas station. Unfortunately, his last kidnap victim, a ten-year-old girl, hadn't been with him. She was presumed to be alive . . . which is why they had tried to raise him.

"Okay, first off, any serial killer zombie is going to be angry." I smiled at the memory of how spectacularly Dane had acted once the raiser told him he was dead. Liam Sinclair, celebrity practitioner and TV host, liked to get the recently deceased to acknowledge their shortcomings in life and commit to self-improvement in the afterlife. This approach might give closure to the families of expired drug addicts and be spectacular for ratings, but it really wasn't the tack you wanted to take with a serial killer.

Serial killers kill people for sport. They are the definition of unrepentant. Scratch that—their life's regret is that they can't kill people anymore. Raising Dane gave him one last chance to commit murder, and Liam happened to be standing right in front of him with the TV cameras rolling. What the hell other outcome would you expect? The only surprising part was that Liam had survived.

Now, convincing the serial killer he's still alive and that co-operating and telling you where his last victim is will get him off death row, and therefore secure another chance someday to kill someone? That took finesse beyond the capability of a half-rate pseudo-celebrity zombie raiser.

Aaron, a Seattle detective who worked afterlife cases—and my ex-boyfriend—had been right about one thing: I'd been insulted that Liam, a practitioner with no criminal experience, had been asked to raise Dane and not me. Why hire a professional with a track record when you could hire a camera-friendly, D-list celebrity with a syndicated TV show?

Not that I was going to bother telling Cody any of that. Instead, I said, "Do you want this will settled in the next fifteen minutes or not?" If we didn't get the will revoked soon, no one got paid, including me . . . well, except Graeme's mistress.

Cody didn't nod, but his eyes shifted back to Graeme's widow. I took that as an affirmative.

"Then stick to the sleazeball lawyering and leave me to wrangle the zombie." I pulled my sleeve free and turned back to Mr. Graeme, and shivered against a fresh gust of cold wind. The sooner this will was signed, the sooner I could get back to my apartment and take a hot shower . . . and deal with my own personal zombie complication, one Nathan Cade.

Still holding his medical folder, Graeme had started examining his surroundings: the gravestones, falling leaves, and the freshly dug-up grave and coffin where he'd been buried until a few minutes ago. He was looking a hell of a lot less confident about the whole alive thing.

"I'm really dead?" he said to me, pointing at the tombstone.

I nodded. "You bet you are, Graeme." I held out my hand. Now was as good a time as any to make introductions. He took it, albeit reluctantly.

"I'm Kincaid Strange, voodoo practitioner." I inhaled deeply. There's never an easy way to broach this one . . . "I raised you as a zombie this evening so we could address some business you left unsettled before you died."

KRISTI CHARISH has a background in archeology and a PhD in zoology from the University of British Columbia. She has worked as a scientific advisor on projects such as fantasy and science fiction writer Diana Rowland's series, White Trash Zombie, and is the author of *Owl and the Japanese Circus* and *Owl and the City of Angels*. She co-hosts the *Adventures in Sci-Fi Publishing* podcast and lives in Vancouver. www.kristicharish.com